I/S
4/11

D1330721

**Newcastle College**
Library Services

## To be returned by the date stamped below
If you wish to renew your books please call 0191 200 4020

24 NOV 2011        − 8 JAN 2014   9 JUN 2016

    13 JUN 2012              21 SEP 2010

                  − 8        21 SEP 2018

                2 7 JAN 2014

23 OCT 2012    2 7 JAN 2014

04 DEC 2012

The Haunted

ALSO BY JESSICA VERDAY

*The Hollow*

# The Haunted

## JESSICA VERDAY

**SIMON AND SCHUSTER**

BARCODE

A **pulse** book

Simon Pulse and its colophon are registered trademarks of Simon and Schuster UK Ltd

First published in the USA in 2010 by Simon Pulse,
an imprint of Simon & Schuster Children's Publishing Division.

First published in Great Britain in 2010 by Simon and Schuster UK Ltd,
A CBS COMPANY

Copyright © Jessica Miller 2010

This book is copyright under the Berne Convention.
No reproduction without permission.
All rights reserved.

The right of Jessica Miller to be identified as the author of this work
has been asserted by her in accordance with sections 77 and 78 of the
Copyright, Design and Patents Act, 1988.

Simon & Schuster UK Ltd
1st Floor, 222 Gray's Inn Road
London WC1X 8HB

This book is a work of fiction. Names, characters, places and incidents are either the
product of the author's imagination or are used fictitiously. Any resemblance to actual
people living or dead, events or locales is entirely coincidental.

A CIP catalogue record for this book is available from the British Library.

ISBN 978-1-84738-499-7

1 3 5 7 9 10 8 6 4 2

Printed in the UK by CPI Cox & Wyman, Reading, Berkshire RG1 8EX

www.simonandschuster.co.uk
www.jessicaverday.com

LIBRARY
NEWCASTLE COLLEGE
NEWCASTLE UPON TYNE

Class    Fic

BARCODE  02815215

*For Lee—You man the lifeboat and row me to shore when my arms get tired. Thanks.*

# PREFACE

I was so lost when Kristen left. When she died. Then Caspian found me. I got to know him. Fell in love with him. He helped me deal with the fact that my best friend was never coming back. And when I found out that she'd been keeping so much hidden from me, he helped me try to understand.

But he had a secret too. A secret he should have told me from the beginning. Now I don't even know if he's real, or if I dreamt him up to help me process the pain. I can't stay away from Sleepy Hollow forever.

Will he be waiting for me?

*Chapter One*

# NOT READY

Besides, there is no encouragement for ghosts in most of our villages . . .

—"The Legend of Sleepy Hollow" by Washington Irving"

*I*'*m not ready to go back.* "Can I just stay here forever?" I leaned my head against the seat of Aunt Marjorie's car. "I don't eat very much, and really, who needs to graduate from high school?"

Aunt Marjorie laughed. "*You* need to graduate, for one thing. And don't you miss home? Your parents? Friends?"

I looked out the window. I *did* miss Sleepy Hollow. But not much else. I missed my best friend, but Kristen wasn't there anymore. Only her grave was. "I think farm living is the life for me. Mom and Dad can come visit, and I'll just stay here. There's a lot I still need to learn about flying your plane."

Her brown eyes sparkled. "We should take her out again

tomorrow. We've only got a couple of weeks left until you *do* have to go home."

"Aunt Marjorie, that's what I'm trying *not* to think about," I groaned. "Help me out here."

"Okay, okay," she said. "You don't think about how *not* ready you are to go back home, and I won't mention how many chances we have left to take the plane up together. Deal?"

"Deal."

"So, how was the visit with Dr. Pendleton this morning?"

"It was good. Really good." A big red barn came into view. We were almost back to Aunt Marjorie's house. She turned onto a rutted road, and we bumped our way down the grassy lane. "He thinks I've made a lot of progress, and I agree."

"Will you be seeing any doctors when you return home?"

"I don't think so. I feel like I've finally gotten a handle on . . . things." *Well, as much of a handle as you can have on thinking you were in love with a dead boy, and that you'd had afternoon tea with Katrina Van Tassel and the Headless Horseman from "The Legend of Sleepy Hollow."* "I feel like I can deal with it all and put it in its place."

We pulled up to the old farmhouse with its faded black shutters, and Aunt Marjorie parked the car under a metal carport right next to the front door. "And what place would that be?"

I unbuckled my seat belt and shrugged at her question before getting out. Aunt Marjorie still didn't know the whole story—just the parts about how I needed time away from Sleepy Hollow and professional help because I couldn't deal with Kristen's death. Which was technically, sort of, true. Everything that *had* happened to me all started on the day of Kristen's funeral.

"Just . . . in their place," I said. "Head grasping facts, heart dealing with emotions. Death is a natural part of life, and I don't have to feel guilty about living because Kristen isn't here to share it anymore." I was spouting psychobabble I'd lifted almost word for word from Dr. Pendleton, but it sounded good.

And sometimes I could almost convince myself that it was true.

Aunt Marjorie nodded and held the screen door open for me as I followed her into the house. "He sounds like a smart fella. I think I'd like him."

"I think you would too, Aunt Marj. Call me down for dinner?" She agreed, and I headed up to my room. It was formerly part of the attic, a section that had been converted and walled off into a tiny reading nook. I'd begged Aunt Marjorie to let me have it the instant I'd seen it. She'd wanted to give me a larger, "more comfortable" guest room downstairs, but I told her this room was perfect. It had a window seat, like my room at home, and a round, leaded-glass window with a view that stretched across the entire farm.

It was absolute heaven to curl up and read there while warm sun slanted in on my shoulders, making me feel like a fat, lazy cat. Cats don't have any worries.

I threw my messenger bag down onto the neatly made bed and crossed over to the lone bookcase that stood directly across from the window, propped up next to a dormer arch. Perusing the wooden shelves like I'd done at least a dozen times over the last three months, I pulled down *Jane Eyre*.

Turning to the ribbon that marked my place, I kicked off my shoes and climbed onto the seat, tucking my feet up underneath me. Where could I find myself a Mr. Rochester? Preferably one who *didn't* have a crazy wife hidden away in his attic . . . But a sexy and mysterious hero to call my own? Sign me up.

*You found a sexy and mysterious hero to call your own,* my subconscious whispered. But I ruthlessly pushed that thought away. *One who* isn't *dead and a figment of my hallucinations, please.* Finding my last stopping point, I began to read . . . and was promptly jerked away from the page by the sound of my cell phone ringing.

I glanced over at it lying on the small nightstand next to the bed. Something told me not to pick it up. Not to go over and see who it was. But I did.

"Hello?"

"Hi, Abbey, it's Dad. How are you, sweetie?"

Waves of homesickness washed over me at the sound of his voice. I really *did* miss my bed. And my room. And the rest of my perfume supplies. "I'm good, Dad. I'm doing good." Yeah, and okay, maybe I missed Mom and Dad a little bit too. "What's up?"

"Well . . ." He hesitated. "Your mother and I wanted to talk to you about something."

I could hear Mom in the background telling him to hand her the receiver.

"What is it, Dad?" My stomach did nervous flip-flops. "Just tell me." I hated drawn-out phone calls. Especially *these* types of phone calls.

"They finished the work on the Washington Irving Bridge," he said. "It's all done."

I had a quick flashback to a memory of sitting with Kristen under that bridge before the construction work had ever started. Before she'd fallen into the Crane River. "That's great, Dad." *But why is it significant enough to call and tell me about?*

Mom picked up the other line. "Abbey, what your father is trying to say is that the town council will be holding a ceremony there soon, to celebrate the finished project. I told them that I'd make arrangements for you to be a part of it. To say something about Kristen and to dedicate the bridge to her memory."

A loud ringing filled my ears, and for a second I thought it was coming from the phone. Holding the receiver away from my ear, I shook my head to stop the noise.

Dad spoke up now. "Your mother and I think that this would be really good for you, sweetie. To help you get over your . . . issues."

The buzzing was growing fainter, but my stomach was still flip-flopping. "I can't," I blurted out. Thinking as quickly as I could, I added, "I'm not supposed to come home until the end of June."

"We know it's earlier than expected, but you've made remarkable progress," said Mom. "The weekly reports from your therapist have shown *such* improvement." Her tone was enthusiastic, but I couldn't tell if she was trying to convince me, or herself. Mom never called Dr. Pendleton my psychologist. He was always my "therapist."

She was obviously where I got my avoidance issues from.

"Dad, I . . . I . . . can't. Tell Mom that I can't do this. I'm not ready. I need more time."

"I know, I know." He sighed heavily. "It's just that the town council wants you to be a part of this, and it would really please your mother. . . ."

"I've been working on it for weeks. We've already cleared it with your doctor," Mom said. "The dedication ceremony will be on the twelfth."

*What?* "You talked to Dr. Pendleton about this before you talked to *me*?"

"Well, we didn't want to impede your progress. We wanted to make sure that something like this wouldn't be harmful."

"Don't you think that I have a right to be talked to first? Since *I'm* the one being asked to do it?"

"Don't you think that it's appropriate for you to be there for Kristen? She was *your* best friend."

Guilt-trip city. Mom was pulling out the big guns now. But two could play at that game.

"But isn't my *therapy* more important, Mother?" I asked sweetly. "Are you telling me to come home and *not* finish all of my arranged sessions with Dr. Pendleton?"

If eyebrows made noises, I swear hers were making one right now as they shot up.

"I don't think coming home a couple of weeks early is too much to ask," Mom huffed. "Your doctor—"

"Dad?" I interrupted her. "Dad, please? Please don't make me do this. Don't make me go back to the spot where my best friend died. I need more time to make sure I'm all better."

"I know this is difficult for you, but your mother . . ." Dad sighed again. "Just think about it, okay, sweetie? That's all we're asking for right now."

Mom started to say something, but he stopped her. "Just take tonight to think it over, and we'll discuss it again in the morning."

I sniffled. I tried to hold it back, but the tears were breaking through anyway. Kristen . . . the river . . . The wound was still so fresh. The ache in my heart still so unbearable.

"Okay, Dad. I'll thi—" My voice broke. "I'll think about it."

"That's good, Abbey. Really good. We'll talk tomorrow," he murmured.

I forced out a quick good-bye and hung up the phone. Just before the backlight grew dark, I caught the date on the tiny screen below me. *June ninth.* The same day that Kristen went missing last year. The same day that my life changed forever. And here it was, changing again when I didn't want it to.

June ninths were really starting to suck.

I picked up the phone again and called Dr. Pendleton's office before I lost my nerve. His secretary answered and put me through. A half second later his voice-mail greeting started to play.

I waited for the beep and then spoke in a rush. "Hi, Dr. Pendleton, this is Abbey . . . um, Abigail Browning. I was calling to speak to you about my parents. They want me to go home early, and they said you told them that I could. Why wasn't this brought up in our session today? Please call me back. . . ." I left my name again and my phone number, then hung up.

How could they do this to me? Was I ready? What if I couldn't go back? What if I couldn't be a part of that ceremony? What if I wasn't better?

Would *they* still be there?

Would *he*?

I dropped the phone on the bed and moved to the door. I needed to talk to Aunt Marjorie about this. She would know what to do.

I found her on the porch swing outside, moving slowly back and forth. She stopped for a moment at my unspoken request and I sat down. It didn't take very long for her to start swinging again, and the chains supporting us squeaked as we moved in silence. In the fields large sunflower stalks with furled green leaves and heavy sagging heads dipped and swayed in the breeze as it danced around them. The sun gilded everything it touched, and a haze of gold settled down like a finely spun cloak draped across the land.

A sudden buzzing noise caught my attention, and the massive dome light over the big red barn started kicking on. It wasn't dark yet. Not even dusk, but it would be. Soon. The light steadied and burned bright, and the buzzing slowed.

Everything felt safe here. *Normal.* I didn't want to admit to myself that something was missing. There was a small hole inside of me. But unlike the black void that had been left behind when Kristen died, this empty space felt like it could be filled again.

"I got a call from Mom and Dad," I told Aunt Marjorie, looking down at my bare feet.

"Weekly update?"

"No."

I traced a crack in the porch floor with my eyes, following it as it disappeared under my heel. "They want me to go home early."

She didn't say anything, and I knew she was waiting for me to carry the conversation.

"They want to have this dedication ceremony at the bridge,

where Kristen . . . died. And they sprung it on me at the last minute." I shifted my body so that I could see her face. "Do you think I'm ready?"

She faced me too, and I could see years of wisdom in her eyes. "Do *you* think you're ready?"

"I don't know."

"What would be some of the benefits?"

I thought about it for a minute. "Well, I'd be home, for one thing. Back in my own room. Able to work with all of my perfume supplies again."

She nodded. "And?"

"I'd get to see Mom and Dad and Mr. and Mrs. M."

"And you might get some closure," she said. "You'd be surrounded by the love and support of family and friends as you honored Kristen's memory."

Now it was my turn to nod.

"Good. Now what would be some of the drawbacks?"

I had a whole list of answers for that one. "I could break down again. Have nightmares. Lose sleep." She put her hand on mine and squeezed gently. I kept going. "I could go completely insane. Freak out my parents. Have everyone in town start talking about me. Lose it in front of the Maxwells. I just thought I'd have more time—"

She squeezed my hand harder, and I broke off.

"That's quite the list of negatives."

"Yes, but all things that could possibly happen," I pointed out. "If it happened before, it can happen again."

"That's true," she said. "But if it did, you would be better prepared to handle it now. You have your parents, Dr. Pendleton, me . . . So, what's your gut telling you? Do you think you're ready to go back?"

I sat quietly, contemplating her question. My gut told me that sooner or later I was going to have to go home. I couldn't stay away forever.

It also told me that I needed to be there for Kristen. First and foremost, she was more important than me. And Caspian . . .

I had to face that truth too.

"I need to go back," I said softly.

She nodded. "I thought that would be your choice."

The seat beneath us shifted in an easy rhythm, and there was a gentle pull on the back of my calf muscles every time my knees stretched to propel us forward. The motion was soothing, a relaxing kind of ache that made me think of riding a bike for the first time after the winter snow had melted.

"There are a lot of nee-deeps this year," Aunt Marjorie commented, and I turned my head toward the dark line of trees that swallowed the back of the barn. A swampy forest lay within a dozen feet of the trees, and the toads that lived there swelled in a symphony, croaking out a cacophony of sound that started and ended in a blur of syllables that made up their nickname.

"Great," I replied. "Guess I'll be sleeping with headphones on again tonight."

She chuckled. "I actually like them. They remind me of hot summer nights with your uncle. Cool breezes, the rasp of an overhead fan, rumpled bedsheets." She grinned at me, and I felt my cheeks flame.

"And moving on to other subjects . . . Thanks for letting me stay with you, Aunt Marjorie. Being here . . . away from everything there . . . was exactly what I needed." I planted my feet firmly on the ground, and the swing came to a halt. Then I reached over and wrapped my arms around her.

She hugged me back and rested her chin on top of my head. "You're welcome to come and watch *Murder, She Wrote* with me anytime, Abbey. I'll get the other episodes on DVD."

I closed my eyes and enjoyed the simple comfort of her embrace. We sat there in silence for a few minutes before I started to pull away. "I guess I need to go call Dad. Let him know about my decision."

She stood too. "I'm off to the kitchen. Dinner should be ready soon."

I followed her into the house and inhaled deeply. The aroma of fried chicken hung in the air, and I spotted two striped cardboard buckets sitting on the table.

"Is the chicken from Frankie's Restaurant?"

"Yup. It'll be ready in about ten minutes."

Aunt Marjorie *never* cooked. She had told me once that she preferred to let the professionals do their jobs, and she'd be glad to pay them handsomely for it. I hurried up the stairs and went to my room. I found the phone in the covers and flipped it open. There was one missed call from Dr. Pendleton. I ignored it and pushed the button to call home. Dad picked up on the third ring.

"Hi, sweetie. I thought we weren't going to talk until tomorrow. What's up?"

I was so relieved to hear his voice instead of Mom's that I let out a breath I didn't even realize I'd been holding.

"Hey, Dad. I just wanted to let you know that I thought about what you said and . . . I'm ready. I'm ready to come home."

"Are you sure? Don't you want to sleep on it? You don't have to make your decision right now, you know." Now *he* sounded unsure. "I don't want you to regret this, Abbey. Why don't you call me tomorrow and we'll discuss it some more."

"No, Dad." I said. "My mind is made up. Can you guys come pick me up tomorrow?" The last thing I needed was time to reconsider.

"I guess. Then you'll have a day or two to get settled before the ceremony. I'll go tell your mother."

I hung up the phone and heaved a frustrated sigh. First he was trying to talk me into going back, and now he almost sounded like he was trying to talk me out of it? I didn't get it.

But at least the decision was made now.

I was going back.

Music seemed to be nudging me awake. Soft and faint, bare wisps of song floated along, and I could barely make them out. I thought I was dreaming.

I lay very still and opened my eyes wide. I don't know why I thought not blinking would help me hear better, but it seemed to make some sort of sense as I held my breath in that hushed darkness.

*There it is again.*

It was old-fashioned sounding, like something that would play during an epic love scene of a black-and-white movie.

Silvery strains slipped through the crack under my door, and I waited in anticipation. It was lovely and haunting.

But still too faint.

I threw back the covers, slid my feet to the floor, and tiptoed over to the door. *Maybe I can hear it better this way.* With one hand on the knob I turned it gently, easing the door open.

I followed the sound until it stopped. There was a pause, a shift, and the music changed to a Cat Power song. Her voice ached with longing and sadness. I closed my eyes, overcome by emotions the song evoked.

A soft clinking of glass interrupted the moment, and I found myself moving forward again, peeking through the sliver of opened door into Aunt Marjorie's room. It was open far enough that I could see in without having to press my face close, but not wide enough for her to see me if she should happen to glance over.

Aunt Marjorie was standing in front of a vanity, pouring a drink from a glass bottle. The amber liquid splashed into the bottom of a tumbler, barely filling it half an inch. Then she picked it up and toasted a large picture frame of Uncle Gerald that hung over the vanity mirror. An instant later she tipped her head to one side and put the glass back down. A low murmur and a giggle escaped her, and she put her arms up like she was getting ready to waltz with someone.

Cat's voice soared, and the words "Oh, oh, I do believe . . ." filled the room as Aunt Marjorie started dancing.

Once, twice, three times she slowly moved back and forth in a triangle pattern. She wore a long, flowing white nightgown, and I noticed that her hair was down. I'd never seen it that way before. She normally wore it tied back in a bun, but now the dark brown waves gently bobbed around her shoulders as she swayed in time to the music.

I smiled. *So this is where I get my crazy dancing-with-imaginary-partners gene from.* It was kind of nice to know it came from her.

Then the song ended. The room grew still.

Stumbling to an abrupt halt, she stood, arms frozen in place. Waiting for a partner who was not there. Who would never *be* there. Her shoulders shook, and a harsh sob echoed throughout the room. Within seconds it multiplied, and she started to cry like her heart was breaking.

I moved to go to her, and my toe bumped into the bottom of the door. I froze at the sound. What if she didn't want me to see her like this?

She glanced up, her eyes meeting mine. I held my breath,

waiting to see what she would say, or do. But she only wrapped her arms around herself and sank to the floor, a lonely old woman trying to make it through life with a piece of her heart missing. In some ways I knew exactly what she was feeling. As hard as I tried to forget, there was a Caspian-shaped hole inside me, too.

Slowly, I retreated. Her sobs echoed in my ears the whole way back, and even as I shut my door, I could not escape them. They followed me into my dreams.

I flung myself forward, sitting straight up in bed. I don't know how long I'd been asleep, but a nightmare had startled me awake. My eyes searched the dark corners, flew to the clock blinking 3:12 a.m., and scanned the ceiling. Looking for whatever it was that had my heart racing.

My mind frantically tried to reassemble the jumbled pieces of my dream.

I'd been . . . running? *No.* More like stumbling, really. Hands outstretched in the darkness. There were things all around me, and I could tell by their shape and feel that they were tomb-stones. Sharp edges and jagged pieces that left my bumbling knees and shins bruised, my fingers scratched.

I shook my head, looking for the missing scenes.

*Stumbling . . . stumbling . . . almost falling, always moving.* I knew I had to keep moving. What was after me? What was I running from? I saw myself try to glance behind, but it was too dark. I couldn't make out what was there.

The dream started fading, and I knew I was losing it. Already the bare fragments of memory were slipping through my fingers.

With a final glance at the room around me, I slid back down onto the sheets and pillows, closing my eyes. *Stupid dreams. I should* not *have drunk that Mountain Dew at dinner.* It always gave me the jitters.

And then I sat bolt upright again.

I knew. I knew what the dream meant.

I wasn't running *from* some*thing*. I was running *to* some*one*.

*Chapter Two*

# OUT OF PLACE

To turn and fly was now too late . . .

—"The Legend of Sleepy Hollow"

Late the next morning I waited impatiently with my bags by the front door for Mom and Dad to come pick me up. Time was dragging.

I gave my suitcase a kick and nudged it over on its side before sitting down on it. Aunt Marjorie was in the kitchen heating up a store-bought pie so that it would look like it just came out of the oven. She wanted to impress Mom. I scanned the distance through the glass door for the three hundred thirty-seventh time. *When will they get here?*

A horn beeped.

I jumped up and waited for them to pull in. As soon as they reached the house, car doors started swinging open and then slamming shut. Mom got to me first. I ran into her arms too, and hugged her for all I was worth. Sure, I was still a little mad at her for pushing the issue that I come home early, but she was my *mom*. And I'd missed her.

Dad came over and put his arms around both of us, and I turned to squeeze him tight.

"Hi, sweetie, we missed you," he said.

"I missed you too, Dad."

"Where's Aunt Marjorie?" Mom asked. "I want to say hello."

"She's in the kitchen. I think she wants you to stay for pie."

"Ooh, pie! How nice."

Mom wandered into the house, and Dad leaned over to pick up my stuff. Suddenly I felt shy and awkward around him. Did he think I was still crazy?

"So how did the football game go last week?" I asked.

"Football season hasn't started yet," he replied. "But baseball season has, and last week the Yankees beat the Sox."

I picked up my backpack and put it on the backseat. "I totally knew that. I was just testing you."

We smiled at each other, and in that moment I knew everything was okay. Even though he'd been the one I'd gone to when I needed help, Dad didn't think I was a freak.

He shut the back door and then turned to me. "So, your aunt made a pie, huh?"

"*Made*, not so much. Bought is more like it. I think it's cherry."

His smile widened. "Well then, let's not keep her waiting."

An hour later we were back at the car again, this time saying good-byes.

I hugged Aunt Marjorie one last time, pretending that I didn't notice the way her eyes were getting all teary. "I'll come back and visit again soon," I promised. "You still owe me a couple more plane rides."

She nodded. "You bet. Call me if you need anything." She lowered her voice and looked me right in the eye. "*Anything*, okay, Abbey?"

"Okay," I said. *And I promise, your midnight secret is safe with me.* I didn't say it out loud, but she gave me an almost imperceptible nod, and then we were climbing into the van, waving as we backed out of the driveway and pulled onto the open road.

I leaned my head back and settled in, sad to leave Aunt Marjorie behind. Anxious for everything I would be returning to. And nervous about what my future might hold.

Up front Mom chattered away. "We're so excited to have

you back home, Abbey! I can't wait to show you the new colors I painted the dining room in. And last week I replaced the drapes in the front hallway . . ." I tuned her out.

I didn't *care* about paint colors or new hall drapes. I only cared about what the rest of my summer was going to be like. Had word gotten out about the meltdown I'd had? Did anyone know where I'd been these past couple of months? What were they saying about me?

Trees zipped by, and so did several cars. The clouds shifted overhead, and I peered up at them. The shadows they cast seemed to stretch for miles, and for a while I amused myself with the what-does-that-cloud-look-like game. For some reason I kept seeing hippopotamuses.

Then my thoughts switched course. School was out now. What would everyone else be doing over the summer? Getting part-time jobs? Throwing pool parties? Hanging out at the beach? Driving around in their cars?

Would *I* be doing any of those things? I didn't know what this summer would bring, but I didn't think it was going to go down as "the one to remember." Not with Kristen being gone. Not with me being . . . me. *I wonder what Ben is doing. . . .*

He'd called my cell phone once or twice while I was at Aunt Marjorie's, but I still hadn't called him back. I didn't know what to say or how to act. Not only had I ditched him in the middle of our science-fair project, but then I had to go and have a mental breakdown on top of it. How do you explain *that*? Baffled as to what to do about Ben, I thought about it until we were almost home.

Dad had to say my name three times to get my attention, and I think he was amused by my obvious daydreaming.

"We're going to cross the new bridge," he told me. "In about ten minutes."

I turned to look out my window, grateful for the distraction from my thoughts. I kept my neck craned and didn't have to wait long. Dad pulled onto the main cemetery road, and even from a distance I could see the massive, looming structure.

The covered part of the bridge appeared to be at least twenty feet tall, and it had been made to look like it was a hundred years old. I couldn't figure out why it was so *big* until we crossed it and an eighteen-wheeler drove past us. Of course, trucks would need the extra room.

Thick wooden beams crisscrossed each side, and a rumbling sound echoed underneath us. It was the quintessential covered-bridge experience . . . and I hated it. It felt ugly and out of place. A big, jarring reminder of what had happened to my best friend at this spot.

"So?" Mom turned around in her seat to see my face. "What do you think?"

"It's, um, new. And huge. And kind of seems . . . like it will take some getting used to."

Mom waved her hand. "You'll get used to it in no time. And it's already increased tourist traffic by thirteen percent."

I returned to looking out my window. *Great.* Like I was really in the mood to be around more strangers. All I wanted was for Sleepy Hollow to be exactly the way it had been when I'd left it. Minus the crazy.

We pulled up to our house, and Dad parked out front by the mailbox. I climbed slowly out of the car and stood looking up at the white siding. It seemed . . . smaller than I remembered. The green shutters weren't as dark as they'd once been either. In fact most of them looked like they could use a fresh coat of paint.

Mom came and put an arm around me. "Aren't you glad to be home, Abbey? We have a special surprise for you. It's up in your room."

I nodded, and we started walking toward the house. Inside, everything felt weird. I had the oddest sense of something being not quite right . . . or out of place . . . and a sinking suspicion that the not-quite-right thing was me.

But I shook my head and tried to resist the urge to stand

in one place for too long. I grabbed on to the stair banister for support. My knees felt funny.

Mom was grinning at me, and I started to get slightly nervous. *Oh God, what if she rearranged my room or something?* Was that the surprise?

When I got to the top of the stairs and stood in front of my closed bedroom door, I found myself shutting my eyes. I stood there for a moment before I felt Mom move away from me and then I heard the door open.

"Come on, Abbey," Mom said, laughing. "You don't have to close your eyes."

*Yes. Yes I do*, I wanted to tell her. Instead, I took a step forward and opened one eye at the same time. Everything *looked* okay. With the exception of my floor being clean. Which was not how I'd left it. But if all she'd done was pick up my dirty laundry, then that was fine by me.

I shot a glance over at my freshly made bed. *Not how I left that, either*. Okayyyy . . . so maybe she changed the sheets, too?

Mom was still grinning, so I put a fake smile on. "You cleaned my room. Thanks, Mom." I tried to look genuinely happy.

"You don't see it yet, do you?"

"Sure I do—" I stopped and my jaw dropped open as I

turned to my right and looked over at my work desk. Sitting on the floor next to it was the most *amazing* curio cabinet I'd ever seen. It looked like a giant old-fashioned card catalog.

"Oh. My. *God*." I ran toward it. "Mom! Where did you guys get this? I love it!"

I don't think her smile could have gotten any bigger. "Uncle Bob found it in pieces at one of the supply places he gets his storage crates from. So he called your dad and asked if we wanted it. We went and picked it up; Dad glued it back together and fixed all the split ends. Then I painted it."

I ran my fingers over the gilded edges. They were a pale cream color and sanded down in spots to appear worn with age. The cabinet was at least three feet tall, and there were rows upon rows of little drawers, all stacked up on top of one another. Each drawer had a tiny gold rectangular handle, with a two-inch space above the handle to add in a nameplate. When I opened one of the drawers, I saw that it had been painted a deep gold inside.

"I added some gold flaking to the bottom of each one," Mom said. "I wanted it to have that special feel to it. It's for all of your perfume supplies."

Stunned gratitude and sheer amazement took over when I realized how many painstaking hours she must have put into it. "Mom, I can't even . . . I don't know what to say. *Thank you.*" I leaned over and wrapped her in a giant hug. She squeezed me back, and for a moment I pretended everything was normal again.

Then she pulled away, and I saw a desperate look in her eyes. She tried to hide it. Tried to put on a smile, but I could see what she was thinking. She wasn't sure if I was better yet.

"I'll let you get settled in and unpack your things," she said. "Dinner's in an hour. I'm making your favorite—lasagna."

"Thanks, Mom," I said again. "Sounds good!"

She gave me one last glance and then left my room. I let my smile drop as soon as she was gone, and I quickly shut the door. It was so strange to be back here. Back *home.*

I moved slowly around the room, pausing at my desk to shuffle through an old stack of perfume notes. Running my hands over the computer screen. Picking up a small glass paperweight and rolling it round and round. My stuff. My *things.* Every little piece that made me was represented here. Somehow.

Then I moved on to my bed. Sitting cautiously so I wouldn't wrinkle the sheets, I placed both hands on the comforter, palms down. It was cool beneath my fingertips, and I got lost in thought there for a while. I stared at the red striped walls, the fireplace mantel with the silver swirly frame, my telescope in one corner . . .

Mom's voice broke through my thoughts, calling that dinner was in thirty minutes, and I stood up to move to my window. Sinking down onto the window seat, I grabbed Mr. Hamm, a stuffed bear resting next to Jolly the penguin and Spots, a giraffe, musing that *I* hadn't left them so neatly arranged, and hugged him to my chest.

My eyes traveled to the closed closet door. *Is the black prom dress Mom got me still in there?* I'd never even checked it to see if she'd had all the tiny tears mended from when I'd worn it last, on Halloween night. When I'd gone to the cemetery and danced in the rain. That night I'd lain in the river and Caspian had walked me home and then we—

*No! He's not real. Caspian is dead.*

A shout outside drew my attention away from the closet door, and I turned to look out the window. On the street below me a little boy was running after a small, white, fluffy dog and yelling for him to stop. The dog kept trotting right along, dragging a blue leash behind him.

I smiled and watched them for a minute until something else caught my eye. Heart pounding, I sat straight up and put one hand to the glass. A figure dressed all in black darted toward the trees that stood by the side of our house. The sunlight shone on his white-blond hair.

"No," I whispered. "No!" My hand turned into a fist and I pounded once on the window pane. But he was moving fast, and an instant later I lost sight of him.

I stood up and sprinted out of the room. Clamoring down the stairs, I threw open the front door and ran outside. My eyes scanned side to side, taking in the trees, the sidewalk, and the fence up the road. I forced myself to walk calmly to the edge of our yard. After taking a deep breath, I called out softly, "Caspian?"

There was no answer.

I tried again, but this time I moved closer to the trees when I said his name. The result was the same.

Gathering up all of my courage, I pushed my way through the foliage and ended up in someone else's yard. A door slammed, and Mr. Travertine waved to me. He started wheeling his lawn mower out of his garage, and I waved back, glancing around. There was nothing but houses and empty yards as far as I could see.

*But I could have sworn I saw him. . . .*

Casually changing direction, I went back through the trees and started walking to the mailbox. Making a great show of acting like I was checking it, I reached in, expecting to come up empty. To my surprise, and somewhat relief, there were a couple of envelopes in there, and I grabbed them to take with me.

I walked back to the house, stopping by the kitchen to deposit the mail on the table. Mom turned to me. "I thought that was you, Abbey. Why did you go stampeding out the front door like that?"

*Because I saw the person I'm not supposed to be seeing, who wasn't really there anyway?* Yeah, that wouldn't work. "I, uh, saw a little boy out there chasing his dog. Thought I could help him catch it." Then I remembered the mail in my hands and held it up. "And I brought this in."

She smiled at me. "That's good. Want to set the table for me?"

"Okay." Anything to make things seem normal again.

After I set the table, Mom called Dad in from the living room, and we all sat down for dinner. I kept my replies to Mom's never-ending conversation light and happy, all the while silently longing for the safe haven of my room. Nothing even remotely close to the topic of my recent "away time" came up, and it was just like any other boring family dinner.

So then why did I want to *scream*?

Luckily, dinner ended quickly, and I only had to make it through one bowl of cookie-dough ice cream—"because I know it's your favorite," Mom said—before I begged off and told them good night.

As I climbed the stairs to my room, I was struck with that out-of-place feeling again. When I went to bed, I was afraid to go to sleep. Afraid that the feeling of not quite belonging would never go away. Afraid that everyone in town would find out where I'd been and what was wrong with me. Afraid of what I'd see and who I'd talk to. But mostly . . . afraid of what I'd dream.

*Hard snow crunched under my feet, packed and icy, and I stepped carefully. The sensation of walking on frozen water struck me as absurdly funny, but I stifled my laughter. Something told me this wasn't the time or place for giggles.*

*A single grave was in front of me. My destination. And it felt familiar, yet I knew I'd never seen it before. The perfectly carved stone angel resting on top of it had delicate features and arching wings. One side of her face was cast in shadows, and there was a red cloak draped over her shoulders.*

*My lips made the sound before my voice caught up to it. "Kristen."*

*Reaching out a hand, I touched her face. Her hair. Her wings. The likeness was stunning. She was caught forever in stone and dust. Etched out of hard lines and impossible granite. "Are you waiting for me?" I whispered. "You said you'd always be here."*

*Suddenly the statue turned cold. Freezing. As harsh as any winter wind, and I feared my fingers would be stuck in place. "No!" I cried out. "Please . . ."*

*Her wings cracked. The stone sighed. And from her eyes a tear fell.*

I rolled over and punched my pillow, knowing that I'd have a hard time getting back to sleep again after that dream. I hadn't dreamt about Kristen at all at Aunt Marjorie's. Now I knew I was *really* home.

After bringing me a snack (ten minutes after lunch) and finding half a dozen other reasons to come check on me, Mom interrupted me yet again the next afternoon.

I sighed and pushed my chair away from the computer screen, trying to hide my irritation as she knocked on the door frame. "Abbey, there's a call for you."

Well, I certainly wasn't expecting *that*. "Who is it?"

She had one hand on the phone receiver and held it out to me. "It's Ben. He called here while you were"—she lowered her voice—"*away*, and I told him that you'd call him back as soon as you had a chance. I think you should talk to him now."

My stomach dropped to my toes, and I shook my head

vehemently. He'd called the house, *too*? "I'm really not up to it, Mom." I forced my tone to stay calm and even.

She thrust the phone at me again. "Just talk to the poor boy, Abbey. He won't bite."

"No, I—"

"Ben?" Mom took the phone back and spoke into it. "Here she is, just one second." She placed it forcefully into my hand, then turned to leave the room and shut the door behind her.

Partly to soothe my nerves and partly to give Mom enough time to move away so she wouldn't hear me, I counted to five before I answered. "Hello?" I closed my eyes and waited in horrified suspense for his voice.

"Hey, Abbey? It's, uh, it's Ben. Ben Bennett."

"Hi, Ben . . . Um, how are you?" My fist unclenched, and I flexed my aching fingers. I'd been holding them closed so tightly that all the color had leached out of my digits.

"I'm good. It sounds like you're doing a lot better too."

That put me instantly back on alert. *What does he know?*

"Yeah, I guess I am . . ." I let that statement trail off, and an awkward silence filled the space between us.

"My cousin got mono once. It wrecked him for like four months straight," he said.

*Mono? He thinks I had mono?*

"It's too bad you missed the science fair, though. We took second place."

"Ben, that's great!" I said. "I'm so happy for you." And I was surprised to realize that I actually *was* happy for him. "I'm sorry I had to miss out too. But you know . . . mono and all that." I gave a weak cough. Did people who had mono cough? I had no clue.

"Paul Jamison and Ronald Howers took first place. They built a conversion kit that turned compost into an energy source. They actually managed to power a lightbulb with it."

"I bet it was rigged," I offered up.

He laughed. "Or they're just geeks with way too much time on their hands."

I laughed with him, and it was nice. It reminded me of the afternoons we'd spent together at school working on stuff for the science fair. Ben always could make me laugh.

"I called before," he suddenly admitted. "And your cell phone, too. I wanted to, you know, stop by and show you the trophy we won. But your mom told me you were sleeping a lot."

"Yeah . . . sorry about that. The . . . mono sure did a number on me. But at least I got to catch up on all my beauty sleep. Which I needed," I joked.

But the remark seemed to fall flat, and another moment of

uncomfortable silence stretched out between us. I tried to think up something else to talk about.

Ben came to the rescue on that one. "Are you going to be at that bridge thing?" he asked.

"Yeah, I'll be saying something about Kristen."

More silence.

"You know, I really miss her," he said quietly.

"Me too." I sighed. "I'm kind of nervous about the whole thing. Like, what if I mess up? Or say something stupid? Or . . ." I didn't want to say break down, so instead I said, "Forget her name, or something completely idiotic like that. Plus, I *hate* crowds."

"I'll be there to cheer you on," he said. "And you can always do the whole picturing-them-in-their-underwear trick. Except me. Don't picture me in my underwear, or that will just be awkward."

I laughed again, glad he couldn't see my reddening face. "You won't let me forget her name, will you?" I asked.

"Nope. I'll bring a cue card and hold it up for you in the back."

A couple of minutes later I was hanging up the phone with a smile on my face. At least some things hadn't changed.

Returning to my desk, I sat down and tried to get back into

what I was doing before the phone call had interrupted me. But I wasn't in the mood to be on the computer anymore. Deleting Spam e-mails and catching up on celebrity gossip could wait.

I wandered over to my new cabinet and briefly thought about transferring over all of my perfume stuff, but I didn't feel like doing that, either. Cataloging and labeling bottle after bottle of essential oils was a task better left for a day when I wasn't so distracted. I halfheartedly hung up a couple of shirts from my still-packed suitcase and then put away a pair of shoes.

Ben had brought up Kristen. . . .

I hadn't gone to see her yet since I'd been home. What kind of best friend was I?

I left my room and went downstairs to tell Mom that I was going for a walk. She made me promise to keep my cell phone on me and wouldn't let me leave until I told her that I'd "stay safe."

Enduring another one of her smothering hugs, I tried not to squirm out of her embrace. *This won't last long,* I told myself. *This is all because you've just come back home. It'll die down eventually. Hopefully.*

Finally, I headed outside. Even though I hadn't walked these streets for months, my feet knew where they were going. When I came to the big iron gates that marked the main entrance to the Sleepy Hollow Cemetery, I didn't allow myself to hesitate.

If I stopped now, I might not go in. This was the place where I'd played with Kristen, met Nikolas and Katy, spent time with Caspian . . .

Walking slowly, I followed the pathways as they bled into one another. There were a lot of people in the cemetery today. More than I'd ever seen before, and it made me uncomfortable. Were they watching me? Were any of them going to start whispering about the weird pale girl wandering among the tombstones? What if one of them tried to talk to me?

The cemetery was different. It didn't feel like my safe haven anymore.

I passed the empty wrought-iron chair where I'd sat the day of Kristen's funeral. It was still resting beside its plot, the grass now fully grown in and freshly mowed. Casting a glance over my shoulder, I paused and whispered hello to it. But I didn't say anything more than that, and I didn't stay.

The next place I stopped was Washington Irving's burial spot. There were fewer people on this side of the cemetery, and no one was in sight when I finally reached it. I knelt down, digging my fingers into the neatly trimmed grass along the bottom edges of his headstone.

"I'm back," I said. "Just like I promised." The marker looked like it had been freshly scrubbed: All previous bits of moss and dirt were gone, and a small American flag had been planted next to it.

"My . . . trip . . . went well," I said. I'd once felt comfortable speaking to him here like this, but things were different now. "It was nice to get away from everything, and just take some time to deal with it all."

I tugged a blade of grass out of the ground and rolled it between my fingertips. "Aunt Marjorie's house was great. She lives on a farm, and it's really nice there. She took me up in her plane, too, and let me fly it."

Voices echoed in the distance, and I scrambled to my feet. People were coming, and the last thing I needed was to be caught talking out loud to a tombstone. "I'll try to stop by again soon," I said. I touched the stone briefly and then turned to walk down the steps, away from his family plot. A small group of people came around the corner and waited for me to pass.

I went in the direction of Kristen's grave, but ran into two more groups on the way there. One of them stopped at the stone right next to Kristen's, and I tried to hang back to give them enough time so they'd move on and I could be alone. But they didn't seem to be moving on.

After what felt like at least twenty minutes, I finally stepped up to her stone.

The first thing I noticed was that the area immediately surrounding her headstone looked well manicured. Although the grass in the cemetery was usually kept short, a lot of the graves had scraggly weeds that grew up close to them. Kristen's plot was obviously being taken care of.

The second thing I noticed was a freshly plucked four-leaf clover sitting at the bottom of the stone. It was the first time I'd ever *seen* a four-leaf clover in real life, and I touched it, counting all four petals to make sure it wasn't just a trick of the light or something.

I glanced down at the grass surrounding the tombstone and then scanned the area around it. There weren't any patches of clover nearby. In fact there weren't any patches of clover *anywhere*. It must have been found somewhere else and placed here.

Goose bumps stood up along my arms, and I whispered a good-bye to Kristen. Leaving the cemetery behind, I wondered what that four-leaf clover meant.

And who had put it there. . . .

*Chapter Three*

# DEDICATION

To pass this bridge was the severest trial.

—"The Legend of Sleepy Hollow"

I couldn't sleep at all the next night. I was too hot, then too cold. The mattress too lumpy, then too firm. I scrunched up my covers one minute and cast them aside the next. At 6:54 I finally gave up and crawled out of bed to go downstairs. Today felt like a coffee kind of day.

Luckily, there were already some coffee grounds inside the coffeemaker, so all I had to do was fill it with water. It trickled down into the glass pot, its steady stream a rich, dark brown. The first couple of drops hissed and splattered until the coffee began to fill up the bottom of the carafe. I shook my head once and moved to grab an empty mug.

The taste was sharp and bitter, and I added another heaping

spoonful of sugar. Then I poured in some more milk for good measure. It didn't help very much.

I walked over to a large window in the living room, snagging a padded chair along the way and dragging it with me. The sky was bland and gloomy. It didn't look like rain, but the sun wasn't out either. Sinking down onto the chair, I stared outside, sipping as I watched several birds pecking the ground in search of worms.

*Early bird gets the worm.* I held my mug up and toasted the birds. Then I readjusted myself and got comfortable. I didn't even notice when my head began drooping and my eyes started to close.

When Mom woke me up two hours later, baffled as to why I was sleeping in the chair, I was more baffled at how I'd managed to put my half-full cup of coffee down on the floor next to me without remembering that I'd done it *or* spilling a single drop. Apparently, I was some kind of sleep juggler or something.

I staggered back to my room, rubbing my eyes the whole way. *You can't go back to bed,* I told myself. *The ceremony is less than six hours away, and you have to think about what you're going to say.*

Grabbing a spiral-bound notebook and a pen from the desk,

I sat down on the window seat. But the pen wouldn't work, and it took me a good five minutes before I finally gave up and grabbed a different one. Putting pen to paper, I tried to sort out my thoughts.

*Kristen Maxwell, who had a tragic drowning accident . . .* I crossed that out. Everyone who was going to be at the bridge probably already knew what had happened there. No need to state the obvious.

*Today we are here to celebrate . . .* Another scratch line. That sounded too happy. This needed to be more . . . somber.

*The Good Book says that there is a season to be born and a season to die. . . .* Too preachy.

I balled up the piece of paper and sat back. What was I *really* trying to say here? Was this about her death? Or her life?

Trying a different angle, I bent over the notebook and wrote down some of the things I'd admired about Kristen. Her laugh. Her infectious smile. Her kindness. Her loyalty. Her fierce protection of our friendship. If only people could see *those* sides of her, my job would be done. She had been an easy person to love.

Satisfied with what I'd come up with, I took another short nap and woke up with plenty of time to get ready. I knew right away what to wear. It only seemed right to put on her favorite maroon corset-style top—the one I'd taken from her bedroom after I'd found the diaries—and a flowing black skirt. She would have liked that outfit.

"Boots or flats, Kristen?" I debated, as I rummaged through my closet. One heavy black boot fell at my feet with a solid *thump*, and I looked down. "Okay. Boots it is." I laced them up and moved to the bathroom to style my hair. I was finished ten minutes later.

I almost forgot my notebook as we got in the van to leave, but I hurried back to my room and grabbed it. Dread tied my stomach into knots, and the short trip to the bridge passed all too quickly.

"How many people are going to be there?" I asked Mom as Dad pulled into the Old Dutch Church parking lot. The church was next to the bridge, and it looked like that was where everyone was parking.

"Fifty, a hundred. I'm not really sure. I don't think any more than that."

Swallowing hard, I locked my hands together and squeezed until they turned white. The fierce pressure was a welcome distraction from the mind-numbing fear that was threatening to take over at the thought of "fifty, a hundred" people all listening to what I had to say.

"Are you *sure* I have to do this?" I asked. "Why does it have to be me that says something about her?"

Mom opened her door and stood up, smoothing out the edges of her wrinkle-free black pantsuit. Pausing for a moment to look back at me, she said in a soft tone, "Because *you* were her best friend, Abbey. You knew her better than anyone."

Unlocking my hands, I released my seat belt and climbed out of the car. I gripped the sides of my skirt. The parking lot was full. It reminded me of Kristen's funeral. *There was standing room only that day. And it was raining.*

If I turned to glance at the mausoleum on the hill, would he be standing there? Watching me? White-blond hair and a black suit. Green eyes and an easy smile. *Caspian . . .*

Forcing those thoughts away, I clutched my skirt harder. A bead of sweat ran down my back, and I shifted uncomfortably. Several people stood by their cars, most of them smoking and talking with one another, while a local TV van idled nearby. A reporter was clipping some sort of wire pack under her suit jacket.

Mom said something to me, but I didn't hear her. I was focused on just making it through this and getting it over with. All I could think about was how much I *didn't* want to be here.

We crossed the street and passed by a police officer who was directing traffic and holding up a SLOW sign. When we walked closer to the huge wooden beams that made up the main arch of the new bridge, I glanced up. There weren't any windows cut into the sides of the bridge, and it seemed oddly cumbersome and wrong. All sharp angles and rough seams. Not at all what I'd imagined from the Sleepy Hollow legend.

It was out of place. . . . Like me.

A podium had been set up on the sidewalk off to the side of the bridge entrance, and the man standing behind it waved us over. We had to push our way through several groups of people clustered tightly together. There wasn't much room for anyone else to stand on the small patch of concrete.

The man introduced himself as Robert, the master of cere-monies, and then he and Mom started talking. As far as I could tell, he wasn't going to actually be *doing* anything during the ceremony, but he seemed to like his title. I turned away and went to stand closer to the water.

Bracing myself with one hand on the edge of a beam, I stared down into the Crane River. It was calm and clear. Tiny pockets of current swirled and danced as they rushed farther and farther downstream.

My fingers found each crack and split that made up the

wood grain and followed the scattered, random squiggles and lines that blended into one another. As I traced across the wood, my pinkie snagged on a piece of cold metal.

*Wood and metal. Tough and strong.* Things that could stand the test of time. Things that hadn't been here a couple of months ago. What if they had? Would things be different? Would Kristen not have fallen into the river? *Would those thick beams have caught her? Stopped her . . . ?*

I pondered that over and over again, running my pinkie round and round the screw head, until I felt something catch. Quickly pulling my hand away from the beam, I looked down. The skin had split, right down the middle of the finger pad.

Holding my breath in anticipation, I waited for that dark red drop to well up. For some sign of life to come pulsing out of me.

It didn't.

Surely I would bleed. I was cut. But the blood didn't come. Instead my pinkie just began to throb.

I held it up and watched as my finger pulsed, each movement in sync with my heartbeat, like there was a gossamer string attached from my heart to my hand. The noise of the traffic and reverberation of people began to fade. Only white static filled my ears, and I couldn't turn away.

"Abigail!"

The sound of my name shook my concentration, and I blinked once. Mom was standing to my right, one hand gesturing for me to come over to her, and I realized what a freak I must look like, standing there with one finger raised in the air.

I blinked again. Noises started returning, and I came back to where I was and what I was supposed to be doing. The low buzz of people resumed, and I lowered my hand. Wiping my palms hastily on the sides of my skirt, I found myself repeating Mom's earlier actions and smoothing out a nonexistent wrinkle.

*Get it together, Abbey. You're in public.*

I made my way over to Mom. She was nodding and smiling, talking to a reporter, while also casting discreet *Is everything okay?* glances my way.

I grabbed Mom's hand and squeezed it tight, trying to send her my best *I'm fine* vibe. Her grip tightened and then relaxed, and I could tell she got the message. I tried to stay out of the reporter's way, but then she must have realized I was another person to talk to. Her body language changed, and she started to inch the microphone away from Mom's face.

Mom just compensated by smiling wider and moving her head forward each time the mike moved backward. Mom hated to give up the spotlight. By the time she was done answering a question about how the town council had arranged the cere-mony, her neck was craned at such an angle that she looked like a giraffe. It would have been comical if I hadn't been concen-trating so hard on trying to keep up my smile and decide what I would say if the reporter asked me about Kristen.

I didn't have much time to rehearse.

"And I understand that you were a friend of Kristen Maxwell's?" A big, round foam piece was stuck in my face, and the reporter turned my way simply by shifting her pad-ded shoulders. It was seriously impressive. "You two went to school together, correct?"

Picturing the little caption with my name spelled wrong that might appear on the TV screen if this piece ran on the news, I leaned forward to speak directly into the foam covering. "Yes," I said a bit too loudly.

The woman's face got kind of pinched around the eyes, and she tilted the microphone down and away from me.

Mom quickly slid into the picture and put one arm around me in a gesture of sympathy. "Abbey and Kristen were best friends since they were seven years old. I think it's wonderful that Kristen will be remembered this way." Her arm tightened, and I tried to keep my smile on.

"And how do you feel about the fact that this tragedy

occurred? Do you think the town of Sleepy Hollow could have done more to prevent it?" She didn't pause for me to answer. "Do you think that construction-site safety needs to become a higher priority for our city?"

I froze. She redirected the foam at me, and I just stood there with a blank smile. What was I supposed to say here? Did she want me to answer *all* of those questions? Or just the last one? Mom's grip turned into an anaconda death squeeze, and I got the hint that she wanted me to stay quiet.

"I'm sure all of us wonder, *Could we have done more?* when tragedy strikes," Mom said. "As concerned citizens, we always want to learn how we can prevent something like this from *ever* happening again. We just have to do our best to make sure safety rules are followed to the fullest extent and push for better laws to protect our communities."

Mom was a real pro.

The cameraman made some sort of *Wrap it up* gesture with his hand, and the reporter stepped back in. "Truer words have never been spoken. I'm Cara Macklyn with Channel Eight News, reporting from the dedication ceremony at the Washington Irving Bridge."

We stood with frozen smiles on our faces until the camera guy called, "*Aaaaand* we're out." Then Mom complimented the reporter on her lovely outfit, the reporter complimented Mom on her lovely daughter, and I stood in the middle of it all, not knowing when would be the right time to stop smiling.

Finally we all shook hands, and then Mom shuffled me toward the podium. Mayor Archer was there now, studying several note cards, but he looked up as we approached. I said hello and went through another round of handshakes.

Mom stood by my side, looking so proud of me. But all I could think was, *Why did I agree to do this? What if I mess up?*

More perspiration trickled down my back, and immediately, I wanted a shower. It was hot and sticky out, and the growing crowd was adding to my overwhelming feeling of clamminess and unease.

Then it hit me.

*I can't do this! This is a lot of people. I can't speak in front of crowds!*

Taking deep breaths, I tried not to hyperventilate. But I could hear little gusts of air being sucked in and out as I started breathing faster and faster. Mom turned to me, and I saw the color leave her face.

"Are you okay?" she asked. "You look like you're going to throw up."

"Crowds ... can't do it ... feeling sick ..."

"Yes, you can, Abbey," she said. "It will be over before you know it. Just say a couple of words about Kristen, and then you're through."

I shook my head at her. "Can't . . . do . . . it." I looked around me. I needed to leave. I had to get out of here.

Mom must have realized my intentions to bolt, because she latched on to my arm and squeezed gently. The pressure actually managed to distract me from hyperventilating . . . a bit.

"You wrote down what you're going to say, right?"

I nodded.

"Then you're going to be fine. As soon as the mayor calls you, just read what you wrote. I'll be standing right here next to you to give you my support. Okay?"

I nodded again, and then Mayor Archer started talking. He greeted the crowd and thanked everyone for coming. Naming all the members of the town council and the building committee, who had "worked tirelessly on this project and shown true community service and pride," he encouraged a round of applause and then announced that I would be coming up to give the dedication.

Mom had to propel me toward the podium, but true to her word she stood up next to me. Mayor Archer introduced me as Kristen's best friend, and then everything fell silent.

I glanced down at the paper I held clenched in one fist, then placed it on the podium and flattened out a folded edge. Everything I wanted to say was there. In front of me. All I had to do was open my mouth and read the words. They were waiting for me.

"Kristen Maxwell was . . ." I broke off, and then tried again. "She was a . . ."

Someone near the front shifted and distracted me, and I felt the urge to clench my fists. I tried to spot Ben but couldn't. So instead I decided to try his trick. I looked out at the crowd, picturing everyone in ridiculous underwear.

It kind of helped.

"I could tell you . . . all the good things that Kristen Maxwell was," I read hesitantly. "A good daughter. A good friend. A good student. A good person. But that's what you'd expect to hear. Who ever talks about all the bad qualities someone had after they've died?" My voice wavered, but I continued on. "But what was really important about Kristen was that she loved life. She loved living, and smiling, and just enjoying everything that came her way. *That* was her best trait."

I looked over at the bridge. "We used to come here before the construction started. We'd hang out underneath the bridge and look at the water. Just talking and laughing. Spending time together. She really liked it here." I started to get choked up, and

I fought to hold it back. "Even though she'll never get to enjoy the simple things in life again, *I've* decided to enjoy them for her. To live each day to its fullest, and to always try to find the happiness in small things. Like Kristen did."

Several people were dabbing at the corners of their eyes, and then thunderous applause broke out. They kept clapping and clapping, and I looked up into the cloud-covered sky. *These people are clapping for you, Kris.*

Mayor Archer returned to the podium and the applause died down. "I'd like to thank Abigail Browning for her touching words," he said, "and all of you for coming out. This bridge is hereby declared the Washington Irving Bridge, and is dedicated to the memory of Kristen Maxwell."

The mayor smiled out at the crowd, but already people were starting to shift. Ready to move on. They separated into two distinct groups: Those who were moving toward us, no doubt looking for conversation, and those who were moving toward the parking lot in a polite stampede. They worked against each other, and it looked like everyone was gridlocked.

Mom and I just stood there, waiting for the incoming tidal wave until finally Dad reached us. I was in a sort of haze, blindly shaking proffered hands and saying "Thank you" as people told me what a great job I did, or how I had their sympathies. As soon as I could, I latched on to Dad and put my arm around him.

It felt nice to have something solid to hold on to and just that small gesture helped me immediately feel more grounded.

Dad shook hands too, and he was able to reach more of them faster than I could. Eventually people stopped coming, and I took a moment to scan who was left. I didn't see the Maxwells or Ben, but I managed to catch Mom's attention for a second. "Did the Maxwells come?"

She shook her head. "They must have decided they just couldn't do it." She put a hand on my arm. "You did a great job, Abbey."

I smiled at her. "Thanks, Mom. And thanks for standing up there with me."

We were the last ones by the bridge now, except for Mayor Archer, and I figured that Mom and Dad would want to talk to him before we left. "I'm going to wait by the car," I told her. "Don't be long, okay?"

"Of course, of course," she said, but I knew her thoughts were already elsewhere.

The traffic cop was gone, and I had to wait for several cars to pass before I could cross the street to the Old Dutch Church. Entering the parking lot, I noticed that there were only a handful of cars left, and no one seemed to be around. I moved to the side of the church that was hidden from the main road and hopped up onto a low masonry rock wall that jutted out from the stone foundation.

It was quiet back here, and I had a full view of the older gravestones that made up this part of the cemetery. They were ornately carved and beautifully decorated with flowing cursive script that stood out in sharp relief against the granite. Many of the stones were doubles—final resting places for a husband and wife—and those always made my heart ache just a little bit.

I leaned back. The sun was peeking out from the clouds, and the rocks were pleasantly warm. I stretched my hands out behind me, feeling the contrasting smooth stone and rough mortar edges. Tipping my face upward, I closed my eyes. I was finally alone and comfortable.

A mosquito buzzed near my ear, and I swatted it away. I turned my head, thinking that it was just that. Nothing more than a bug.

But then I saw *them*.

A weird, shivery feeling passed through me, as goose bumps suddenly covered my whole body. My fingers tightened reflexively on the rocks, and I forced myself to relax. *It's just a couple of people. No big deal.*

They were walking among the graves on the far side of the cemetery. Weaving in and out around them. As they came closer, I could see what they were wearing. It was ... *odd*. Even in a town that has its fair share of Goths and vampire wannabes, they definitely stuck out.

The guy wore baggy black skater shorts with a wallet chain attached, several layered long-sleeved red and black shirts that looked way too hot for summer, and carefully smudged Johnny Depp guyliner. A black Mohawk was the crowning touch.

The girl had on a black-and-purple plaid miniskirt, torn fishnets, and biker boots laced with teal shoelaces that matched her mini tee. Her hair was shoulder length, neon purple, with the bottom a pale blond about six inches up.

I didn't know either of them, so I stayed sitting, hoping that they would keep moving on.

But my gut told me they wouldn't.

Pasting on the fake smile that had served me so well at the bridge ceremony, I waited for them. They got within arm's length and then stopped.

Both of them were extremely pale. Their skin was almost translucent. And it had the strangest sheen to it. Like vellum paper. *And I thought I was sun deficient.* Their eyes were strange too. Very wide, and clear. If they had any hint of color to them, it was only the faintest shade of gray. They had to be brother and sister.

"Do you know where the nearest gas station is?" the girl asked. "I'm dying for a Coke."

Her voice was *incredible*. Absolutely crystalline. I had the strangest notion that she'd just sung her question to me, and I felt all shivery again. Then my head cleared, and I tried to hide my simultaneously awed and weirded-out feelings.

"It's um . . . well, there's um . . ." It was like all my sense of direction was gone. My brain felt hazy. I tried again. "There's, um, a gas station a couple blocks up here on your right. Just keep following the sidewalk . . . I think. . . ."

The guy smiled at me, and the girl chirped her thanks. They both stared until I dropped my gaze.

"Do you live around here?" the songstress asked me.

"Yeah, I'm Abbey Browning." The words flew out of my mouth before I could stop them.

She smiled, revealing a perfect row of dainty white teeth. "I'm Cacey, and this is Uri."

I nodded, wondering if I should, like, shake their hands or something. They both watched me with their pale eyes, and it was incredibly unnerving.

"You don't really want a Coke, do you?" I said, not even realizing why I was saying it.

Uri shot a glance over at Cacey, then said, "Maybe. Maybe not." His voice was low pitched, with a beautiful timbre to it. Like warm chocolate sliding over rich velvet.

My entire scalp broke out in creepy crawlies. It felt like dozens of baby spiders were suddenly swarming across my head and tap dancing down my spine.

It was *not* a pleasant feeling.

"Well, it was nice to meet you guys." I stood up. "But I have to go. My parents are waiting for me."

"Okay," Cacey said. It didn't look like she was blinking at all. "We just have one more question for you."

I should have walked away. I should have left them behind and gone to Mom and Dad and told them to drive me away from there as fast as they could.

But I didn't. I stayed.

"Were you friends with Kristen Maxwell?" Uri asked. "The girl who drowned in the river here?"

I froze. This was beyond creepy now. Even though I'd just given a speech about Kristen's death, this just felt *wrong*. Very, very wrong. Like they shouldn't have *known* that. "Why do you want to know?" My voice was almost a whisper.

"We heard about what happened. That's all," he said.

Suddenly, a completely carefree, everything's-fine-now feeling washed over me. I had the most insane urge to laugh everything off. But it almost felt . . . forced. I knew I *shouldn't* be feeling all fine and dandy. What was going on here? All I could think to say was, "Okay. Well, I really do have to get going. See ya."

My mouth felt funny, and I swallowed hard. Someone must have been burning leaves or something, because I could taste it on my tongue.

"Bye, Abbey," Cacey trilled. "Catch you later."

The spiders came back and did double time on my spine, and I walked away as fast as I could.

*Chapter Four*

# NEW PLANS

From hence the low murmur of his pupils' voices . . . might be heard in a drowsy summer's day . . .

—"The Legend of Sleepy Hollow"

I wanted to visit the cemetery the next day, but I had to take a trip to Hollow High to return my junior-year textbooks.

When I'd left school in February to go stay with Aunt Marjorie, all of the teachers gave me schoolwork to take with me so I wouldn't have to make everything up when I returned. But science had been an issue. I'd had a really tough time with my assignments, and I hadn't gotten very good grades.

Mom and Dad had been pretty lenient, since I had extenuating circumstances and all, but now Mr. Knickerbocker and I were going to have to talk. I didn't want to repeat chemistry my senior year.

It was weird being inside the school with no students. Emptiness hung in the halls. Rows of silver lockers stood barren and waiting for the next batch of teenagers that would call them home for nine months. Wooden floors squeaked under my feet, and I looked down, realizing they were freshly buffed and polished.

Hiking up my book bag, I walked to the administration office. It was a small room, painted in a warm vanilla shade, with lots of pictures on the wall. Mrs. Frantz sat behind the desk with a pencil tucked behind one ear and glasses falling off the tip of her nose. She looked up from her computer and gave me an easy smile.

"Hi, dear. What can I do for you?"

I unzipped my bag and pulled out a stack of books. "Just need to return these." I piled them onto the desk, where they took up almost the entire surface.

She gave me a wry look and sighed. "I'll take care of them."

I turned to leave.

"Wait," she said. "Let me get you a return slip." She opened up a side drawer and dug through for a minute, then pulled out a sheet of paper. After cutting off one side of it, she scribbled her name and then handed it to me.

I tucked the paper into my back pocket. "Thanks. Do you know if Mr. Knickerbocker is still here?"

"Mmm-hmm." She had already returned to her computer work. "Check the gymnasium. Sometimes he helps coach the track team. They have practice today."

Leaving the administration office behind, I hurried to the gym to find him. As I got closer, I could hear sounds spilling out through the open doors. I poked my head in and saw a group of kids doing leg stretches in the corner. They each wore matching blue-and-gold warm-up suits with the logo of the Headless Horseman mascot emblazoned on the side.

But Mr. Knickerbocker wasn't there.

I walked in anyway, figuring that I'd ask one of the runners if they knew where he was, and was surprised to see a girl I sort of recognized from English class. She was standing apart from the main group, bending over to touch her toes. Her long, dark brown hair was gathered in a ponytail, and her smooth skin glowed like she had a permanent tan. I waited for her to notice me.

It took about five seconds.

"Abbey?" She stood up and came over to me. "Are you joining the track team?"

"Me? No. I'm looking for Mr. Knickerbocker. Do you know where he is?"

She leaned into a side stretch. "Nope. Why?"

"I have to talk to him about something." My brain spazzed as I tried to remember her name. *Beth.* That was it.

Beth turned and cupped her hands around her mouth. "Lewis! Yo! Come here."

A tall boy with shaggy black hair and the biggest smile I had ever seen left the leg-stretching group and came to join us. "What's up?" Then he turned to look at me. "Hey, I thought you transferred or something."

I could feel my face turning red. "No. I was, um, sick. Mono."

"Do you know where Mr. Knickerbocker is?" Beth asked him. "She's looking for him."

"He's in his office," Lewis replied. "Or he was, like ten minutes ago."

"Okay, thanks. I'll head there."

"Hey, Abbey," Beth said suddenly. "I'm glad you're back."

"Me too," I said. "See you guys in September."

I found Mr. Knickerbocker in his office just like Lewis had said. He had two neatly stacked piles of paper in front of him and was methodically rearranging them.

He glanced up at me when I cleared my throat. "Abigail. Come in. Have a seat." He pointed to a chair by his desk, and I sat. "How are you . . . feeling?"

Mr. Knickerbocker wasn't dressed in his usual polyester shirt and bad tie; instead he had on a T-shirt and jeans and looked like a total stranger. I didn't even *know* teachers were allowed to wear those types of clothes.

"I'm good. Better, I mean. Feeling better."

He folded his hands in front of him and looked out at me from behind horn-rimmed glasses. "I'm sure you heard about the science fair. Your partner, Mr. Bennett, took second place."

"Yes, I heard. I was happy for him." I moved my foot restlessly against the edge of the chair. *How should I bring this up?*

"Actually, I'm glad you stopped by here today, Miss Browning," he said. "We need to discuss your chemistry grades."

"Well, um, see, that's why I'm here, Mr. Knickerbocker," I blurted out. "I know I've been having a hard time, and I wanted to see if there was any way I could maybe do some extra-credit work, or something? I really don't want to have to take chem again next year."

Instead of answering that, he asked me, "What are your future goals? College? Career? What do you want to do with your life?"

I thought about just telling him that I didn't know, or wasn't sure yet . . . but something prompted me to be truthful. "I'm a perfumer. I create perfumes, and I want to have my own business making them for people."

His eyes lit up. "*Really*. How interesting. Then you must have a particular interest in chemistry, and perhaps botany?"

I nodded. "Granted, I'm more of an experimenter than a strict by-the-book person when I make new perfumes, but the science is fascinating." Then I shook my head. "Fascinating, but totally overwhelming. I have a hard time really grasping all the mechanics behind it."

"All it takes is patience and a willingness to learn, Miss Browning. I've found that the real problem for most students is that they aren't willing to apply themselves. Are you willing to apply yourself?"

Was he talking about extra-credit stuff now? "Um, I guess. . . ." *Maybe*. It all depended on how much it was going to cut into my summer vacation.

Exhaling loudly, he adjusted his glasses. "I was hoping it wouldn't come to this, as you are the *only* student who needs the extra attention this year, but with your future career goals in mind, and your . . . absence . . . during the school year, it can't be avoided."

Now I was getting nervous.

"I'm talking summer school, Miss Browning."

*What?* No way. "But, Mr. Knickerbocker . . . I can't. I'm . . ." *Think, think, think, Abbey. Helping the poor? Going on a mission trip? Working in a soup kitchen?* "Surely there has to be another way . . . ," I protested. "*Summer* school?"

He frowned. "I'm not happy about it either. Do you think I want to spend my only free time *here*? I had plans to spend the entire summer floating in my pool, drink in hand."

*Mental image: Mr. Knickerbocker in a swimsuit. YUCK.*

"What if I . . . But what about . . . Ben!" I said. "Ben's really good at this stuff. What if he tutors me? And then at the end of the summer I can take another test. Like a final exam. Would that work?"

He gave me a look. "Do you think he'd do it?"

*Ben? Absolutely.* "Yup."

"I'd put together some notes, of course, for what *could* be on the test," Mr. Knickerbocker mused. "That way I'll know you're going over everything." He stuck out his hand for me to shake. "You'll have to *pass* this exam, Miss Browning. If you don't, I'll give you a failing grade for the entire year, and then you'll repeat the class. Is it a deal?"

Like that wasn't a ton of pressure or anything. But at least it beat summer school. I shook his hand. "It's a deal."

Five minutes later I was climbing into Mom's car, trying

to tell myself that I'd done the right thing. A couple of tutoring sessions with Ben were *infinitely* better than summer school with Mr. Knickerbocker. Now all I had to do was convince Ben to give up part of his vacation. . . .

As soon as we got home, I went up to my room to call him. I dialed his number, let it ring once, and then hung up.

Tapping my phone against my forehead, I took a deep breath, then dialed again . . . and promptly hung up again.

I threw the phone on my bed and paced back and forth. It was just a question. A simple "Will you do this?" He wouldn't say no. *Would he?*

Bracing myself, I picked the phone back up. I . . . needed a snack first.

I headed downstairs and moved toward the fridge. My phone rang, and I stared at it. Ben's number flashed on the caller ID. *Maybe I should . . . No, no thinking. Just talking.* "Hello?"

"Hi, Abbey," he said. "Did you just try to call me?"

"Um, yeah. Sorry, I must have had a bad connection or something. The call kept dropping." Distracting myself with the food in front of me, I pushed a bottle of juice aside and reached for a can of soda.

"Okay. What's up?"

I moved to a cabinet and gazed up at a row of snack bags. "I wanted to ask you something, Ben." There was silence, and I pulled down a bag of pretzel sticks. I ripped it open and quickly ate one, trying to think of the best way to ask him for this favor. "Do you . . . want to get some pizza with me downtown? In, like, thirty minutes?"

"Yeah. Are you home? I'll come pick you up."

"Okay. I'll, uh, I'll see you in half an hour, then."

So I was a chicken. *But I will ask him over pizza,* I vowed to myself. I just hoped his answer would be yes.

Right on time, Ben pulled up in his battered green Jeep Cherokee, Candy Christine. I'd teased him about the name when he'd first told me, but now I thought it was kind of cute. He honked once, and I climbed into his car with a shy "Hey."

"Don't forget the sweet spot," Ben reminded me.

I flashed him a grin. "I won't." The seat belt had to be pulled down at just the right angle and then snapped in. Once it clicked, Ben threw the car into gear and we pulled away from the curb.

Turning slightly toward him, I sized him up. He looked . . . different. Taller, maybe? Although it was hard to tell sitting down. And he was *very* tan. He'd obviously spent some time out in the sun. His darkened skin really set off his brown eyes.

"So . . . what are your summer plans?" I said. God, that was ten kinds of lame, but I had to ask him *something*. If I continued to stare at him much longer, he might get the wrong idea.

"I'm still working at the Horseman's Haunt. But I'll be helping my dad out too. He has this grand idea to plant Christmas trees for next year, and I've been roped into slave labor." He smiled, showing off his pearly whites.

A spark of awareness ran through me. I didn't remember him being so *cute*.

We drove down Main Street, and he pulled off to park at a meter outside of Tony's Pizzeria. Once we were both out of the car, he fished a handful of change from his pocket, then fed the meter. "Ready?"

"Ready."

Tony himself called hello to us as we stepped in, and we headed for a table near the back. The orange plastic tabletop had definitely seen better days, and the faux wooden bench creaked when we sat down.

"What do you want?" Ben asked. "A couple of slices, or a whole pie?"

"I'm pretty hungry. A whole pie sounds good to me."

"Let me guess, you're a pepperoni type of girl."

I shook my head. "I like mine loaded."

"Seriously?"

"Yup."

He didn't look like he believed me.

"You don't think I can handle it?" I raised one eyebrow at him.

Ben laughed. "No, no. I like mine loaded too. That's what we'll get." He moved to order, and I grabbed a soda from a nearby cooler, carefully reaching around the Coke for a root beer.

"What do you want to drink?" I asked him.

"The same."

I scooped up another root beer, then popped the top of my soda and waited for Ben to return. He came to sit down a second later.

"Pizza's in. One large, with the works."

I nodded and took a sip. Now that we were here, I was losing my nerve again.

"So," Ben said, opening his can, "what are *your* summer plans?"

"I don't know. Since it took so long to get over my ... mono, I'm not really sure what I'm going to do." Okay, so that wasn't *technically* true. I sort of knew one thing I was going to be doing, if Ben agreed to it.

"Gonna work at your uncle's ice cream place again?"

I shrugged. "Don't know. Haven't talked to him about it yet."

"Will that be . . . okay? Can anyone get sick if your mono isn't all gone?"

I almost snorted soda up my nose. "No, no," I sputtered, reaching for a napkin. "The doctor, um, gave me the all-clear. I'm . . . better."

"Oh, cool," he said. "That's good."

"Hey, I didn't see you at the bridge thing." I changed the subject. Too much talk about mono and I might blow it.

"Yeah, sorry about that. I got called in to work. I tried to get out of it—"

Tony came bearing our pizza and interrupted him, placing the round aluminum tray in front of us. "One large, with the works! Youse enjoy it now, 'kay?"

"Looks great, Tony," Ben said. He slid a steaming slice onto a paper plate and handed it over to me, then did the same for himself.

My slice was way too hot to eat yet, but Ben didn't seem to have a problem.

"So how did it go?" he asked, around a mouthful of cheese.

"It was okay. The mayor said something, I said something, and then we left."

"I wish I could have been there," he said softly. He poked the crust of his pizza and then ate the rest of it in two bites.

"I was just sad you weren't there to hold up your cue card like you promised," I teased. "But, um . . . there *is* something else you can help me out with." I glanced down and said the rest in a rush. "I might have to go to summer school, but I talked Mr. Knickerbocker out of it if you'll agree to tutor me so I can pass a big test at the end of summer."

Ben reached for a second slice. "What? That was like a crazy rush of Abbeyspeak. You have to go to summer school?"

I nodded. "Because I basically failed chem."

"But you talked Mr. Knickerbocker out of it?"

"He said that if you'll agree to tutor me over the summer, I can just take another final exam instead." I peeked up at him. "I know it's asking a lot of you, Ben, since you're going to have two summer jobs and all. But I really need the help."

"Well, I *am* good at science," he said slowly, and I grinned at him.

"Does that mean you'll do it? Mr. Knickerbocker will give you notes and everything."

He paused like he had to think for a moment, then nodded. "Sure. I'll do it."

I almost jumped up and hugged him right there. "Really?

*Really,* really? Seriously, I have no idea how to repay you."

His eyes glinted mischievously, and he had a wicked grin. "I'm sure I'll think of something."

Going for my slice of pizza, I stopped mid-grab and gave a mock sigh. "I know. That's what I'm afraid of."

*Chapter Five*

# HAUNTED

A drowsy, dreamy influence seems to hang over the land, and to pervade the very atmosphere.

—"The Legend of Sleepy Hollow"

I didn't know what it was that woke me up, but one minute I was sleeping peacefully, and the next I was lying there, staring at the dark wall. Rolling over on my back, I threw off the covers and draped one arm over my eyes. All I wanted was to go back to *sleep*. Why was I awake?

I shut my eyes and tried to relax. Forcing every muscle in my body to go still, I inhaled and exhaled deeply. But my neck was uncomfortable, and I knew I couldn't stay that way. I flipped my pillow over and felt the smooth, cool side of a pillowcase that had been resting against the sheet. It was heavenly, and I buried my face into it. The scent of fresh laundry still clung there, and the smell was already making me feel sleepy again.

I grabbed for my second pillow to do the same thing with it, but part of it had slipped down in the space between the mattress and the headboard. I had to give it a good, hard yank. It came free, and I slid a hand underneath to flip it over too.

There was something cold and hard there.

My fingers grasped the small square, and my mind recoiled in recognition of what it was. One of the necklaces Caspian had made for me. Almost compulsively, I stroked the smooth glass plates and found the black satin ribbon attached.

I pulled it out and held it in my palm, horror stealing over me. *How can this be real?* He *wasn't real. It doesn't make any sense.*

A dreadful urge came next and whispered in my ear, *Put it on. . . .* My hand shook slightly with the willpower it took not to listen. I couldn't. I didn't know how it had gotten there, but there had to be some other explanation for it.

I held it to my cheek. The glass was cold and gentle. *Like a dying lover's kiss.*

I threw it to the floor. It was making me crazy. These were irrational thoughts and feelings. What was I doing? It was haunting me.

Huddling back under my covers, I squeezed my eyes closed.

*Sleep. Go to sleep.* Everything would be better in the morning. I just needed sleep. My head nestled deeper into the pillow, and I slipped down into a dream.

*Wind blew my hair into my face, and I laughed out loud as I tried to shove the black curls away. The radio blasted out a rhythm of earth-shaking bass beats and soaring guitar riffs as we raced down the highway. Eyes closed, I leaned my head back and felt the vibrations moving through my entire body. My toes curled in my boots and tingled with pleasure.*

*Throwing my arms wide, I caught the breeze and rode the wind. There was no barrier between the sky and me. We were one.*

*A shriek of pure joy escaped my lips, and I felt as light as air. If I wanted to, any second now I could float away, out of the car. The music was the only thing holding me down. The only thing anchoring my soul.*

*A hand reached out and caught mine. Our fingertips snagged, intertwined. I turned my head and held that hand close to my cheek. When my eyes opened, there was no surprise as I registered brown eyes. Curly brown hair.*

*No surprise . . . but no heat, either.*

*Ben grinned at me, and the wild music faltered, sputtered out. Only for a second, but it happened.*

"Let's take a break, babe," he called.

I nodded. The music played on. A different song now, but one with the same driving urgency behind it. The car slowed and came to a stop. I looked down, surprised to see that we weren't in Ben's green Jeep, but in a red sports car instead.

The scenery around us shimmered and changed from an endless orange desert to a fifties-style silver boxcar diner. We were inside now, and I took in the kitschy decor.

Plastic-covered menus, their sides greasy and flecked with dried bits of food, sat on round red vinyl tables. The floor was covered in black-and-white-checkered linoleum with curled and peeling edges. A jukebox was on, and the song "I Only Have Eyes for You" echoed through the small room.

Ben grabbed my hand again and flipped it over, palm side up. He began to trace it, following the lines that crisscrossed there. A sense of déjà vu came over me, and my stomach tied in knots and dropped to the floor.

I jerked my hand away. I should tell him not to . . . not to . . . something. I had to tell him something.

But then he smiled at me, and all my misgivings vanished. "Want to dance?"

Of course. This was happy. This was fun.

. . . right?

He pulled me close, and suddenly the music was louder, completely enveloping us. I glanced around and noticed that the diner was empty. No waitresses, no staff, not even any other customers.

He steered us to a corner. Hidden from view of the register, the counter, even the kitchen, it was our own private stage. The music pushed in, crowding around us and filling my ears. My head ached at the sound of it. Over and over again, the same song played.

Ben spun me once, and I landed against the wall. Dizzy and out of breath. He came closer. "You're so beautiful, Abbey. Have I ever told you that? I don't know. . . ."

Those words sent a shiver down my spine, and I closed my eyes. Was this the feeling I'd been waiting for? His feet nudged mine as he slid one leg closer. I pressed my back to the wall and arched my spine. I don't know why I did it, but it felt good . . . right.

He accepted my wordless invitation and came up flush against me. I blushed when I looked down and realized I was straddling his leg.

I started to move away, pull back. . . .

"Don't," he whispered, catching both of my hands, pinning them to the wall on either side of me. "Stay. . . ."

I was helpless in his grip. I didn't feel trapped, yet he was holding me in place. Bending down, he started kissing my neck, and my knees went limp.

"*Abbey, Abbey . . . ,*" *he said.*

*The music flared and then died down to a low buzz. It was like it was playing directly on a soundtrack inside my brain. Again and again the loop repeated: "I only have eyes . . . for you . . . for you . . . for you . . ."*

*His murmurs bled together, and I closed my eyes again, feeling the beat of my heart thumping in tune with his words. "Abbey . . . Abbey . . . Abbey . . .*

*"Astrid."*

*My eyes flew open, and I held desperately still.* What did he say? What did he just call me?

*Ben must have felt my body go rigid, because he raised his head too.*

*"What did you . . ."*—*I licked lips gone instantly dry*—*"say?"*

*"Abbey," he replied, clearly puzzled. "I called you Abbey."*

*I held his gaze and searched his eyes, looking for something . . . anything.*

*He smiled at me again and leaned in until his lips were just a fraction of an inch away from mine. "Do you prefer Goddess? Light of my life? All that I desire? I'll gladly name you any of those things."*

*That shiver came back again. This was what I wanted. This was real, and I wanted it. . . . Him.*

I slid my hands out from underneath his and wrapped them around his neck.

"I like Goddess," I whispered back.

He grinned, a very sexy grin. "Goddess it is." And then his eyes changed to green.

I slammed back against the wall, wrenching myself away from him. Horror clawed its way up from the pit of my stomach and lodged in my throat.

Brown eyes gazed at me in concern.

"Abbey, what's—"

"Why did you do that?!" I screeched.

"Do what?" he asked.

Change your eyes to green! *my mind screamed.* You changed your eyes! *But I couldn't force the words past the lump in my throat.*

I took in every square inch of his face. It was *his* face. Not Caspian's. It was just me and Ben. Here. Together. Didn't I want this? This was normal. *I was being normal.*

I took a step closer and threw my arms around him again. "Forget it," I whispered in his ear. "Bad memory. Now, where were we?"

He turned his head and our lips met. I pushed away the feeling that I was doing something wrong. Reaching up, I threaded my fingers through his hair. But instead of curly, his hair was long and smooth.

*It flashed in and out before me. Changing from dark brown to that shocking, shocking pale blond. I moaned from the confusion and frustration of it all, and Ben moaned too. Then deepened the kiss.*

*I was frozen in place when his eyes changed again.* Green eyes, blond hair. *A strand of black appeared, and my stomach dipped. My blood pressure soared. I was hot and achy and feverish.* Caspian. *He was what I wanted.*

*I lost control. Only for a second, but I wanted to feel him. To taste him.*

*I crushed my mouth to his and teased the edge of his lips with my tongue. Instantly, he granted me entry, and the back of my brain exploded from the pleasure. There was no mistaking it. This was the reprieve I sought so desperately.*

*My eyes fluttered open and shut while Caspian weaved in and out of existence.*

*Brown eyes, brown hair.*

Ben ...

*Green eyes. Blond hair.*

Caspian ...

*Green ... brown ...*

*I caught myself. Was this wrong? To use Ben this way?* Yes. *I knew the answer to that question was a thousand times yes.*

*Tearing myself away, this time for good, I stepped out of his arms* and away from the wall. "I can't . . . I'm sorry." And then I was running.

Out of the diner, out to the car. I jumped in the passenger seat and put my head between my knees.

I was going crazy . . . again.

Ben came bursting out of the diner and called my name. I raised my head and lifted a hand—whether to call him over or warn him to stay away, I didn't know. But suddenly the car roared to life.

Caspian was sitting in the driver's seat.

I did a double take to make sure it wasn't really Ben doing that weird flashing again, but Ben was still by the diner. We peeled out of the gravel driveway, spitting stones as we went, and I noticed that my hand was still up. Now it was catching the wind again. . . .

"What's happening?" I choked out. My throat was dry and scratchy. "Why is this happening to me?"

Caspian didn't answer; instead he turned on the radio. A violin wept in sadness. "Don't you know, my love?" a female voice crooned, soft and full of emotion. "Would you die, my love? I am waiting, waiting for you. These ashes turned bone. Waiting, waiting for you. Waiting . . . waiting for you."

As the violin echoed the singer's dying last words, Caspian turned his gaze to mine and looked straight into my eyes. "I'm waiting, waiting for you."

I sat up straight, chest heaving, breath sawing in and out of me. Shoving heavy fistfuls of damp hair away from my face, I tried to slow everything down. My pulse was raging and it felt like I had a fever. And then I had a crazy thought.

I swung my legs out of bed, walked to the bathroom, and switched on the light. Of course my hair wasn't windblown. My lips weren't bruised and looking like they'd just been kissed.

But my eyes were wide, and my cheeks were pale. I pinched some color into them and leaned over the sink, replaying that crazy dream.

Was I having another breakdown? Or was my subconscious trying to tell me something?

I stood there a minute longer and then went back to the bedroom. But one glance at my rumpled sheets and I knew I wasn't going to be able to sleep again anytime soon. My foot bumped the necklace on the floor, but I gave it a sharp kick under the bed. As far as I was concerned, it didn't exist.

I turned on my desk light and moved over to my new perfume cabinet. Reaching into the desk drawer, I pulled out a pen, a pair of scissors, and some unused paper that looked like old parchment. Then I opened my supply briefcase. Starting with the bottom row first, I made a label for each tiny bottle so that it would have its own drawer in the cabinet.

As I copied the names, the haunting melody of a violin echoed in my ears, and I started thinking about the sample notes of a perfume to match it.

Lavender. Honeysuckle. Jasmine. Wild violets. Something with just a hint of longing and heartbreak. Old roses left on a lover's grave. A wilted carnation pressed between the pages of a prom program. Forgotten baby's breath hastily discarded along with the bouquet's green wax paper . . .

Jotting down possible formulations on a piece of the parchment paper, I came up with the perfect name for this new fragrance. I'd call it Ashes Turned Bone.

Later that morning I filled my cereal bowl and drank down a large glass of juice along with a cup of tea. I hadn't been back to bed since the dream, but I felt oddly exhilarated in spite of my exhaustion. My fingers were itching to get back to my perfumes upstairs.

Mom entered the kitchen and made a pit stop at the coffee-maker before sitting down next to me. "Hungry?"

I smiled at her. "Working on a new perfume."

She smiled back, a genuinely happy smile, and I could see the relief in her eyes that I was working with my perfumes again. "What's the inspiration?"

*Ashes, bones, haunting music, lost love.* Probably not the answer she was looking for. "Violins." I bit into a piece of toast and crunched loudly.

"Ooh, I get it. Strings, old wood, and furniture polish?"

"Right." *Hmmm . . .* Actually, now that I thought about it, that wasn't a bad combo. I should make that one too.

"Oh, hey, guess what," I said, suddenly remembering my recent conversation with Mr. Knickerbocker. "You know how I had to drop my books back off at school?"

Mom nodded.

"I talked to Mr. Knickerbocker while I was there about what I could do to help improve my chem grade."

Now she looked intrigued.

"My friend Ben, the one who was my science-fair partner and is supersmart, offered to tutor me. Then I'm going to take a test at the end of summer, and that will help average out my numbers." I left out the whole by-the-way-my-entire-year's-grade-is-riding-on-the-test thing.

"So it's going to be just you and Ben?" Mom asked. "Where is this tutoring going to be taking place?"

I hadn't thought about that. "Um, I guess here? That would probably be the easiest."

Her face turned disapproving. "And how often?"

"A couple of times a week?" I thought she'd be happy about this, but she was looking decidedly *un*happy. Time to do some damage control. "It was really sweet of Ben to say that he'll tutor me. He already has a job at the Horseman's Haunt, plus he's going to be helping out his dad with some farm stuff."

She looked impressed. "He *was* a very polite young man when your father and I met him." Then she nodded. "And you're almost seventeen. It's hardly like you'd need a babysitter."

I smiled to myself. I was *good*.

*Chapter Six*

# CHNOPS AND SHOPS

He was a kind and thankful creature . . . whose spirits rose with eating . . .

—"The Legend of Sleepy Hollow"

When Ben came over three days later for our first science session, his arms were loaded down with papers. He greeted me and entered the living room.

"Hey . . . Ben," I said. Unfortunately, all the steamiest parts of my recent dream chose *that* moment to come flooding back in excruciating detail, and my face flamed.

"Ready to get started?" he asked.

*It was just a dream, just a stupid dream.* "Yeah, sure. What's all that?"

He glanced down. "I brought some of my old notes so you could look them over." Dropping the stack onto the floor, he took a seat and held up one finger in a dead-on imitation of Mr. Knickerbocker. "It's science time. Have a seat, Miss Browning."

I rolled my eyes but did as he instructed. Snaking one hand forward, I picked up a composition book he had lying on top of the pile. The inside pages were covered with his handwriting. I groaned. "Do we have to cover *all* of this?"

"Yes. It's divided into different sections." He took the book from my hands and started reading from it. "Acids and their base chemistry, the elements, basic atomic structure, quantum theory, CHNOPS . . ."

"CHNOPS? What's that?"

"The six elements that make up all living matter. Carbon, hydrogen, nitrogen, oxygen, phosphorus, and sulfur. CHNOPS is an acronym."

I buried my face in my hands. He was speaking Greek. "Why can't we just do something simple, like making a LEGO replica of the solar system or something? God, I hate chemistry."

Ben grinned and started to do that excited-jumpy thing he'd done once before in the library when we were researching projects for the science fair. "You know, in sixth grade I made one of those out of meatballs. It was great. The entire solar system was edible."

The look on Ben's face was so ridiculous that I had to laugh. He was *very* pleased with himself.

"Why does that not surprise me?" I got up. "Before we get started, I want to show you something. Come here."

He followed me to the kitchen. "Think of it as my way of paying you back." Throwing open one of the cabinets above the sink, I revealed that it was stuffed with Doritos, cheese curls, pretzels, microwave popcorn, and a dozen other snacks. "Behold, the Ben Cabinet."

His eyes grew huge. "I think I love you. Are those Funyuns?" He pulled out a yellow-and-green bag. "*These* are the snack food of the gods."

"They're all yours. I hate Funyuns."

We moved back into the living room and took a seat on the floor next to the papers. Ben placed the bag of Funyuns between us and ripped them open. He scooped up a handful and started to crunch.

"I wish Kristen was here," I said. "She was *so* much better at science than me."

Ben stopped eating and looked over. I thought for a moment he was going to say something about how he missed Kristen too, but then he said, "Do you remember when we had that debate over evolution versus creationism in biology?

You were in that class with me and Kristen, right?"

Of course I remembered that day. I couldn't forget it. Two buttons on the top of my shirt had popped off right when I was getting ready to argue my side of the debate. Luckily, thanks to Kristen standing in front of me and literally covering for me, no one else saw it.

"Yeah, I was," I said. "Kristen was amazing. I've never seen anyone think so fast on their feet."

"She was really good at that," he added. "When she was switched to my team and only had like five minutes to prepare, she had a list of points already made. Even though she was supposed to be debating *against* creationism, she'd made arguments for both sides."

I smiled at him. "That was Kris. Always prepared."

"Did she ever tell you that the only reason I got so many points was because she let me have most of the arguments on her list?"

"*No.*" Even *I* could hear the surprise in my voice. "She never told me that."

"Yup. She said that since I was the captain, her answers were there to benefit the entire team, and I was the one 'leading the boat.' I'll never forget that phrase. I always thought it was funny. 'Leading the boat'. . ."

His eyes took on a faraway look. "After that, I knew she wasn't just some airhead who relied on her looks, or copying someone else's homework the morning of class, to get by. She really took it seriously, you know?"

I looked down at the floor and tugged on a loose carpet fiber. I'd been guilty of copying Kristen's homework in homeroom on more than one occasion.

"And when she finally did make an argument," he continued on, "man, it just blew me away. She said something about how it came down to faith versus science, and even scientists had to have faith every now and then."

I smiled and we sat there in silence for a while. Finally, Ben cleared his throat. "Okay, let's actually get started sometime today."

I nodded and then we got to work.

The next time Ben came over we spent two hours diagramming atoms and protons and neutrons, and it felt like my brain was going to start melting.

"I can't do this," I said.

"Want to take a break?"

"*Yes,*" I replied eagerly. "Let's get out of the house."

We left everything where it was and headed in the general direction of downtown. I steered him toward the end of the block, where my storefront was waiting, and we passed an antique store along the way.

Ben glanced over at the window and then turned to me. "If you ever go in there, do *not* buy the giant blue urn near the back."

"Okay. Although I'm not planning on buying an urn anytime soon.... Why not?"

"Because I went in there once with my mom, and I had just eaten this chili corn dog from the street fair. It must have been undercooked, or it was the heat, or something ..."

As soon as he said the words "it must have been undercooked," I realized I did *not* want to hear the end of this story.

"...but I knew I was gonna puke, and the only thing around was that urn."

*Talk about gross.*

"No one saw, so I just put the lid back on and didn't say anything."

I shook my head, feeling slightly queasy myself. "That's not right. That's *so* not right, Ben."

Then we came to my shop, and I pointed at the bay window, glad to have something else to talk about. "Look there. Isn't it gorgeous?"

I pressed my face against the glass and cupped my hands around my eyes to block out the sun's glare. It looked . . . different. "Does this place look clean to you? Do you think they're cleaning it up?" I asked him.

He walked over to my side and peered in. "Umm, it kind of just looks old and crappy to me."

Taking a step back, I tried to see it how he was seeing it. Yeah, the glass was cracked. And there were cobwebs in one corner of the room. Plus, several lightbulbs needed replacing.

But the window itself was actually clean, not grimy like it had been the last time I was here, during Christmas. The floorboards looked freshly scrubbed and polished too.

Some spray bottles and rags were sitting near the back door. I jabbed a finger in their direction. "Look, over there!" I said. "Someone's definitely been *cleaning*."

Suddenly, something moved inside the store.

"Did you see that?" I asked.

Ben nodded, and we both looked closer, trying to make out what it was. A figure moved in and out of the light, then disappeared into a back room.

"Come on." I motioned for Ben to follow me.

"What? What's up, Abbey? Why does it matter who that is?"

"Because this is *my* store! I mean, the store I'm going to

open one day for my perfume business. And I want to make sure that someone else isn't renting it."

He followed me reluctantly to the alley around back. The door was propped open with a plastic milk crate, and I stepped up to look inside the store. "Hello—"

I was cut off as a large person came barreling out of the store and nearly collided with me. He was holding a stack of boxes.

"Sorry," I said, jumping out of the way. He jumped too, but managed to keep hold of his boxes.

"Oh, my. I didn't even see you there. Just let me set these down over yonder."

The man sat the boxes near the wall and then came back to me. "Now, what can I do for you, little missy?"

He swept off the tall black hat he wore, and bowed low. A short red jacket stretched tightly across his shoulders, and I noticed that his black pants were oddly shiny. He looked sort of like a ringmaster from a circus.

"I noticed that someone was cleaning up the store here, and I wondered if it was going to be occupied. I just love the shops downtown." I widened my smile and gazed up at him.

The man chuckled. "She's still vacant for now. I was just prettying her up a bit."

"Do you need any help with that?" I put on my I-am-a-very-polite-teenager voice.

"Ain't you the nicest thing," he said. "Thank you for your offer, but I do believe I can manage."

"Do you own this store?"

"Oh, it's mine." He gave me a calculating smile, revealing a large set of white teeth.

"Lovely," I said. "So since it's been available for a while, would you be willing to offer a discount to the next person who rented it?" I thought I heard Ben snort, but I ignored him.

"Well, I can't promise anything, since certain terms would have to be discussed. But I'm a generous landlord."

"I'll be graduating soon, so you might be hearing from me. *If* the terms are acceptable."

"You *are* a clever little thing," he said. "I think I like you." Digging into his back pocket, he pulled out a business card and handed it to me with a wink. "Here's my card."

I accepted it and looked down. "Thank you, Mr.—"

"Melchom," he supplied.

"Nice to meet you, Mr. Melchom. I'm Abbey Browning." I stuck out a hand, and we shook. "Good luck with your store."

I turned to Ben, who had remained amazingly quiet the whole time. "Ready to go?"

He nodded.

Once we were clear of the back entrance, Ben leaned in to me and drawled, "Why, you southern belle, you."

"Oh, please. I was just being nice."

Ben scoffed. "You were totally sweet-talking him! I was waiting for you to bat your eyelashes and break out the sweet tea."

"It's called using my God-given charm, Ben. Haven't you ever seen *Gone with the Wind*?"

He just shook his head at me. "Chick flick." Then he froze mid-step. "Wait a minute."

"What?"

He leaned in close and inspected my hair. "A bit of straw from the barn jest stuck right in there," he said, plucking out an imaginary.

I couldn't help the laughter that bubbled out of me. "You? Are a dork."

*Chapter Seven*

# AN EMBARRASSMENT

However wide awake they may have been before they entered that sleepy region, they are sure, in a little time, to inhale the witching influence of the air . . .

—"The Legend of Sleepy Hollow"

I sat up groggily as Mom knocked on the door, and then glanced over at the clock. 9:34 a.m.

"Do you know that at this time, seventeen years ago on June twenty-first, you arrived after fourteen hours of labor?" she said.

Groaning, I pulled the covers over my head. I had totally forgotten what day it was. "Not the fourteen-hours-of-labor story, Mom."

She sat down on the bed, and I poked my head out. In her hands was a tray that held plates of French toast, chocolate chip pancakes, a Belgian waffle, and a little bowl of strawberries. She put it on the comforter beside me. "Happy birthday, sweetie."

She kissed my cheek before looking sappily into my eyes. "My little baby. So grown up."

"Mom, please." I sat up and dug into the waffle, taking a moment to scatter some of the strawberries on top of it first.

"I know, I know. I'm sorry. What do you want to do today?"

I thought about it for a minute, then said, "Mani-pedis, lunch at Callenini's, and then a trip to that supply store up by the cabin, A Thyme and Reason."

"Sounds good," she said. "Finish your breakfast, get dressed, and we'll hit the road."

I swallowed and then asked, "Are you and Dad going to have a birthday dinner for me tonight?" That was Mom's usual custom, before everything with Kristen happened.

"Of course we are."

"Nothing too sappy, Mom," I begged. *"Pleeease?"*

"And here I was looking forward to the slide show of all your naked baby pictures."

*"Mom!"*

She laughed. "Okay, okay, I'll cancel the slide show and the tribute band."

I cut off a small piece of pancake and waved it at her. "Thank you, Mother. Now go, so I can eat in peace."

~ ~ ~

Three hours later Mom and I had freshly painted fingers and toes (her color: Pretty in Pink, mine: Rock Me Red), our stomachs were full of delicious Italian food, and we were on our way to A Thyme and Reason.

"I can't believe how long it's been since we've stopped in here," I said. "Too long."

"It was last year, right?" Mom asked.

"Yup. You wanted me to make you that Christmasy perfume."

Mom smiled. "Ahhh, I love that one. You captured the scents of winter perfectly. You're such a great perfumer, Abbey."

"You're just saying that because it's my birthday."

Keeping one hand on the wheel, she turned and gave me a serious look. "No. I'm *not* just saying that. Your perfumes are amazing. I know I don't tell you this very often, but you make me proud." She switched lanes. "And I'm glad you've already decided what you want to do with your life. Although I hope you'll rethink the whole college thing, I won't push. I want you to be happy."

I glanced out the window so she wouldn't see me getting all choked up. "Thanks, Mom. You make me pretty proud too."

We pulled into the parking lot, where a glossy green sign proclaimed the store's name. I got out of the car and just took everything in for a minute. The store was located inside a gorgeous old-fashioned house that was painted in stunning shades of green and magenta. A quaint wrought-iron sign post had been added to the front porch with an ALL WELCOME banner hanging from it.

"Have I mentioned yet how much I love this place?" I sighed happily. "I can't wait to have my own store."

Mom followed me inside. "Anything in particular you're looking to stock up on? Maybe some oils for your violin perfume?"

"Yeah," I said automatically. "And I need a few more oils to fill my new supply cabinet."

"How many is *a few*?" Mom asked suspiciously as she eyed the very large essential-oil aisle.

*She knows me so well.* "Birthday girl," I reminded her.

She put both hands up and retreated. "I'll leave you to your shopping. Call me when you're ready."

"Okay." I grabbed an empty basket from a nearby display and started at the *A*'s. *Amyris, angelica, anise, basil, black pepper, cardamom, cedarwood, cilantro, clary sage, dill seed, Douglas fir, eucalyptus . . .*

My basket started to fill up and quickly became superheavy. I stopped at *L* with a deep sigh. I was going to have to come back for the rest another time. I probably had too many already.

Browsing for a moment by the bottles and vials, I looked at what they had, but didn't pick anything up. I had plenty of bottles at home. Then I hauled the basket up to the front register to leave it there while I called for Mom.

But she was already there, talking to the lady behind the counter, and her eyes widened when she saw what I had.

"It's just a couple . . . ," I said defensively. *Couple dozen.* "It's a really big cabinet."

There was a split second when I thought she was going to refuse to pay, but then she nodded and gestured for the clerk to start ringing everything up. I breathed a silent sigh of relief.

*Why can't birthdays be every day?*

"I remember you," the lady behind the counter said. "You came here before and liked our selection because you only had a smaller store by your house." She started scanning items and punching in totals.

I grinned. "Yup, that's me."

She started wrapping the oils in tissue paper and placed several of the small bundles into a handled brown paper bag. "Well, I hope you're still happy with our products."

"Oh, definitely. Although, I did want to ask you about this

honey absolute. Is it just a packaging change, or has it been reformulated, too?"

"Ahhh." She looked pleased. "You're the first customer to notice that. The packaging has been updated *because* they reformulated it. Personally, I think it's a vast improvement over the previous version. It's spicier. Truer to real honeycomb."

I nodded eagerly. "I've always had trouble with the honey holding its true scent. It degraded too quickly."

"I bet this one will work better for you," she said.

Poor Mom stood by looking like we were speaking a foreign language, but at least she was being a good sport about it. The register kept working, the total climbing higher and higher, and I watched it with a growing unease. There was no *way* Mom was going to let me keep everything. I started to prioritize what I could and couldn't live without. Any second now she was bound to draw the line.

"What do you think of the new E151 distiller?" the sales clerk asked. "It's been redesigned to leave less of the plant oils behind."

"What's an E151 distiller?"

"It's for harvesting your own essential oils." She turned to the counter behind her. When she turned back to face us again, a large, square glass box was in her hands. My eyes widened, and she laughed. "You mean you don't make any of your own oils?"

I shook my head. "No. I've considered it once or twice, but always thought it would be too expensive."

She held the contraption closer for my inspection. "Normally, that's true. The large distilling machines can cost thousands of dollars. But this little baby is for home use, and it's designed to make the process ten times easier. You just put your flowers or plants inside the humidifier box and add some water to this jar here." She turned it so that I could see the back. A maze of tubes ran from one end to the other, all connecting to and criss-crossing each other. A tiny bronze knob was at the end of the tubing. "Turn this knob to increase the heat and boil the water; then the plant oils are released and funneled into a collection tube. Making your own oils really adds that extra personal touch. A lot of people swear it's the only way to go."

*Oh, man.* I was sold.

Trying *very* hard not to look at Mom with puppy-dog eyes, I asked, "How much does it cost?"

"It's normally one ninety-nine, but this week we're having a discount of forty percent off on it. So the price would only be one nineteen."

*Only.*

I couldn't help it, I caved. I turned the full force of my *OMG I have to have this gaze* on Mom.

She sighed. "Go ahead; add it to the bill."

"Okay, then," the clerk chirped. "Your total will be two twenty-five eighty-seven."

I almost choked. *Two hundred dollars for some perfume supplies?!*

But Mom only shot me the tiniest of glances before she reached into her purse and pulled out a credit card. I gleefully picked up my bags and whispered, "Love you, Mom" as she paid. I'm pretty sure I heard her mutter, "Thank God it's not your birthday *every* day," and I grinned all the way out to the car.

Sometimes she could be a very good mom.

Ten minutes before I was supposed to be downstairs for my birthday dinner, I was still trying to figure out what outfit to wear. I didn't want to look too dressy, yet Mom had pleaded with me to wear something nice.

Searching my closet for the millionth time, I finally chose a white cotton sundress and slid it on. The hem was decorated with black satin ribbon, and tiny daisies danced across the straps. It was dressy, but not fussy. Then I threaded a white ribbon through my black curls and pulled my hair up into a low ponytail. A couple of strands immediately escaped, but I tucked them safely behind my ears.

Black strappy shoes were next, and then the last thing I needed was some jewelry. Dipping into the holder on my desk, I picked through necklace after necklace. But none of them seemed to fit my mood. *I'll just go without.*

Then my pinkie got snagged on a tangled chain, and I tried to free my finger.

A silver star on a delicate chain spilled out, and I stopped for a second. I'd only worn it once before it had gotten lost in the depths of the jewelry pit. It seemed perfect for tonight, though. Kristen had given me the star-shaped necklace for my fifteenth birthday.

"Okay, Kristen," I whispered, smoothing out the tiny tangles and fastening it around my neck. "I can take a hint."

Checking myself over one last time, I straightened the necklace, tugged at the bottom of my skirt, and messed with my hair a bit. Time to go.

I felt oddly nervous as I made my way to the stairs. *It's just dinner. No big deal,* I told myself. But that didn't stop the slightly nauseous feeling that was creeping up. I hoped Mom and Dad weren't going to do anything *too* embarrassing.

Forcing myself to put one foot in front of the other, I froze mid-step when I heard voices. It sounded like they were talking to someone. *Who's here? Mom said it would only be us tonight.* She'd thought about inviting Aunt Marjorie and Mr. and Mrs. M. but had decided against it so that we could have some "family time."

Slowly descending the rest of the way, I peeked into the living room. It was Ben. Ben was *here*, sitting across from Mom and Dad on the couch. He had on a long-sleeved button-down shirt and a *tie*.

I was horrified.

Mom spotted me first and came over to greet me. "Here she is. The birthday girl."

I put on a fake smile and whispered through gritted teeth, "Mom! What's Ben doing here?"

"I wanted to surprise you, Abbey." She lowered her voice. "He's such a nice boy."

Ben stood up, and so did Dad. "Hey, Abbey. Happy birthday. I hope you don't mind that I'm here."

"Of course not," I said. "I'm glad to see you."

"Ben here was just telling us all about his college plans," Dad said.

"Isn't that *wonderful*, Abbey?" Mom added. "He has his *whole life* planned out."

I looked closely at her. Something was . . . off. "Yes, that's nice, Mom. I'm sure he has a bright future ahead of him." Then I changed the subject. "Is dinner ready?"

Mom nodded and teetered over to Ben, putting her arm through his. "Why don't you escort me into the dining room?" she said to him with a smile. "I hear you have very good mannersh."

*Oh. My. God.* Mom was tipsy. I gave Ben an apologetic look, but he played along.

"I'd be honored, Mrs. Browning." He led her out of the living room, and Dad came over to escort me.

"Is Mom *drunk*?" I hissed to him.

At least *he* had the decency to look slightly embarrassed. "She's not . . . It's just that . . . She was so excited after you guys came home from shopping, and she kept talking about what a great bonding experience it was . . . so I suggested a drink to celebrate. One drink turned into a couple, and, well . . . she really shouldn't have had that last one."

Nice. *This* was going to be fun.

"Can you watch her, Dad?" I pleaded. "Try not to let her do anything too embarrassing, okay?"

We entered the dining room, and Mom was giggling at something Ben was saying. I sighed, and Dad threw me a helpless look before we sat down.

Mom had outdone herself with the decorations. The whole room looked like something out of a Martha Stewart magazine. Gleaming silverware, tall candelabras with red tapers, maroon wine goblets, and a black-and-white damask tablecloth were all part of the setting. Confetti was scattered across the table, and fancy deckle-edged place cards sat at each plate. A large crystal bowl filled with strawberries was the centerpiece, and my excitement grew when I saw the telltale long-handled forks sitting nearby.

I *might* be able to forgive Mom's tipsiness for fondue. *Maybe.*

"Oh, by the way, I brought you a present," Ben said. "But I left it in the living room."

Mom brought over a silver tray loaded with little white fluted paper cups. "Well, isn't that nice of you?" she said. "That was very thoughtful."

Ben was seated across from me, and he leaned forward conspiratorially. "It's a Barbie. Doctor Barbie. I looked, but they didn't have Perfumer Barbie, or even Artist Barbie. I thought about getting you Hippie Barbie, but I didn't want you to get the wrong idea. At least Doctor Barbie is a businesswoman."

I laughed. "Thank you, Ben. That's a great gift."

Dad looked baffled by the whole thing. "Aren't you kind of old for Barbies, Abbey?" he said.

"It's an inside joke, Dad. Something Ben told me at the library when we were working on the science-fair project last year. It was about his sister and Barbies."

"Ohhhhh, okay."

He totally didn't get it, but I did. It was sweet.

Mom passed the silver tray to me, and I reached for one of the paper cups. It had a round brown disc filled with something green inside of it. "What is it?" I asked.

"It's spinach-stuffed portobello," she said with a hopeful grin.

I put the blobby thing back down. "But . . . I don't like mushrooms, Mom. You know that."

Her face fell, and she looked crushed. "You don't? I could have sworn you liked them."

A moment of stunned silence filled the dining room, and everyone waited for me to make a move.

"Don't worry about it." I passed the tray on to Ben. "Leaves more room for . . ." I scanned the table and saw the edge of a garlic knot peeking out from a cloth-covered serving dish. "Garlic knots! Mmmmm, I love garlic knots! Pass me those, please."

Ben took three of the stuffed mushrooms, and as soon as Dad passed me the garlic knots, I loaded my plate.

Within seconds we were all crunching and chewing and

discreetly wiping our fingers on our napkins. Then we moved on to some chilled tomato basil soup (which I actually did like), and Mom poured herself a glass of wine.

I shot a worried glance over at Dad, but he didn't seem to notice.

"So Ben, why don't you tell my parents about your summer jobs?" I said. *Anything to keep the conversation from turning to me and my naked baby pictures, or something equally embarrassing.*

Ben gamely joined in. "I'm a busboy at the Horseman's Haunt. Nothing important about that, but they *do* let me take home the special of the day after each shift. Great perks, there." He stopped talking while Mom brought out the main course, lasagna, and dished out a piece to each of us.

"Go on," she told him, spatula in hand, "I'm lishening." She giggled. "Oops! I mean, I'm listening."

I clutched a fistful of skirt under the table and sent up a prayer to the lasagna gods that she wouldn't accidentally drop Ben's dinner into his lap. Luckily, Dad sprang into action.

"Why don't you have a seat, dear?" he said to her. "You've worked so hard on this dinner; let me help you."

Mom beamed at him and patted his face. "Okay."

*Thank you, oh lasagna gods.*

"So, the um, other job . . . ," Ben said.

"Yes, yes, go on," Mom urged, wine glass in hand.

*Dear wine gods . . .*

"I'm going to be helping my dad. He wants to plant some Christmas trees, and I'm going to work for him."

A piece of lasagna landed on my plate, and I thanked Dad. It looked *really* good, and I couldn't wait to dig in.

"What's involved in Christmas-tree farming?" Dad asked. He took his seat and lifted his fork.

I bit into my food as I waited for Ben's answer.

And two seconds later I almost spit it back out again. *Good Lord, that was* nasty.

"I'm not really sure," Ben said. He took a big bite of his lasagna and chewed enthusiastically. "I'm guessing it will be a lot of digging holes and planting trees. Then watering, and maybe fertilizing them?"

Dad nodded, and I took a second to look down at my plate. White filling oozed out of the bitten edges, and my stomach turned.

*Great.* Another thing Mom had screwed up.

I peeked over at her, but she seemed blissfully unaware of her mistake.

"I think ish verrry exciting to have a Christmas-tree farm here. It will be an asset to our *community*!"

Ahhh, she wasn't wasted enough to stop thinking about her precious town council, though. A lump started forming in my throat, and I had to blink back tears. *Nice, Mom. This birthday sucks. . . . My food sucks. . . .*

"I know that my dad is looking forward to it," Ben said. "I just hope he'll be able to share his trees with the rest of the town—"

Suddenly, Mom sat straight up. "Oh, no!" she wailed. "No, no, no!"

Ben, Dad, and I traded puzzled glances. *What's wrong now?*

"This has ricotta cheese in it!" Mom held up her fork with a piece of the offending meal on it. "Abbey hates ricotta cheese!"

And she promptly burst into tears.

All my feelings of hurt and anger immediately left, and I was filled with shame instead. "Mom, no." I put out a hand, but Dad was already reaching for her. "Look, Mom, I love it."

With Herculean effort I lifted another forkful to my mouth. *Don't grimace, don't grimace . . .* I shoveled it in and gouged my thumbnail into my leg under the table at the same time.

*Focus on the pain. Something else to think about . . .*

*Chew, chew, swallow . . . done.*

I reached for my water glass, took a very large sip, and smiled widely at her. "See?"

She stopped crying and gazed at me through wet eyes. "Are you . . . sure?" She sniffled once. "You really like it?"

I nodded. "It's great, Mom."

She clumsily got up and came to give me a hug.

When she sat down, I looked at what was left on my plate. *It's times like these we could really use a dog*. After cutting up the remaining piece into smaller bits, I pushed them around a lot, moving them from side to side to make it look like I'd eaten more than I actually had. I think it worked. Mom didn't seem to notice.

Mercifully, everyone ate quickly, and then Dad suggested that I open my presents. I wholeheartedly agreed. He came around and gathered the dishes, starting with mine first, and I mouthed a silent *Thank you*. Then he sent Mom off to get the gifts.

I leaned across the table to Ben. "I'm *so* sorry." I had to fight back tears. "My mom's totally not like this. It's just that today was an emotional day for her, and . . ."

He just shook his head. "It's cool, Abbey. Don't worry about it." It looked like he was going to say more, but then Mom came back in with a small pile and sat it in front of me.

"Here we go," she announced, grinning from ear to ear. "Happy, happy birthday, Abbey!"

Dad finished with the plates and came to stand beside her. Discreetly, he pushed her half-full glass of wine out of her reach.

"Happy birthday, Abbey," he said. "Go ahead and open the small one first. Leave the big one for last."

I reached for the present on top, a flat, rectangular box wrapped in bright blue and red paper. It was the cherry on a bizarrely colored birthday sundae, adorned with carefully curled ribbons in a multitude of colors. I ripped open one end, pulled out a smaller brown box, and slid back the lid. Nestled on a plump square of white cotton was a gift card for a clothing store at the mall.

"I picked that one up," Dad said proudly.

"Thanks, Dad. It's great."

Next up was an iTunes gift card, a new messenger bag, a pair of shoes . . . and then I got to the big one on the bottom. It was square and kind of heavy, and wrapped in green polka-dotted paper. As I tore off the wrapping, I was absolutely shocked to find a brand-new laptop staring up at me.

"Wow, guys! I don't even know what to say. Thank you, thank you!" I jumped up and gave them both a hug. Mom held on a little too long, and I was afraid that she'd start crying again, but she didn't.

"Ish red," Mom said. "Your *favorite* color."

Dad jumped in. "That should help you with your business plan."

"You're going to let me have more time?" I thought our deal was over since I hadn't finished it by the end of the school year.

"Yup. Since things"—he shot a look at Ben—"came up . . . I figured that we can make a new deal. Same terms as before. Finish the plan, and I'll give you some start-up money, but let's make the deadline the first of September. Sound good?"

"Yeah," I said, smiling back. "It does."

Mom threw her arms around me again. "This calls for a toast!"

"No, Mom . . . really, it's okay—"

"I'll get the glasses! Dennis, you go get the cake."

She moved quicker than I thought she could, and didn't wait for Dad, instead bringing the cake over herself. As she plopped it down on the table, I watched the golden edges of a custard chiffon quiver with the force of her movement.

*Here we go. . . .*

Next she moved for the bottle of wine.

"Some for me, some for your father, and here . . ." She pulled my goblet, then Ben's, closer to her. "A little bit for both of you. Not too mush now."

I grimaced and was extremely grateful when she finally put the bottle down. I glanced over at Dad, but he didn't seem to know what to do.

Mom picked up her glass and waited for the rest of us to follow suit. "Come on, come on," she urged. "A toast."

I lifted my goblet and Ben did the same. That queasy feeling was back, and I prayed for this to be over quickly.

"Seventeen years ago," started Mom, "my preshus little girl was born. And I couldn't have been happier. My beautiful daughter, Abigail Amelia . . ." I cringed when she said my middle name. No one knew my middle name.

Well, strike that. Now one person knew it.

"From your first step, to your first word. Your first day of school, and your first loose tooth . . ." She lost her train of thought and stared off into space. A moment later she came back and took a deep sip of her wine.

"And now look at you," she said suddenly. "All grown up. Making business plans. And life plans. Here on your birthday, with a boy . . ." She grinned at Ben.

*Oh God, this is going downhill fast.* I cleared my throat.

"I'm just so glad you're back with ush again, Abbey," she said, turning her gaze to me. "I'm so glad you're home. And not seeing a doctor. I really missed—"

"What I think your mother's trying to say is that of course we're proud of the girl you used to be, but we're even prouder of the young woman you're becoming. Hear, hear!"

Thank God Dad stepped in and cut her off. I was starting to sweat bullets.

"Hear, hear!" said Mom, raising her wine glass.

I raised mine, too, and downed what little was in there in one gulp. I noticed that Ben did the same thing.

"And now I'll cut the cake," Mom crowed.

Dad reached out and plucked the glass from her hand. "That's okay, dear. Why don't we let Abbey and Ben have some time together? I need your help with something in the . . . living room."

Mom nodded and put one finger in front of her lips. "Shhh, it's time for some alone time." She giggled. "I understand."

Giving us a not-so-subtle wink, she let Dad steer her out of the room.

Desperate for something else to take the attention off the situation, I grasped at the first thing that came to mind. "Do you want to go outside and get some fresh air?" I asked Ben. "God, I could really use some fresh air right now."

Ben nodded and put his goblet down. I did the same and turned to lead the way out. Then my stomach growled loudly.

"Why don't you bring the cake?" Ben suggested. "We'll eat some out there."

I reached for the cake and picked it up. "Forks?"

"That's what God made fingers for," he replied.

The cake quivered in my hands, tiny blobs of lemon custard sliding around on the plate, and Ben held open the door. With a deep breath I took a step out into the muggy night air. And wondered if this night could get any worse.

# Chapter Eight

# MORSE CODE

Every sound of nature, at that witching hour, fluttered his excited imagination ...
The fire-flies, too, which sparkled most vividly in the darkest places, now and then
startled him ...

—"The Legend of Sleepy Hollow"

We sat down on the porch steps—Ben on the first one and me on the third. I placed the cake on the step between us and stared at it, watching its glistening sides in the pale glow of a dim bulb above us. Bugs fluttered and hovered around the light, their wings making oversized shadow puppets on the wall next to us.

I didn't even know where to start, what to offer as an excuse for why Mom had said what she'd said, how to explain ... So I just sat there, running my thumb and forefinger back and forth across my necklace. *What do I say? What's he thinking?*

I poked a finger at the cake and swiped off some stray custard. Maybe sugar would give me courage. Licking my fingertip, I sat back and prepared myself to come up with something clever. "Ben, I . . ."

"You don't have to explain your parents, Abbey. Mine freak out all the time. I think it's a side effect of getting old or something," he said.

I laughed, and he smiled. "The really important thing here is where your finger's been."

"What?" I looked at him in confusion.

"You just swiped some icing," Ben said. "I saw you. Do you know how many germs are on your hands?"

"But I thought you didn't want to use a fork."

He reached out and tore off a hunk of the cake. "I don't. I just wanted the first piece."

But then he graciously offered his prize to me, and I accepted. Grinning, he shoved a smaller bite into his mouth and started chewing. "That," Ben said, sucking bits of frosting off his fingers, "is good cake."

I bit into my piece. "We got it from this great little bakery over on DeWalt Street. They have the *best* desserts there."

Ben scooped up another bite and offered me half. I had to scoot closer to take it from him. "So what did you do for your birthday last year?" he asked.

I sat there for a minute. Fireflies winked on and off in the grassy yard near us. "Last year I didn't really do anything. Kristen was . . . missing, and I wasn't in the mood to celebrate." Looking down at my lap, I brushed away a speck of a crumb. Those memories were sad, and I didn't want to think about that. So I said, "But the year before, Kristen and I went into the city to see *Rent*. My parents got us this limo, and we took it all over Manhattan. Nothing like seeing the sights while you're stuck in rush-hour traffic. We saw a whole bunch of alleys and backs of buildings."

"I bet you had a great time, though," Ben said.

"Yeah, we really did." I stroked my star necklace. *I wish she could have been here for this birthday. I wish I would have gotten to share it with her.*

The fireflies glowed, and I closed one eye. It almost looked like they were blinking in Morse code.

"Do you know Morse code?" I mused out loud.

Ben must have been distracted, because he looked startled. "What?"

"Do you know Morse code?" I repeated, standing up. "*Look.* The fireflies are blinking in Morse code. It's some kind of secret message." I stepped out into the yard and glanced back at him. "Help me catch one."

He looked at me with an amused smile. "What is this? Your eighth-birthday party?"

"Don't make me pout. Or cry. Cuz it's my party, and I'll cry if I want to."

Ben laughed and stood up. Then he lunged at me. "Almost had one there."

"You did not." I punched his arm lightly. "You just wanted to scare me."

He shrugged and turned away. "Maybe."

I spotted one flying toward the trees and started after it. With my hands cupped together, I combed the air and then quickly closed them. Moving back to the light, I cracked them open to see if I'd caught the glowing prize.

But my hands were empty. "Aww, I thought I had one." Sudden movement in the corner of my eye had me spinning around again, and I scooped my hands through the air. I felt something small catch. "I got one! I got one!"

Ben came over, and I opened my hands wider so that we could both see in. A small, black winged bug crawled steadily across my cupped palm.

"Bring it here, out of the light, so we can see it blink," he suggested.

Holding my tiny captive carefully so that I didn't squish

him, I followed Ben back toward the trees. My hands lit up every couple of seconds.

Ben leaned in closer and cupped his hands around mine. "Wait, he's saying something."

I leaned in too and held my breath. *Does he really know Morse code?*

"Happy … birth … day … Happy birthday … Abbey." Ben looked up at me and smiled. "The lightning bug wanted to wish you a happy birthday."

Our hands were touching, but now our heads were almost touching too. My eyes were finally adjusting to the darkness, and I could see the outline of his eyes, his nose, and his lips. He was staring at me, and I could tell he was noticing the lack of space between us.

Shifting my weight, I moved slightly closer. *Is this … ? Are we going to … ?*

A buzzing sensation drew my attention from Ben, and I realized that the firefly was trying to escape. "Oh!" I moved my hands away from his. The flapping of tiny insect wings against my skin was giving me the creepy crawlies.

Ben looked confused.

"Sorry," I said. "It wanted to get loose and was moving against my hand. Kind of gross."

"Kind of gross, huh?" He laughed.

I nodded. *What should I do now?*

Then I felt his warm fingertips brushing against my collarbone, and I looked down, shocked to see his hand on my necklace.

He took a step closer, and was practically touching me. Standing so close, I had to look up at him to see his face.

"Your star was crooked," he whispered.

But he'd straightened it.

. . . and still had his hand there.

A strange feeling flooded over me, and immediately I knew what was going to happen next. In that split second I saw it all playing out in front of me. Like a scene from a movie.

It should have been a moment of shivery breathlessness, yet I only felt . . . betrayal? *Wait. That can't be right.*

Ben tilted his head down, and I said the first thing that came to mind. "It was a gift."

He paused, and smiled. "Oh, yeah? From who?"

"Kristen."

As soon as I said her name, I knew *that* was where the feeling was coming from. I was betraying Kristen. Or more so, I was betraying the fact that Ben once had a crush on Kristen, probably still *did* to some extent, and if I kissed him right now it would be like kissing my dead best friend's almost boy-friend.

Not cool.

Ben stiffened and jerked his head back, almost like he was thinking the same thing. Then he ran his fingers through his hair, a gesture I found oddly familiar but couldn't place. "Abbey," he said suddenly. "It's getting late. I should go."

*Could he tell what I was feeling?* "Okay," I said. "Well, um, thanks for coming and all that." Now it was going to get awk-ward.

Clearly, he didn't know what to do either, because he kind of leaned in for a half hug and patted me on the back. "So, happy birthday. And I guess I'll see you at our next science session."

"Yeah. Thanks for coming, Ben."

He nodded once and then turned back toward the house, disappearing inside. I headed to the porch and sat down again on the second step next to what was left of my birthday cake.

"That was weird," I said out loud. "Really weird."

Overhead, the distinct rumbling sound of thunder broke through the distance, and seconds later a jagged piece of green-ish lightning lit up the sky. The loud boom that came after the lightning made me jump, but I stayed where I was.

I wasn't ready to go inside yet. I had more cake to finish.

~ ~ ~

I stared out my bedroom window, watching sheets of rain cascade down the glass pane. Mom and Dad had said good night an hour ago, with Mom tipping slightly to one side, and I'd been getting ready to change for bed when the lightning had lured me over.

There was something strangely beautiful about this storm. The trees outside were swaying in the wind, dipping low as they bowed to one another. A scattering of leaves lay on the streets, and every now and then one got caught up in the current of shallow runoff and went dancing merrily along its way. Although it was pitch-black in the yard below, I could almost see the wet, spiky blades of grass and new flower buds turning their faces up, eagerly soaking in the moisture.

I needed to create a perfume that evoked a summer storm. Cut grass, frantic wind, the heady scent of rain . . . with just a touch of fresh sheets drying on the wind. And I needed something powerful and strong, a dry scent to mimic thunder. Perhaps vetivert or fennel?

A yawn interrupted my thoughts, and I stretched my arms over my head. The soft pounding of rain on the roof was like a soothing melody, something rhythmic and primal. I gathered several pillows, moved them to the end of the bed, and lay down with my head where my feet should go. I could watch the storm better that way.

I felt safe and warm in my little cocoon. And when I closed my eyes, lightning still played behind my eyelids. Dancing and leaping in strange, crackling patterns . . .

*Thunder rolled and echoed all around me, but I knew I was dreaming, because the storm was inside my room. White forks of lightning crackled and spread across the ceiling, and climbed down the walls like vines. Every time the thunder sounded, it spread through the vines with tiny pulses of electricity.*

*Then I noticed a cloaked figure sitting on the edge of my bed. It was Kristen.*

*"Take a walk with me, Abbey." I could hear her voice as clear as day, but her lips weren't moving. "Let's take a walk."*

*And suddenly we were in the cemetery. On the far side. Away from the main gates.*

*My feet were moving even though I tried to stop. The tips of my toes dragged along the hard ground as I floated along. Hovering, just above the bare earth, yet still touching.*

*"Where are we going, Kristen?" I asked.*

*She turned her cloaked face to me and pointed straight ahead. I recognized the twisting path immediately. It led to Nikolas and Katy's house.*

*I sucked in a breath. Nikolas and Katy weren't real. Having tea with the Headless Horseman and Katrina Van Tassel from "The Legend of Sleepy Hollow" was just something that I'd made up. We had to be going somewhere else.*

*We walked on. It felt like hours, and gradually I noticed that everything around me was damp. The ground, the trees, the springy ferns that reached for our legs. It was raining, but I wasn't getting wet.*

*Neither was Kristen.*

*We came to a heap of old stones and rotting shingles. Dead wisteria clung to what was left of the fallen-in stone fireplace, and chills ran down my spine. What had happened to their house?*

*Kristen stopped and turned, pushing back the hood from her face. Her hair was soaking wet. "Go," she said.*

*I shook my head. "Not without you, Kristen. Come with me. Please come with me?"*

*"I can't, Abbey. I can't go with you. You're all alone."*

A clap of thunder woke me up, this time for real, and I was seconds away from screaming. *It's in my room. The thunder is in my bedroom!* Lightning illuminated the outline of my bed for a moment, clearly showing that the storm was outside where it was supposed to be. I gazed around me. *It's not in here. It was just a dream. Nothing to be afraid of.*

Sometime during the night, the rain had turned softer. Instead of sounding like a fleet of soldiers marching across the roof, now it was only a steady drum in the background. I flicked on my nightstand lamp and got up to go look out the window.

The bushes next to the trees moved a little, and I watched, waiting to see what was there. Then they moved again. I grabbed a blanket off the edge of my bed and started walking to the stairs. The porch swing was covered, so it would be dry, and had a better view. I could sit there and see what it was.

As soon as I stepped out the front door, a cool breeze reminded me that all I had on was my thin white summer dress, and I wrapped the blanket around myself.

I sat down on the swing and drew my feet up underneath me. Gradually, I was able to make out each tree and bush separating our yard from Mr. Travertine's. Within a couple of minutes the bushes moved again, and then a deer came forward. He was all spindly legs and white spots and showed a sleek neck as he nibbled on some wet grass.

A bunny hopped out next to him, and I couldn't stop the little "awww" that escaped me as he nibbled on the grass too and they ate side by side. It was like watching live-action-theater *Bambi*.

But something must have spooked the deer, because all of a sudden he looked up and then ran away. I tilted my head slightly to watch it. Were deer afraid of other deer?

Except . . . the shadow that moved now wasn't a deer. It appeared to be more . . . human-shaped. I held very still. *Is someone out there? Maybe they haven't noticed me.*

But I knew who it was. With every fiber of my being, I knew it was him. Caspian.

He took a step forward, and I *swear* I felt his eyes burning holes into me. Even in the darkness I could see his white-blond hair. His silhouette stood out against the trees, and somehow I knew this wasn't a dream or a hallucination.

He was *here*.

Blanket left behind, I stood up and moved across the grass. With every step I took, I dug my bare feet into the wet earth, forcing myself to feel. Every move I was making was *real*. This was *real*.

He disappeared again, back into the shadows, but I saw him as soon as I reached the trees. He was leaning up against the broad trunk of a solid oak.

Squeezing my eyes tightly shut, I choked back tears. Did this mean I was still crazy? That I always was? "Caspian . . . ," I heard myself whisper.

He didn't respond, but there was a rustling sound, and I opened my eyes again.

He'd moved closer, and in the darkness I could see bright green eyes. Their shocking color tore right through me, and my world tilted crazily. *I'm falling.* . . .

Grabbing on to the tree for support, I stopped myself from pitching over. I cursed as I saw everything so clearly. It was happening again.

"I missed you, Abbey," Caspian said quietly. "I know it's wrong. That I shouldn't be here—" He stopped and ran his hands jerkily through his hair. "God, Abbey, I missed you."

My heart somersaulted, and I wanted to fly into his arms. Started to, then stopped myself. Remembering. "I don't even know if you're *real*. How can I see you? You're dead."

"I don't know why you can see me. We're both just . . . here."

"But *why* are you here? I had to leave town. I had to go see a specialist. I thought I was crazy. Seeing things that weren't there. You, and Nikolas and Katy . . ."

"Is that where you were? I thought you just stopped coming to the cemetery."

"*Of course* I stopped going to the cemetery. Last time I went there, the boy I *thought* I was dating told me that he couldn't love me because he was dead! I don't know if I'm more pissed off at you for making me think I was crazy or for making me think you were alive."

"I thought you'd be mad that I lied about not loving you," he said softly.

"You lied about . . . not . . . loving . . . me . . . ?"

He nodded, and the stripe of black hair that normally angled across his forehead fell into one eye.

"You love me?" I whispered.

He looked at me and said very clearly, "I think I've loved you from the moment I first saw you, last year in the cemetery."

I stared down at my hands. Once, I would have been happy to hear those words. Now they just left me feeling even more confused.

"But you . . . I'm . . . You said that—"

"If you're mad, be mad," Caspian said. "I'll take that over . . ." He shook his head. "The last time I saw you, I thought I . . . broke you, Abbey." His voice came out in a whisper.

"You did."

His eyes were horrified, and I wanted to explain, to make it all better . . . but I couldn't.

"You really messed with my head, Caspian." I laughed quietly. "Obviously, you are *still* messing with my head if I can see you again. I don't know what's wrong with me. Some part of my brain is messed up."

"Maybe it's not such a bad thing," he offered.

"How can it *not* be a bad thing? I see dead people."

Caspian looked away, and shoved his hands into his pant pockets. "Who was that guy here earlier?" he asked, changing the subject. "The one you were getting hot and heavy with."

He almost sounded jealous, and I wanted to laugh at the absurdity of it. "I was *not* getting hot and heavy. And his name is Ben. He's just a friend." I flushed with the memory of what had almost happened. "He was here for my birthday dinner."

"Today's your birthday?"

I shrugged. "It was."

"Happy birthday, Astrid."

His words filled me with warmth, but I tamped down on the feeling. "So now what, are you stalking me? Hiding out in the bushes, watching?" I thought about the day I came home, with the kid and the dog. "Have you been here before? In the daytime?"

"Sometimes I stop by when I'm out just walking around," he admitted. "At first it was to look for you. But then I thought you were avoiding me, so I tried to stay away." He kicked at a loose branch by his foot. "I guess I couldn't stay away tonight."

A loud bark suddenly had both of us lifting our heads. Nearby, Mr. Travertine shuffled sleepily along the perimeter of his porch, clearly not very happy about the task of letting his dog out for an early-morning walk.

The dog barked again, and it sounded like he was coming closer.

"I'm gonna go," Caspian said. "And you should get back inside. You'll get sick if you stay out here too long."

He stepped away from me and gave me a sad, final look.

"Where does this leave us, Caspian?" I called out softly. "What do we do now?"

"I don't know, Abbey," he replied. "But whatever it is, I guess we're not meant to do it together."

# Chapter Nine

# SHELTER

To look upon its grass-grown yard, where the sunbeams seem to sleep so quietly, one would think that there at least the dead might rest in peace.

—"The Legend of Sleepy Hollow"

The next morning I woke up full of confusion. Last night had really happened. I'd washed mud and grass from the bottom of my feet. Caspian was *real*. And he'd said he loved me ... But did it mean anything? *Could* it mean anything? He was dead. That threw a slight complication into the mix.

I got out of bed and knelt down, feeling underneath it for the necklace. Looking at it in the daylight, I traced the red cursive letters, spelling out the name Astrid, trapped forever beneath tiny glass squares. The edges were soldered all the way around with a shiny metal, and a black satin ribbon hung from a small O-shaped ring at the top. The other necklace he'd given me was tucked away in the back of my sock drawer.

Very slowly, I put it on.

It felt like it belonged. Like it was meant to be there.


The house was curiously quiet when I went downstairs. I couldn't tell if Mom and Dad were gone, or just sleeping off the effects of last night. I ate a quick bowl of cereal and then scrawled *"Going out. Be back later."* on a notepad next to the fridge. I didn't need Mom freaking out if she woke up and couldn't find me.

I capped the pen and slid it back into the little clip that held it in place, then made my way out the door. I headed up the hill and started walking toward the cemetery. I wanted to see Caspian again. I had so many questions.

The warmth of the sun felt good at first, but it didn't take long for me to start getting hot and sticky. I pulled my damp shirt away from my back and used my hand to fan my neck. *Almost there. It won't be much longer now.*

I just hoped that I'd be able to find him, or at least a *sign* of him.

The cemetery gates came into view, and I breathed a sigh of relief. Weeping willows, cherry trees, and great oaks lined each pathway. A profusion of fresh green buds and flowers bursting with new life filled the grounds. A mower sounded, and suddenly I craved the scent of freshly cut grass.

I checked down by the river first. We'd met there so many times that it seemed like that was where he would be. I scanned underneath the bridge, and the top of it too, but he wasn't there.

I walked slowly through the cemetery, checking behind upright tombs for any type of crawl space or cubbyhole that he might have found. Several mausoleums were next, and I tried each door latch. But they weren't giving up their secrets, or their dead, and I was forced to move on.

The mower sounds grew closer, and I sat down in a clearing of grass to wait while it went by. Keeping my eyes peeled, I scanned the hillside looking for him. A flash of his clothing, or hair . . . Caspian had to be here somewhere. *Of course, he has acres and acres of room to roam, and I could never run into him. . . .* I pushed that thought aside.

Something told me to head in the direction of the Old Dutch Church next, so I went that way. There was an old shed behind it. Maybe he would be there.

It was chained, but one of the doors was loose and wobbled back and forth when I nudged it. I stuck my face up to the crack and peered into the semidarkness. There were a couple of tools inside, and some lumpy covered things in the back. *If I could just see a little more.* I wiggled the door on its hinge, and it gave up a new position. Sunlight streamed in toward the back revealing . . . a bunch of wheelbarrows and one rusty lawn mower that looked like it hadn't been in service for a long time.

I didn't know what to do next. Should I wander around some more? Go to the other side? Or maybe I should head back to the main gate. He *could* be over there. . . .

Sudden movement caught my eye, and I lifted my head. It was a flash of white-blond hair. A figure was standing next to a giant mausoleum built into the hill near Washington Irving's grave.

Trying *very* hard not to get my hopes up, I watched him walk toward the far side of the cemetery. Once he was just a speck on the horizon, I started up the path to the mausoleum.

Excitement warred with nervousness when I reached the top of the hill and came face-to-face with the crypt. It was a familiar one. I'd passed it every time I'd come to see Washington Irving's grave.

Glancing around to make sure that no one was watching, I moved closer to the door and put my hand on the latch. It gave way, and the door swung inward with surprisingly little resistance. I found myself in a large, windowless stone chamber. Several stubby candles littered the walls and were burning steadily.

The change in temperature was palpable, and instantly the

sweat puddles on the small of my back dried. I had a sudden flash of fear as I envisioned the crypt looming up and closing around me, swallowing me into the bowels of the earth while I screamed for help. . . . *Don't think that!*

I shook off the mental image and put out a hand for balance. The walls were cobwebby and I yanked back fingers covered in strings of spider filament. I tried to brush them off on the rough denim of my shorts, but they seemed to stick to everything.

I looked closer at one of the candles. They were dusty and yellowed with age. Clearly from an earlier era. Tracing my finger along the trail of wax drippings, I noticed that they had a heavier, grittier feel than the smooth remnants that dripped off the candles I burned. What were they made of? Lard? Tallow?

Not all of the candles were lit, but they lined the room from top to bottom, and I realized that they were place markers. One for each person that was buried here. This had been one *large* family.

A giant rectangular stone rested near me, and I pried loose one of the candles. Moving closer, I saw that it was a black marble slab. Even under the thick layers of dust, bright veins of gold shot through the heavy stone and sparkled at me. I swiped a hand over the dirt-encrusted name plaque and read MONTGOMERY ABBOTT 1759–1824. With such a large monument, he must have been the patriarch of the family.

Nodding my head in respect, I paused for a moment. Should I say a prayer or something? Bits and pieces of a Catholic benediction rambled through my brain, but as I tested the words on my tongue, they felt foreign and out of place. I made the sign of the cross instead and whispered, "Rest in peace." Hopefully Mr. Abbott wouldn't mind me poking around his family's final resting place *too* much.

Of course, if he did decide to visit me from the beyond, what was one more ghost?

A small iron bench was to the right of the stone and spread across one end was a . . . jacket? It had to be Caspian's. The urge to put it on came over me, and I almost did. . . .

But then I saw the pictures.

They were drawings of me. Dozens of them. Almost covering the entire wall beside the bench. Black-and-white charcoal sketches that showed me standing, sitting, smiling, frowning, scowling, crying . . . They were amazing.

I lifted a finger and gently traced the outline of one of them. Who *was* this girl? She was sad and beautiful all at once. It couldn't be me. I wasn't that pretty.

A bit of wax suddenly rolled down my thumb, leaving a burning trail. The light dipped and wavered, casting dancing shadows across the room. Several boxes were piled nearby, and I turned to them, curiosity aroused.

Two of them were overturned and being used like tables, but a couple of smaller ones had stuff inside. I sat the candle down and knelt to take a look.

There was an alarm clock, a picture frame with an old school picture in it, a couple of books, and some clothes. I picked up the frame, feeling a thrill run through me. It was almost like being in his room. I smiled when I saw a copy of "The Legend of Sleepy Hollow" sitting next to the alarm clock. *Guess he's finally gotten around to reading it.*

On the nearest overturned box rested a sketch pad, a set of charcoals, and another book. It was one of the Christmas gifts I'd given him. I opened it, flipping through the illustrations of stars.

An abrupt scraping noise had me scrambling to my feet, and the door opened. I dropped the book and the candle. The candle rolled and sputtered once before dying.

Caspian looked surprised to see me. "Abbey?"

I didn't know what to say. Glancing down at my feet, I saw the book sprawled open with several of the pages sticking out at an odd angle. I bent to pick it up and put it back on the box.

I waited for him to confront me, but he just turned away.

"How did you find this place?" he asked.

"I—I saw you. I, um, sort of came looking for you."

"Why?"

"I don't know. I guess I just . . . After last night, I wanted to see you again."

"So you came in here and went through my stuff?"

I could feel my face flushing, even in the semidarkness. Then I got mad. "Well, *you* were hanging around *my* house. And . . ." I glanced over at the drawings. "And you've been stalking me!"

Caspian glanced at the pictures too. "You saw those? What did . . . what did you think?" The hopeful look in his eyes completely threw me off balance.

"I . . . um . . . I thought the drawings were really good. I mean, there's no way I look like that. That pretty, I mean. . . ." I blushed. Then I decided to be truthful. "It was kind of weird, actually."

"I'm *not* stalking you," he said. I raised an eyebrow at him. "I'm not!" he protested. "Everything I drew, I drew from memory. It's kind of like my way of having you here with me."

At that moment I wished desperately that I still held the candle. I wanted to see his face clearer. Did he mean it? He drew them so that I would be "here"? I didn't know if that was totally creepy or totally swoonworthy.

"They really are good," I said again. I didn't know what to say beyond that, so I waited for him to speak. Instead he moved to the bench and sat down. I just waited. For what, I didn't know, but now I was here. He had to do *something*.

The "something" he did was ignore me. Finally I couldn't take it anymore.

"Are you hoping that if you don't talk to me long enough, I'll turn into a pile of bones like all the other ones in here?" I flung my arms out in exasperation. "Sorry, but it won't happen."

"No, I was hoping that if I stayed quiet long enough, you'd take the hint and leave," he said.

Wow. That hurt. "If you want someone to leave, just tell them." I turned and started to storm off, then stopped. "Oh, and since we're on the subject of people leaving, this is a *tomb*, if you haven't noticed. Not a place for squatters. You shouldn't be here either."

I was breathing fast and getting all worked up. The space around me felt like it was growing smaller and warmer every second.

"I know," he said quietly. "I shouldn't be here. But I don't have anywhere else to go."

The loneliness I heard behind those few short words made my heart ache. "I'm sorry. I shouldn't have said that."

"Just leave, Astrid. Please."

"Why?" I asked him. "I want to stay."

Caspian shook his head. "We discussed this last night, remember?"

His voice was so hollow. He'd given up already. Rash impulses filled me, and I crouched before him. We were face-to-face, and I could see his shadowed eyes. "Don't do this, Caspian. Don't give up on yourself."

"Don't give up on myself?" He laughed weakly. "What is this, an after-school special? I don't *have* anything to give up on. I'm nothing."

"That's not true. If I can see you, that means you're something. We just have to figure out what."

"I've already played that game, Abbey. When I first met you. It didn't turn out so well, remember? I broke you."

I slammed my hand against the hard floor, surprising both of us. "Don't throw that back at me. I had every right to be upset."

"And I don't?"

"Yes! Yes, you do. That's the point. Get upset. Get pissed off. Yell at me for coming into your place and going through your stuff. *Feel* emotions. If you have that, then you're *not* nothing."

Caspian suddenly leaned forward. Startled, I stood up.

He echoed my movement, placing both hands on the bench and pushing himself to a standing position. We were inches apart, and I took a nervous step backward. I don't know why I did that, but his eyes looked strange. *Wild.* My stomach fluttered. What was he going to . . . do?

He took a step forward. I took a second step back. He advanced, and I retreated, until I felt a wall behind me. He took another step forward and slid his hands on either side of me. Bracing himself against the wall, he had me pinned in.

My throat went dry, and I swallowed. My legs turned to water, and my clothing felt like it was sticking to me. I swallowed again, burning everywhere. It was so warm in here.

Caspian leaned in and put his lips right next to my ear. I fought very hard not to shiver. "You want me to have feelings?" he said. "I already told you that I love you. What else should I say? That I long to be near you every second of every day? I see colors, only around you. . . . I smell perfume, only around you. God, it's like . . . like I'm *alive* again. Sometimes I go crazy just wondering if I've imagined it all, and I wait to see when it . . . *you* . . . will be taken away from me."

The sputtering of a dying candle nearby distracted him, and then we were plunged into darkness over in the corner of our little world. The sound of his voice in my ear and the soft darkness blanketing around us had me biting my lip to hold back a moan. My skin was growing hotter. Aching for his touch, for *any* part of him to fuse with me and make this terrible need go away.

How could I do this? How could I feel this way, *knowing* that nothing could be done about it?

"I feel all these things, Abbey," he continued on. "Rage that I can't run my fingers through your hair. Sorrow that I can't lay my face next to yours. Agony that I can't steal the breath from your lips. I can't eat or breathe or sleep for wanting to touch you, and yet I don't eat or breathe or sleep. I'm just here. Stuck in between."

A tear rolled down my cheek and I closed my eyes, turning my head away from him. This was too much. I couldn't handle this longing and emotion. This much pain. I broke too easily.

"I crave your companionship, your friendship, your conversation," he said. "Do you have any idea what it's like to go from having everyone see you and talk to you, to having them all ignore you? You're left with nothing but your thoughts and a whole lot of free time."

He moved his arms, and the prison lifted. I cleared my throat and tried to find my voice. "I want you to feel those things, Caspian. Feeling means you're human. Hold on to that. Grab on and don't let it go."

He was drawing away from me. I felt it, and I was desperate to make him stay.

"I don't know if I can," he said, mumbling. "It's too hard to pretend. I get too angry. . . ." He trailed off, and I was lost.

"What do you mean? Does something . . . happen?"

Caspian laughed bitterly. "Yeah, it's called my temper. When I first found out what happened to me, I was really angry about it. Pissed off at everyone. And I did some stuff. Stuff I'm not proud of. It's not like I hurt anyone, but I damaged property and things. I just don't want to go to that place again. I don't want to become . . . destructive."

My brain was on overload. I'd bounced from confusion to anger to lust and now back to confusion again. I leaned against the wall and massaged my temples. He was watching me.

"I don't know how to process any of this," I said. "So I'm just going to leave now and think about it. Can I . . . will you . . . *be* here tomorrow? Can I come back?"

"Yes," he said. "If you want to."

"I do." My voice cracked, and I tried again, saying firmly, "I want to come back."

*Chapter Ten*

# CRAZY BEAUTIFUL

He would delight them equally by his anecdotes of witchcraft, and of the direful omens and portentous sights and sounds in the air . . .

—"The Legend of Sleepy Hollow"

When I first stepped out of the mausoleum, the bright sun shocked me, rendering me temporarily blind. But now the darkness was fading, and I suddenly felt weary. I put my hands to the back of my neck and massaged the muscles. They were all tense and knotted up, and my head ached. I stopped for a moment to release my hair from its ponytail and ran my fingers through the tangled curls.

I didn't pass anyone as I exited the cemetery. Not even the landscaper. Everything was still and silent, and I wondered where they'd gone.

The house, however, was *not* silent when I got home.

Mom was talking loudly on the phone, with the TV blaring in the background. I let the back door slam behind me and then angled toward the couch. Plopping down, I stretched out my feet. They were aching too. I picked up the remote and flipped through all the channels twice but there was nothing on. Summer television sucks.

Mom came into the living room, and I turned the TV off. She had that look on her face that said she wanted to "talk."

"Where did you go?"

I shrugged. "Took a walk."

She sat down beside me. "Abbey, I wanted to apologize to you for last night. I'm sorry your birthday dinner wasn't to your liking."

"You're apologizing for the *food*? What about the other stuff?"

She looked dumbfounded. "What other stuff?"

"Well . . . how about the fact that you completely embarrassed me and got drunk in front of my friend?"

"I was *not* drunk," she sputtered. "I only had a couple of sips—not enough to do any damage."

"Could have fooled me," I mumbled.

"What's that?"

I stood up. "Nothing, Mom. I'm going to my room."

"But don't you want to hear what else I had to—"

"No. Not interested."

That was *clearly* the wrong thing to say.

"Fine then . . . just fine. If you're not interested, I won't waste my breath."

"Okay, Mom." *Whatever*. I couldn't believe she didn't see anything wrong with the way she'd acted.

I left the living room and climbed the stairs, shaking my head the whole way. Once I reached my bedroom, I kicked off my sandals and padded over to the bed. Rolling my head from side to side, I slid down onto the edge and closed my eyes.

I felt all tight and itchy on the outside. I couldn't tell *what* I was feeling on the inside.

A soft beeping noise sounded, and I opened one eye. My phone was on the desk, its red light flashing to signal that the battery was dying.

Getting up, I grabbed the phone and plugged it into the wall charger. Then I flipped it open and saw I had a voice mail. Hitting the button to connect me to the mailbox, I put it to my ear and listened.

"Hey, Abbey, it's Beth. I just got back from babysitting the Wilson kids, and I heard that you babysit for them sometimes too. I wanted to let you know that they have this new trick to lock you in the bathroom. Whatever you do, don't let Eli show you his magic numbers game." There was a pause, and then, "So, uh, that's all. I just wanted to tell you that. You can call me later . . ."

Beth rattled off her number, and the phone prompted me to press nine if I wanted to save, or seven if I wanted to delete. I hit nine, staring down at the keypad. *How did she get my number?*

I placed the phone back on the charger and pulled my hand away, but I accidentally knocked into a large bottle of apricot-kernel oil that was sitting on the desk. I tried to reach it in time but couldn't. It fell, and the loose cork top bounced off.

Liquid started to seep across the papers that were scattered there.

"Damn it! Those are my notes for the Ashes Turned Bone perfume," I said.

Lunging to sweep my papers out of the way, I hit a test tube, and it fell too, splintering into a dozen pieces. Quickly righting the apricot oil bottle, I held the damp notes to my chest with one hand and reached down to the floor with the other, groping blindly for something I could use to clean up the mess. My hand struck what felt like a crumpled T-shirt, and I threw it down on top of the puddle slowly inching its way across my desk.

I carried the papers over to my bed and used the corner of a pillowcase to dab at the excess oil as I spread them out to dry. Then I went back over to clean up the broken glass.

I picked up my garbage can along the way and carefully deposited the fractured glass into it. It didn't look like there were any small splinters to worry about, but as I picked up the last piece, it sliced across my thumb. Immediately, blood welled up, and I wrapped my finger in the bottom of my tank top to stop the bleeding.

Only after my hand started turning white from applying so much pressure did I look down to assess the damage. My tank top stuck to the wound, and when it finally pulled free, it was spotted with bright red splotches of blood. *Lots* of blood.

I felt a curious sense of detachment as I gazed down at it. Blood had never bothered me before, and it was almost like I was looking at someone else's injury. More bright beads welled to the surface of my thumb, and I shuffled over to the bathroom. First-aid kit was in there.

I opened the medicine cabinet one-handed and pulled out a small plastic container, then flipped the latch and grabbed some antibiotic ointment and a large square bandage. I squeezed a line of thick ointment across the cut. The gel clotted with the blood, tinting the mixture pink. After peeling back the white plastic strips of the bandage, I wrapped the sticky ends first around one edge of my thumb and then the other.

Satisfied with my patch-up job, I stuffed the antibiotic ointment back into the first-aid kit and returned it to the medicine cabinet. I caught a glimpse of myself in the mirror then and stared at my reflection. I was a mess.

Blood speckled the bottom of my shirt, while apricot oil stained the top. My hair was ratty and tangled, and my cheeks were bright red. I turned to the left and checked out my exposed shoulders. They were red too. *Sunburn.* The indent left behind by my thumb turned white and then red. *Ouch. That's going to peel.*

Feeling all sticky and dirty, I stripped out of my clothes and jumped into the shower. It hurt my shoulders at first, but after a couple of minutes they grew numb to the stinging sensation. I reached for the shampoo bottle and turned it over, preparing to squirt some of it into my palm. My thumb had bled through the bandage in a small crimson circle, darker at the edges and lighter in the middle. The spray of water was making it soggy, and I wondered if it would bleed again when I replaced the bandage after the shower.

My mind jumped to Caspian. Did he bleed? He was dead, so the logical answer should be no. Yet he was solid in some ways. Could his skin crack or peel? What would be underneath? Could he feel hot and cold? Did he shower?

Water drummed off the edge of the shampoo bottle, forcing my attention back to what I was doing. I had so many questions for him. Which ones would he answer? Which ones *could* he answer?

I turned off the water, wrapped myself in towels, and grabbed a pair of gym shorts and a new T-shirt. It felt *so* good to be clean again.

The sunlight in my room was shifting and changing, slanting away from me and toward the walls. I stopped at my desk to finish cleaning up the rest of the mess.

Pushing the crumpled T-shirt once more over the sections where the oil had spilled, I noticed that several dark stains had bloomed. The spots felt smooth and slick, not wet, under my finger, and I knew the wood had absorbed the oil. Sighing, I threw the ruined shirt into the garbage.

On impulse I picked up the phone and decided to dial Aunt Marjorie's number. She answered right away.

"Hey, Aunt Marjorie, it's me." I glanced at the clock. "I hope I didn't interrupt dinner."

"You didn't interrupt anything that can't be heated up later. You know that. It's good to hear from you. How did the bridge ceremony go?"

"It was okay. There were a lot of people there, but I managed to make it through the whole thing. Other than that I'm just making up some science work with a friend from school who's tutoring me."

"They're making you do *more* homework?" She sounded outraged, and I smiled. "But the whole time you were here, practically all you did was school stuff."

"I know. But my science grades really suck. I have to take this big test at the end of summer and pass it, or else I'll fail for the year."

"You can do it," she said. "I have complete confidence in you." Then she turned serious. "Summertime is for having fun. Are you having fun, Abbey?"

I looked out the window by my desk, thinking hard about my answer. "I don't know. Saturday was my birthday, and it was hard without Kristen here, you know? But my friend Ben came over; that was kind of awkward. And I just . . . I don't know. I have a lot to think about."

"Oh! I have your birthday card here somewhere. I'm sorry it's late."

"Hush," I said. "You don't need to worry about that."

"So what's the *real* reason for this phone call?" Aunt Marjorie asked.

"I wanted to talk to you about something. You didn't question why I came to stay with you, and believe me, you'll never know how grateful I am for that. But what if the reason I had to leave here isn't valid anymore? What if I'm not as broken as I thought I was? Is that even possible?"

"I'm not sure I understand what you're saying, Abbey. Whatever your reasons were, I'm sure they were valid. That doesn't mean that things can't change, get better. Maybe part of realizing where you are now is all because of where you were three months ago."

"So you think . . . *what*? That I had to . . . experience what I experienced to get better?"

"I don't know," she said. "Just don't be too hard on yourself for working through whatever needed to be worked through. You don't have to carry it around with you forever, you know."

"How did you get so smart, Aunt Marjorie?"

She laughed. "I can't tell you all of my secrets. Where's the fun in that?"

"Okay, okay. I'll bow to your wisdom and hope to learn your methods one day."

"That's what I'm talking 'bout," she said.

I laughed so hard at that, I had to hold the phone away from my mouth for a second. "Where did you hear *that?*"

"From a movie."

*Of course.*

"Hey . . . Aunt Marjorie . . . what was it like for you?" I asked. "Um . . . falling in love?"

She took my sudden change of topic in stride. "It was exhilarating. And terrifying. The scariest thing I've ever done in my whole life. I didn't know how I could I be so sure."

"What if you've never had a boyfriend before?" I rushed out. "How can you know then?"

"Ahh," Aunt Marjorie said. "Your *friend*, hmm?"

"I guess I'm just confused about a lot of stuff right now." *Like how I can be in love with someone who's dead.*

"I've always thought that maybe it's different for everyone," she said. "But for me, I had to trust my gut. One instant I was seeing your Uncle Gerald as just this good-looking fella, and then *bam*! It was almost like everything around me slowed down. And I knew."

I knew *exactly* what she was describing. I felt that same stopping of time around Caspian, too.

"If you had the chance to spend one more hour with Uncle Gerald, knowing that the pain of losing him would happen all over again, would you do it?"

"Without a doubt," she said. "I'd give anything to have one

more minute with him. I'd take him by the hand, look him in the eye, and tell him that I love him." Her voice broke on the last word, and I felt the ache of tears gathering. Blinking rapidly, I tried not to let them fall.

"Thanks, Aunt Marjorie." I cleared my throat. "You're the best great-aunt I've ever had."

"You're welcome, sweetheart. Anytime you need me, you call. And you're the best great-niece I've ever had too."

She said her good-byes, and I hung up the phone. I had a full mind and heavy heart.


I bided my time the next day, willing two thirty to come faster. For some odd reason I'd decided that two thirty was the perfect time to head to the cemetery, and I was counting down the seconds.

Finally, at two p.m., I changed into a red-and-white check-ered sundress and spent an inordinate amount of time on my hair. It was precisely 2:32 when I left the house, and I told myself to try to walk at a normal pace.

But when those cemetery gates came into view, my heart flip-flopped inside my chest, and I quickened my speed. My feet flew as I followed the path, and I found myself standing in front of Caspian's mausoleum.

Tugging nervously at my dress, I moved to the door and opened it. Then I realized what I'd forgotten to do, and stopped to glance behind me. No one was in sight, so I slipped inside.

I noticed right away that he'd lit more candles. The room was now clearly illuminated. Caspian was bent over one of his makeshift tables, with a candle resting on the box before him. He held up a finger to motion for me to wait.

"I didn't know when you'd get here. I'm almost done." His hands were shaping something. Flashes of silver caught the light, and I noticed a peculiar scent in the air. Like a wire burning.

"What's that smell?"

"It's my soldering iron. I was using it earlier." He held whatever it was he'd been working on up to the light and inspected it. A moment later he nodded and then turned to me.

I suddenly grew shy. "Hi. . . ."

"Hi." He palmed the item and walked over. "I thought you might change your mind. Why'd you come back, Abbey?"

*How do I answer* that? "Curiosity," I blurted out. "I have lots of questions."

"Oh. Right." His face fell, and he turned away. I took a step forward and put a hand out to touch him, then let it fall to my side.

"What do you want to know?" He shoved the item he'd been holding into his back pocket.

"Tell me what that first day was like. The car crash. And after. What do you remember? How did you get here?" *Are you buried here?* was on the tip of my tongue, but I held it back.

Caspian glanced up and then ran his fingers through his hair. "You don't start with the easy ones, do you? What's my favorite color, when's my birthday . . ."

"Oh, I want to know those things too, but later."

He closed his eyes. "It was the day after Halloween. I remember that. . . . My dad wanted me to get a part for him at a junkyard. I went to go pick it up, but I got the wrong one. When I got home, Dad yelled that I'd never learn, never get a real job, if I didn't start paying attention. I shot back some smart-ass comment about how I didn't want to be a grease-monkey like him. Didn't want dirty fingernails and split knuckles for the rest of my life. Then I took off."

He opened his eyes and looked at me, but I could tell he wasn't really seeing me.

"I was going to go back and get the right part. I don't know if he ever knew that. I never told him. . . ." Sadness was all over his face, and I ached to put my arms around him.

But I couldn't.

"The next thing I remember . . . I was sitting on the side of the road. Just sitting there. It was dark, and when I tried to figure out where I was, I had this big, gaping hole in my memory. It was like the hangover from hell without the nausea."

Since my alcohol experience was limited to occasional sips of wine at special dinners and weddings, I didn't know what the hangover from hell felt like. But I *did* know about that gaping black hole. I'd experienced the same thing when Kristen died.

"Was there anyone around? Cops, firemen, random people?"

Caspian shook his head. "No. I was alone, and my car was gone. Now that I think about it, there wasn't even any glass or anything the road. I don't know how much time had passed. I just ended up walking back to the house. Dad was asleep when I got there, so I went to bed too. Figured I'd get my car back in the morning."

He hesitated, then started pacing back and forth. "I must have slept . . . or something . . . for a while, because I think it was a couple of days later when I woke up. I'm not sure why, but time passes differently for me now. Faster." He glanced over at one of the boxes, and I followed his gaze to the alarm clock sitting in there.

"That's why I have *that*," he said, pointing to it. "I had to set it to go off every time I was supposed to be meeting you."

"Time moves *faster*? How?"

"I can't explain it. But when I close my eyes, I kind of fall into this void. I don't know what it is. Maybe it's my body going to an astral plane, or heaven . . . or wherever it is I'm supposed to be."

"Do you find yourself visiting yourself in the past or future?" I joked. "Are you wearing chains? Or do you hang out in the attic of old houses?"

He looked at me blankly.

"You know. Ghosts of Christmas Past and Christmas Future? Haven't you ever seen that Bill Murray movie *Scrooged*? And the chains and the attic are from haunted houses. Technically, you *are* a ghost."

"Thanks for the reminder," Caspian said.

*Open mouth, insert foot.*

"But no, no chains or haunted houses. Just calendar pages flipping faster and faster. What's a day for you can be a week for me. Or a month. Whenever I said I'd meet you at a specific time, I'd have to set the alarm to make sure I didn't miss it."

"Why close your eyes and go into this black void thingy at all then? Why not just stay awake the entire time? Do you *need* to sleep?"

He looked me directly in the eye. "It's not like when I was

alive. I don't need sleep. Sometimes, this weariness comes over me ..." He paused, then said, "Have you ever felt time crawling? Have you ever been so desperate to make the hours disappear that you'll do anything? Do you know what that feels like?"

"Yes," I whispered. "When Kristen died. After her funeral. After I met you ... I couldn't sleep. My dreams were awful, so I forced myself to stay awake. It got so bad that I started to think that Kristen was there with me. That she'd ... come back."

His eyes were understanding. "Sometimes I'd go weeks at a time and not wake up."

"What changed?" I held my breath waiting for his answer.

*"You,"* he said. "I saw you and Kristen here, and around you I could see *color*. I knew that meant you were different."

I cracked a smile. "What did you see—my aura?"

"No. I saw your beauty."

My heart lurched and started beating triple time. It was thumping so hard that I put one hand to my chest, afraid it would break right through.

"Are you okay?" he asked. "What's wrong? Do you need to sit down?"

His concern for me was adorable. "I'm fine. I don't need to sit down. You just need to give a girl some warning when you're going to say something like that. It sends my heart into quivers."

Caspian suddenly looked all bashful and shy. I liked that almost as much as I liked him being worried about me. But I took pity on the poor boy. "Tell me what happened with your dad. When you finally woke up."

"I tried to talk to him, but he wouldn't answer. I thought maybe he was just pissed about the car thing, so I went outside to give him some space. Saw some people on the sidewalk and said something to them. They ignored me too."

He paced over to the bench and sat down. He looked sad. I moved toward the bench too and sat next to him.

"For days . . . or weeks . . . I don't really know which, I walked the streets. Screaming at the top of my lungs. Trying to stop every person I came across. Searching for someone to tell me what was going on. I even went to the police station. Threw myself in one of their chairs and waited all day. Nothing changed."

I shook my head, horrified at what he was saying. "Did you . . . did things . . . *people* . . . pass through you?"

Caspian didn't answer. Just looked at me. I wanted to touch him so badly that I locked my fingers together so I didn't forget again and reach out. "You must have felt like you were going crazy," I whispered. "Like everyone around you was a part of something connected, but you had broken loose."

"That's exactly what it felt like."

"How did you get here? To the cemetery?" I asked him. "Are you . . . ?"

"I'm not buried here. And for a while I just stayed in my old room. It wasn't hard. I didn't get hungry or thirsty, so I never needed food. I tried not to move anything in case my dad noticed, but he wouldn't come into my room, so eventually I just stopped caring. That worked until—" He broke off.

"Until?" I prodded.

He got a funny look on his face, somewhere between horror and frustration. "Have you ever watched all of your stuff being hauled away? Seen your parents put the contents of your life into garbage bags and set them outside at the curb? Like yesterday's trash? He put a tarp over the bags . . . ," he said slowly.

I forgot then, or remembered, but I just didn't care. I grabbed for his hand.

And hit solid bench as it went right through.

He looked down, startled.

"Sorry," I said. "It's just . . . Oh God, Caspian. That's awful. And terrible. No parent should ever do that."

Caspian shook his head. "I don't blame my dad. He waited long enough. It was time to move on with his life."

He traced the ornate scrollwork on the arm of the bench

before speaking again. "I followed the trucks that took my stuff. I thought they were going to the dump, but they went to Goodwill. So I waited until it got dark and jimmied the lock on the store. Filled one of the bags with my art stuff, some clothes, and a couple of books."

"I went to the high school and stayed there for a while. Sometimes I'd wander the halls when the bell rang, just to feel like I was a part of something again. I thought that if I tried hard enough, brushed shoulders with them long enough, that someone would know. Someone *had* to see me or feel me."

A mischievous look spread across his face, and I was struck again by his gorgeousness. My heart was rapidly melting at the sight of him.

"I have to admit though, it wasn't *that* bad there. Perhaps you've heard of the urban legend about my school?"

I cocked my head to one side. "Enlighten me."

"The legend says that the White Plains High School boys' bathroom is haunted. Oddly enough, strange things only happen when the jocks are beating up on the freshmen."

"I take it that was you?"

"Maybe. Nothing makes a football player scream faster than the words 'You are going to end up with bad hair plugs and tiny balls by the time you're thirty' suddenly appearing on the mirror."

"Steroids?"

He flashed a smile. "Exactly. That's why the biggest ones always screamed the loudest. The plumbing is awful too. Sinks randomly turning on, toilets that won't flush at the most *inopportune* times."

"Why didn't you stay there? Practicing random acts of . . . non–toilet flushing?"

"Summer came. School let out. Everything was stale and tired. Then eventually I started growing more and more used to the quiet. The dust. I knew that when school let back in, I wouldn't want to be around all those people anymore. This place came to mind, and I figured it would be perfect. It took me three days of searching to find a mausoleum that was open."

"So then . . . you just keep your stuff here and in your spare time hang out with the crazy girl who can see you?"

"Crazy beautiful," he said with a half smile. "Yeah, that's pretty much it."

# Chapter Eleven

# SHADOW PUPPETS

The sequestered situation of this church seems always to have made it a favorite haunt of troubled spirits.

—"The Legend of Sleepy Hollow"

While waiting for Ben at our next tutoring session, I was practically vibrating with energy. Things were going *so well* with Caspian, and Mom and Dad were being cool too. And if sometimes, late at night in bed, I questioned whether or not I truly *was* insane, I told myself that it didn't matter. I was too happy to care.

Ben came in and sat down, but I noticed right away that he was acting fidgety. "Ben?" I said. "What's up? You look worried."

He glanced at the table. "I just, uh, didn't want things to be awkward . . . after the other night."

"I am *so* sorry about that. My mom—"

"No, not that. Your mom was fine. I meant me. Us. Me leaving. I'm sorry."

I'd already forgotten about that. "No big. We're cool."

"Are you sure?"

"Yup. Now let's get started."

"Okay. Do you have a highlighter? We're going to need one for this next section."

"Let me check the junk drawer," I said. "I think there's one in there."

I dug through a pile of old batteries, rubber bands, burned-out lightbulbs (*Seriously? Why are we keeping those?*), and years-past-their-expiration-date coupons, but I couldn't locate a highlighter.

"Not here," I told him. "Let me run upstairs. I know I have one in my room."

When I reached my bedroom, I went right for the supply box that was stashed under my work desk. As soon as I felt the capped end of a highlighter, I pulled it free. A small piece of paper was stuck to it, and drifted to the floor. I recognized it right away.

It was the recipe for peppermint tea that Katy had given me for Christmas last year. I'd never even noticed it was missing.

*That's because you didn't* want *to notice,* my subconscious whispered. *Noticing it was missing meant noticing that it was real.*

I held it in one hand and ran my thumb over the crinkly texture. Even though Nikolas and Katy had claimed to be ghosts, or Shades, as they called it, and said they were characters from "The Legend of Sleepy Hollow," they *were* real, in some sense. I'd visited their home. Drunk their tea. Exchanged gifts with them.

Slowly, I sat the recipe back on the desk. My eyes and fingers involuntarily went to the dainty gilt-edged, rose-covered teacup sitting there. They gave that to me too. Barely visible, and crammed next to several full bottles of perfume that I was aging, it had collected a fine layer of dust.

*I should go visit Nikolas and Katy. Prove to myself . . .*

Prove to myself what? I didn't know. But I was going to get proof . . . of something.


The doorbell rang later that afternoon, just as I was getting ready to go see Caspian again. I was literally at the front door with my hand on the doorknob, when the chimes echoed through the house. Spiders raced along my scalp when I saw who was there, and immediately I remembered our last encounter.

It was the odd-looking boy and girl I'd met at the cemetery.

This time they were dressed in khakis—pants for him, long skirt for her—and white polo shirts. They looked like private-school kids or Jehovah's Witnesses.

Except for their hair.

The guy still had the Mohawk, only it was red this time, and the girl's purple-and-blond hair had been dyed completely turquoise.

As soon as I saw them, I took a step back. I couldn't help it; my legs were no longer in my control.

"Hello, Abbey," the girl sing-sang in that gorgeous, high-pitched, melodic voice. "Do you remember us?"

Something pushed at the edges of my memory. It made me sick to my stomach. "Cacey and Uri," I replied.

"That's right," Uri said. His voice was musical too, but in a different way. A hidden timbre ran in his tone, stretched thin like a silver current. "Can we come in?"

"That's, um . . . I have to . . . I really should . . ." I lost all train of thought, and the empty house loomed at my back. Dad was at work, and Mom was at a meeting. I had the strangest urge to call 911, but what was I going to say? "Help, there are two kids dressed in khaki and being polite at my front door"?

Hysterical laughter bubbled up, and I pushed the thought

away. I was feeling much calmer now. Happy, even. Everything was going to be fine.

"Sure!" I said, throwing the door wide open. "Come on in. Do you want anything to drink?"

First Cacey, then Uri crossed the threshold and followed me in. "I'll take a Coke, if you have some," Cacey said. I entered the kitchen and fetched her one from the fridge. Bringing it back in, I turned to Uri. "Anything for you?"

"No, I'm good."

They both sat on the couch, and I sat in the recliner across from them. Cacey popped the top of her can and guzzled the entire thing in three sips. She turned her wide, clear eyes to me as I watched in astonishment.

"I just *love* that beverage," she trilled. "Co-ca-Co-la. Makes me want to write songs about it."

*Well*, that *was definitely one of the weirdest things I've ever heard.* I glanced at Uri. He was smiling indulgently at her. Then, suddenly, he turned his gaze to me.

"Do you like Coca-Cola, Abbey?" he asked. "Is it one of your favorite things?"

"Um, well, yeah."

"What about potato chips? Hershey bars? Doritos? Pizza? Those are all typical teenage vices, aren't they?"

*Vices.* That was an interesting choice of words. "Yeah, I guess . . ."

Cacey leaned forward. "Cigarettes? Booze? A little gin and tonic after school to help ease the stress of peer pressure?"

*What? Ew.* "Those are all generally considered vices, but they're not mine." Why was I answering them? Why were they here? What did they want?

I opened my mouth to turn the question-asking tables on *them*, but Cacey intercepted me. "I know! Sex with boys . . . in fast cars, and on your parents' bed. Or with girls. I'm not judging."

I stood up. "Who *are* you people? Why are you asking me these things?"

Cacey looked at Uri and grinned. Her eyes were paler, if that was even possible. There was absolutely no color in them now, not even the tiniest hint of gray. It was like staring into crystal-clear water. "We're from a local college," she said. "Just gathering statistics and data. Can't you tell by our clothes?"

They were lying. I knew they were lying, but I didn't call them on it. "Oh, okay."

"Do you have any plans for your future? College and what-not?" Uri asked me.

I looked back and forth between them. A sick feeling blossomed in the pit of my stomach, and I desperately wanted them to leave. "Shouldn't you . . . I mean, don't you have someplace else to be?" I glanced at the door.

"You want us to *leave*?" Cacey said, a delighted tone in her voice. "Oh, I get it. *No*."

"Why don't you just answer our questions?" Uri asked me. His tone was soothing, and I almost closed my eyes for a second to catch that melody. "Don't you *want* to answer them?"

*Yes. No.* A migraine was starting to throb in the back of my skull. "I really don't think it's any of your business. . . ."

Cacey and Uri both leveled glares at me. Every single hair on my arms and on the back of my neck stood straight up. The dancing spiders did triple time, and I almost gasped out loud at the shivery sensation.

Putting one hand to my pulsing temples, I didn't recognize the whispery voice that came out of me. "Please, don't ask me these things. I can't . . . Just please . . . don't."

Uri broke his gaze and turned to look at Cacey. She shook her head at him. "*No.*"

"It's too much," he argued. "Later."

Cacey gave a disgusted sigh and then began to examine her nails. "Fine, whatever."

Uri looked like he wanted to grab her by the arm and haul her to her feet, but she shot him a deadly look. My head was splitting, but I felt that weird sense of calm coming over me again. In one swift movement Cacey stood up and strode to the door. Uri was by her side a heartbeat later.

"See you around, Abbey," Cacey said, wiggling her fingers in an approximation of a wave. "Next time."

Uri reached around her and opened the door. The sunlight streamed in, illuminating both of them in glowing silhouettes of white. "Oh, and try some baking soda for the aftertaste. Takes away the burn," she called out before they stepped into the daylight.

I sat on the couch, staring at the door like I could see through it. Like I could see them walking down the street, and away from my house.

All the while tasting burnt ash on my tongue.

*Red eyes and dark, leathery things chased me down cramped alleys and dirty side streets. Every time I tried to scream, they'd come swooping toward me, cackling and spitting fire.*

*I turned blindly, searching for something to fend them off with, but every brick or stone or piece of wood I could find turned to ashes in my hands. Disintegrated at my touch.*

*Somewhere, in the back of my mind, I knew this was a nightmare. Knew that I lay on my bed, trapped beneath stifling sheets. Shivering as sweat cooled on my skin.*

*I opened my mouth again to scream. In my mind, my vocal chords flexed and stretched. I felt the strain as a hoarse cry edged its way past my lips. It was almost there . . . almost free . . .*

*The dark thing flew low, and I took a step back. Threw up my hands, tried to protect my face . . .*

*And swallowed it whole.*


I sat up, feverishly clutching the covers in the dark. It was here. It was in me. It was . . . a dream.

I took in my surroundings. Closet, bathroom, desk, door. No hulking shapes. No dark shadows. No red eyes. But just to be on the safe side, I reached over and flipped on my light. A warm, buttery glow filled the room and swept aside my wave of panic.

Looking down at my twisted sheets, I slowly unclenched my fingers. My legs were sweaty and stuck together when I moved. I took several steps toward the bathroom and fumbled for the light switch. The tile was cool on my bare feet as I shuffled in and stood in front of the sink, gripping both edges.

Staring at the reflection in the mirror, I turned my head from side to side and looked at my throat. There weren't any . . . marks, or anything. Feeling slightly foolish, I opened my mouth and looked inside. Nothing dark or scary there either.

I shuddered as I thought about that thing swooping toward me. Forcing its way past my throat. It had screeched the most god-awful sound. . . . I shuddered again and ran my hands under some cold water. Pressing them to my cheeks, I tried to calm my racing thoughts. It was only a dream, but it had *felt* so real.

A single thought crossed my mind, and without questioning it, I followed through.

Leaving the bathroom behind, I changed into some jeans and a dark hoodie. Then I went over to the window seat and looked at the ground outside. There was a section of flat roof right below my window, attached to a hanging trellis. The drop down to the ground didn't look too bad, and I was pretty sure I could make it.

I raised the window halfway and leaned my head out into the darkness. *I'll have to be careful not to bump into anything down there and wake up Mom and Dad.*

I pulled my head back in. What was I thinking? Could I really sneak out of the house? If they caught me, I'd be *so* dead.

I glanced back over at my bed and tasted burnt ash again. *No way.* I didn't care what happened. I wasn't going back to bed, and I didn't want to stay here.

Lifting the window a little bit higher, I threw my leg over the edge. One toe touched the roof, and I put my other leg through. Balancing on tiptoes, I pulled the window back down, leaving it open just enough so that I could get back in, but not too much so that it looked suspicious. Belatedly, I realized that I probably should have stuffed some pillows under my sheets to make it look like I was still there in case Mom came in to check on me.

But I wasn't going to climb back in just to do that. Besides, I wouldn't be gone very long anyway.

Moving over to the edge where the lattice was, I stuck my feet into the crisscrossed holes. It settled when I put my whole weight on it, and I froze, but a second later it was still. I gripped it and gave a tug to double-check. It held firm.

Climbing down was a lot easier than I'd expected, and my feet hit solid ground in no time. It looked like everything was clear, and I moved stealthily across the yard and out into the street.

Most of the houses were dark except for a porch light, and a wicked thrill went through me at what I was doing. When the massive iron cemetery gates rose up before me, I took another peek around, then slipped through them.

The cemetery was beautiful and eerie in the moonlight, the bleached-bone color of the aged tombstones turned milky and luminescent. The pathways were dark, but my feet knew the one that would take me to him. It was peaceful and quiet as I passed by small metal fences and lopsided angel statues, but then I felt a tiny frisson of fear when I pictured red eyes and things on wings swooping after me.

I quickened my pace to a half run, and I reached his mausoleum. Slipping through the door, I saw that there weren't any candles lit. *What if he's not here? What if he goes wandering at night?*

Terror started to clog the back of my throat, and I willed my eyes to get used to the darkness. The total, complete darkness, which was black . . . and empty . . . and yawning in front of me.

A rustling sound caught my attention. Were there rats in here? *Rats have beady eyes. Red. Beady. Eyes.*

The sound came closer, and I tried to breathe slower. If it didn't hear me, it couldn't find me. But my heart wouldn't stop pounding, and my pulse was racing. I wanted desperately to close my eyes, but I couldn't even do that.

The noise stopped. "Abbey?"

His voice was right next to my ear, and I turned my head, groping blindly for him in the dark. A spark of electricity tingled faintly in my hands, and I knew he was there.

"What's wrong?" Caspian said.

 182

I wanted to run into his arms and be told everything was okay. "I had a bad dream. Couldn't sleep."

"So you came *here*?"

Had I made a mistake? "Sorry," I whispered. "I just wanted to see you, but I shouldn't have—"

"No, no, it's good. I'm glad you came to see me. But won't your parents find out?"

I shook my head, then realized he probably couldn't see it in the dark. "I snuck out my window. They'll never notice, and I won't stay long." I shifted awkwardly. "Can you, um, light some candles? My dream was pretty scary."

"Oh, yeah." He moved, and then there was a soft scratching sound. The bright flare of a flame burst to life at the end of a match, and he lit two candles on my left. "Do you want to sit down on the bench?"

I nodded and followed him, waiting as he lit several more candles that sputtered and shed their light across the empty tomb. He slid down into a sitting position against the wall next to me. It was deadly quiet in our little space, and I tried to imagine him here day after day, all alone. It would drive me to the edge in no time.

"Want to talk about it?" he asked. "The dream?"

I draped my arm across the back of the bench. The metal was

cool through the thickness of my sweatshirt. "It was awful. Dark things were chasing me into dark alleys. And I couldn't defend myself. Then this monster swooped down on me, and . . ."

Caspian got up and moved over to one of the boxes. Reaching down, he pulled out two items and then came back to me. "Here." He held out a shirt. "You're cold. You're shivering."

I wasn't going to argue that it was just because of the dream, so I took it. It was a button-down, and felt like fleece under my fingertips. Tilting my head back, I said, "Thank you."

Then he placed a small brown paper bag next to me. "Second, a distraction. Sorry it's not wrapped nicer. This was the best I could do. Happy birthday, Astrid."

He'd *gotten* me something? I opened the bag and looked down into it. A book with a colorful illustration of Ichabod Crane and the Headless Horseman lay there. "Ohhhhh," I whispered, pulling it out reverently.

"It's a kids'-book version," he admitted, with a bashful smile. "I hope that's okay."

I flipped through the pages. It was an old book, copyright 1932, and crisp with age. Every third page had a gorgeous black-and-white illustration on it. It was the most beautiful thing I'd ever seen. "It's *perfect*," I said. "'Thank you' seems so inadequate. Where did you get it?"

"Don't worry about that," he replied. "I'm just glad you like it."

I hugged it to my chest. "I love it."

He stood over me for a minute, looking down with a strange expression on his face. "Every guy's dream," he muttered softly. "To be the one the girl comes running to when she wants to be saved. And I can't even do anything about it. . . ."

His eyes were intense, holding me captive. My breath caught in my throat. "You can come sit by me," I offered. "Keep me company." But he moved back toward the wall, reclaiming his seat on the floor.

"It's better if I stay here. Easier that way."

*Better for who?* I wanted to say, but I tried not to let the disappointment show on my face and busied myself with wrapping his shirt around me. "So how come you can touch things, but not me? Um . . . people. People, I mean."

Caspian spread his hands out in front of him and looked at them. "I don't know why I can move boxes, pick up my charcoal, snap a pencil, break a twig . . . but can't touch you. Maybe it's the rule of this place, or whatever I am. I'm not sure."

"Have you tried to touch anyone else?"

"Yeah. Kids at the high school, my dad, strangers on the street . . . Hell, I even went church-hopping. Figured for sure that if anyone could see me or touch me, it would be a priest. But they slipped between my hands just as easy as the rest."

I thought back to that night in my room, and the next day at the library when he'd kissed me. "How were you able to . . . ?" I felt myself blushing. "How could you kiss me at the library? Shouldn't that have been impossible? And before I left, that day at the river when I found you in the rain, you said you could only touch me for one day. What does that mean?"

He looked away, and I had to strain to hear his answer. "I can only touch you on my death day. November first. I touched your face in your room because it was after midnight. And that's why I wanted you to meet me at the library that day. Why I was so adamant that you didn't forget."

"Why didn't you stay longer? In my room? If you could only touch me then, why were you in such a hurry to . . . leave?"

"I wasn't sure how much, *exactly*, I could . . . do," he said. "That's why I picked the library. Public place and all."

My ears grew warmer as I realized what he meant. I coughed once and cleared my throat. "How did you figure it out? The first time. How did you know you could touch me on that day?"

"On the first anniversary of my death, the year before, I was downtown. I didn't even know what day it was, but I bumped into someone. Literally. Normally, I'd just pass right through them, but that day I didn't.

"At first I thought something had changed. People saw me. They heard me. For the first time in a whole year." His eyes grew sad. "Then I passed a newspaper stand and saw that it was November first. I put two and two together."

He looked up at me. "I wanted to go see my dad. Almost did, too. I wanted to tell him what had happened to me, and that I was sorry. But then I thought about how traumatic it would be seeing your dead son a year after his car accident, so I didn't. I ended up just sitting in a park all day. Doing what I did every other day. Watching the people go by."

"That must have been hard," I said. "To finally be a part of it, and yet still be on the outside."

Caspian nodded.

"And then the next day? It was the same again?"

Another nod. "Back to being a ghost."

I looked down at my hands. "When did you find me?"

"Last year. It was spring. I followed you, but then you left. I remember, because I could see the flowers blooming. They were pink. I knew right away that something with you was different."

"What is it with colors? You said something before about seeing colors around me."

He nodded and ran his fingers through his hair. In the half-light, the white-blond strands were muted. But that black streak was still as bold as ever.

"I can't see colors anywhere else except around you. Normally everything I see is gray. It's like living in this shadow world. But around you . . ." He made an arching shape with his hands. "There's a . . . bubble or something that surrounds you. Your eyes, your hair, your clothes." He laughed. "Even the tree you stood next to shared your color. When you moved, I could see the green grass under your feet."

He stopped suddenly and leaned forward, saying very intently, "It's exhilarating, Abbey. *You* exhilarate me."

My heart lurched, and I gave him a stern look. "There you go again. Saying things that make me—"A huge yawn interrupted me, and I broke off, embarrassed beyond belief.

"Why don't you lie down on the bench?" Caspian suggested. "I have a pillow." He stood up again and went to a spot on the far side of the room. Then he brought back not only a pillow, but also the black jacket I'd picked up before.

He held both out to me. "Even though I don't need to sleep, it helps to have something that reminds me of . . . before. Sorry, I don't have a blanket. Will this jacket be okay?"

"Yes, on one condition."

He cocked his head at me, waiting for me to go on.

"Can you come over here? To sit on the floor by the bench?"

He came closer, and I took the pillow first. Then I took the jacket and pulled my feet up, shifting to a lying-down position. Caspian knelt on the floor beside me, smiling as he tugged on a piece of the jacket that was hanging on the floor.

*Good* Lord, *he is gorgeous when he smiles.*

I smiled shyly back at him and arranged the jacket around me before turning to put my head on the pillow. He was close enough to reach out and touch ... and I bit my lip at the sudden sadness that overwhelmed me.

"Can you do shadow puppets?" I whispered to him, desperate to make the sad feeling go away.

He hooked his two thumbs together and flapped his fingers, angling his body so that the shape he was creating showed up on the wall. "Kee-yar, kee-yar," he said softly.

"What's that?" I asked.

"It's the sound a hawk makes. That's what my shadow puppet was—a hawk."

"I thought it was a bluebird," I teased. "Do it again."

He made the shadow again, this time making it flap its wings fiercely. I giggled, and then he moved his fingers, casting some bizarre round-shaped thing on the wall. "Three guesses what this one is."

I studied it carefully. "Bunny?"

"Nope." He wiggled his hand to simulate movement.

"Puppy?"

He laughed. "*Where* did you see a puppy there?"

"I don't know. Okay, last guess, um . . . a turtle?"

"Ehhhhhhh, wrong answer. It's an armadillo."

"An *armadillo*? How did you learn how to make an armadillo shadow puppet?"

His face turned bashful. "Okay, you got me. I made that up. I didn't know *what* that one was."

I snuggled deeper under his jacket. My eyelids were starting to get heavy. Caspian arranged his fingers into an intricate pattern.

"There you go. I'll make 'em, and then tell you what they are. No more guessing."

I fought back another yawn. "Okay."

"First obligatory shadow puppet is . . . an incredibly self-conscious clown." He wiggled his fingers. "Second one . . ."

My left eyelid drooped. Then my right. I blinked heavily, and the walls shifted around him.

". . . Three-legged panda bear."

My eyes stayed closed, and I felt myself sliding toward the edge of sleep.

"Scrambled eggs ... bacon on the side." His voice ebbed and flowed around me. "Are you falling asleep, Abbey?"

I fought to stay awake. "Noooo ... ," I heard myself saying. "Caspian, don't leave, 'kay? I don't want them to get me."

"Don't worry. I'll stay with you."

Everything was fuzzy now, but I tried to stay awake long enough to tell him one more thing. "Glad you ... see ... my colors, Caspian."

"Me too, Abbey," he said softly. "Sweet dreams."

*Chapter Twelve*

# OLD FRIENDS

The chief part of the stories, however, turned upon the favorite spectre of Sleepy Hollow, the Headless Horseman, who had been heard several times of late . . . ; and, it was said, tethered his horse nightly among the graves in the churchyard.

—"The Legend of Sleepy Hollow"

"Abbey . . . Abbey . . ."

My eyes opened slowly, and Caspian's face came into view. "What are you doing here?" I asked, rubbing one eye. My hair was in my face, and I pushed it away.

"I'm here because this is my place, remember? You came to see me."

*Right.* I'd snuck out of the house. "Crap! I have to get back. What time is it? My parents are going to kill me!"

"It's okay. You've only been asleep for an hour. You have plenty of time to get back before they wake up."

I groaned and rolled my stiff neck from side to side. Already my brain was waking up and slamming into overdrive. *Is my hair a mess? Do I have morning breath? What about drool . . . I hope I didn't drool. Oh God, do I snore?*

Not knowing what to say, I carefully folded up the jacket and then the shirt. Would "Thanks for letting me sleep in your crypt" work?

But what came out was, "Did you stay awake the whole time?" I wanted to kick myself as soon as I said those words. *Why can't I be witty?* I was perpetually cursed with nonwittiness.

Caspian smiled at me. "Yeah, I stayed awake. I didn't want to close my eyes and fall into the . . . darkness." Then he blurted, "I didn't, uh, sit here looking at you, or anything weird like that. I had a book."

Well, that was oddly comforting and disappointing at the same time. "I hope I didn't snore."

"Nope. Did you have any more bad dreams?"

"No. No more dreams."

He stood up and shuffled his feet. "I don't want you to think I'm kicking you out or anything, but you should probably be on your way home before your parents wake up."

"Yeah, you're right." I handed him back the jacket, then glanced down at his shirt I still had on. "Can I, um . . . Would it be okay if I . . . keep this?" That sounded so lame, but I wanted to have some small piece of him.

"Sure. Although I don't know why you'd want to."

*Because it's yours* . . . I kept that thought to myself. "Thanks."

Caspian walked me out of the mausoleum, and the early-morning air was cool. We both moved in silence until we got to the gate.

Jamming my hands into the pockets of my hoodie, I turned to face him. "Thanks for letting me sleep over. It was . . . nice."

He snorted. "Yeah. I'm sure spending the night in a creepy tomb is every girl's idea of the perfect date."

"It wasn't creepy. *You* were there."

"That's why it was creepy. Because of me."

I rolled my eyes at him. "It wasn't you. Don't say that. Besides, you're going to ruin my happy memories of shadow puppets."

"I *am* pretty great at shadow puppetry. Maybe I should start my own business." He grinned, and I felt warmth spreading through me.

I looked up at the brightening sky. "I really *do* have to go." I dug my shoe into the ground. "But if I, maybe, came back later today . . . would you be here?"

Caspian nodded, then turned and started to walk away, pausing long enough to say, "You know where to find me."

I stood there watching his retreating figure, then shook my head. We'd pretty much just spent the night together, and he was able to act that casual about it? Boys were so hard to figure out sometimes.

Movement on the path to my left caught my eye, and I turned and saw a person. A person with a little wire brush and a trash bag sticking out of his back pocket. A person with gray hair, a faded blue shirt, and patched overalls. *Nikolas.*

He spotted me, too, and paused. I walked toward him and threw my arms open for a hug when I reached him. Nikolas patted my shoulder in that rusty way of his, and hesitantly hugged me back.

I squeezed him tight, suddenly realizing how much I'd missed him. It was like seeing my long-lost grandfather.

"I'm kind of mad at you," I told him, drawing back. "But I really missed you, Nikolas."

I could see his eyes were misty, and he scrubbed a rough hand over his face. "Forgive an old man whose eyes leak," he told me. "I missed you too, Abbey. We thought you had decided to abandon this place."

A sliver of guilt and shame wormed its way into my heart. I *had* intended to leave them all behind. "I had a lot to work through, Nikolas. I'm still working through some of it, I think.

But I couldn't stay away. In fact I was going to come see you again. How is Katy?"

"My lady is well. Her garden has been blooming these past few weeks, and she is happy to be in her element of picking flowers."

I laughed. "I bet she is. Does she still have them covering every surface of the house?"

Nikolas nodded. "I cannot take a step or make my seat without fear of crushing some fragile bloom." A gentle look came over his face. "But that is what pleases her, and so I tread carefully."

A warm feeling settled over my heart. It was nice to hear that they were still so happy together. The sky lightened to a shade of pink with faint fingers of yellow. Daylight was racing toward us, and I needed to get home.

"Is it okay if I come over later today?" I asked him. "I have a lot of questions for you."

He followed my gaze toward the sun. "Why don't you come with me now? Katy is at home, and I'm sure she will be happy to make us some tea. We have peppermint." His look was hopeful, and I hated to turn him down, but I could get *seriously* grounded if Mom or Dad found out that I snuck out of the house.

I tried to think fast. I could always tell Mom that I went

for a walk early this morning. Technically, it *was* early morning when I went to see Caspian, and I *had* walked to get there. I turned my attention back to Nikolas. "I guess I could come for a short visit."

"Good! Let us go now."

He turned, and I followed him to the far side of the cemetery. We reached the woods and set off down the overgrown path that would lead us to their cottage. An angry chipmunk scolded us when we trampled dangerously close to the tree he called home, and I smiled at the absurdity of his chattering. Chipmunks had it easy. Gather a couple of nuts, make your home in a tree, wave your tail at the giant humans invading your space . . .

The path widened, and a little bridge came into view. Beyond that was Nikolas and Katy's home. I held my breath. Would it still look like the enchanted little storybook cottage that I'd visited before? Or would it look different to me in any way?

But the thatched roof was still the same, and the giant round stones that made up the exterior were still there. Even the wisteria growing on the stone chimney looked colorful and vibrant. I exhaled in relief.

Nikolas led me around back, where Katy was kneeling in a garden among daisies and bluebonnets. She had on a wide straw hat and an old-fashioned, yellowish summer dress. I stopped for a second and mentally kicked myself for not seeing it before. She was the picture of someone straight out of Washington Irving's tale, right down to the bouffant hair she had rolled up under her hat in a loose bun.

I felt shy all of a sudden. But as soon as she heard Nikolas call out, Katy looked up, and a large smile broke out on her face.

Gracefully rising to her feet, she hurried over to me, arms outstretched. Seconds later I was smothered in a hug that smelled like peppermint and honeysuckle. "How wonderful to see you, Abbey!" she said. "What a pleasant surprise. It has been so long."

"I was gone for a while. I'll tell you all about it inside. Can we go talk?"

She nodded. "I'll make some tea."

I stepped back, and Nikolas came around to her other side, offering his arm. She leaned on it, and they started toward the front of the house.

Entering the kitchen, I crossed the room and went to the large slate table by the fireplace. I pulled out a glossy cherry-colored chair and sat down. Nikolas sat too, and Katy went to the cupboard.

I stopped her before she made the tea. "Can that wait for a minute? I'd like to talk first."

She sat at the table and bent to pick up yarn and needles from a basket on the floor. Within seconds her fingers were flying.

I decided to start from the beginning. "I left Sleepy Hollow to go see a specialist. A doctor who helps people who ... see and hear ... things that don't exist." I wasn't sure how much to tell them, how much to admit to, but I didn't want to hold anything back. "See, I thought I was crazy. You guys told me that you're Katrina Van Tassel and the Headless Horseman from 'The Legend of Sleepy Hollow,' and the father of the boy I'd been spending time with told me that his son was dead. I couldn't cope with any of that."

Katy paused from her knitting and put one hand on mine. "I know how you feel, Abbey. I, too, was once in the same position. When Nikolas and I first met and I learned he was dead, I didn't handle it very well. I ignored him for a month."

"After she tossed an entire Sunday dinner through my head," Nikolas muttered.

"So wait," I said, "you *did* have a head?"

"I could see him in his true form. How he was before," Katy said.

"Will you tell me, then? About your story?"

Katy looked to Nikolas. "Do you want to start?"

He nodded. "The tale is true that I *was* a Hessian soldier. During the Revolutionary War, I made my living as a mercenary. A soldier for hire. Alas, I had an unfortunate meeting with a cannonball. It took my head, and my horse dropped over with it. They buried me in this cemetery, because I saved a child once . . . but that is a story for another day.

"When I found Stagmont nuzzling at the cemetery grass, I realized he had followed me over. My story spread, became the stuff of legend, if you will, and that is how I became the Galloping Hessian of the Hollow."

"So you keep a horse here too?" I said. "Where is he? Can I see him?"

"Sometimes we go on midnight rides through the cemetery, but I do not keep him here. It isn't fair to him. He prefers to wander."

Katy spoke up. "As for me, everything changed when Ichabod Crane came to town. He gave me singing lessons and seemed very interested in me. I tried to remain kind in my refusals of his attention, though."

"Bah. That proud peacock knew you were no more going to choose him than that bag of bones Brom," Nikolas said.

I leaned forward, looking back and forth between the two. "Wait. I thought Brom Bones was the sturdy one and Ichabod

Crane was the skinny one. That's what the legend says."

"Yes," Katy said. "That's how it was written, but as we told you before, the legend was changed from reality. Most notably the ending, to protect Nikolas and me, but other aspects were changed as well."

"Then one day I saw her and fell instantly in love," Nikolas replied.

"I was *not* very pleased by that," Katy said. "I thought I was having fits or a case of the vapors, seeing things that no one else could see. Thank goodness I never told anyone. They would have sent me to a convent." A faraway look came into her eyes. "Although I did often think about telling Father. I always thought that he might be the one person to understand."

She shook her head as if to clear her thoughts. "Imagine having a lovesick ghost as your constant companion. I threw my needlepoint at him, my books at him, even my slippers at him! But he followed me everywhere. Then Brom pulled that silly stunt, dressing up like a headless horseman, and chased Ichabod over the bridge."

"What happened next?" I asked.

"Ichabod left town, and Brom married someone else. Eventually I was able to woo the fair Katrina, and she said she loved me," said Nikolas.

"So you never married Brom?" I asked Katy.

She shook her head no. Pushing her needles to the side, she stood up. "I think I will make the tea now, if that is agreeable with you?"

I nodded.

As she passed by Nikolas, he reached out an arm, and she took his hand, gently kissing the back of it. A twisting sensation filled me, and I looked away.

Sounds filled the kitchen as she started to prepare the tea—the scrape of a bowl being moved, a cabinet door banging open, water filling the kettle. There wasn't a fire in the hearth this time, since it was summer, but Katy put the metal teapot onto an old stove. When she turned the knob, a fine ring of blue fire lit up under the burner, and she came back to sit at the table.

I still had so many questions. "How was Washington Irving involved in all of this? Besides writing the story."

Nikolas was the one to answer. "He played in the cemetery as a little boy and had a penchant for telling stories, even as a lad. I was his companion, and we spent hours talking together. He grew up listening to our story. I was honored when he asked me if he could write it down."

"Washington Irving could *see* you? How?"

"He was one of us. A Shade."

I looked at Katy. "Could he see you, too? Is he still, um . . . *here*? Somewhere?"

"Oh yes, he could see me, too. We talked fairly often. But he didn't stay. His love moved on, and then so did he."

"Wow." I said. "So you guys are like *really* old then, huh?"

They both laughed. "Yes," Katy replied. "I suppose we are rather old." The teakettle whistled, and she got up to remove it from the stove.

"What about the other stuff?" I looked down at the table, suddenly unsure of what I was asking. "With Caspian . . . the boy from the cemetery." I thought back to the last time I had seen them, right before I left for Aunt Marjorie's. "You told me that he was a Shade like you—because of the black streak in his hair. What exactly *is* a Shade?"

"A Shade is just a name we've given ourselves. We're like shadows, living within the shade of real life. I think it fits," Nikolas said.

"Why not just call yourselves ghosts?"

"We are different from ghosts," said Katy. "It's hard to explain, but we are."

Nikolas stood up and went to gather the small silver pots that held sugar and honey. Katy poured the tea into three teacups and brought two of them over to the table, and Nikolas followed closely behind with the server that held milk.

"How?" I persisted.

"Ghosts," he said, "are tied to memories, or places they frequented. Most of them are only capable of repeating one action over and over again. There are a small few who can cause minor disruptions, but they are still playing a role. If they are troubled in death, then they were troubled in life, too."

He sat a teacup in front of me and then reached for his own. "It was different for me, because I wasn't tied to one place. That didn't come till . . . after. Of course, I had my favorite spots, the bridge and the cemetery, but I could go all over this valley. And I followed Katy around quite a bit too." He winked at her and grinned.

"What about touching? Could you and Katy touch each other from the start?" I stirred some honey into my tea and looked down at the amber liquid as I asked my question.

"No, we couldn't touch each other," Katy said.

"You couldn't? Why not?"

"I don't know. That's just the way it was."

"Did you guys know that Caspian was dead when you first saw him?" I asked.

They exchanged a long look.

"Yes," Nikolas said slowly. "We can sense those things. And . . ." Nikolas pointed behind his ear. "What do you see here?"

I peered at him. "You have a black streak too. Like Caspian?"

He nodded. "When I saw it on him, I knew."

"Do you have one too, Katy?" I turned to her.

"Yes. Although mine is white."

"But what if someone dyes their hair?" I asked. "I dye mine all the time."

"It is easy to see through what is natural and what is not," Nikolas said. "Caspian sensed something about me as well. Since I could see him, he thought I was dangerous. He didn't know what he was feeling."

He continued on. "I could sense that *you* were special too. Sometimes small children and those who are especially sensitive can almost tell that I am there, but you could see me right away. And when you were able to hug me, that was a confirmation in itself."

I sipped my tea slowly, trying to take it all in. "So what happened after you . . . passed, Katy? You and Nikolas simply found each other again? Just like that?"

She stirred her tea and glanced away from me. "Yes, that's pretty much the story."

I got the feeling that there was something else she didn't want to say. *She doesn't want to talk about her death. Take a hint, Abbey.*

"At least you both got to come live here together," I said, looking around at the cozy cottage. "A happy ever after."

Suddenly Katy asked, "Would you like to see some of our keepsakes? We have documents and personal items."

I said yes, and Nikolas pulled down a small wooden box from the top of the fireplace mantle. I sat in awe as they showed me Katrina's birth certificate (an ornately hand written parchment dated *In the Year of Our Lord 1775*) and painted portraits. There was Katy sitting stiff and posed next to a table and vase, Nikolas proudly showing off his Hessian uniform, another of Katy as a baby in a bassinet . . .

It was amazing to be holding such historic items, and I handled them carefully, worried that the wrong movement would suddenly reduce them to dust. Then it hit me, a thought that went splintering through my brain like lightning. "Oh!" I gasped. "I have to get home! My parents are going to kill me."

I hurried to my feet. How could I have lost track of time like this? I had to get back.

"I'll come visit again soon," I promised, rushing to the door. "Thanks for telling me everything."

Katy called out a good-bye, and Nikolas followed me as I stepped across the threshold. I was stricken at how bright it was outside.

"Abbey," Nikolas said. "Abbey, be careful. I know at the river that night I told you to go to Caspian, but you need to be careful. Perhaps . . . perhaps it would be best if you did not see him again."

"I'm glad you care, Nikolas," I told him. "Really. It means a lot to me. But I'll be fine."

Instead of looking relieved, though, he looked even more worried.

*Chapter Thirteen*

# ACTING NORMAL

And then the lady gave him her hand as a matter of course.

—"The Legend of Sleepy Hollow"

I ran home as fast as I could, but Mom was pacing the front hallway when I got in. "Where have you *been*?!" she practically shrieked at me. I padded into the kitchen, sweaty and out of breath, and made a beeline for the fridge.

"Abigail, I'm *talking* to you!"

I poured some orange juice and guzzled it down in one long swallow.

"Are you purposefully ignoring me?" she said.

"Mom, chill." I sat the empty cup down and reached for more OJ. "I was just getting a drink." She put both hands on her hips and raised an eyebrow.

I was *so* not in the mood for this right now. *She knows how to turn everything into a bigger deal than it really is.*

"You can't just go . . . go . . . ," she sputtered.

"Go where, Mom? For a walk around the same streets I've been walking up and down since I was eight years old? I'm seventeen. I'm allowed to go for a run, if I want to." It slipped out before I had a chance to even think about it.

"A run?" she said. "You went for a run this morning?"

I pointed to my wet hairline. "Do you see the sweat? That's generally what happens when you exert yourself."

She was at a loss now, and we both knew it. I put the juice back in the fridge and grabbed my cup to take with me. "I'm going to go take a shower now. See ya." She followed me out of the kitchen.

*God, is she going to watch me shower, too?*

But she only followed me to the bottom of the stairs.

"Next time, leave a note or something!" she said. "And you have a phone call to return. Dr. Pendleton called."

"Fine, Mom," I called down, slamming my door shut for emphasis. I'd call him *after* my shower.


An hour later, when I was clean and dry and dressed again, I sat down to call Dr. Pendleton. His phone rang twice, and my eyes wandered to a row of cobalt bottles lined up on my desk.

I reached for one marked FALLOWEEN and rolled it around in my hand to mix it up.

The receptionist picked up on the fifth ring. "Doctor's office."

"Hi, this is Abigail Browning. I'm returning Dr. Pendleton's call."

"One second, please," she said cheerfully, and then flute music was playing in my ear. I twisted off the top of the bottle in my hand and inhaled deeply. The scent was warm and musty, with hints of dry leaves and crackling bonfires. I was instantly transported to October. Seeing the leaves turning colors in the cemetery, pulling my jacket closer around me, tucking my scarf against my throat . . .

*This* was what fall smelled like.

I pulled back, studying the bottle, and then reached for one of my notebooks. Maybe I should add a drop or two of tart-apple fragrance oil. That would spice it up just a bit.

A deep voice interrupted my thoughts. "This is Dr. Pendleton."

I fumbled with the phone and almost dropped it.

"Hi, Dr. Pendleton. This is Abbey, returning your call."

"Yes, Abbey, how are you doing? How was the bridge ceremony?"

The ceremony. It had only been a couple of weeks ago, but

it felt like months had passed. "I didn't throw up on anyone, so that's good."

He chuckled. "How did you feel afterward? Did it feel like closure?"

"Not really," I admitted. "But I didn't have any breakdown moments, so I guess that's progress, right?"

"Any time we feel like we have transcended a moment, then we are moving beyond our limitations."

*So is that a yes or a no?* He never gave me a straight answer. "Okay, then."

"And what about our other issues?" he asked. "Have you been back to the cemetery? To Kristen's grave?"

"Yeah, I've been back to visit her grave. It was before the ceremony, just to kind of say hello."

He made an *mmm-hmm*ing noise on the other end. "Any hallucinations?"

"No. I've been working with a classmate on some extra-credit school stuff, and taking walks. I even talked with my dad about my business plan for my shop, and I'm going to be working on that. It's been a great summer so far." *Please, please let that be a good enough answer.*

"That sounds like excellent progress." A door opened in the background, and the receptionist said something about his twelve o'clock being there. "I'm glad to hear you're adjusting so well, Abbey. If you need anything else, don't hesitate to call."

"Okay, Dr. Pendleton. I won't."

He murmured a good-bye and hung up.

As soon as I put the phone down, I went over to my supply box and dug through my oils until I found the one labeled MACINTOSH APPLE. Then I pulled out a bottle of Burnt Vanilla and returned to my desk.

Flipping to a fresh notebook page, I jotted down the ingredients from the back of the FALLOWEEN label: one part cinnamon leaf, one part clove, two parts patchouli, and two parts Peru Balsam. Filling a new transfer pipette with some of the apple oil, I carefully squeezed two drops into the bottle. Then I grabbed a second pipette and added one drop of the vanilla. Re-capping it, I gently shook it again.

When I smelled it for the second time, it had a nice hint of apple resting on the edges of smoke and leaves. But it wasn't quite where I wanted it yet, and I knew some aging would be necessary.

I placed the bottle back on my desk and glanced through my notebook. On one of the pages I had scribbled some notes for an idea to make perfumes based on "The Legend of Sleepy

Hollow." Specific scents for Katrina, Ichabod, Brom, and the Horseman. It was actually a pretty good idea. Tourists could come tour the cemetery and town, and then stop by Abbey's Hollow and take home a sampler pack of perfumes based on the legend.

I could design the packaging to look like old-fashioned apothecary bottles with medicinal-type labels, and set up a section of the store to mimic the Sleepy Hollow setting. I'd have vintage schoolbooks, and pumpkins, with scatterings of dried leaves. Maybe I could offer hot cider and pumpkin pie when people came in.

I tried to capture some of my thoughts, and suddenly my fingers were flying across the page. My mind was racing a mile a minute, and my handwriting grew wilder and wilder as I wrote down everything I could think of. *Pumpkin pie? Old books? Apothecary bottles? Nikolas?* But my pen stilled when I wrote Nikolas's name. What would a scent for him be like?

Immediately, chocolate came to mind. Warm and sweet. And almonds. Something that added an edge. Leather was an obvious choice. Remnants of old boots and a horse saddle, worn with age. Maybe taffy, or cotton candy and caramel-covered apples. Sticky Halloween treats that made you sick to your stomach and set your teeth on edge. Danger wrapped in a sugary coating.

But Katy . . . Katy was gingerbread cookies and lemon tea. Lavender sachets, or honeysuckle growing wild on the vine. And fresh peppermint, of course.

I wrote and wrote until my fingers cramped up and my eyes were crossing. I could feel the lack of solid sleep starting to catch up with me. And when I finally put my head down, I found myself dreaming of cemetery dirt and snickerdoodle cookies.


Several hours later I woke up with a pounding headache. It was probably due to the fact that I hadn't eaten anything yet. I went downstairs and found Dad at the kitchen table, holding a newspaper.

"Hey, Dad." I sat down next to him. "Watcha reading?"

"An article on greenhouse gases and produce. Scientists are starting to study the link between them. Some farmers have reported that mutant tomatoes are being grown."

I looked at him and raised an eyebrow. "Mutant tomatoes? How do they know that's because of greenhouse gases? What if it's due to water pollutants, or the fertilizers they use? Or maybe it's the giant, unexplained asteroid that crash-landed near their fields."

"That's just silly," he said. "This is a very particular study that they spent a lot of money on, and it's their duty to report their findings."

"It's their *duty* not to spend so much money on stupid reports," I mumbled. "How do they choose where to do these studies, anyway? If I grow a giant mutant tomato, do you think they'll pay *me* to study it?"

"I'm sure they have their methods for choosing people and towns. They probably look for ones that are produce-y and . . . gassy." He looked at me and cracked a smile. "Okay, I give up."

Yawning, I leaned back in my chair. "You *do* know that you can find updated news online anytime, right? Instead of day-old articles. It's called the *internets*."

He looked aghast. "And not read the newspaper? But it's tradition. Plus, online you don't get that crinkle of paper and smell of ink."

I shook my head and smiled back at him. Clearly, he was where I got my love of scents from.

Dad flipped over the page and scanned the weather report. "Looks like rain this weekend. Bring an umbrella with you to the picnic."

My stomach grumbled loudly, and I got up to find something to eat. "Picnic?" I grabbed the bread bag and plopped it on the counter next to the stove. "What picnic?"

"The Fourth of July picnic your Uncle Bob is having."

*Family get-togethers. I hate family get-togethers.* "Daaaaad, do I *have* to go? Can't I just stay here?" After buttering two slices, I threw on a piece of cheese and put the sandwich on a plate.

He was already shaking his head. "Nope. Your mother wants you there. End of story. Besides, it won't be so bad. A couple of hours with your extended family, and a potluck dinner."

"Every teenager's dream. Watch me as I leap around with joy." I grimaced as I fished out a pan from the drawer and turned a burner on.

Dad stood up and came over to me. Kissing my forehead, he said, "Do it for your dear old dad, huh, Abbey?"

"Yeah, yeah, dear old Dad," I grumbled. "Just remember, *I'm* going to be the one picking your retirement home."

He smiled and turned to leave, then stopped and looked back. "I wouldn't eat tomato soup with that grilled cheese, if I were you. It could have come from mutant tomatoes."

I tossed a pot holder at his head. He just ducked and moved out of the kitchen, laughing the whole way.

After I ate, I changed into a pair of shorts and a cute black T-shirt, and slid on some red flip-flops. Thoughts of perfumes and cookies were still floating around in the back of my brain, so I pulled out the scent I'd accidentally made last year that smelled like snickerdoodles. It reminded me of when I'd made Caspian the cookies and how he'd seemed to like them so much.

I dabbed some of the scent on my fingertips and stroked them over my pulse points; then I ran my fingers through my hair to add some there, too. *Now* I was ready to go.

I left the house quickly, but walked slowly toward the cemetery. It was another hot day, and I didn't want to get all sweaty any sooner than I had to. Several cars were parked inside the cemetery, and people were standing around. *Must be for funeral preparations or something.*

They seemed to be too busy to notice me, though, and I followed the path down to the mausoleum. Casting a glance around to make sure no one would see me go in, I slipped through the door and pulled it shut behind me.

Caspian was sitting on the edge of the black marble slab, hunched over a book, with a candle resting next to him. He looked up when he heard my footsteps. For a moment he just smiled at me, the black stripe of hair hanging in one eye.

"Hi," I said, staring at him.

"Hi."

"You're going to need to get some more candles if you keep burning them like this."

He put his book down to one side. "I don't light them all the time. I just didn't want you to be afraid of the dark."

I sat on the marble slab next to him. There was less than an inch of space between us, but it felt like a mile. "I'm not afraid of the dark."

Caspian wiggled his eyebrows at me. "You should be."

*No, what I should be afraid of is the fact that I'm falling in love with someone who's dead.* "You should get out more," I said instead. "Take a walk downtown. We could go together. Since no one can see you, then it would look like it's just me walking around. I promise not to talk to you in public or anything."

"Okay," he said. "Now, close your eyes."

I did as he asked, and saw shadows playing behind my eyelids. "What are you going to do to me . . . in your crypt . . . in the *dark*?" I teased.

"Stick around until November first and you just might find out," he whispered. His voice was close, and instinctively I turned my head to follow it.

"Wait," he said softly. "Mmmm, just hold still."

I shivered at the tone of his voice. It was raw and edgy and unbelievably sexy. "What?" I asked. "What is it?"

"You smell good. Like cookies. Just . . . let me . . ." His tone turned rueful. "Sorry. This is probably weird for you. But it's like the colors. At certain times it's like my senses are heightened. And I just . . . noticed."

"It's a perfume I made that reminded me of you," I said. "I made it accidentally, but it's a snickerdoodle scent. Like the ones I gave you."

"I still have those," he admitted.

I opened my eyes. "You still have them? Didn't you eat them?"

"No. I mean, I ate the one in front of you, but I saved the rest."

"Why did you do that?" I asked. "Acted like you ate them?"

He ducked his head and looked at the ground. "I didn't want you to be upset if I refused them. And I was still acting . . . normal."

"So you *pretended* to eat my cookies? What did you do, spit it out later?"

"I didn't pretend to eat the cookie," he said. "I really *did* eat it. But just the one. Eating is uncomfortable for me. Everything tastes like ashes."

Something in the back of my brain snapped to full alert when he said those words, but I couldn't pinpoint what it was.

"So, you knew it would taste bad . . . but you ate it anyway?"

He nodded.

"And then you kept the rest of them?"

He looked up, straight into my eyes. "It was a gift from you. The first thing you ever gave me. Why wouldn't I keep it?"

My heart did a little pitter-patter and lurched. I had to bite my lip to keep sudden tears at bay. His gesture was beyond words. "I'm glad you kept them," I said. "And that you ate one in front of me. That was really sweet." I could almost feel his exhale of relieved breath, and I glanced at him with curiosity. "Why did you invite me to go out for pizza, then? What were you going to do if I said yes?"

"Convince you to get it to go?" He shrugged. "Then tell you I wasn't very hungry? I don't know ... I just wanted to do something normal with you."

I understood that feeling. I leaned forward until we were face to face, almost nose to nose. "Next time we *will* do something normal. And you won't have to pretend to eat, okay?"

"Okay. Now, close your eyes again."

I closed them.

"Hand."

I held out my hand and was rewarded with something dropped into it. "I hope you don't mind another one," Caspian said. "It's sort of what I do."

I looked down. Another necklace was resting in my palm. I held it up and saw a perfect four-leaf clover pressed between two small squares of glass. The edges were soldered shut with silver metal, and a black ribbon had been attached to a tiny O-ring.

"I know you already have two," he said in a rush of words, "but I—"

"Caspian," I said, cutting him off. "It's beautiful. Thank you." The clover was *amazing*, each leaf gently rounded and vibrantly green. "But how did you find a four-leaf clover? And where do you get the supplies for the necklaces from?"

He glanced back at the boxes that held his stuff. "I have my soldering iron and supplies from before, when I helped my dad in his garage. The glass pieces are slides I, uh, borrowed from the school science lab. I found the four-leaf clover in the cemetery. I'm kind of good at finding them."

After tying the necklace around my neck, I lifted it up and held on to it. "That's funny. I found a four-leaf clover on Kristen's stone the last time I was there."

"I know," he said. "I put it there. I was kind of watching over her when you were gone and thought she might like it."

I dropped the necklace and stared at him. "You left that there? Because you were watching over her?"

"Yes," he said softly.

Everything was making sense now. All the puzzle pieces were fitting together. The reason why he kept making these gorgeous necklaces for me . . . "Since you can't touch me, you made something that could, didn't you?" I said.

"Yes."

My world slowed and I closed my eyes. "I am going to give you my heart now," I whispered. "Please don't break it again."

*Chapter Fourteen*

# MAKING PROMISES

It is remarkable that the visionary propensity I have mentioned is not confined to the native inhabitants of the valley, but is unconsciously imbibed by every one who resides there for a time.

—"The Legend of Sleepy Hollow"

I woke up on Thursday morning from dreams of white dresses and picket fences—the same dream I'd had about Caspian during school last year—and stretched lazily in bed, grinning at the ceiling. Life was grand.

But a ringing doorbell broke through my happy thoughts and echoed throughout the house. I counted the chimes going off six times before I finally rolled out of bed, calling for Mom to answer it.

There was no response, and as I stumbled down the stairs, I realized that the house must be empty. "I'm coming, I'm coming," I grumbled, hurrying toward the incessant ringing. "Give it a rest."

I threw open the door and was shocked to find Ben standing there.

"Crap," I muttered. "I completely forgot about our class today, Ben."

He looked at me with hesitancy. "Does that mean you want me to leave?"

"No, no. Come drop your stuff off on the table." Suddenly aware of the fact that I was still wearing the ratty T-shirt and gym shorts I'd thrown on last night, I glanced down at my bare feet. "I'm going to get changed. Be back down in ten."

He followed me in and disappeared into the kitchen. I ran upstairs and quickly put on some capris and a tank top, then brushed my teeth. My hair was a wild mess, but I didn't feel like fighting with my curls, so I just spritzed them with some water and threw one last hopeless look over my shoulder.

Tangled hair it was, then.

When I made it back downstairs, Ben had several papers spread out on the table in front of him and was making this weird humming noise in the back of his throat. "Stop that," I ordered, coming to take a seat beside him.

He looked up at me. "Stop what?"

"That humming thing. It's annoying."

"Oh, sorry. I do that sometimes when I'm reading. Ready to get started?"

I rested my chin on my fists. "I guess. What's on the schedule for today?"

"Reports. It'll help with the memorization process. I've brought several books for you to use as reference material. So . . . go."

"'Go?' What is this, a race or something?"

Ben tapped his fingers on the table. "You can either keep stalling, or get cracking."

I groaned. "Can you help me with them? At least one of them?"

He shook his head. "This is where my tutorship ends. Do you have any more Funyuns? I'm going to need a snack to keep myself awake just sitting here."

I got up and dragged myself over to the Ben Cabinet. It was in bad need of replenishment, and I felt a momentary pang of guilt. I moved a couple of bags of chips around, but I didn't see any Funyuns. "Nope. Your choices are Doritos, cheese puffs, or pretzels."

His tone was mournful. "I guess I'll take Doritos."

"Next time I'll have some Funyuns," I promised, grabbing the bag of Doritos. He had no problem digging into them, and I sat back down to get started on my report.

"If your crunching gets too loud, I'm banishing you to the living room," I warned.

"Okay," he said, through a mouthful of chips.

I picked up the nearest science book and cracked it open, groaning internally at the mountain of homework lying in front of me. Why couldn't this be over already?

Ben just gave me a goofy smile and continued crunching.

Two hours later I snapped my book shut and gave in. "This is torture," I said. Ben had a science book in his hands, and it looked like he was reading it. *For fun.*

"Enjoying that?" I asked.

He looked up and wiggled in his seat like a crazed monkey. "There's a fascinating section here on storm-cloud formations."

"Are you kidding me? You actually *are* enjoying that?"

Ben nodded.

"Kristen used to be like that too," I said. "But her subject was math. I always told her that there had to be something wrong with her brain to get so much pleasure out of reading a math book for fun."

"She was going to get her degree in accounting, right? Become a CPA?"

"Yeah," I said. "But how did you know that?"

"We shared a study hall once, and I saw her looking at college brochures. She wanted to go to DeVry or Northern Illinois. I told her to go to Cornell. Great science program there."

I sat back and studied him. "I didn't know that. Kristen never told me."

"It was because of her brother. She said he was a whiz at numbers and wanted to study at Brown."

I frowned at him. *He knows an awful lot about Kristen.* "Yeah. She—"

The phone rang and I reached for it, glad for the distraction. "Hello?"

"Abbey, I need you to check on something for me."

I turned my back to Ben, but I could still feel the frown on my face. "Yeah, Mom. What is it?" Glancing out the window into the yard, I almost fell off my seat.

Caspian was standing next to the house.

Mom was prattling on about something, so I covered the receiver and turned back to Ben. "I'll be . . . right back." Without waiting for his response, I flew out the back door and gestured for Caspian to follow me into the covering of trees we'd met under before.

"What are you doing here?" I hissed at him, the phone cradled next to my shoulder so that I could still sort of hear Mom but she couldn't hear me.

Caspian looked at the house and then stepped closer to me. "I thought I'd come see you for a change. Did he do something to you?"

"What? *No*. Why?"

"You were frowning."

Mom's voice grew silent, and some part of me was vaguely aware that she was waiting for an answer from me. "Um, Mom," I said. "Can you repeat that again?"

She said something about eggs and salad and waiting for me to go check, and I put the phone back against my shoulder.

"Ben's fine," I said to Caspian. "He just mentioned something about Kristen that surprised me, that's all."

Caspian's face turned thunderous, and he took a step toward the house.

"No, no," I told him. "Really, it's okay." *Ahhh, protective boyfriends*. The tiny part of me that wasn't furiously trying to multitask was very much enjoying this.

"—and I can just check then." Mom's voice caught my attention again.

I held up one finger to Caspian and turned back to the phone. "What was that, Mom? Sorry, Ben and I are studying, and it's hard to concentrate on two things at once." *Make that three things.*

"I said never mind about the egg salad," Mom repeated. "I'm on my way home right now. Oh, and don't forget to pack an overnight bag. We're leaving tomorrow to spend an extra day at Aunt Cindy's before the picnic. Bye."

She hung up, and I stared down at the phone. Overnight bag? Extra day? When had that little detail been agreed upon?

But I knew by Mom's tone that her mind was made up. If Dad wouldn't let me skip the family picnic, there was no *way* he would let me bail on an overnight trip. I was doomed.

Sighing heavily, I put one hand to my head and rubbed my temple.

"Are you okay?" Caspian asked.

"Headache. Thanks to my mother."

He looked sympathetic. "Why don't you come take a walk with me? We can go downtown. What do you say?"

What did I say? I wasn't going to get the chance to see him

again until after we got back from the picnic. Of *course* I wanted to spend the afternoon with him.

I hit the redial button, and it went to voice mail. "Hey, Mom, Ben and I are going to finish studying at his house. I'll see you in a couple hours, and I'll leave enough time to get my bag packed."

"Okay," I said, turning to Caspian. "I'm in. Let me just go talk to Ben and get him to cover. You can . . . follow me, I guess."

I held the back door open for a couple of extra seconds when I walked into the house, and Caspian came in. *I'm totally not letting my invisible boyfriend in. The hinge was just stuck. Or something.*

Facing Ben, I tried to pretend that Caspian wasn't right behind me. "Ben, I need you to do me a favor."

Ben was still scarfing down chips, and he paused with the bag in midair. "What?"

*"Nice,"* Caspian murmured.

I forced myself not to let any reaction show on my face. "I need to get out for a while. I have something to take care of. But my mom's coming home, and I told her I'd be going to your house to finish studying. So can you cover for me?"

He looked down at the half-started report. "But we have to work on this."

"Please, Ben? You'll be on my top-friends list forever. I *really* need this favor."

Caspian snorted, but Ben stood up and started gathering his books. "Okay, fine. But you owe me." He came around the table and was dangerously close to going through Caspian, but I moved to help him pick up his stuff and stopped him from getting any closer.

I led the way around the opposite side of the kitchen and held the door open for him. Ben walked through it, and then stopped outside. "Abbey, I . . ." He gave me a funny look. With his free hand, he brushed a piece of my hair away from my face.

I pulled back and cast a quick glance over my shoulder. Caspian's face was furious.

"Don't even *think* about it," he warned Ben.

But Ben had no idea what was going on. "I have to talk to you about something soon, okay?" His gaze dropped to my mouth, and instantly, vivid memories from the diner dream slammed into me.

Good Lord, this was really not going well.

"Okay," I said. "Thanks for helping me out with this, Ben." He turned and stumbled before regaining his balance, then moved toward his car. I slammed the back door shut and gave Caspian a look.

He put both hands up in the air. "What? I didn't do anything."

"No, but you *wanted* to. And besides, we don't really know yet what you *can* do."

"Well, I know I can't make people disappear," he muttered darkly. "Or else he would have been gone a half an hour ago."

I was a bit shocked at how serious he sounded, and then I looked into his eyes. "You're jealous!"

"He wanted to *kiss* you!"

Now I was dumbfounded. "How do you know that?"

"Because," he said, running a hand through his hair and pushing it back. "It's what I'd want to do."

"You'd want to kiss me?" I teased. "I never could've guessed." He shook his head and I laughed. "Come on, green eyes. Let's get out of here before my mom gets home. Take me downtown; I'm all yours."

"Promise?" he said, holding my gaze steady.

"Promise," I whispered.

We walked side by side downtown, moving quickly from store to store. At first it was strange for me to see him walking among people while no one else noticed he was there. I kept wondering what would happen if someone suddenly moved right through him. I didn't think I was ready to see *that* yet. But Caspian moved aside when anyone got too close, and eventually it almost felt normal.

*Normal.*

I was walking downtown with someone only *I* could see. There really was something wrong with me.

We passed an antique store and the pizza place, but another building was coming up, and I felt a happy smile creep over my face. It wasn't rented yet. My shop was still available.

"Follow me," I whispered to Caspian, moving across the street and toward the shop. He was right behind me, and we ducked down the alley.

"There's a trick to it, if you want to go inside," Caspian said, sizing up the door frame in front of us. He leaned down to mess with something at the bottom of the door.

"I don't think it's going to work. I was here before, and the owner was too, and he—" A scraping sound and then a clicking noise interrupted me. Caspian smiled as the door swung open. "How did you . . . ?"

"There's a piece of cracked wood at the bottom. When the door is closed, it's wedged into place, and the lock stays. But loosen the wood, and the door sags a little, slipping out of the lock." He held the door open and ushered me in. I stepped into my shop and closed my eyes, imagining it all set up the way I would have it.

When I opened my eyes again, Caspian was leaning against one of the walls, looking at me. I suddenly grew shy. "Why are you looking at me like that?"

"I like seeing you happy, Abbey." He placed a hand on the middle of his chest. "It makes me feel . . ."

"Feel what?"

"Just feel. I don't know what, but I like it." The look in his eyes changed, and he leaned away from the wall, coming to stand next to me. "Tell me about your plans for your shop. Come on, start over here."

Caspian led me to a wide wall space, and I studied it for a moment. "Here I'll put the reading section. I'll bring in a fireplace mantel, arrange some chairs around it, maybe even an ottoman, and put out some of Irving's books. People can read or just lounge while I create their perfumes."

He spun and pointed to the open floor space behind us. "What about there?"

"An armoire that holds perfumes based on Ichabod Crane, Katrina Van Tassel, Brom Bones, and the Headless Horseman. With a scattering of fall leaves on the floor, and white baby pumpkins to decorate it. Nearby, I'll have a tray that holds apple cider and warm pumpkin pie. Or caramel apples and roasted pumpkin seeds!"

My mind was filling with pictures, and I could see it all. I pointed to our left. "I'd put an old-fashioned register there, with a big metal scale that holds Halloween candy. And, next to the register, three giant glass jars filled with bath salts, soap samples, and black licorice sticks."

I frowned then. "Hmm . . . I can't have the candy so close to the bath stuff. It will pick up the scent." I paced closer to the door. "Here," I said. "I'll have jars of candy set up here by the door on a row of wooden egg crates."

"And what about the windows?" Caspian asked. "What will your grand display there be?"

"A cast-iron claw-foot bathtub filled with soaps," I said, without hesitation. "All wrapped in bits of parchment paper and old string. Shades of robin's-egg blue, soft dusky rose, coffee bean-brown, and aged yellow books."

I turned to him and wanted to throw my arms around him. "Can you see it? Can you see all of it? I want this so badly, Caspian. Without Kristen I thought . . . I didn't think I would want this anymore. I thought my dream would be empty and hollow. But now . . . it's like, I don't know, it all feels like I can *do* this suddenly. Like I can share it with someone new."

"Did you feel like this when you were working at the tattoo place? Or when you were talking to your dad about his shop?"

Caspian slid down to the floor and patted the ground next to him. I took a seat and waited for his answer. "Yes, I did," he said. "I felt that way too."

"Do you think you could . . . ?" I looked down at my hands and tugged at a loose string on the bottom of my shirt. "Ever feel that way again? Maybe . . . about *my* shop?"

He looked away, and I heard him sigh. The floor we sat on was warm, and tiny, almost invisible dust motes swirled around us in the rows of sunlight that slanted through the window. *What's he thinking?*

Time crawled by, and still he didn't speak.

"I'm kind of putting myself out here," I said eventually, "asking . . . well, I don't know what I'm asking. . . ."

Caspian started tracing an outline on the floorboard next to him, a triangular pattern that he made over and over again. Finally, he turned to face me. "I'm not so great with the mixed-signals thing, am I?"

I shook my head no.

"I'm really sorry, Astrid," he said. "Really, I am. I know I'm the one asking for more, but I just don't know how to deal with any of this." His face was serious. "I need you to know that I want to be with you every second of every day, Abbey. I *want* that. I *crave* it."

He made a fist and slowly unclenched his fingers one by one. "But I don't know what's right. Before, when I was pretending to be normal, I thought it would be okay. You were so real, and here, and I wanted it so much . . . and then I broke you. I thought the reason why you went away was to punish me."

His eyes turned glassy and far away. "I spent those months in the dark. In my tomb. I hid away and went to sleep. I don't think I dreamed, but I *felt*. Vast and endless and alone. Always alone."

I nudged my knee closer to his, and passed through him. A dull hum of sensation rippled through me, and I knew he could feel it too. His eyes focused, and he came back to me.

"I just don't want to hold you back from anything," he said. "I don't want you to forget, and speak to me in front of someone, make people think you're crazy. *I* don't want to forget, and freak someone out by helping you move boxes or something." He laughed a dark, harsh laugh. "Although maybe that would be good for business, a haunted store and all that."

"We won't forget," I insisted. "And you don't have to do anything you don't want to. We don't even have to make any decisions right now. There's plenty of time."

He just looked at me, with heartache and hopelessness in his eyes, and a sense of determination filled me. "Let's go talk sometime to Nikolas and Katy," I suggested. "They've dealt with this. I went to visit them, and it was good. They know a lot."

His face turned skeptical, but he agreed. "If you come with me, I'll go. I won't promise to believe them, but I'll listen to what they have to say."

I could feel my face light up with a grin, and I made a vow. "We'll make it work, Caspian. I promise. Somehow, we'll make it work."

If you are interested in joining a reading group, please fill in your details below.

Name and student number

_____

Email address

_____

Favourite genre (romance, historical, thriller etc.)

_____

Preferred day and time (Mon, Tues etc.)

_____

*Chapter Fifteen*

# THE BIG DIPPER

Stars shoot and meteors glare oftener across the valley than in any other part of the country . . .

—"The Legend of Sleepy Hollow"

"Time to get up," Mom said, knocking on the wall above the sofa I'd fallen asleep on at Aunt Cindy's house.

"Later," I mumbled. "Why so early? Picnics are in the afternoon."

"Your father's grandmother Lurlene is going to be at the picnic," she said. "And we want to leave early so we can spend some quality time with her."

I groaned and stuffed my face into the cushions. An hour later Mom yelled at me again, and I rolled off the couch. "I'm up, I'm up!" I yelled back. After fumbling my way into clean clothes, I hurried to the car and went back to sleep.

When I opened my eyes again, we were pulling up to Uncle Bob's house. Three cars were already parked in the too-small driveway, and I realized that this was going to be more of a family reunion than I wanted.

We came to a stop, and I got out, stretching each leg as I stood. Mom carried two Tupperware containers of egg salad to the house, muttering the whole way about how Uncle Bob's fridge wasn't going to be big enough. I grabbed my iPod from the car, then walked around the house to the backyard.

A big white tent was set up with several picnic tables underneath it, and there was only one other person sitting out there, an old lady.

*Must be Lurlene.*

I lifted up a netted tent flap, ducked under it, and chose a table next to her. I didn't want to sit close enough so that she could talk my ear off, but I didn't want her to think I was rude, either. Being a teenager is a tricky balance.

I sat down and gave her a friendly smile before angling my body in the opposite direction. She had a four-legged cane resting next to her, and immediately I felt bad. So I put only one earbud in and turned my iPod on low. I thought the banging that I started feeling was part of the bass, until I realized she was trying to get my attention.

Pulling the wire from my ear, I turned to her. "Yes?"

She had a mean look on her face, probably due to the fact that it was July and she was wearing a long-sleeved maroon sweater over a pinkish frilly blouse. That *had* to be suffocating. "I was trying to get your attention, girl. But I didn't want to yell. Not polite, mind you."

I smiled my best *You're old; I understand and will be nice to you anyway* smile. "Well, you have my attention now. What can I do for you?"

She raised her cane and then thumped it on the ground. "For starters, you can come sit next to me so I don't have to keep yelling. It isn't polite."

*Yeah, well, it isn't polite that I have to put up with you, either.* I got up and moved closer. I thought about sneaking my earbud back into my ear so I could just ignore her, but then she poked me in the right foot with her cane.

"Hey!" I said. "Watch—"

"Eh? What's that?" She grinned a toothy, denture-filled smile, and I could have sworn the smell of Polident wafted out at me. "Speak up. I'm an old lady; I can't hear as well as I used to."

I rubbed my right foot against the back of my left shin. "Watch out for mosquitoes. I think I just felt a big one bite me on the foot."

Her eyes filled with an unholy delight, and I waited for the evil cackle that I was sure would be coming out of her any minute now. I needed an exit strategy. *Fast.*

"My mom probably needs some help with the—"

"Your mother is here? Which one is she?"

"Julie Browning."

"Aha!" she crowed. "What's your name then?"

Apparently, I didn't answer fast enough, because she poked me with her cane again.

"Abigail," I said through gritted teeth. "But everyone calls me Abbey."

"I shall call you Abigail. I despise nicknames. Tell me, do you have a middle name? Everyone civilized has a middle name."

I didn't want to tell her, but I wasn't sure how many more thumps my poor toe could take. "Amelia," I replied.

"You're not still contagious are you?" She leaned away from me a little and put the cane in between us as a buffer. Like that would do any good.

"Contagious?"

"I heard you had that disease, the momo."

*Does she mean mono? Mom's still telling that one, huh?* I coughed. "I don't know. The doctors say they can't be sure, but the weak"—I forced myself not to smile—"and the elderly are highly susceptible. I should probably go," I said. "I wouldn't want to be responsible for you getting sick from being around me."

"Bah," she said. "I'm an old lady who has lived her life. If the good Lord says it's my time to go because of the momo, who am I to argue? Stay and keep me company."

She clamped a bony yet surprisingly strong hand on my arm, and it took everything I had not to shake it off. "So tell me, girl, Abigail Amelia, what grade are you in school? Seventh? Eighth?" she said.

"I'm going to be a senior."

"Aha! A senior, eh? What college are you going to?"

A slight panic welled up in me, but I tamped it down. I could totally handle this. "It's still early yet, and I'm gathering information."

"Couldn't get in to any of them, eh?" she cackled.

"No!" My temper flared. "I haven't applied to any yet."

"You better get on that, girl. Time's a-wasting. I'm sure lots of hardworking kids are already making their plans."

"Yeah, but it doesn't matter. With my plans for my shop, I don't really need to go to college."

Her hand tightened on my arm at the same time the thump came.

*"What?"* she squawked. "You're not going to college? What kind of plans are those? Everyone in this family has gone to

college, and by George so will you." She exhaled heavily. "I don't even know what kind of nonsense this is."

My arm and foot were stinging now, and I was mentally cursing out Mom with everything I had. "I never said I wasn't *going* to college. I'm going to take some business courses, and my mind isn't definitely made up . . . definitely . . . yet . . . ," I finished weakly.

She made an angry sound and opened her mouth, but a swarm of people started to descend upon us from the house. Mom was leading the pack of distant cousins or something, and they were all talking excitedly.

Mom smiled at us. "I see you've met Abbey, Lurlene; I'm so glad," she said loudly.

I grimaced at Mom and silently promised her payback with my eyes.

"That's right," Lurlene said. "I know about the momo, but I decided to risk it."

Worry flashed across Mom's face, then disappeared just as quickly. "Yes, it's such a . . . terrible . . . disease. We're just glad that Abbey's doing so much better now." Her eyes pleaded with me to play along, and I was forced to stay where I was.

Not the least because I still had a velociraptor claw attached to my arm.

The cousins came and crowded around us, making me feel even more boxed in. "We were just discussing Abigail Amelia's future plans," Lurlene told them. "Seems she's not going to college."

Mom's face pinched. "Oh, well," she said. "Nothing final has been decided. It's still early yet . . . and you know kids!" She gave a fake laugh. "Always changing their minds from one minute to the next."

*Gee, thanks, Mom.*

She turned to me. "Abbey, why don't you go find your uncle. There's something that he needs to talk to you about."

She didn't need to tell me twice. I pried Lurlene's hand off my arm and moved my legs away from striking distance of her cane. Mom drew her into a discussion about a recipe for egg salad as I stood up and walked quickly to the house.

Uncle Bob was in the kitchen, standing by the fridge. "Hey, Uncle Bob," I said. "Mom told me you wanted to talk?"

"Yeah, I wanted to ask you something, Abbey."

"What's up?" I took a seat at the small table next to the fridge. "How's the ice cream biz? I never got the chance to tell you that I'm sorry I had to bail on you."

Uncle Bob cleared his throat. "It's busy. Which is a good thing. Actually, that's what I wanted to talk to you about. I wouldn't normally ask this of you. Your mom said you have summer-school classes and all that, but I'm shorthanded at the shop. One of my regulars just quit, and the other one broke her wrist, so she can't work. But I'm going to be hiring some new people soon."

"You need someone to help out now, though, right?" I guessed.

"Only until the first week of August. Then my other regular, Steph, will be back. She's taking the month off to go backpacking through Europe."

*Oh, man.* "Uncle Bob, I don't know. I have school stuff on Tuesdays and Thursdays, and I'm working on my business plan for Dad...."

His face fell. "I understand. I know it's last minute and all. I never should have mentioned it. No big deal."

Now I felt terrible. I'd already ditched him once when I'd left Sleepy Hollow to go stay with Aunt Marjorie, and now it was like I was ditching him all over again.

"When would you need me?"

Uncle Bob looked hopeful. "Mondays?" he said. "And maybe Wednesdays and Fridays?"

Working three days a week for Uncle Bob and having science sessions with Ben on the other two days was going to *seriously* cut into my time with Caspian.

"I'll pay you the same amount as before," he said quickly, "when you were helping me in the back office. Ten dollars an hour. But don't tell the other employees. Counter staff are supposed to start at eight."

Ugh. This wasn't going to be easy work like filing papers; now I'd be stuck scooping all day? But this *was* Uncle Bob, and he looked desperate. "I'll start Monday," I said. "But only until August. After that you're on your own."

He grinned and came over to give me a bear hug. "Thanks, Abbey. It really means a lot to your old uncle."

"Yeah, yeah," I grumbled. "You just remember this when I come around asking for a loan to buy a car."

He winked, and I followed him out of the house, back toward the tent.

"Don't let Lurlene get her claws into you," I whispered. "She's got a wicked grip. And a cane."

"I know," he said. "I've already felt it."

We approached the tables, and I hid behind Uncle Bob, trying to use his girth as a shield. But it didn't work.

"Abigail Amelia!" Lurlene crowed as soon as she spotted me. "Come sit over here by me and your father, girl. I want you to be the one to get my food."

I thought about refusing. Or using the momo excuse. But

Mom was giving me the look, and I knew I was doomed.

Dragging feet that felt like they were encased in cement shoes, I made my way over to Lurlene and sat down next to her. Her vulture claw descended rapidly, and she squeezed with delight, sending me a toothy grin.

I just sat there, counting down the seconds until this stupid picnic would be over, and wishing to God that I had a pair of steel-toed boots and arm guards on.

Later that night we finally pulled into our own driveway, and I breathed a happy sigh of relief. "Did I tell you that she pinched my arm?" I asked Mom on the way inside the house.

"Yes, Abbey. Three times."

"I'll probably have bruises tomorrow. And my toe will be black and blue." Mom unlocked the door, and Dad was right behind us. "That's child abuse, you know. I could tell social services."

They both headed to the stairs and started up.

"Good night, Abbey. See you in the morning," Dad said. They were clearly not hearing me.

"If I'm still here," I called after them. "I might be with the agency. That's all I'm saying."

A slamming door was the only response I got, and I wandered over to the couch. I turned the TV on and flipped through it, finally landing on a *Friends* rerun. I wasn't the least bit tired yet....

When I woke up, it was almost three a.m., and I had to drag myself upstairs to my bedroom. I kept yawning the whole way, and I pitched headfirst onto my bed, not even bothering to take off my shoes or crawl under the covers. All I wanted to do was go back to sleep.

Of course, then my shoulder started cramping, twisted at an odd angle, and my pillow was lumpy. I rearranged myself and punched my pillow into a new shape.

Then I started to get too hot, and it felt like I was suffocating. Rolling myself over, I kicked off my sandals and threw my arms over my head. The rush of open air was cool across my face, and I breathed in deeply.

But my clothes were too confining. I sat up and started to take my shirt off, when something greenish caught the corner of my eye. *That's weird.* Tilting my head back, I looked up ... and gasped when I saw the maze of stars that covered my bedroom ceiling.

Stars, moons, planets ... It was my own personal solar system located directly above my bed.

I pulled my shirt back down and got up to turn on a light.

As soon as the lamp flickered on, the constellations disappeared, and little waxy pieces of plastic were left in their place.

Standing on the bed, I reached up to touch one. It was stuck fast. I turned the light off and watched as the room glowed again. Clapping my hands together in delight, I stood in the middle of the bed and just stared and stared and stared at them.

Stars stretched from one end of the room to the other. I'd never seen so many all in one place. My father had bought me a pack of glow-in-the-dark stars once at an air-and-space museum, but there had only been five or six of them in there. This had to be dozens upon dozens of stars.

I couldn't believe it. *Did Caspian do this? Who else would have?*

Happiness flooded through me. I wanted to dance around the room. This was wonderful. And romantic. And perfect.

A sharp, crackling noise at the window had me spinning around. Then it came again, and it sounded like the glass was going to break. I moved closer to it, wary that I might come face to face with some crazed flying nocturnal animal.

I peeked out the window but didn't see anything, so I cracked it open and looked out.

A small pebble suddenly came flying up out of nowhere and

flew right past my head, landing with a soft thump on the floor next to me.

"Hey!" I said, leaning out even further, to get a clearer glimpse all the way down. Caspian was standing there, next to the house, with his hand lifted, ready to throw another rock.

"Abbey!" he said. "Sorry, I was trying to get your attention." He looked sheepish. "I didn't hit you, did I?"

I shook my head no. "Why don't you come up?"

He quickly dumped his handful of rocks on the ground, then climbed up the lattice. I stepped back from the window once he reached the low roof, and he hauled himself into the room.

With him here, standing in my room, I suddenly felt vulnerable. *Come on, Abbey,* I told myself. *It's not like he's never been here before.*

"Astrid," Caspian said, smiling slowly at me.

I smiled back. "Have you come to look at the stars with me?"

He nodded, and I walked toward him, immensely grateful that I'd kept my clothes on. That would have been . . . awkward. *Fun,* my mind whispered. *But awkward.*

My cheeks burned, and I hoped it was dark enough that he couldn't see me blushing or read my expression. I spread one hand out and waved it around me. "This? You? *How?*"

He grinned a wide, happy grin then. "Happy belated birthday. I thought you'd like it."

"Are you kidding me? Who *wouldn't* like it? But how did you get in? And how did you put them up? And where did you get them all?"

"Your window doesn't close all the way," he said. "I noticed it while you were gone. I just climbed up and opened it a little. Luckily, your mom keeps a step stool in the kitchen. I don't think I could have gotten them up without it."

"So you climbed into my room while I was gone, used one of our step stools, and stuck plastic stars to my ceiling?"

He ducked his head. "Yeah. Are you mad?"

"Mad? No. This is the coolest thing *ever*. I'm just surprised you didn't, I don't know, wait for me or something."

Caspian looked horrified now. "Wait in your room *without* you? It's one thing to stop by for a surprise project, but I'd never stay here without permission."

I shook my head at him and smiled. "You are a strange boy, Caspian Vander. But you have my permission to come in here whenever you want."

He looked uncomfortable. "I think I'll wait for you." Then he looked mischievous. "Unless I have another surprise planned, of course."

"Surprise me anytime." I turned to the bed and sat on the edge, patting the space next to me. "Let's look at the stars."

Without waiting for him, I lay down with my feet toward the headboard and my head near the bottom of the bed.

Moments later he joined me, lying carefully next to me.

I flattened my hands out and felt the cool cotton beneath my palms. Neither of us spoke, and I concentrated on keeping my breathing normal. The stars glowed a steady green above us.

But I didn't want him to think that I was ignoring him, so I said again, "Where did you get them all? There are soooo many."

His voice was low. "I found like fifty packages in a huge bag at the Salvation Army. Some fast-food place must have been giving them away in kids' meals or something. I felt kind of bad about taking them, but I figured they were donated for someone to use, right? And I had a use for them."

My eyes traced a path from one star to the next, and I started to see shapes and patterns. "I can't believe you did this for me, Caspian. Now every night when I'm in bed I'll think of you."

"That's what I was hoping for," he said. "For you to dream of me."

"Look," I said, directing the conversation away from *that* topic. "A shooting star."

"I see," said Caspian. "Right next to the Big Dipper over there."

"Where?"

He pointed to a clump of stars. "There. You just have to do some creative rearranging with your eyes."

"Ohhh, is that what it's called?"

"Yeah. It's right next to that line of stars. What are those three in a row called?"

"Orion's Belt?"

"That's it." He tilted his head. "Although, it looks more like Orion's toga to me. See how they kind of trail up and out?"

Laughing, I said. "Orion's *toga*? I've never heard of that one. What about Orion's cape?" He grinned at me, and even in the darkness I could still see the vibrant green of his eyes.

"Yup, that's right there along with the slightly less famous— but still featured on *Jeopardy!*—Orion's bathrobe."

We shared a smile, and then I shifted so I could prop my head up on my hand. "Tell me a story," I whispered. "A secret. Something you've never told anyone else."

His face turned blank, unreadable. Then he turned to me. "When I was little, I thought I could fly. My aunt took me to this rehearsal for a play she was helping out with—I think they were doing *Arabian Nights*—and I climbed up on this big floating carpet that was there as a prop.

"I remember it distinctly. I sat on this carpet and folded my arms genie style, while repeating 'ALASHAZAM,' and then the carpet started moving. It probably should have freaked me out or something, but it didn't. And I just . . . floated . . . back and forth."

His story made my heart give a little sigh. It wasn't a sad story by any means, but there was something about the way he told it. Something about getting a glimpse of the boy he used to be that made me want to go back in time and see it for myself.

"Now that I'm older, I realize that the carpet was on a moving platform, or wheels or something," he said. "But back then? It was the greatest feeling in the world. I was flying."

His smile grew wistful, and he closed his eyes for a moment. When he opened them again, he said, "Now it's your turn. Tell me a secret."

I didn't really *have* any secrets. Sure, there was silly stuff, like stuffing my bra with socks when I was twelve, or having a crush on my teacher in fifth grade. But that all felt too small and trivial for this moment.

Then I thought about Kristen.

*She'd* certainly kept secrets. A boyfriend she purposely didn't tell me about. Conversations with him behind my back.

All those times she was hanging out with me, when she really wanted to be with *him*.

I didn't have any of *those* kinds of secrets. But there was one thing. . . .

I began slowly. "When I was nine or ten, I was waiting for Kristen in her yard. She was at the dentist, so she wasn't home yet, but there were these kids playing in the next yard over. A bunch of neighborhood kids."

My stomach started churning. I hadn't thought about this memory in a long time.

"They were playing in the mud with those large dump-truck toys, you know, the heavy metal yellow ones, with big wheels?" He nodded. "I sort of moved closer. Curious about what they were doing, but I didn't really want to be noticed. Then I saw that they weren't just playing with dump trucks. There was this huge toad being held down, and they just kept squishing it with the tires, over and over again."

I could hear my voice growing fainter, but I was lost in that awful memory of bulging toad guts and muddy ground.

"It was *horrible*. I was horrified by what they were doing, and even more horrified that I wasn't saying anything. But I was scared. I felt powerless and mute. And it was just a stupid frog. I wasn't hurting it, so what did it matter? Or at least that's what I kept telling myself." I let out a shaky breath. "I never told that to anyone else. Not even Kristen. I didn't want her to be ashamed of me."

Caspian nodded slowly.

"Nice, huh?" I said. "I could have saved that frog and I didn't. I'm a frog killer. Bet you always wanted to know that."

I tried to read his face. Was he thinking I was an awful person? Did he hate me for what I'd just told him?

"You're not going to get it," he said, shaking his head.

"I'm not going to get what?"

"Condemnation. You're not going to get that from me. I know you want me to tell you how bad and awful of a thing that was. But you were just a little kid. Forgive yourself for it, and let it go."

I flopped back down on the bed, stretching my legs and flexing my toes. Anger at myself ran through my veins like hot fire. I didn't know if I *could* just let it go.

"Don't pout," Caspian said.

"I'm not pouting," I replied. "I don't pout."

"That looks like a pout to me," he said. He shifted so that he was facing me now, propping himself up on one hand. His grin was contagious, and I grinned back, feeling silly and romantic and wonderful.

"Black," Caspian said abruptly.

I raised my eyebrow at him. "Black?"

"It's my favorite color. You never asked, so I'm telling you."

"But that's not really a color. It's all the colors put together."

He pointed to his shirt, which was black. "It's a color. Oh, and I don't have one."

"Don't have . . . a pet skunk?" I guessed.

Caspian laughed. "A middle name. I don't have a middle name."

"Mine's Amelia," I said. "But I prefer Astrid." I sat up slightly. "Hey, you need a nickname."

He shook his head. "I don't think I'm a nickname kind of guy."

"No, really, you are. Let me think about it. Caspian . . . Casp . . . Casper . . . There you go, Casper! Has a nice ring to it. Plus, you're friendly *and* you're a ghost."

"A cartoon character?" He gave a mock sigh. "Seriously?"

I lay back down and folded my arms under my head, trying to keep my face straight. "Get used to it, Casper. At least I didn't suggest Shaggy or Scooby-Doo. Although . . ."

"Don't get any ideas," he mumbled.

I closed my eyes then, and let the laughter that was building up take over me.

~ ~ ~

When I awoke, the sky outside was gray and ominous. The sure signs of a summer storm about to hit. The clock said nine thirty, and I couldn't figure out why I was sleeping at the foot of my bed. Then I remembered the stars.

Glancing around the room, I looked for Caspian. He wasn't there, but a folded note next to my pillow had *Astrid* written on the outside. I reached for it, stomach clenched.

It was short and sweet.

Hope you had pleasant dreams, beautiful. I stayed until you fell asleep, and then let myself out. I'll be thinking of you . . .

Love, Caspian

I read it a dozen times and then tucked it safely under my pillow so I could read it again later. Hopping out of bed with a smile on my face, I didn't even mind the crack of thunder that followed me as I got in the shower. The hot water was delicious, and I found myself humming a song as I lathered up my hair.

After I got dressed, I decided to grab sturdier shoes than my flip-flops, and I went to the closet. Lifting the pile of extra pillows and blankets that were stashed in there, I dug around for a pair of sneakers. My hand hit something solid, and I pulled back, seeing two small books, one red and one black.

My knees gave out in a slow fall. My good mood vanished.

Kristen's diaries. The ones I'd found in her room. I touched the edge of one, and a jolt of memory ran through me.

*Kristen and me shopping for new shoes at the mall. Hanging out under the bridge after the first day of school. Leaving letters for Washington Irving at his grave on Halloween night. Roaming through the cemetery and making up stories . . .*

I needed to see her again. I needed to go see Kristen.

# Chapter Sixteen

# INTRODUCTIONS

There was something in the moody and dogged silence of this pertinacious companion that was mysterious and appalling.

—"The Legend of Sleepy Hollow"

It looked like rain the entire way to the cemetery, but that didn't bother me. I'd grabbed my yellow raincoat in case the storm hit while I was out.

When I reached Kristen's stone, I saw that a pot of red tulips had been left there. I knelt down to read the card sticking out of a long, pronged plastic stake. *Love, Mom and Dad*, it said.

I smiled to myself. That was typical of Kristen's parents. Bringing something to make the place look pretty. *I should really go visit them sometime soon. See how they're doing.*

There were loose grass clippings stuck to the face of her tombstone—evidence of careless lawn-maintenance people—

and I brushed them away, taking a minute to trace the carved letters of her name with my pinkie.

"Hey, Kristen," I whispered.

I tucked my legs up under me and rested one palm on the top of the granite marker. "I found your diaries again today. They were in the back of my closet, and I saw them when I was looking for my shoes." I took a deep breath. "I really miss you. I miss hanging out with you. I miss calling you. I miss seeing how your face lights up when I have something funny to say. . . ."

Thunder rumbled, and a breeze blew past me, causing the nearby tree limbs to shiver. I shivered too.

"You know, when I first found your diaries and read about the secret boyfriend you were always trying to find ways to be with, a part of me was really mad at you, Kristen. I couldn't understand why you kept him a secret from me. Why you didn't tell me about someone who made you so happy." I ran my thumb back and forth over the center of my clover neck-lace. "I would have been there for you. I would have been happy for you. . . .

"But you didn't let me in. And when I found out, I hated you for that." I bowed my head, and the tears came, slipping down my nose and falling to the ground below. "I'm sorry, Kristen. I'm *so sorry* I felt that way. I shouldn't have. You were my best friend. How could I ever hate you?"

A heavy raindrop landed on the back of my head, and before I had the chance to put on my coat, the sky opened up. Sheets of rain cascaded down around me, and within seconds my hair and clothes were soaked. But I wasn't done talking yet.

"Whoever D. is, I'm sorry that he hurt you," I told her, over the sound of the storm. "It must have been heartbreaking, to have to hold it all inside. And I'm sorry I couldn't be there to talk about . . . after . . . your first time." Rain pounded down on me, echoing off of the plastic jacket I struggled to put on, and splattering on the hard ground. "Oh, Kristen, your words were so full of regret, and that's not how love is supposed to be."

A smile crept across my face. "Love is supposed to be wonderful, and thrilling, and exciting, and nerve-wracking. It's amazing, Kristen. I have someone now too, and I can talk to him like I can't talk to anyone else. Not anyone since . . . you.

"He's the boy I told you about on prom night, when I wrote you that letter. He's gorgeous and funny, and smart. He's an artist, too. He makes me these necklaces that are just unbelievable. And last night? He climbed into my room and put glow-in-the-dark stars on my ceiling. Can you believe that?"

Then I frowned as I realized I'd left something out. An

important something. "This next part is going to sound crazy. Believe me, I know. But it's the truth. He's . . ." My voice faltered, and I cleared my throat. "He's . . . dead. I'm in love with a ghost."

I waited for lightning to strike, or the ground to split open. But nothing happened. No sign from the heavens, or rupture of reality as I knew it.

Nothing happened at all.

I shook my head back and forth. "I don't understand it. I just know that I love him. However wrong . . . or right . . . that may be. He makes me happy." I let out a quiet laugh. "Crazy, right? I know. God, I wish you were here to talk to." Something pinched in the pit of my stomach. "I wish I could share this with you, Kristen. Because that's the difference between you and me. I would have told you about him instead of keeping it a secret."

Sorrow overwhelmed me, and my tears came faster. Gasping for breath, I turned my face to the sky. The rain was cool and clean, and I just wanted it to wash away my pain. To make everything better. I thought I'd been able to put this all behind me, but apparently not. The wound was still fresh. It still burned.

Monday morning Mom woke me up with a reminder that I had to go help Uncle Bob. I'd completely forgotten about my promise and was *not* very happy to remember. But I climbed out of bed and quickly threw some clothes on. At least I'd get a paycheck out of the deal.

Mom dropped me off at the front door of the ice cream store and said she'd be back at five, then sped away. I forced myself to enter the shop, already regretting this decision. Working in a back office once a week was one thing—that kind of felt like I'd been doing admin stuff for my own store—but handing over melted ice cream cones to sticky-fingered children all day long was another.

The bells over the door announced my arrival, and Uncle Bob came running from the back. His gray hair was standing up at weird angles, like he'd been pulling at it, and a ring of sweat lined his collar.

"Abbey, I'm so glad to see you."

I noticed several customers were already in line with impatient looks on their faces, while a brunette who had her back to us was busily scooping away.

Uncle Bob motioned for me to follow him, and we went over to a small supply closet. "One of my freezers quit working, and I have to run in to the city to find another one." He reached for a box that was sitting on a shelf, and pulled it down. "There are some shirts in here, part of the uniform and all, so you can choose your size and use the bathroom to change."

He stuck one hand in the box and lifted out a bunch of shirts. "Here's an extra large . . . an extra large . . . another extra large . . . Damn it, are these all extra large?" He rifled through, scanning tag after tag. "I thought I had some more sizes in here." He looked at me in defeat.

"Don't worry about it, Uncle Bob," I said. "An extra large is fine."

He smiled at me and handed over a shirt. Abandoning the box to the floor, he hustled me out of there. "After you're changed, I'll show you around the counter area."

The shirt was a hopeless disaster. I pulled it on in the bathroom, and it hung to my knees, the sleeves practically going to my wrists. I tried to tuck it into my shorts, but that bulged in all the wrong places.

Finally, I just tucked in the front of the shirt and tied the back into a knot. It was the best I could do.

As soon as I exited the bathroom, Uncle Bob shuffled me off to the counter. He directed my attention to the tubs of ice cream lined up in a cooler beneath a clear lid. "Ice cream's here," he said. "Scoopers are kept in a water trough there." He pointed behind him. "The counter has all your toppings: peanuts, sprinkles, M&M's, Reese's Pieces, coconut, gummies . . . Hot toppings are kept in the warmers."

He opened the lid of a small silver pot, and I saw a long-handled ladle bobbing up and down in some brown goo.

"Caramel," Uncle Bob said. I nodded, and he leaned down to open a mini fridge located under the countertop that held the silver warmers. "Your cold toppings are kept in here: whipped cream, marshmallows, strawberries, pineapples, et cetera."

The brunette girl turned to us, and my heart sank.

It was Aubra Stanton. A cheerleader from school.

I had a momentary flashback to that first day of school last year, when Principal Meeker had announced Kristen's death to everyone during an assembly. Then Aubra and two other cheerleaders had stood up and acted like they were her BFFs and said they would miss her *soooo* much.

They hadn't even gotten her name right.

A tortured groan slipped out of me before I could hold it back, but Uncle Bob must not have heard, because he turned to her with a big smile on his face. "Aubra, this is my niece, Abbey. She's going to help us out. Abbey, Aubra will show you the ropes. She can take care of the cash register while you handle the customers."

Rumbling noises suddenly emerged from the room where the freezers were kept. Uncle Bob cast a worried glance in the direction of the sound.

"That's the freezer giving up the ghost. I'm gonna have to go check it out. Will you two be able to hold down the fort?"

*No, Uncle Bob. Don't leave me here with her!* "Sure," I said instead.

"Absolutely," Aubra replied.

Uncle Bob gave us both a wide grin and then disappeared into the back.

Aubra and I turned to face each other, standing off like two skittish gazelles in the middle of a pack of lions, waiting to see who would make the first move. Aubra looked me up and down. "You look kind of familiar. Your name is Abbey?"

*Here we go . . .* "Yeah, we go to the same school."

"Oh." She tossed her head. Clearly now *she* was the lion and *I* was the gazelle. "And you're the boss's niece, huh? I hope that doesn't make you think you're going to get any special privileges. Cuz you're not."

*Right. Because I'm sure she's never used her position on the cheerleading squad, or her short skirt, to get special privileges.* "I'm not—"

"Whatever. Look, just stay out of my way and do what I say, *comprende?*"

"Yeah, sure. Okay." I sighed. The doorbell chimed, and a man and a little boy walked in.

Aubra sneered at me, muttered, "Nice shirt," and then stalked away to go greet them. I looked down at my baggy shirt and pushed the sleeves up. This day needed to go by *fast*, or else I wasn't going to make it.

I slipped behind the counter and waited while Aubra smiled and chatted up the man. He kept cocking his head to one side and bragging about his ride—probably a flashy red sports car that just screamed *midlife crisis!*—while his kid ran grimy fingers over the window that covered the ice cream tubs.

Finally, Aubra glanced over at me and told me to grab a scooper.

I reached for one, trying to fling off the beads of water that clung to it without spraying myself in the face, and stood by the cooler.

"What kind do you want, Billy?" the man asked.

Billy pressed his dirty face against the glass, then finally said, "Chocolate."

Aubra glared at me. "You heard him. Are you going to scoop?"

I leaned down over the chocolate, digging the scooper into ice cream that was hard as a rock. I tried again, angling the scooper a bit more. That was unsuccessful too. So I started hacking at it. Eventually, little slivers of ice cream started flaking away, and I gathered several of them into a pathetically small ball.

"I want vanilla!" Billy suddenly yelled.

Pausing, I looked over to Aubra. "Vanilla with chocolate? Like two scoops?"

But the dad was already shaking his head no. "I told you only one scoop, Billy. Do you want vanilla *instead of* chocolate?"

Billy stomped his foot and shook his head too. Apparently, he wanted both. The father knelt down in front of him and took what seemed like forever to calm him down. My back was *killing* me from staying bent over, and the flakes of chocolate I'd managed to hack off were starting to melt.

"We'll take vanilla," the man said, standing to face Aubra.

I didn't know what to do with the ice cream I already had, so I tried to put it back. The scooper refused to give it up though, until finally Aubra gave a disgusted sigh and reached over to take it out of my hand. She threw the scooper back into the water trough and told me to get a new one.

Fresh utensil in hand, I bent down to get the vanilla.

"Watch it!" Aubra cried. "Your sleeves are getting into the ice cream."

I looked down and saw my sleeve trailing through orange sherbet *and* mint chocolate chip. *Impressive.*

My cheeks flamed, and I pulled back. Aubra took the scooper from my hand again and scraped out a perfect ball of vanilla ice cream. Lifting a small cup from a nearby stack, she released the ice cream and handed it over to the boy. "Sorry about that," she said to the dad. "She's new."

An obligatory eye roll and a sympathetic glance (directed at her, not me) passed between them, and she went to ring him up at the register.

I made my way to the bathroom to go clean up. Once safely inside, I told my mirrored reflection that this was only for a couple of weeks. I just had to keep reminding myself of that.

I blotted off my sticky sleeve with a damp paper towel, then tried to dry it the best I could. Finally, I rolled both sleeves all the way up. I looked like some wannabe jock heading to the gym to work out, but at least I wouldn't be dangling my shirt into the ice cream anymore.

Making my way back out, I saw three more people lined up, and Aubra gestured impatiently for me to come over. It took several tries, but finally I got the hang of the scooper and was able to dish up the ice cream without any major mishaps. Aubra worked the register, and for anything more complicated than a triple scoop, took over my duties. We even managed to make it through a Little League baseball team that came in without anyone getting *too* upset.

After a couple of hours had passed, Uncle Bob came out and told us that he'd man the counter while we took a fifteen-minute break. I followed Aubra out to a little sitting area in an alley behind the store. I kept my distance from her, though, and she did the same.

Taking out my cell phone, I checked the time and saw that I still had three more hours to go. *Wonderful.* I scrolled through my missed-calls folder and noticed a strange number listed there. Was it Caspian? Had he used a pay phone or something to call me from?

I hit redial and listened with bated breath as it began to ring. A female voice picked up. "Hello?"

*Well, I wasn't expecting that.*

"Hello?" I said. "Who is this? I mean, this number called my phone, and . . ."

"Is this Abbey? It's Beth. From school."

Right. The same Beth whose call I hadn't returned before. I was completely embarrassed. "Oh God, Beth. Hey, I'm sorry I didn't call you back."

She laughed. "No big. I thought you'd appreciate the tip if you're ever stuck with the Wilson kids again."

"Oh yeah, I do. Those kids will eat you up and spit you out." Aubra turned and glared at me, but I just looked the other way.

"Tell me about it. So listen, Lewis and I are going to a movie on Saturday night. Do you and Ben want to come?"

"Oh," I said. "Ben and I aren't—"

"I know," Beth said. "We're not a thing either. I'm giving Lewis a test run. Try before you buy. He's cute and all, but does the boy have *stamina*? I need to know these things."

I laughed. "Okay, I get it."

"So will you come? I've already asked Ben, and he said yes."

I hesitated. Beth was being really nice, but would Ben get the wrong idea? Would *Caspian*?

Beth must have heard my pause. "Please, please, *please*? You can't leave me alone with him, girl. What if it doesn't work out and I need a quick excuse?"

"Let me check my schedule," I said hesitantly. "Okay?"

She let out a whoop of joy. "I'll be calling you, girl. Wednesday. Don't flake on me."

"All right, all right. I'll talk to you then."

She said good-bye, and I closed the phone. A movie *did*

sound like fun. But what about Caspian? I wanted *him* to be there with me. Not Ben.

Aubra interrupted my thoughts. "We have to go back sometime. Come on."

Reluctantly, I stood up and followed her in. A line of customers had formed in front of the counter, and Uncle Bob was frantically waving to us. I paused for a minute to roll my falling sleeves back into place and then went to grab a scooper. Only two hours and forty-five more minutes to go.

When the customer traffic finally died down, Uncle Bob came out of the back room and said that he'd found some new freezer parts he needed to go pick up. He'd be back in an hour. Two, tops.

I watched him go, feeling abandoned and slightly hopeless as I turned back to Aubra.

She exhaled loudly and said, "The store will be dead for a while now. Prepare to be bored out of your mind."

Leaning on the counter, I stared out the window at all the people walking by and willed them to come in and prove her wrong. But she was right. Only twenty-two minutes had passed, and I thought I was going to die of boredom. *This must be what it's like for Caspian. Watching every second crawl by with nothing to help pass the time. No wonder he likes to read.*

Finally I couldn't take it anymore, and I glanced over at Aubra. She was texting furiously on her phone. "Does anything need to be done?" I asked. "Like the floors swept, or napkin holders filled or something?"

"No." She never even looked up.

I wandered out from behind the counter. I thought about going back to Uncle Bob's office and hanging out there, but I felt bad about leaving Aubra alone.

Grabbing a bottle of cleaner and a roll of paper towels, I headed to the tables. They weren't really all that dirty, but it was something to do. I cleaned each one and the chairs, too, taking my time to make sure that every speck of dirt was gone.

The doorbells went off again and I looked up, happy to see a customer at last. But my happiness vanished when a guy in cargo pants and a looks-vintage-but-costs-five-hundred-bucks T-shirt walked through the door. A silver Rolex gleamed on his wrist.

His hair was different, black now instead of the carefully highlighted blond spikes, but I still recognized him. It was the jerk I'd met here once before during Thanksgiving break.

Aubra squealed and came flying out from behind the counter. The boy smiled at her, flashing a perfect dimple.

Immediately my hackles rose. I really did *not* like this guy.

"Baby!" Aubra cooed, jumping into his arms for a hug. He

held her at a distance, being sure not to let her press too tightly against the front of his shirt. Aubra composed herself and flipped the OPEN sign on the front door to CLOSED. She glanced over at me. "Time for another break."

I wasn't going to argue. Even if I wanted to, I couldn't run the cash register on my own.

She started to walk away, then said sharply, "Abbey, come on."

I looked up at her, surprised. "Me? I'm, uh, fine here. You two go ahead."

Aubra planted both hands on her hips and gave me a cold glare. "You can't *stay* out here." She paused, and I could almost hear the "stupid" she wanted to add in there. "If people *see* you, they'll think we're *open*. Come on."

Dropping the cleaner onto the table, I followed both of them. When we came to the room that held the freezers, she tossed her hair and said, "We're going in here. You can go wherever. Just don't go out front."

I nodded and headed to Uncle Bob's office. At least he had a couch in there. *How long is this "break" going to last, exactly?*

Several stacks of newspapers were scattered across the surface of the couch, but I just swept them to the floor. Stretching out, I closed my eyes to take a short nap. Let Aubra come find me when she was ready.

But I couldn't sleep. Loud voices kept waking me.

"Fine!" someone shouted. It sounded like Aubra, and then there was a thump. Muffled noises came next, and it ended in weeping. I didn't know what to do. Should I stay out of it? Or go check on her?

I shifted to a sitting position. But I didn't have a chance to do any more than that, because Ex-Blondie-Turned-Goth-Boy suddenly appeared at the door.

He sauntered in and ran one finger down the edge of Uncle Bob's desk as he came toward me. Never breaking eye contact, never missing a step. Which was an impressive feat in an office as cluttered as Uncle Bob's. He stopped less than a foot away from the couch, holding up his finger to inspect it.

"Tsk, tsk. I do so *hate* a messy work area." Neatly sidestepping one of the stacks of papers, he sat down next to me. My skin crawled, and I forced myself to let out a breath I didn't even know I'd been holding.

"I like things neat and tidy," he said. "Do you?" I nodded, and swallowed. "Have we met before? Aubra said your name was . . . Abbey?"

"Thanksgiving," I heard someone say. Then I realized it was coming from me. "You dropped some papers off for my uncle, and I took them from you."

"Ahhh, yes." He extended a hand. "I'm Vincent."

I hesitated for a moment, but didn't want him to see how much I didn't like him, so I capitulated. He reached past my hand and slid his fingers down my wrist before shaking. The sensation made me feel queasy, and my gut reaction was to immediately let go.

But he held firm.

"You won't hold my earlier behavior against me, I trust. And I won't hold it against *you* that you left me out in the cold." He flashed a perfect white smile, but all I could see were sleazy car salesmen ads, infomercial hosts, and bad come-on lines all rolled into one. I was *so* not going to be another notch on his bedpost.

I pulled my hand free and resisted the urge to wipe it across my shorts. That could wait until he left. Instead, I stood up. "It was nice to meet you, Vincent. I have to go help Aubra now."

He stood up too, in one fluid motion.

"I guess I'll see you later, Abbey," he said, pausing to flash me another smile. I followed him out, and watched as he stopped to talk briefly with Aubra, who was back behind the counter. She shook her head once, and then gave him a hug, all smiles again.

As soon as he left, I wanted to ask Aubra what had happened, and why she was with someone who was such a jerk. But she pinned me with a steely, slightly red-rimmed glare.

"This will be our little secret, right, Abbey?" She glanced away and went to go flip the CLOSED sign back around. "It better be. I wouldn't want to see you accidentally "misplace" some money from the register drawer."

*So that's how it's going to be?* Ignoring her, I went to gather up the cleaning supplies I'd left on the table. *I should have known.*

At ten after five Mom rolled up to the door, and I headed back to Uncle Bob's office to tell him I was leaving. And that I wasn't coming back.

After Aubra's little boyfriend break, she'd given me even more of the cold-shoulder treatment and left me to clean up a huge pile of puke on the floor after some overeager kid had told his buddies that he could eat ten scoops of ice cream in a row.

He'd been wrong.

Uncle Bob was sitting at his desk, and he looked up as soon as I entered. "Mom's here, so I'm gonna head out, and . . ." I lost my nerve for a second, but then looked down and saw puke remnants on my shoes. "I'm not going to be able to . . ."

He held up something and pointed to it. "Look what I still have." It was the WORLD'S BEST BOSS mug I'd given him for Christmas last year. "I use it every day. It's my favorite."

All my thoughts of telling him that I was quitting instantly vanished, and I gave him a feeble smile. "Glad to hear it, Uncle Bob. See you on Wednesday." He beamed at me and I turned to leave, telling myself that no matter *how* desperate someone acted, in the future I was going to just say *no*.

Out in the car Mom asked me how my first day went. I flopped wearily onto the passenger's seat. "Long. Never-ending. With an eternal time suck in the middle of the day." As I said it, I couldn't help but think of Caspian, who had nothing *but* time on his hands.

Mom patted my knee. "I'm sure it wasn't that bad."

"You're right," I said. "It was worse."

She turned the wheel and pulled away from the store. "I know what will make you feel better. The library is having a book sale. You can get one to bring with you for next time."

I perked up. That actually wasn't a bad idea, and I knew someone else who could probably use some new books to help pass the time too.

# Chapter Seventeen

# A FORGOTTEN DATE

Fain would I pause to dwell upon the world of charms that burst upon the enrap-
tured gaze of my hero . . .

—"The Legend of Sleepy Hollow"

The rest of the week passed by in a blur of science sessions and long hours at Uncle Bob's, until Saturday finally came. I'd only gotten to see Caspian once during the week, stopping by the cemetery to explain my prolonged absence, and I'd totally forgotten to bring the books with me. Or tell him about my evening movie plans.

But now I had time to remedy that, and I walked swiftly to the cemetery. I was glad I'd worn a long, loose, red cotton skirt and my sheer white peasant blouse. Thanks to that, I wasn't turning into a puddle of sweat just yet.

Switching the small pile of books and some of Mom's

unused dinner-party candles from my left arm to my right, I passed by the gates and hurried toward the mausoleum. When I entered, Caspian was bent over his cardboard-box table, working on a drawing. He was so engrossed in what he was doing that he didn't hear me come in.

"Hey, Casper," I whispered, leaning in close. He jumped and looked embarrassed, and I caught sight of what was in front of him.

It was a half-finished scene of the two of us, lying on the grass, looking up at a sky filled with stars. My hair was wild and loose, spread all around me in crazy waves, and my face . . . "I'm not that beautiful," I murmured, captivated by the gorgeous girl he'd drawn there.

"Yes, you are, Abbey," his tone was hushed and reverent. "Raven hair, red lips, porcelain skin. You're like my own personal Snow White. And your eyes . . . they haunt me."

I sucked in a deep breath. He haunted my thoughts too.

He reached out a hand like he was going to touch my face, but then caught himself. Switching course, he ran the hand through his hair instead. "Snow White always was my favorite," he said.

"Are you calling me a princess?"

He shrugged. "If the shoe fits."

I groaned and he laughed. "Okay, yeah, that one was bad." Then he glanced down at my books. "What are those for?"

"These"—I sat the small pile on the box, being careful not to wrinkle his drawing—"are for you. Since you were sweet enough to leave me a surprise in my bedroom, I thought I'd bring you something. The candles are for when you run out of the ones in here, and I got the books at a library sale. So . . . happy birthday. Late. Or early. When *is* your birthday?"

Caspian grinned as he picked up the first book from the top of the pile and squinted at the title. "December twenty-second. *Jane Eyre*, huh?"

"Yeah, it's a good one. There's a crazy old lady, and a mad wife. Ooh! And a fire."

He opened it and scanned the front page. "That settles it then. I'll read this one first." His words made me ridiculously pleased, and I could feel my entire face light up with happiness. "If all I have to do to get a smile like that is read your books, then I promise to read one every day," he said.

"Stop it. You're going to give me heart palpitations."

He leaned closer. "That's what I'm trying to do. Your face is absolutely adorable when you blush."

My ears burned. *Oh great, am I the color of a tomato now?*

"Yeah, well, I can make *you* blush," I retorted. "By telling you how hot you are, and that when that little piece of black hair falls into your eyes, it's so sexy it makes me forget my words, and . . ." I stopped, suddenly aware of how warm the mausoleum was.

"Go on," Caspian prodded, shaking his head so that his hair covered one green eye.

I blushed again, and glanced around me, slowly backing away from him. I just needed some . . . space to clear my head.

He followed me, stalking my every move. My blood felt like pure oxygen racing through my veins, fizzy and bubbling and making me want to float away. A hard wall at my back stopped me, but Caspian kept coming. I thought desperately of some way to change the subject. "I got you *Moby-Dick*," I blurted out.

He gave me a sly smile. "Mmmm, did you? How . . . interesting."

"And *Treasure Island*, and *The Count of Monte Cristo*." I babbled on. "I thought you might like some boy books."

He stopped an inch away from me. I felt like I was his prisoner.

"Let's go back to the sexy and hot thing," Caspian said. "Could we add a gorgeous or mysterious in there, too?"

I gulped. "Like you don't already know you're all of those things. You probably had girls falling all over you before."

Caspian cocked his head to one side. "True. But I always thought it was because I was the quiet new guy. And besides, there's only one person I was ever *really* interested in."

"*Was*?" I squeaked. Then I cleared my throat and tried again. "I mean—"

"Am," Caspian corrected himself. "Technically, I guess it's both. I *was* interested the first day I saw her, and I still *am* interested in her." His eyes glowed in the soft candlelight around us, and every last ounce of coherent thought left me.

"It's ... um ... really. It's ..." My head felt like it was thickening and my body was overheating, every word dragged from somewhere in the depths of my fuzzy brain. I waved a hand in front of my face to fan myself, and finally spit out what I was trying to say. "It's hot in here. Don't you think? It's really warm."

"I only feel warmth when I'm standing next to you," Caspian said. He stepped half an inch closer. "Like right now."

I flapped my hand harder, desperately trying to get some air, when I felt something tug at my arm.

"Hey ..." I lifted my arm, trying to pull free, and my shirt rose up. It was caught on one of the unlit candles at my back. "I'm stuck."

Caspian glanced down. I followed his gaze and saw that my hip bone was peeking out above my low riding skirt, my shirt pulled high enough to show a wide expanse of flesh.

I was completely mortified until Caspian glanced back up at me and we locked eyes. "What are you doing?" I whispered.

"Enjoying the view." His voice was shaky, and he closed his eyes for a minute, taking a deep breath.

"*How* much longer until your death day?" I asked.

"Too long."

"And you're *sure*, that for a whole day you can . . ."

"Touch? Yes. And I'll definitely be spending that day with *you*." His voice was hoarse, and it seemed to take a lot of effort for him to speak.

I raised an eyebrow at him. "Promise?"

"Promise."

A high-pitched beep broke the silence and cut through the tension. Caspian pulled himself upright with an almost audible snap, and I freed my shirt. Shoving one hand into my skirt pocket, I pulled out my phone and turned it off.

"Sorry," I said. "It's my alarm. I have to go."

I hadn't told him about my movie plans yet, and now I *really* didn't know what to say. So of course, per my usual brain-mouth-no-filter method, I just blurted it right out. "I'm going to the movies tonight with some friends." I hesitated. "And . . . Ben."

He pulled back even farther, and everything in me yelled for him to stop. I had to clench my fists to keep from reaching out.

"It's totally just this friend thing," I tried to explain. "I felt bad because this girl, Beth, called me and begged me to go so she wouldn't be alone."

Caspian smiled, but it didn't reach his eyes. "You don't have to explain yourself to me, Abbey. It's cool. Go. Have fun." He took a step away and turned his back.

"You could come." I said. "And sit next to me. No one will know you're there."

He shook his head. "That could get awkward. It's fine. I'll see you later."

I hesitated, unsure of what to do. I wanted to stay with him, but he *was* telling me to go and have fun. "All right," I said finally. "Can we meet at the bridge? Tomorrow morning?"

"You're on," he replied. "Bye, Abbey."

I tried to tell myself the whole way home that he didn't *really* look at me with hopelessness in his eyes when I left. It must have been a trick of the light. That's all.

Just a trick of the light.


At the theater that night I had to admit that I actually was having fun, and the movie was pretty good too. Beth and Lewis were so cute together, and every time Beth and I took a quick bathroom break to talk about everything, she couldn't stop gushing over how sweet he was.

Ben kept cracking jokes the entire evening and making us all laugh. Afterward we went for some pizza, and I didn't think about Caspian the whole time. It wasn't until I was standing in line to buy a bottle of iced tea to take home with me that my thoughts turned to him.

Glancing outside at Ben, Lewis, and Beth standing on the sidewalk, I thought about how much fun he would have had. If he could have been here. If he was as real to everyone else as he was to me . . .

The clerk snapped his fingers to get my attention, and I jerked out of my daydream. "Sorry," I said with an embarrassed smile.

"Is that all?" he asked.

"Yup."

"That'll be a buck twenty-five."

I handed him two ones and waited for my change, glancing outside again. Ben was doing a crazy version of the robot, and Beth was almost in tears from laughing so hard.

"Here you go. Want a bag?"

"Um, no. I'll just carry it. Thanks."

He nodded, then handed me my receipt and something

else. "This is your friend's. He dropped it when he was paying for the pizza."

Ben had been the one to pay, so I said thanks and took the plastic card, then shoved it along with the receipt into my back pocket. Leaving the pizza place, I joined my friends outside, and we headed for my house, laughing the whole way.

Ten minutes after they dropped me off, the phone rang.

"Hey girl, it's Beth. I just got in."

"Oh, hey."

"So?!" she squealed. "What do you think? Is Lewis worth it? I mean, he's the total package, right?"

I sat down on my bed and pulled off my shoes. "Definitely. Brains *and* muscles." I didn't even know if that made any sense, but it sounded good.

"Oh, he's got muscles all right. Big, and well built in every way. And I do mean *every* way."

This was turning wayyy too personal for my tastes. "Go for it."

She squealed again, and I held the phone away from my ear. There was some shouting in the background, and I heard Beth yell, "Just a minute!" Then she said to me, "Okay. I have to go. Thanks for coming with us tonight, Abbey."

"No problem." I yawned. "Night."

Crawling under the covers, I kissed the cool glass of the four-leaf clover necklace I still had on. "Good night, Caspian," I whispered. "Wish you could have been with me." I fell asleep to dreams of starry skies and green eyes.

But sometime during the night my dreams changed.

*It was a party, with decorations and streamers and fairy lights strung everywhere. The floor was covered in a sea of pink and red balloons, and I had to kick them out of the way. Kristen was there, sitting next to a giant three-tiered cake, her back turned to me. Her red hair was longer than it had been in real life, and hanging loose.*

*"Kristen!" I yelled to her. "Happy birthday!" She tilted her head and laughed, but she didn't turn around.*

*A tugging at my ankles distracted me, and I looked down. The balloons had crowded around me again. A band started playing, and couples suddenly appeared out of nowhere, dressed in old-fashioned clothing. They swept between the balloons, gliding back and forth, all of them executing perfect dance steps.*

*Every time I tried to move, closer at first, then farther away, they'd stop in unison and turn to stare at me. Every single face was hidden behind a mask.*

*The balloons swelled again, climbing higher and higher. Burying me deeper and deeper. I tried to dig my way out, flinging them to the sides, but the balloons grew heavy. Suddenly, one of them burst, and water came slowly leaking out.*

*It was like a special effect. As soon as the trickling stream touched another balloon, it burst in slow motion, and then another and another would go off.*

*The crowd kept dancing. Moving along a balloon remnant–littered floor. None of them seemed to notice the puddles under their feet.*

*Finally I broke free. Enough balloons had popped that I was no longer weighed down, and I rushed to Kristen's side. "Did you see that?" I asked her. "Is this a masquerade?"*

*She turned to face me, eyes downcast, with a pout on her lips. "Where's your mask, Abbey?"*

*"I don't have one," I said.*

*She stroked one hand along the black dress she was wearing. "Do you like this? I wore it to my funeral."*

*I drew back, horrified. "Why would you say that, Kristen?"*

*She leaned down and put one finger to her lips, making a* shhh *sound. "I'm waiting for someone. Now put on your mask, Abbey."*

*I was getting frustrated now, and angry. "I don't have a damn mask, Kristen."*

*"Sure you do. Everyone does. I'm wearing* mine." *Her face*

turned tight, pinched, like she was schooling her features. Then a single trumpet blared, announcing the arrival of someone, and Kristen clapped her hands together. "He's here! My brother is here. And he's wearing his mask."

Turning, I saw the outline of a dark figure in the doorway with the sun behind him, casting a silhouette. I couldn't make out his features.

"But Kristen, Thomas is dead. . . ."

And then the balloons were back, clustering around me, sweeping me away. They brought me closer to the door, and I cried out, "Thomas, help me!"

Kristen was there by his side. Wearing a black mask now. "He can't save you," she said. "He couldn't even save himself."

I woke from my dream shaking and covered in sweat. After changing into a pair of jeans, I paced around my room. Why had I dreamt about Kristen like that? What did it mean? And why was Thomas there?

Weak morning light filtered across my floor, and I kept pacing back and forth. Lost in my own head. Every way seemed wrong and I just couldn't figure it out.

Then I realized something. I padded over to my desk and scanned a calendar that was sitting there; then I checked my phone to be sure.

It was July twelfth. Thomas's birthday.

I went back to pacing around the room, feeling all out of sorts. Last year I hadn't gotten the chance to spend the day with Kristen because she'd been missing. But this year it would be different.

I threw on some shoes and a sweatshirt and went to my closet to grab a blanket. I was going to the cemetery, and the grass there might be damp.

Caspian found me an hour later.

"How did you know where I was?" I asked him, not looking up from Kristen's grave.

"I don't know. I just sensed it. When you weren't at the bridge, I came to check here. I guess you make my Spidey senses tingle."

I knew he wanted me to laugh or smile, but I wasn't in the mood.

"Hey," he asked. "What's wrong? Did something happen last night?"

I looked up then. "At the movies? No. It's not that. I just had a bad dream last night about Kristen and . . ." A car drove slowly up the path next to us, and I stopped talking, trying to look like I was just a normal teenager sitting alone by a tombstone.

Like there was anything *normal* about that.

"Do you want to go sit under the bridge?" Caspian asked quietly. "I don't think we'll be bothered there."

I nodded and stood, folding the blanket as I went. Resolutely, we walked past the church.

"Wait just a minute," I told Caspian, when we reached the bridge. "Let me check on something." Dropping the blanket, I walked over to the section where Kristen and I used to sit. Then I grabbed on to the support pillar, used several chunks of exposed concrete as footholds, and climbed up under the bottom of the bridge. "Come on," I called softly down to Caspian. "We can sit up here."

He climbed up as I settled myself on the support beams. An extra beam had been added near the front, so it wasn't as open and as much of a drop down into the water below as it used to be when Kristen and I would sit there, but it was still a long way to fall.

Caspian wedged himself in next to me, and for a moment his knee disappeared into mine. "Sorry," he said, readjusting. I shrugged and looked out over the water, falling back into my dark mood. "So, what about this dream?" he asked.

"It was a weird birthday dream about Kristen. But this time her brother, Thomas, was in it."

He waited for me to continue. Never once prodding me to

speak faster. I liked that. "Today is Thomas's birthday," I confessed. "I think that's why he was in the dream."

"Okay."

Just one word. One simple sound, and it completely undid me. Suddenly, the words were spilling out of me. "Ever since he died, Kristen and I used to spend his birthday together every year. But last year we didn't get to because she was . . . gone. And I missed *her* birthday this year because I was at Aunt Marjorie's. It was May fifth."

Caspian just watched me with wide eyes, patiently listening.

"I feel terrible," I said. "I mean, I thought about her, and I wrote her a note. I even sang 'Happy Birthday' to her before I went to bed that night. But I wasn't here. *With* her."

"I'm sure she knew you were with her in spirit," Caspian said.

"Maybe." I dug one finger into the fabric of my jeans and traced a random pattern on my leg. "But maybe she doesn't. Maybe that's why I had the dream. Because she's mad at me, or something."

Caspian shook his head. "No. I know that's not true."

"But *how* can you know?" I said. "Last time I checked, she wasn't exactly hanging around here to give us her opinion."

"I know because of the type of friendship you had. I saw it firsthand."

"You did?"

He looked sheepish. "I told you before that I saw you here at the cemetery, and . . . sometimes I would follow you guys."

I watched him closely. Fascinated by his admission.

"I mean," he said, "I didn't like peek over your shoulder or anything. But sometimes when you would sit by Irving's grave, I sort of stuck around. It was like I was a part of it too." His face suddenly changed. "Your expression said it all. Your laugh spoke volumes." Caspian looked down at his hands. "I could tell how close you two were. She loved you."

My eyes grew moist, and a tear leaked out before I had the chance to wipe it away. "You think so?"

He nodded, and a quiet laugh escaped me as a memory surfaced. "You know, this one time, on Easter, Kristen thought it would be neat to hide some eggs for the people that 'lived' here. We were like ten, by the way." I laughed again. "So we took three dozen painted eggs and hid them all around. But when we were done, all the hiding places looked the same, and we couldn't remember where we'd put them."

"It took weeks for poor John, the caretaker, to find them. A couple of them must have been eaten by animals, because we never did find them all. But every time the wind blew, you knew you were close to one. The stench of rotten eggs was horrendous."

He laughed, and I joined him. "Of course, now I feel bad for all the people that just wanted to come visit their loved ones, but it was pretty funny at the time."

Caspian grew silent and studied me with a serious look on his face. "Your love for Kristen shines through when you speak about her."

I nodded and spread my hands wide. "She was the best."

"Tell me about her brother."

Leaning back, I looked up at the underbelly of the bridge overhead, feeling the vibrations of a passing car rumble through me. "He was her devoted big brother and she was his baby sister. Even with an eight-year age difference between them, they were super close. They had their moments, of course. But they were few and far between."

He leaned back too, and I glanced over at him. "It's weird, right? I can't imagine having a brother or sister. I mean, Kristen and I were close, but to have someone who shares your *blood*?" I shook my head.

"I always wanted a brother," Caspian said.

"Me too," I admitted. "Someone to take care of the bullies and stand up for me at school. When I was younger, Mom and Dad talked once about adopting a baby. But then they just sort of dropped it. I don't know what happened."

He caught my eye. "What happened to him? To Thomas?"

Sadness filled me. Even though it had happened years ago, it was still hard to talk about. "He died of a drug overdose. Everyone thought it was accidental, but I think Kristen's family . . . they knew."

"Knew what?"

"That it might not have been accidental." I waited a moment for that to sink in, for the heaviness of it to reverberate. "See, Kristen's brother had an addiction to pain pills. When she was three, Thomas was holding her, and he sat her down for a minute on this table. She started to fall off, and he caught her and put her on the ground, but then he tripped over a chair leg and fell out the window."

Caspian cringed, and an ache went through me. It was an awful story to tell.

"They were living in a third-floor apartment at the time, and he fell all the way to the ground. He only needed twelve stitches for the cuts on his face and hands, but he broke his back."

Caspian nodded once. "So that was why he had the pain pills."

"Yeah. He had two surgeries, but he needed more, and they couldn't afford it at the time. So he took pills when it got to be too much to handle.

"Poor Kristen. She always thought it was her fault. No

298

matter how many times I tried to tell her it wasn't, she never believed me. And whenever Thomas needed anything—a heating pad, or a new pillow—she was the first to get it for him.

"When he died, she cried for months. Luckily, she was in the hospital for bronchitis when it happened, and she didn't find him or anything. That would have been awful." I shuddered. "I just tried my best to be there for her. She always went with her mom and dad to go visit his gravestone on the anniversary of his death every year, but I was never far away."

"I know how that is," he whispered.

I smiled sadly at him. "He's buried in the town where they used to live. Out by Buffalo. They already had family plots there and couldn't get one closer." Another car passed overhead and the support beams of the bridge trembled.

"You know what's really ironic?" I whispered. "When Kristen died, people spread rumors that it was because she was into drugs. But Kristen never took anything stronger than a Tylenol. Refused to, because of what happened to her brother. Once, in eighth grade, she suffered through this terrible toothache because the dentist couldn't squeeze her in for twenty-four hours. He prescribed her a Vicodin for the pain, but she wouldn't take it. I sat by her side and held her hand while she cried the whole night."

My tears came hard, and suddenly, I couldn't stop. I missed my best friend and I missed her brother, and I cried for both of them.

Caspian sat there with me until my sobs died down to a slow hiccup. Then he whispered, "I'd hold *your* hand right now if I could."

His eyes were so wide and earnest that I couldn't help but smile at him. "Thanks," I said, trying to hold back more tears. "It's the thought that counts."

*Chapter Eighteen*

# A REVELATION

In the dark shadow of the grove, on the margin of the brook, he beheld something huge, misshapen, black, and towering.

—"The Legend of Sleepy Hollow"

When I got home from work on Monday evening, I was tired and moody and sore. Every time I moved my arm or flexed my hand, it hurt. I seriously needed to talk to Uncle Bob about dialing back the settings on his coolers. Soft ice cream would be *much* easier to scoop.

I dropped my phone on the desk and turned toward the bed. A piece of notebook paper was resting there, held in place by a violet—like the ones that grew wild in the cemetery. I picked it up and stroked the soft purple petals of the flower.

As I unfolded the note, a four-leaf clover fell out and

dropped to the floor. I left it there for a minute as I scanned the words in front of me.

Abigail Astrid,

I hope your day scooping ice cream and making children of all ages deliriously happy went well. May I request the pleasure of your company at Kristen's spot tomorrow morning, 7 a.m.? Until then, I'll see you under the stars.

-Caspian

P.S. I hope you don't mind another four-leaf clover. For some reason, they keep finding me.

There were drawings of stars and leaves covering the back side of the paper, and I smiled to myself, holding it close to my heart. I bent down to pick up the clover and placed it on the desk next to the flower. *I'm going to have to start pressing these to put in a scrapbook if he keeps giving them to me. . . .*

I fell asleep early that night, and slept deeply. When my alarm went off at six forty-five the next morning, I had to drag myself out of bed, and I hoped that a shower would help wake me up.

I was still pretty sleepy as I walked to the cemetery, but the closer I got, the more my excitement grew. What did he have planned? My stomach was in knots, and I tried to tell myself to calm down. It wasn't like he was proposing. . . .

*Oh God.*

I came to a screeching halt. That was ridiculous. *He's not . . . I'm only* . . . I shook my head to clear my thoughts and pushed that idea firmly from my mind. It *was* ridiculous. And I wasn't going to think about it.

Forcing myself to act cool and collected, I strode through the gates and made my way to Kristen's grave. Caspian was standing next to her stone, holding something in his hands.

"Ah, Abbey." His face lit up. "I see you got my note."

"You're starting to haunt my bedroom," I teased.

"All I did was leave the note," he said. "I swear. That's it."

I raised my eyebrow.

"*Maybe* I stopped for a second to check out the stars," he admitted. "On my way out, of course."

I grinned at him, then looked around me. "Why are we here so early? And what are you holding?"

Caspian glanced down and held out a piece of cake wrapped in saran wrap, with a twenty-five-cent sticker on it. He pulled up a corner of the plastic, and a nutty smell wafted out. The cake was an orange, crumbly mess. "Sorry. It's carrot. I know, not the best, but it's all they had."

He produced two candles from his pocket and stuck them in the cake. "We'll have to pretend they're lit; I forgot my lighter. But, ta-da!"

I was still lost. "Seven a.m. with carrot cake and candles . . . And this means what?"

"I picked seven a.m. because I figured there would be less people around," he said. "And the cake is for Kristen and Thomas. We're going to celebrate their birthdays."

Surprise hit me first, and then an aching sweetness. This was the nicest thing anyone had ever done for me. But how . . . ? "Where did you get the cake? And the candles?"

"I nicked the candles from a kid's birthday party yesterday. They'd already blown out the ones on the cake," he said. "These were just extra." He ducked his head and looked up at me like he was waiting for me to criticize him.

Maybe I should have, but personally, I thought it was a really sweet gesture.

I smiled and he continued. "The cake I got at a yard sale. Found a quarter on the ground and did a switch."

"You could have taken a quarter from Washington Irving's grave," I suggested. "I'm sure he wouldn't have minded."

Caspian looked affronted. "But they're *his*. That would be stealing from the dead."

Well, when he put it *that* way . . .

"Has anyone ever told you that you're the best? Because you are." My eyes grew misty, and it was hard to see, but I didn't cry.

Caspian started to sing softly. "Happy birthday to you . . ." I joined him with a shaky voice, and we sang together. "Happy birthday to you. Happy birthday, dear Thomas and Kristen . . . Happy birthday to you."

"Blow out the candles," Caspian whispered to me. I peeked over at him, feeling a little silly, but blew anyway.

I closed my eyes, a sense of calm coming over me. "You just won *so* many brownie points," I said, opening my eyes and looking straight at him. "More than you'll ever know."

His eyes were shining, and his face looked happy. "It's not over yet. Bring the cake and follow me."

"What?"

But he didn't answer. Just gestured for me to go with him. I started to follow, and then stopped. Breaking off two small pieces of cake, I left them near the tombstone. "Happy belated birthday, Kristen and Thomas," I said. "Enjoy."

Then I turned back and followed him to his mausoleum.

He made me close my eyes as soon as we entered and directed me with his voice so that I wouldn't fall. I bumped into something hard, and I put out a hand, feeling smooth marble under my fingertips.

"Okay," Caspian said. "Now on the count of three, open. One . . . Two . . . Three!"

I steadied myself and opened my eyes. The sight that greeted me was magnificent. And hysterical.

Rows of pink curly streamers crisscrossed the open room, hanging from unlit candles. A SpongeBob SquarePants "Happy Birthday" banner covered one wall, and Caspian was wearing a Teenage Mutant Ninja Turtles party hat tilted at an angle.

My jaw dropped open. "You *decorated*, too?"

He looked pleased. "Did a little shopping at the Salvation Army yesterday. I took back my suit and left it there in exchange for a couple of items. How soon am I going to need it again?" He handed me a party hat. "I saved Spider-Man for you. Sorry there wasn't more girly stuff."

I put the hat on and looked around me. "This is *unreal*, Caspian."

He shrugged. "Dead guys have to work harder to impress girls."

"You certainly impressed *this* girl."

Caspian grinned wickedly. "Hmm, so if the cake and candles got me brownie points, what does *this* earn me?"

"Stick around until your death day, and you might just find out. I'll show you my thanks very, very slowly." I blushed as soon as I heard those words leave my mouth. When had I become such a tease?

Caspian swallowed and looked around him. "Is it hot in here? I think it's warm in here."

"You can't feel anything unless I'm next to you."

"True, but words like that can make *anyone* overheat."

Blushing again, I turned from him and changed the subject. "Do you think they'll mind?" I waved a hand to show I was talking about the occupants of the drawers that lined the mausoleum walls.

"Nah. Who doesn't like a party?" He looked down. "Although I feel like I should be wearing something nicer than this old T-shirt."

He was wearing a gray shirt with a faded red Aerosmith logo.

"I like it," I protested. "In fact, I just realized that you change." *That came out wrong.* "Er, I mean, you . . ."

"Change my clothes?" He looked at me, and I nodded. "At first it was just habit. I don't need to. No sweat or anything. But it felt too weird to stay in the same clothes for weeks at a time. Even for a guy. And then I met you, and I was trying to act normal, so . . ." He shrugged. "It wasn't always easy to remember to wear something different each time we met. Luckily, I had my stash here."

I put the cake I was still holding down on the marble slab next to me. "I still can't believe you did all this, Caspian. Are you *trying* to sweep me off my feet?"

His face turned serious. "I'd like to sweep you off your feet, but the best I can do is ask you to dance with me. Will you?"

He held out a hand, and I suddenly felt nervous. Licking dry lips, I put my hand up next to his and whispered, "Okay." Assuming the position of a proper dancing partner, I held my arm up high, like I would be grasping his hand, and put my other arm around what would have been his waist.

He did the same, and I felt that dull tingle everywhere we would have been touching.

"In my head I'm hearing that Aerosmith song from *Armageddon*, and we're dancing to it," he said. Then he murmured softly, 'I don't want to close my eyes. . . . I don't want to fall asleep. . . . Cuz I'll miss you, babe . . .'"

Moving in small circles, we mimicked two slow-dancers at a prom. Caspian's voice echoed around us, bouncing off the walls of the dead. "'And I don't wanna miss a thing. . . .'"

We came to a halt, eyes locked. Desire, sadness, anger, and fear crashed through me. Like waves pounding on the beach, a violent storm that left nothing behind in its wake. Nothing but black emptiness. And I knew right then and there that, one day, that void would be me. I was the black nothing.

I tilted my face up, gazing at him, and made a secret wish. But it was a wish that would never come true.

Caspian couldn't come back from the dead.


I got home late that afternoon, and my eyes were red and teary. A crying jag had overwhelmed me on the way out of the cemetery, and I'd broken down. I'd stopped several times because I couldn't see where I was going.

Although Caspian and I had spent the rest of our time together talking and even laughing, I couldn't shake the heaviness that felt like it was chained around my heart. A constant shackle that tightened and bruised with every breath I took. A warning that one day I was going to be shattered.

I didn't know how much I could take. How much I could stand before I broke again . . .

A quick nap after lunch helped soothe my mood, and I woke up, determined again, to make it work. I loved Caspian, and that was all that mattered. If Nikolas and Katy could make it work, then so could we.

My phone rang, but I didn't answer it in time, and the voice mail icon flashed, signaling that I had a message. I dialed it to listen.

"Abbey, this is Ben. Call me when you get this, okay?" He sounded upset.

I slapped myself on the forehead. Today was Tuesday. I'd totally bailed on our science session. Hitting the button to call him back, I prepared my excuse.

He picked up on the first ring. "Abbey?"

"Ben, hey. I just got your message, I'm—"

"I came over, but you didn't answer the door. I called you like three times, and you never picked up."

"I know, I'm sorry. I was out and I left my phone here." I felt terrible. "I'm really sorry; it won't happen again."

He made a frustrated sound. "Do you *want* me to keep tutoring you? You've been really distracted lately. Is something wrong?"

*No, nothing. I'm just dealing with the fact that my boyfriend is dead.*

"What's that?" he asked.

I coughed and cleared my throat. Had I said that out loud? "Nothing, it's just . . . my parents. They're really on me about acing this science exam, and I'm nervous about it. . . ."

I crossed my fingers behind my back. "Look, I'm *really*, really sorry, Ben. Let me make it up to you. Come over, and I'll order a pizza."

"Everything on it?"

"Yeah, sure."

"I'll be there in twenty minutes," he said.

I hung up the phone, hoping that I'd made everything better with Ben. He really *was* a great guy.

After I ordered the pizza, I went downstairs to wait. Ben arrived with a big grin and a DVD in one hand. "Movie night."

The pizza guy showed up right behind him, and I paid for the pizza, then ushered Ben inside. "What are we watching?"

"*Star Trek.*"

I stopped in the middle of the hallway, waiting for the punch line. It didn't come. "No, really, Ben. What movie did you bring?"

"*Star Trek,*" he said. "Consider it your way of making it up to me."

I groaned and led the way into the kitchen, setting the pizza box on the table. "You're really going to milk this, aren't you?"

He nodded.

"Okay, fine. I deserve it."

"It's a good movie. Captain Picard meets his clone, and there's a huge explosion . . ."

He talked on and on. I could already feel my brain dying from boredom. But I nodded at all the appropriate times as Ben gave me the rundown on Worf and Troi and Shin-something. And then there was a robot.

"Uh-huh," I said, gathering plates and napkins and cups as he went on. I interrupted: "Grab some sodas from the fridge."

He picked out two cans of Coke and kept talking. I laid everything I had on top of the pizza box, then picked it up and headed to the living room. Ben followed me.

"DVD player is there," I said, pointing, and he put the movie in. Settling down on the floor, I found the remote and pushed play. "Okay," I said to Ben. "Eat pizza now; talk more after the movie."

He promptly grabbed two slices and started in on them. Music blared from the TV, and I leaned back, preparing for two hours of geekdom.

As the end credits rolled, Ben explained everything that I didn't understand, which was . . . a lot.

"But why couldn't they just build another robot?" I asked. "They had an extra one."

"Because Data was a specially designed artificial life form," he said. "One of a kind."

"But his brother, or whatever, was there. . . ."

"Yeah, well that's kind of their way of saying that Data's not really gone."

I looked at Ben skeptically.

"You hated it, didn't you?" he asked.

"Well, not *hated* . . . Okay, yeah. It was pretty boring," I admitted.

He laughed. "That's okay. At least you didn't fall asleep."

*No, but I was pretty damn close. . . .* "So, am I forgiven?"

"Sure," he said. "It's cool." Glancing down at his watch, he sat up straight. "Oh man, I gotta go. My Dad will be home from work soon, and I'm helping him fertilize the Christmas trees tonight."

He moved toward the DVD player to grab his movie. "Thanks for the pizza, Abbey."

The word suddenly jogged something in my brain. "Pizza! Wait. Just a second." I dashed upstairs and rifled through the dirty-clothing pile that held the jeans I'd worn the night we'd gone to the movies. The plastic card was still in the back pocket; I pulled it free and then flew downstairs.

"Here." I held it out to Ben. "The pizza guy gave it to me

the other night. I totally forgot. You dropped it when you paid."

"Library card," he said. "Thanks."

I glanced down, really seeing it for the first time. Ben took it from me and pulled out his wallet with his free hand, but the letters on the card were starting to make sense in my head.

"D. Benjamin Bennett?" I said slowly. "Your first name starts with a *D*?"

"Yeah." He flipped open the wallet and held it so I could see his driver's license. "Daniel. I'm named after my dad, so everyone calls me by my middle name."

Warning bells started crashing in the back of my mind, and a black spot bloomed on the edge of my vision. *D*. Ben was *D*. Ben was Kristen's *secret boyfriend*.

He gave me a strange look and put the library card away. "Are you okay, Abbey?"

All I could see was a black spot over his face, like I'd been blinded by a bright light. I put out one hand and then jerked it away. "Fine . . . I'm . . ." My throat felt funny, tight and constricted. With my vision clearing, I stared at him, my mouth gaping wide.

"You . . . sure?" he asked me.

Bile churned in the back of my throat, and I knew I was going to be sick. "I think the pizza isn't sitting very . . . well,"

I gasped. "Go on. I'll . . . Bye." I waved my hand, desperately hoping that he'd leave before I puked all over his shoes.

Ben must have been able to read what was on my face, because he turned and headed for the door. "Okay. See you later, Abbey," he said.

I waited for half a second, then ran up the stairs for the bathroom before I even heard the front door close. I made it just in time.

The tile floor was a cold comfort against my cheek, and I lay there for a while afterward. My body twitched every now and then, little spasms of aftershock that ran through my veins, making my arms and legs jerk to keep time with some unseen clock of horror. I didn't know how long I lay there. Felt like minutes. Felt like hours.

A door slamming and voices below calling my name broke through my stupor, and prompted me to struggle to a sitting position. I couldn't let them see me like this or I'd never hear the end of it.

Footsteps sounded on the stairs. Using the edge of the sink, I hauled myself up and nudged the bathroom door shut just as a knock came on my bedroom door.

"Abbey?"

*In here.* But it didn't come out, and I tried again. "In here."

"Did you already eat? We found a pizza box downstairs." Mom's voice came through the door.

"Yeah, Ben came over for some pizza, but it didn't agree with me."

"Aww, poor baby. Do you need me to do anything?"

Gripping the sink, my knuckles turned white, and I tried to keep my voice steady. "No, I'll be out in a minute."

"Okay. Come downstairs when you're ready."

I waited until her footsteps faded away before I looked at myself in the mirror. I was almost afraid of what I'd see. But it was just me looking back. My eyes were surprisingly clear and dry. My hair didn't look any different. Though my face was completely white. I was pale as a ghost.

I laughed a little hysterically at that thought and then shoved my fist into my mouth to muffle the sound. *No, stop that. Get a hold of yourself, Abbey.* Turning the cold handle, I splashed some water on my face until the frigid temperature turned my cheeks red.

Drying off, I mentally composed myself to go downstairs. I needed to leave. I needed to go find Caspian.

Mom and Dad were in the kitchen making dinner.

"There she is," Mom said. I smiled wanly at her. She put down the frozen pack of shrimp she held and came over to me.

"You're pale. Do you want to lie down for a little bit?"

"What's wrong? What happened?" Dad asked.

"Food poisoning." Mom held the back of her hand to my forehead.

"I'm feeling better now," I replied. "I think I just need to go for a walk. Get some fresh air." I went over to the door.

"Don't be gone too long," Mom said.

"Okay," I called back, slipping out the door.

I ran to the cemetery, out of breath and out of the ability to think clearly. All I knew was that there was one person who could help me make sense of this. One person who could make it all better. And I was going to find him.

Darkness hadn't fallen yet, so the main gates were still open, and I pounded toward the mausoleum. The overwhelming urge to just find Caspian and tell him about Ben was driving me mad.

"Caspian!" I yelled, pushing open the mausoleum door. A single candle burned by his makeshift table. My voice bounced off the walls and came back to me. "Caspian, where are you?"

He wasn't answering.

I moved to his stuff, calling his name over and over again. Frustration bubbled up in me. *Where is he? I have to see him!*

Something was in my hands, and I looked down to see the

charcoal he used was dangerously close to snapping in half. I hadn't even realized I'd picked it up.

Relaxing my grip, I reached for a nearby drawing pad and tore out a piece of paper. *I need you*, I scrawled, and left it in the middle of his table. He'd see it there when he came back.

I stormed out of the crypt, still reeling from confusion and anger, and decided to head to the bridge. As I ran, I desperately wished for him to be there. I needed to make sense of this. How could Ben have been D. all this time? How could I not have seen it sooner?

The looming wooden structure rose up out of nowhere. I crossed the riverbank, daring to yell his name again. Straining my eyes to make out any shape that could possibly be him. Double- and triple-checking the trestles up under the bridge to see if he was there.

He wasn't.

Digging my fingernails into clenched fists, I threw my head back and screamed, "Why can't I find you?!" My heart was racing, and I tried to calm down, but I couldn't. I pounded the side of my head with my hand as I paced back and forth. "Think! Think, Abbey! Where else would he go?"

*Irving's grave.*

The thought came to me in a crystal-clear flash of inspiration. I left the river behind, and walked quickly to his plot. My heart sank when it came into view. The little fenced area that enclosed his grave was empty. Caspian wasn't there.

I climbed the stone steps and pushed my way through the gate, sinking to my knees at the foot of Washington Irving's tombstone. "I'm lost," I whispered. "I can't find Caspian, and I need him." A bird chirped nearby, sounding like he was saying, "Why? Why? Why?"

A scraping sound made me jerk around. I staggered to my feet. "Nikolas!"

He looked . . . wary, and I stopped short of hugging him.

"Is everything okay, Abbey?"

"Have you seen Caspian?" I asked. Nikolas shook his head, and I reached out to grip his hand. "Are you sure? I have to find him."

"Why?" He said it so abruptly that I took a step back. "Tell me why."

"Because I found out who Kristen's secret boyfriend is! Don't you see, Nikolas? He might have been with her the night she died."

"And you are positive that it was not Caspian here that night with her?"

His question jolted me. "Caspian? No. It wasn't him. He

already told me he wasn't here that night, and besides, Kristen couldn't have seen him and touched him. There's no way it was him." I knew without a shadow of doubt that what I was saying was true.

Nikolas nodded his head. "I do not think that it was your young man either. I just wanted to be sure."

Suddenly, something Nikolas had said once flashed through my mind. "Before I left Sleepy Hollow, when I came to your house, you said Kristen isn't like you. Isn't a Shade. That you saw her die."

He wouldn't look at me then. Wouldn't meet my eyes.

"Nikolas?" I prodded. "What did you see? Please. Tell me. I need to know."

He gazed at me, looking like he'd instantly aged a hundred years. It was as if every horrible thing he'd ever seen or done was etched in the lines across his face. A tear ran down his cheek. "Is it not enough that I saw her die? Why does any more matter?"

I gripped his hand and held on tight. "Was anyone with her?"

He shook his head, as if unable to speak, and I waited.

"I was on my way back to my home," he said slowly. "And I saw her in the water. I felt something. Something dark. But I was too far away." He pulled his hand free, and it was shaking.

"Did I see someone there? I am not sure. It was dark. . . . There were trees. . . . All I know is that I had to watch that poor girl get pulled under, and I could do nothing about it."

Flashes of my dream from the night Kristen died played out in front of my eyes, and I was lost in them. *Cold water. Dull pain. Aching chest. Hopelessness.*

"That is what I saw, Abbey," Nikolas said sadly. "I could do *nothing.* And now you know the worst of it. To see someone die and not be able to cry for help, to be unable to pull them to shore, or to go warn someone of that which you just witnessed . . . It is a hell like no other." He looked off into the distance, at the graveyard behind us, and his voice grew softer. "There is a barrier between their world—*your* world—and mine, and I am unable to breach it."

The tables turned then, and he reached for *my* hand, gripping it with a strength I didn't know he had. "This is my curse. Pay attention, Abbey. It might just save your life."

*Chapter Nineteen*

# COMPANY

Certain it is, the place still continues under the sway of some witching power, that holds a spell over the minds of the good people, causing them to walk in a continual reverie."

—"The Legend of Sleepy Hollow"

I left my window open at home in case Caspian found my note, and I was pacing back and forth in front of it when his face suddenly appeared. I rushed over to him. "I couldn't find you!"

"Abbey, what's wrong?" He looked worried. "I thought that something had ... that you'd ..."

"I found out who Kristen's secret boyfriend is!" I blurted out.

He went completely still. "You did?"

Nodding, I gestured for him to come inside. He climbed through the window, and I backed up a step.

"How did you find out?" Caspian asked. "Who is it?"

"It was on his library card. The initial *D*. I saw it and asked about it. His first name is Daniel." I turned to face him. "It's Ben."

Caspian looked at me in disbelief. "That nerd boy who tried to put the moves on you?"

"Yeah. He came over for pizza today, and we watched a movie because I totally forgot about our tutoring session, and . . ." My words deserted me. I couldn't speak fast enough to keep up with my racing mind.

"God, Caspian! I just can't believe it. All this time."

I started to feel queasy again, and put one hand to my mouth.

"Why don't you sit down?" Caspian came closer and shepherded me to the bed. I followed, and he sat next to me, looking concerned. "Are you sure it's him? Really, *really* sure? I certainly don't want to stick up for the guy, but he doesn't seem like the type to have made her keep such a big secret."

I shook my head. "It has to be him. He knows all this stuff about Kristen. Like where she wanted to go to college, and what her brother was good at . . . And at her funeral? He seemed really upset. Like, *really* upset. More than normal. He probably felt guilty."

Caspian was silent.

"Arrrrrhhhh!" I yelled. "How could I *not* have seen this? All this time. He was always so nice to me. I bet he was just trying to figure out how much I knew." I jumped up to pace again. I couldn't sit still.

"Maybe you should ask him," Caspian suggested.

"What?" I stopped. "No, I can't."

"Why not?"

"Be-because he's just going to lie to me," I stuttered. "He's not going to tell me the truth."

"Maybe he will."

"Yeah, right. Like you did?" As soon as the words were out of my mouth, I regretted them. "I'm sorry. That was below the belt. I didn't mean it."

"Yes, you did. But it's okay. I deserve it." His eyes looked miserable, and it broke my heart.

I sat next to him on the bed. "No you don't," I said. "I'm just being an asshole because I'm pissed at Ben, and I took it out on you. Forgive me?"

"Of course," he said. "Always."

But he wouldn't look at me.

"Caspian." I tried to nudge his arm and felt the tingle. "Hey, Casper."

That was enough to get him to look at me.

"I'd hold your hand right now if I could," I said.

He smiled. "Thanks. It's the thought that counts."

Knowing that I was truly forgiven, I leaned back on the bed and looked up at the stars. "It has to be him . . . right? I mean, it makes too much sense. Everything he knows about her, showing up at her locker last year, being so upset at her memorial. Even making friends with me . . . It all points to classic signs of guilt."

"Or it could just mean that he misses her."

But that didn't make any sense. "I don't think so."

We sat there in silence, and I kept turning everything over in my mind. Replaying bits and pieces of conversations, trying to make all the puzzle pieces fit. It was all so shocking and new. I felt blindsided.

"What are you going to do?" Caspian asked.

"I don't know. How do you bring up something like that? As a question? An accusation? Do I slip it into our next casual conversation?" I laughed bitterly. "Like we're going to have any more of those. And to think that he was in my—" I stopped abruptly and shut my mouth.

"Was in your . . . ?"

I could feel my face heating up, and I shook my head.

"Come on," he prodded. "Was he in your cereal bowl? Tea leaves? What?"

"Nothing." I snapped. He didn't respond, but just sat there quietly. Looking at me. "Oh, all right, fine," I finally sighed. "He was in one of my dreams, okay? But then he sorta turned into you, and it was crazy." His eyes widened. "Can we please get back on track here?" I said. "People can't control their dreams."

He ran his fingers through his hair. "Do you have his phone number? You could call him."

"That's not exactly a conversation best suited to the phone, you know?"

"Do you want to go talk to him about it?" His green eyes held mine. "I'll go with you."

Fear and excitement rose inside of me. "I don't know . . ." I bit down on one thumbnail, worrying the edges with my teeth. "Could I? *Should* I?"

"Asking is the only way you're going to find out for sure. And think of it this way: Without knowing, are you going to be able to sleep tonight?"

*No.* "Good point. But I don't know where he lives." I stood up and went over to my desk, flipping the switch on my computer. "Google."

Nervously tapping my fingers on the edge of my computer monitor, I waited for the computer to start up. But then the tapping noises started to make me irritated, and I switched to rolling one of my perfume bottles back and forth between my hands.

Finally, the computer stopped clicking and whirring, and I pulled up a search engine. Typing in Ben's full name and *Sleepy Hollow, NY* brought up a database listing in no time.

"Looks like he lives over by the high school," I said. "Feel up for a walk?"

Caspian stood. "Let's go."

We climbed out the window and crossed the yard, setting off in the direction of the school. Twenty minutes later we reached Ben's house, and I bounced from side to side on the balls of my feet, trying to psych myself up like a prizefighter getting ready for the ring. I carefully pushed the doorbell and then waited for someone to answer.

A middle-aged woman with brown hair opened it up. She was wearing a light-colored tunic and gray pants. A dish towel was suspended in one of her hands. "Can I help you?"

"Um, hi, Mrs. Bennett?" At her nod I continued. "I'm Abbey Browning. Ben is tutoring me?"

A wide smile broke out across her face. "Oh yes, how are you, Abbey?"

"Good, thanks. Um, do you know where Ben is? I need to talk to him."

Her smile turned to a slight frown, and then it was gone. "He's with his father. At the Christmas-tree farm, about five blocks away from here. Next to a vacant lot."

I nodded. "Okay, thanks." I was already turning away from her.

"Do you want me to call him?" she asked.

I turned back. "No, thanks. I'll surprise him. See ya, Mrs. Bennett." I waved cheerfully and turned away again as soon as she shut the door.

Caspian and I made short work of the five blocks. The Christmas-tree farm, if you could even call it that, was a small strip of land. A *very* small strip of land. There were twenty or thirty baby trees, growing in rows.

A man was there, doing something with a bucket, and at first I didn't see Ben. Then he stood up, and I realized that he'd been bending so low to the ground that I hadn't seen him. But now I could make out his curly hair.

"Ben!" I called, waving my arms in the air. He looked my way, and then said something to his dad before jogging over.

"Remember," Caspian said. "He could have an excuse. Don't fly off the handle right away."

I gave a short, jerky nod.

"Abbey?" Ben said, getting closer. "What's up? Why are you here?"

I took a deep breath and clenched my fists, nails biting deep so that I would have something to distract me. Without waiting, or thinking, I plowed straight ahead. "I know, Ben."

He gave me a puzzled look. "Know what?"

"About you and Kristen. I found her diaries and you were mentioned in them."

*"What?"*

I wanted to yell, to *scream* in his face that I knew, and he needed to stop lying, but I saw Caspian shaking his head. Counting to three, I said very slowly, "I know that you and Kristen were dating, and that you wanted her to keep it a secret from me."

Ben took a step toward me, and even though I felt like flinching, I held my ground. "What are you talking about, Abbey? Kristen and I never dated."

His earnestness threw me for a loop. "But your first name is Daniel, and she was seeing someone named D."

"She was?"

❦ 329 ❦

"Yeah," I replied. "I mean, no. I mean . . . You should know. *You're* D."

He shook his head. "Sorry, Abbey. But it wasn't me."

Caspian watched us, and I stole a glance at him, trying to keep my focus. "I know it was you. She wrote that you guys were meeting at secret places, and . . . and how do you know so much about her if it *wasn't* you?"

Ben blushed a little. "Because I liked her."

"How do you explain all the personal stuff you know about her?"

"We shared a couple of study halls, and I asked her some stuff."

I searched his eyes, trying to see if he was lying.

He wasn't.

"Why didn't she ever tell me?" I asked.

"I don't know. But I *was* going to tell you about my feelings for her. That's what I've been trying to talk to you about." He glanced down, looking embarrassed. "I thought that maybe I had feelings for you. . . . But then I realized—" He broke off and looked up at me.

I stayed silent.

"Then I realized that I, uh, I didn't really have those . . . uh, feelings . . . for you," he said. "It was always Kristen. I guess it was just a temporary transference type of thing."

I unclenched my fists and stared down at my palms. "Where were you?" I asked. "The night she went missing?"

"Out of town. With my dad. We went on a fishing trip upstate. Ask him if you want."

I studied him again. Looking for something . . . anything. "It's *not* you?"

He shook his head. "I almost wish I *was* this guy. Then I could give you some answers. But I'm not. In fact, one of the reasons I was so upset at her memorial was because I missed the search-and-rescue teams. I would have . . . helped." He looked so miserable that I knew there was no way he was faking it.

"You're not D.," I whispered. Half to Ben, half to Caspian. Hanging my head, I felt empty now and drained. "I'm sorry, Ben. I'm just . . . sorry."

He nodded once, and turned away from me to go back to his dad. I didn't know what to say, so I let him go. Now I was even worse off than before. I *still* didn't know who D. was, and I'd possibly cost myself a friend.

The next day at Uncle Bob's shop was long, and I didn't think I'd make it through till the end. My brain and fingers were disconnected, and I felt clumsy and slow. Several times I dropped the scooper onto the floor mid-scoop, and I had to stop each time to get a new one.

Then I hit the wrong button on the register as Aubra was showing me how to use it ("for the fifty-third time!"), and even Uncle Bob couldn't figure out how to fix it. For the rest of the day everyone automatically got their ice cream at half price.

Thursday wasn't much better, and Ben missed our tutoring session. He called me later and said he was sorry, he just got busy, but I knew it was because of our awkward meeting at the tree farm. He wasn't sure how to act around me now.

But at least I had one bright spot at the end of each day. Caspian would come over and stay for an hour or two while we lay on my bed, just talking about nothing at all. Sometimes we didn't talk, but listened to music instead, and that was nice too. Just knowing that he'd be there waiting for me was what kept me going.

Friday, though, was the toughest day of all. Aubra was in rare form, even for her. At first I thought it was just a PMS thing, but she kept taking all these breaks to go text on her phone, and when she'd come back, her eyes were red.

Then I just figured it was a Vincent thing. He didn't exactly seem like the best boyfriend on the planet, so it was no surprise that he'd be making her cry.

I tried to steer clear of her, and actually went to hide out in Uncle Bob's office when it was time for my fifteen-minute break. Uncle Bob snuck up on me and made me jump.

"Staying away from the customers, are we?"

I spun around. "It's my fifteen, and I . . ."

He chuckled. "It's okay. I understand. Sometimes they can be pretty rough. I swear, this summer heat brings out the crazy in people."

*It drives some employees crazy too*, I thought. He gave me an odd half smile, like he'd heard me.

Moving around the desk, he shifted a stack of papers from one side to the other and then sat down in his chair. "You know what I like best about you, Abbey?"

"Um . . . my adorable personality?"

Uncle Bob shook his head. "You change people. That's what I like best about you. Take this office, for instance." He gestured around the room. "When you took it upon yourself to organize it, you changed me."

I started to protest, to say I was sorry for not asking him first when I'd come in here last Thanksgiving and rearranged his stuff, but he held up a hand.

"I mean that in a positive way. I *liked* the fact that you took initiative. Now, granted, not everything took"—his eyes slid over to his messy cabinets, and I grinned at him—"but for the most part you helped me change in a positive way."

He picked up a metal, triangle-shaped paperweight and studied it before looking back at me. "Some of the people will be negative. They'll go out of their way to make you miserable or choose to ignore you."

I glanced down at my feet. It wasn't hard to figure out he was talking about Aubra.

"What's important to remember though, Abbey, *is* the fact that you change people. That overrides all, no matter what. Always remember that."

I looked up at him.

"Do you understand what I mean?" he asked.

"Yup. I got it. Thanks for the pep talk."

He looked pleased and bashful all at once. "It's nothing. Just my way of buttering you up so that I can ask you to stay an extra hour. Busy shift."

I groaned. "Uncle *Bob*. Seriously?"

"Sorry, Abbey. I wouldn't ask if I didn't really need it."

"*Fine.*" I sighed heavily. "I'll call Mom and tell her to pick me up later."

He pushed an old-fashioned, eighties-style professional-office phone my way. "Here you go, you can use this."

I picked up the clunky black receiver and eyed it doubtfully, but dialed Mom's number. "Hey, Mom. Uncle Bob needs me to stay for an extra hour, so you'll have to pick me up at six."

"Okay," she said. Someone was laughing in the background, and she sounded distracted. "Wait, six? But the Maxwells are coming over for dinner, and I told them we'd eat at six thirty."

"They *are*?" I could feel a happy smile cross my face. "I haven't seen them in so long! Oh man, that will be great. Just push dinner back to seven thirty, then."

She didn't say anything, and for a minute I thought the old phone had given up the ghost. Finally, she came back on. "Mmm-hmm, okay. That's fine, Abbey."

There was more laughter, and she laughed too.

"What's going on, Mom?" I said. "Are you having a party or something?"

"What? No. I just have some company over for coffee. See you at six."

I hung up the phone and rolled my eyes at Uncle Bob. "Mom's schmoozing again. Hope there's no wine involved." His booming laughter followed me as I started to head out to the customers. "Just wait," I called back. "You haven't heard the story about my birthday party yet."

~ ~ ~

Mom was about ten minutes late picking me up, and she drove with a lead foot the whole way home, telling me again and again how I had to hurry and change when we got there because we were running so late. I wanted to plug my fingers in my ears and scream.

When we made it home, she rushed into the kitchen, and I took my time heading to the stairs. "Maxwells will be here in ten minutes," she called out. "Hurry, hurry."

When I reached my room, I went straight for the closet. My hand automatically grabbed the first thing that was there, and I saw it was the pink shirtdress I'd worn when Aunt Marjorie had come over for dinner last year.

That would do.

Changing course, I brushed my teeth, detangled my curls, and put on some new deodorant. My ten minutes were close to being up, and I could hear car doors slamming outside. I got dressed quickly and slipped on some black sandals. My toes needed a fresh coat of nail polish, but I didn't have time for that right now.

I ran downstairs, eager to see Kristen's parents. It had been *months*. They were standing by the couch in the living room, and I halted on the third step down as soon as I saw them.

Mrs. M. looked . . . older. Her hair, once scattered with

fashionable gray strands—"stubborn streaks," she'd called them—was now almost entirely gray. And her face looked gaunt, like she'd lost some weight. Mr. M. didn't look as bad, but there were definitely a few new wrinkles at the corners of his eyes. The stress of losing both of their children was clearly catching up to them.

Mrs. M. must have heard me approaching, because almost as soon as I stopped, she looked up. Her face broke into a smile. "Abbey."

I flew down the stairs and threw my arms around her. "Mrs. M.!" She squeezed me tight, and I held on, overwhelmed with happiness. I reached out a hand to Mr. M., and he patted it, beaming at me.

"It's *so good* to see you," she said, taking a step back to size me up. "Look how beautiful you are. How's your summer going? I heard that you're doing some extra-credit science work?"

"It's great," I said, leading her into the dining room. We sat down, and everyone else came in a second later. "I'm helping my uncle out, working at his ice cream store, and Ben, one of our classmates, is tutoring me for this science test I have to take before school starts. It's a whole big thing." *And you know the reason I left? That dead boy I was seeing? He's real. And I love him.* I smiled at her and took a sip of water from the glass in front of me.

The doorbell rang, and I looked over to Mom. "Who's that?"

She stood up quickly. "That must be the rest of our company."

"The rest of our . . . ?" I glanced at Dad. "What company?"

"Oh, just some people that came over today for coffee," Mom replied, going to answer the door.

I waited for Dad to explain, but all he did was shrug. The classic *I don't know; ask your mother* shrug. I shot a look over at Mrs. M., expecting her to be just as curious as I was, but she was paying careful attention to the napkin in her lap. Almost like she was avoiding me.

*Interesting. . . .*

Mom reentered the dining room with a man and a woman behind her. They were both dressed in navy blue, she in a crisp business suit with a breezy red scarf styled artfully around her neck, and he in a navy polo shirt that went perfectly with his pressed khakis. They looked to be about Mom and Dad's age.

"Of course you met my husband today, and the Maxwells." Mom stopped for a moment and gestured across the dining room. Mrs. M. nodded at them, and the business-suit woman was all smiles. "And that's my daughter, Abigail. We call her Abbey."

*We call her Abbey.* What was I, a pet dog? I bristled, but didn't have time to show my displeasure, because they were both coming my way. *Fast.*

"I'm Sophie," the woman said, hand outstretched, "and that's Kame."

I locked eyes with Sophie, getting ready to shake hands, and noticed right away that her eyes were unusually colored. Clear and glasslike. Almost translucent.

The hair on the back of my neck stood up, and something tickled the edges of my brain. They looked vaguely familiar.

Sophie clasped my hand in a firm grip, and it suddenly felt like a million spiders went tap dancing along my spine. I shook her hand for the briefest of seconds and then pulled away, trying not to make it look so obvious that that was what I was doing.

Kame put out his hand. Everything in me *screamed* not to touch it, but I didn't know how to get out of it, so I shook it briefly. "Kame," he reminded me, and I nodded. His voice was deep and lilting; it almost had a musical quality to it. Come to think of it, so did Sophie's.

Mom ushered Sophie and Kame to seats across from me, and as they turned to walk past, I got a whiff of something strange. Like burned toast, or dying ashes.

Wrinkling my nose in distaste, I caught myself and then smoothed out my features. Whatever perfume Sophie was wearing did *not* suit her very well.

Mom disappeared into the kitchen, then returned a couple of minutes later holding a large silver dish. "I hope everyone's hungry. I made pork roast with cardamom mushroom sauce. And I also have meatball soup."

"Personally, I can't wait for the meatballs," Kame said. "I'm sure everything else will be wonderful too, but meatballs are my downfall. They are . . ."—he kissed his fingers to his lips—"*delizioso*."

Mom beamed a *huge* smile. "Well, I hope my meatballs live up to your high standards."

Kame smiled back at her, and I rolled my eyes. *So* gross.

The pork roast moved steadily down the line from Kame to Sophie, and she waited until it was safely passed on to Dad before she said, "So Abbey, I assume you're going to be a senior this year?" I nodded. "I hear the schools around here are just *fantastic*. The teacher-student ratio and academic courses— what an asset to this community. I'm sure that really helps with the value."

Asset to the community? Strong academic courses? What were they, school-board officials?

"Oh, yes," Mom raved. "And we have one of the highest secondary education continuance levels in the state. But of course, we are always seeking new and improved ways to help our students. One of our main goals this year is to encourage our local teens to become active in their community. Big brother/big sister programs, volunteer work with the elderly, community service to improve our parks . . ."

I gave Mom a double take. This was the first time *I'd* ever heard of any of those things.

"That's so important," Sophie agreed.

Kame nodded. "Strong community gives people a better sense of self."

*Okayyyy, so they're . . . self-help gurus?* "How did you say you know my parents?" I asked Sophie.

"They knocked on our door at just the right time," Mom replied. "The Maxwells were here, and we were discussing dinner, so it just turned into one big group meeting when we invited them in."

"We were here to introduce ourselves," Sophie said to me. "We're with the new branch of Hotchkiss Realty."

That explained their outfits, then.

I watched her closely while she went on to talk about real estate, studying her hair as she spoke. It was a bright red color that was so vivid, there was no *way* it was natural. And as I looked closer, I could see little glints of pale blond peeking through here and there. Like the dye hadn't been strong enough to cover up her original color.

Almost perfect, but not quite.

Dad handed me the roast, and I scooped some onto my plate, then passed it on to Mrs. M. I picked up a fork and stabbed one of the squares, then lifted it to my mouth. Just as I was about to take a bite, that burnt smell drifted up to me again.

I moved the fork closer and inspected the food. There weren't any darkened edges. Sniffing again, I got just the barest hint of a smell this time. Everyone else looked like they were enjoying it.

I put the fork to my mouth again, forced it past my lips, and chewed. The taste was fine, if somewhat bland. I reached for another piece and discreetly smelled it. *Smells fine.* I shook my head, hoping to clear whatever was going on in there.

The second bite went down smoothly, and I relaxed. But every now and then I caught a brief trace of it. It was almost like I was tasting Sophie's perfume. *Must be some weird scent-taste-association thing happening.*

Conversation ebbed and flowed around me, with everyone keeping pretty much the same pace. Mrs. M. was a little on the quiet side, but I think I was the only one who noticed. Eventually, the evening wore on, and Sophie and Kame were the first to say they needed to be going.

Sophie came over to Mrs. M., and they shook hands before she slipped Mrs. M. her card. "I know that you said you're not ready to think about anything permanent yet, but when you are, call me. I'll make sure you get top dollar for your house."

Mrs. M. dutifully took the card and murmured a polite thank-you. I wanted to shake my head in pity for Sophie. She wasn't going to get a sale out of the Maxwells. They'd *never* move away from Sleepy Hollow.

Dad and Kame were standing nearby, discussing a baseball game, and I heard Dad say, "So, Kame. That's an unusual name. Family heritage?"

Kame looked over at me before he answered. "Yes. I guess you could say it runs in the family."

Dad shrugged and then clapped him on the shoulder. Suddenly, Sophie appeared next to me, and Kame was right behind her. It kind of surprised me how fast he got away from Dad.

"We're so glad we had a chance to meet you, Abbey," Sophie said, her voice melodic and beautiful. She didn't try to shake my hand again, and I was *extremely* grateful for that. She did, however, keep her gaze directly on me. Kame did the same, and

I felt a prickle of unease run up my spine. It was ... weird and uncomfortable to have them both staring at me.

"Um, yeah," I said finally, taking a small step back. "Nice to meet you, too. Good luck with your new real-estate branch and all that."

Sophie's gaze sharpened, and Kame smiled widely, revealing a surprisingly shiny and sharp-looking set of teeth. "Take care of yourself, Abbey," he said. "Take very good care."

*Chapter Twenty*

# THE MISSING PIECE

And besides, what chance was there of escaping ghost or goblin, if such it was, which could ride upon the wings of the wind?

—"The Legend of Sleepy Hollow"

O ne week later I was sitting in front of my new laptop, working on my business plan. Scribbling down sentences that would hopefully be a part of my mission statement, I let my mind wander. It kept going back to that strange dinner with the real estate agents. I tried to figure out why they seemed so familiar. Had I seen them at the bridge dedication ceremony?

My cell phone rang, and I reached for it, glad for the distraction. "Hello?"

"Abbey? Is this Abbey?"

I didn't recognize the voice. "Yes, who's—"

"It's Aubra Stanton."

You could have knocked me over with a feather. "Um, okay." Or a stiff breeze.

"I got your number from your uncle's office."

"Okay." Gee, I was being a real conversationalist here.

"Look, I need you to come cover the store for an hour."

"But it's Saturday night. I don't work on Saturdays."

Aubra exhaled loudly. "I *know* that, okay? I just need you to come in because I have to go take care of something. Your uncle's not here. He had to go get another part for the freezer."

My thumb moved back and forth over the volume button on the phone. "I'm not sure I can, Aubra. I'll have to ask my Mom for a ride." I felt lame for telling her that, but it was true.

"Please, Abbey?"

Something in her voice tugged at my heart strings. *Push-over.* "I'll try."

She hung up without saying thank you or good-bye, and I sighed. So much for a little gratitude.


Mom dropped me off at Uncle Bob's with fairly little talk along the way, and Aubra was waiting for me by the door.

"Finally!" she exclaimed, the instant I stepped inside. I just looked at her with a raised eyebrow. She ignored it and paced nervously in front of the door, stopping every now and then to peer out of it. I moved toward the counter and grabbed a wet washcloth to wipe up some spilled caramel sauce she'd *obviously* overlooked.

A minute later I heard the doorbells chime, and she was gone. Without saying good-bye. *Again.*

Luckily, the shop stayed pretty quiet, and everyone was patient with me as I slowly worked the register. When there was only half an hour until the shop closed, I kept busy by refilling the toppings jars.

Aubra came back twenty-eight minutes later, not that I was counting or anything, and completely ignored me. Her eyes were red and splotchy, but I wasn't going to give her the pity vote again.

"All right, see ya," I said. "I'm leaving now." She didn't reply, so I headed outside to call Mom and tell her I was ready.

Mom was busy with something, though, and said she'd pick me up as soon as she could. I let out a breath as I hung up, not exactly loving my situation. I walked around the store and went to the alley out back.

It was nice at first, to just sit there and chill in a quiet spot. But then I started to realize how secluded the alley *really* was. A security light sprouted from the middle of the cement wall that was opposite the back of the store, but the light only illuminated a few feet in either direction. I didn't know who, or *what*, could be lurking at the end of the alleyway.

Of course, that was when I started hearing strange noises and seeing things move out of the corner of my eye. I had to laugh at myself when a rat scampered by. "Chill, Abbey," I said out loud.

Pulling out my phone, I lamented the fact that Caspian didn't have one, then scrolled through the games section. I was busy pushing buttons and kicking ass on Tetris when a shadow loomed over me. I looked up.

And then wished I hadn't.

"Hello, Abbey," Vincent said.

I gritted my teeth and forced out a hello before returning to my game. He sat down next to me on the table and bumped his knee into mine. I shifted away from him, and he crowded further into my space.

With exaggerated slowness, I moved farther away from him. His perfect white teeth glowed in the light as he smiled. "Don't be like that," he purred, then he pitched his voice low. "Or rather, *do* be like that. It excites me."

I stopped what I was doing and stared at him. What was his *deal*? Why did he have to be such an asshole?

"I can tell what you're thinking," he said. "You want me."

I made a disgusted sound. "*Please*. I'm taken. Besides, don't you already have a girlfriend?" I gestured toward the shop. "Aubra?"

Vincent sighed, an elegant sound, and looked pained. "I'm getting tired of her. She's becoming a bore." Then he and cocked his head. "Besides, maybe I'm looking for a piece on the side."

"Yeah, well, it's not gonna be me." I stood up and moved away from him to the front of the alley, only noticing then that a black Ford Mustang was blocking the entrance. His footsteps echoed behind me, and with every step I took, they followed.

Panic started curling the edges of my stomach. Whirling around to face him, I planted a fist on my hip. "What's your problem? Go toy with someone else."

He stepped close, and I resisted the urge to shrink back.

"I will *toy* with *you* when and *how* I *want*," he said. His voice was cold . . . and deadly. I knew that this was no game. His face transformed from a perfect mask to seething rage. He gripped my cheeks in one hand, his fingers digging in harshly.

*Please, please,* my mind was whimpering, *don't hurt me.* I bit down on my tongue to keep myself from crying out.

His free hand grabbed my left wrist and shackled it like iron. Vincent's touch made my skin crawl, and I glanced down to see if the flesh was actually starting to curl up and peel away like it so desperately wanted to.

Running one fingernail down my wrist all the way across my open palm, he pressed cruelly and left a deep red scratch in his wake. I tried to put steel in my gaze, but was quickly losing the battle. My hand burned like fire and my mind was still whimpering.

The severity of my situation slammed into me. We were alone. In a dark, dirty alley. No one knew where I was, and no one would come if I screamed. My mind switched gears from *Please, please don't hurt me* to *Please, please let me get through this.*

"Tell me how you are taken," Vincent said suddenly.

My mouth refused to open, my lips clamped shut.

"A boyfriend?" he asked. I nodded mutely, willing the tears not to fall. "I see." He let go of my face.

But I could still feel his finger marks, like brands, on my skin.

He brightened, and flashed a smile at me. "Wonderful, wonderful." As if realizing what he'd done to my hand, he looked down. "My apologies." Bending low, he kissed the scratch mark, and I closed my eyes. I was going to be sick.

Vincent released my arm and straightened, putting one hand to his head like he was tipping an imaginary hat. "My lady." Then he turned and sauntered down the alley, whistling as he got into his car.

I stood there, lost for a moment, as it thundered away. Trying to tell myself that he was really gone . . . I was really okay. . . . And that was when my stomach rebelled. Huddling over a section of yesterday's trash and old cardboard boxes, I couldn't hold it back anymore. Wave after wave of fear and loathing washed over me, and I retched.

I'd only been home for an hour at the end of another long shift on Monday when the second call came. Caspian was sitting nearby on the window seat, feet swinging back and forth, and I was testing some new perfume formulas. I glanced over my shoulder. The phone was on the bed.

"I'll get it," Caspian said, hopping down and reaching it in two long steps. A second later he dropped it next to me.

"Thanks." I smiled up at him and opened the phone.

"Abbey, this is Aubra."

*Oh, no.* My heart sank. I couldn't cover for her again.

"It's over!" she screamed, and I held the phone away from my ear. "I'm finally going to tell that bastard it's over!"

"Okay . . . ," I said.

"I need you to—"

I cut her off before she could finish. "No, Aubra. Sorry."

Her voice turned hysterical. "I *need* you to, Abbey! You don't understand what he's done to me. This is the only way. I can't keep letting him control me like this." She was breathing heavily, and I could hear a note of panic in her voice.

"I have to . . . I have to . . . ," she babbled. "Or else . . . Or I'm going to do something else. I'll end it. I have to."

I sat up straight. "Aubra, what are you saying? You're not going to do anything to yourself, are you?"

She stayed silent, and I had a terrible feeling that was *exactly* what she was saying. I shot a worried look at Caspian, and he made a *What's happening?* gesture. "I'll be right there, Aubra," I said. "You hear me? Give me twenty minutes."

I hung up the phone, and all my nerve endings suddenly came alive. I had to get Mom. I had to hurry and get there. I had to make sure Vincent didn't hurt her. I had to make sure *she* didn't hurt herself.

"I have to go, Caspian. That was the girl from school I work with. She's breaking up with this guy tonight, and I want to make sure she doesn't do anything crazy. She didn't sound right." I rubbed at my left palm. It was burning.

Caspian's face grew concerned. "Will she be okay?"

"I think so."

He looked down. "Hey. Stop. Stop that, Abbey. You're rubbing your hand raw."

I looked down too and saw the red scratch from Vincent standing out in vivid relief on my pale skin. Quickly turning my hand over, I pressed my palm against my leg. I'd been trying to hide that from him.

"What happened?" Caspian asked, his eyebrows arching downward into a frown. "Let me see."

"It's nothing. I just scratched it when I was outside. I have to go. I'm sorry. Can you come by later? Or I can come to you?"

He shrugged, but I turned away from him, grabbing for my phone. I didn't have time for mood swings right now.

"I'm sorry to ditch you," I said again. "Please, wait for me?"

He nodded. "I'll be here."

I blew him a kiss before heading to the stairs, calling for Mom as I went.

When I got to the store, Aubra looked *awful*. Her hair was a mess, and mascara streaked down both cheeks. The store was empty except for a couple finishing their cones, and I grabbed her hand to haul her to the back. "Are you okay? Did he hurt you?"

Aubra gazed at me and sniffled, her eyes wide and glassy. For a moment I thought she was on something.

"Hurt me?" she said woodenly. "He broke my heart, the bastard!" She let out a scream, and I tugged on her arm.

"Aubra! Calm down. There are customers out there." She shut her mouth and looked at me sullenly. "Now, I'm going to ask you some questions. Just shake your head yes or no. Has Vincent been here tonight?"

*No.*

"Is he supposed to come by tonight?"

*Yes.*

"Have you taken anything? Any drugs or pills?"

Silence. Then, "I took a Xanax that I had in my purse. It was my mom's."

That explained the outburst and glassy eyes. "Just *one*?"

*Yes.*

"Do you have any more?"

*No.*

"Good. Okay, listen. I'm going to go out front, and when Vincent gets here, I'll come get you. You can talk to him inside the store. We'll make the customers leave, or put out the CLOSED sign or something. But I'll be here with you. You won't have to face him alone. Okay?"

*Yes.*

I looked around at the freezer room we were in. There didn't seem to be anything she could hurt herself on if she started freaking out again, so I felt relatively comfortable leaving her there. I spotted a wooden chair resting in one corner of the room and dragged it over to us. "You sit here and *wait for me*. Do you want some ice cream?"

Aubra sat in the chair and crossed her arms. "Pistachio."

"Coming right up." I hurried out to the counter, where I grabbed a scooper, loaded up a small cup with the green ice cream, and swiped a spoon from the plastic dispenser. Aubra was still sitting calmly when I returned, and she took the ice cream from me without a word.

I resisted the urge to pat her on the head and tell her to be good as I left the room, and then let out an exhausted sigh when I headed back out front. *What have I done to deserve this headache?* Whatever it was, I sure hoped my good-deed karma was racking up the bonus points.

Vincent never showed up, and I stayed to help Aubra close. We both worked in silence. The tables were really messy, so I decided to put some space between us and grabbed a spray bottle to go wipe them down. Then I glanced out the front window.

Caspian's face was pressed against the glass.

"I'll, uh, be right back," I called over my shoulder to Aubra.

"I need to get some fresh air." I bolted through the door and gestured for Caspian to follow me around back.

"What are you *doing*?" I hissed, facing him. "Not that I'm not happy to see you and all, but how did you get here?"

"I walked."

"You . . . *walked*?"

"Yeah. You know, when you move your legs?"

I made an exasperated noise. "I *know* what walking is. I mean, *why* are you here?"

"I was worried about you. That phone call sounded serious, and that scratch on your hand . . ." He reached out to grab my palm and then drew back. "I just wanted to make sure you were safe."

I tried to keep a stern face on the outside, but on the inside my heart was melting. "I'm fine. Aubra's okay. And the jerk didn't even show up." I took a step closer and peeked up at him. Uncle Bob's store was close to an hour's walk away from home. "You really walked all the way here just to make sure I was safe?"

He ran his fingers through his hair, almost looking bashful, but his gaze was solemn and steady. "I'd go anywhere to find you."

My heart somersaulted and then melted in a puddle at my feet. I gazed at him with a sappy smile. "My protector."

His face fell. "Of sorts."

Suddenly, I remembered Aubra. "I have to get back in. I don't want to leave her alone for too long."

Caspian nodded. "I'll wait for your mom to pick you up before I leave."

"Leave? As in, you're going to walk back home?"

"Yes."

"Um, no. You'll ride back with us."

He opened his mouth to protest, but I shook my head at him. "I'll be more worried about you if you walk home, and you wouldn't want that, would you? Put my mind at ease, okay?"

He grinned. "Okay. You twisted my arm."

"That's why they call me the arm twister," I said. "At least it's better than the alternative, though."

"What's the alternative?" he asked.

"A ball buster."

Caspian looked shocked that I had said such a thing, and I laughed at the expression on his face. I led him back to the store, and he stopped short to take up a watchful stance at the door. Aubra had everything turned off and shut down when I walked in.

"Do you want me to ask my mom to drop you off at home? We can come back later for your car," I said to her.

"Why would you do that?" she asked.

"Because I'm not sure you should be driving after taking a Xanax."

"Me?" She scoffed. "I've taken them before. They don't affect me like that."

*Whatever.* I wasn't going to push her. I had to set my limits somewhere. "Are you still going to break up with Vincent?" I asked instead.

She tossed her head. "I texted him like an hour ago and told him it was over. He never responded. Drake's such an asshole."

My head snapped up. "*Drake*? I thought you were with Vincent?"

Aubra looked at me like I was slow. "*Vincent* Drake. Everyone calls him Drake."

Instantly, an icy sensation filled me. It couldn't be. There was no way. Kristen would never fall for a jerk like him.

A horn honked outside, and I looked up to see Mom's van in the parking lot. Functioning on autopilot, I barely remembered to slide the back door open to let Caspian in. Mom gave me a weird look, but I told her some lame excuse about checking to see if I had my bag in the car or if I'd left it in the store, and she seemed to buy it. With Caspian safely inside the van, I shut the door and then climbed into the passenger seat.

I waited until Mom was all the way in the house before talking to Caspian.

"Do you want me to stay?" he said. "I can."

I wanted him to . . . I didn't want him to . . . I was so confused by everything. "I don't know. . . ."

"It's okay. No pressure. If you want to talk about Aubra, you know where to find me."

I gave him a half smile. "Thanks for coming to check on me."

"I'll always be there," he promised, walking out into the darkness.

"I know you will," I whispered to his retreating form.

In my bed that night I rolled back and forth, trying to find a comfortable position. Tossing one arm above my head, I counted sheep and went through the names of all the vice presidents. Twice. But nothing was working. I couldn't sleep.

I thought for sure I'd drift off and have nightmares about Kristen. But I wasn't dreaming at all, because I wasn't sleeping at all. A fact that became all too evident with every half hour that passed on the clock.

By two thirty I gave up. It was useless to stay in bed any longer.

Sitting by the window, I mulled everything over. Moonlight streamed around me and turned my arms and hands silvery gray. Back and forth I went, worrying the subject like a dog with a bone. *Is Vincent Kristen's D.? Why else would he tell me a different name? And how did they meet?*

It didn't make any sense. No matter how hard I tried, I just couldn't picture *him* being the secret boyfriend Kristen had lied to me about.

I sat there for another hour, not even realizing it until I looked at the clock again. "Screw this," I muttered. I had to go talk to Caspian. My head was going to explode if I kept it all jumbled up in there much longer.

I donned jeans and sneakers, zipped up a hoodie over my tank top, and climbed out the window. After dropping carefully to the ground, I pulled the hood up over my hair and shoved my hands into my pockets. The streets were quiet, and I kept my head down as I walked, contemplating how best to tell Caspian about Vincent. *I hope he's in his mausoleum and not roaming again. We really need to work out some kind of system for how I can find him at times like these.*

Headlights shone at my back as I walked up the hill to the cemetery, and I turned around for a split second. The lights blinded me, and I kept walking, willing the car to hurry up and pass. Instead it slowed down and kept a steady distance.

Just when I was about to turn around again, it veered off onto a side street. My heart thumped erratically, and I waited to see if the car would come back.

It didn't.

Hurrying to the cemetery, I crossed the street to slip in by the main gates. As I was squeezing through, I heard the sound of a car approaching. Flattening myself on the inside of the cemetery gate wall, I held my breath. Something told me that it was the same car that had followed me, and I had a sinking suspicion as to who was in it.

Taking a chance, I poked my head around the gate and saw a black Ford Mustang cruise by. Under the streetlights I could make out the dark hair of the driver. His left arm was hanging out the open window. *Vincent.*

I slammed back around. *Did he recognize me? Did he see me enter the cemetery?*

Palms pressed tight against the wall at my back, I tipped my head and looked up at the night sky. It was completely black. No stars were out, and fear stole over me. A fear like I'd never known before.

The darkness closed in on me, encroaching on my personal space. The misshapen tombstones and gnarled tree branches were grotesque, beckoning me to come closer . . . or stay away.

I imagined that this must have been how Ichabod Crane felt, passing by the cemetery and seeing that fateful bridge. If I were able to look over the high cemetery wall, I'd see that ominous covered bridge waiting for me too.

My breath started coming faster and faster. Deep gasps and painful hitches pulled at my chest and raked my sides. *What was that?* I strained my ears. *Footsteps? Hoofbeats?* Behind closed eyelids I saw fiery breath, a missing head, eyes that glowed red in the dark, and—

And then I opened my eyes.

There was nothing out there. No footsteps. No menacing horseman. Nothing coming after me.

I eased my grip on the wall, and my body relaxed. The cemetery changed back into a peaceful resting place, and the moon came out of hiding, revealing the path in front of me. Clear and unobstructed.

I took a deliberate step away from the wall. And then another. All I had to do was make it to Caspian. And if he wasn't there, I'd go find Nikolas and Katy.

My feet knew the way, and I walked quickly. It was surprisingly cool for an almost-end-of-July night, and a shiver went up my neck. I turned for a second to make sure the shiver wasn't there for any *other* reason, but the cemetery was empty.

I was almost there when I heard it.

A faint *clink*. Metal against stone.

I stopped.

The clink turned to a scratching noise. Someone started whistling.

Turning slowly, I saw a grinning Vincent coming up the path below me, from the Old Dutch Church section. He must have parked his car at the church down there.

The clinking and scratching continued. *Paused*. Continued.

He was walking past a row of tombstones, and in his out-stretched hand was a set of keys. With each stone he passed, he set the keys to granite, dragging them slowly across the surface.

The sound set my teeth on edge. So did the whistling.

I took a step toward my destination, *away* from him, and he kept advancing until we were in this bizarre advance-retreat dance. Glancing over my shoulder, I saw that Caspian's crypt was only a couple of feet away. I prayed for his Spidey senses to start tingling.

Vincent wagged a finger at me like I was a naughty child. "Now, now, now. What are you doing in a cemetery at night, Abbey? Talking to the graves?" He struck a mock prayer pose and clasped his hands together piously. "Or are you visiting a dearly departed friend?"

Rage welled up inside of me, momentarily pushing aside the fear. "What do you know about that, you bastard?"

Vincent laughed. "*Spicy.* I didn't think you had it in you." He looked me up and down. "No, I *really* didn't think you had it in you. Then again, redheads are more my type." He licked his lips slowly and smiled.

"So it was you!" I said. "You were Kristen's secret boyfriend!"

"*Boyfriend.*" He shook his head like he was amused.

"What did you do to her?" I exploded. I didn't care who heard me. "She loved you, and you took advantage of her!"

He spread his hands wide. "I didn't take anything she didn't freely offer."

"Bullshit."

He stepped close, and I flinched involuntarily, remembering the last time. He smiled a beautiful smile, then grabbed my wrist and flipped it, palm side up. "My mark. You still have it. That makes me happy."

I yanked my hand out of his grip.

Studying me carefully, he said, "You know, you and I . . . well, I wouldn't go as far as to say that we're *alike*, because we're not. . . . But we do have . . . common interests, shall I say? We're both connoisseurs. Collectors."

Vincent held up a finger. "*You* collect scents. Oh yes, I know all about you. And me?" His face grew sublime. "I collect noises."

My eyes flickered over to the mausoleum door. Was it my imagination? Or did it move a little? "Noises?" I said.

"Oh, yes. There are any manner of noises that one might *think* would be the ones to collect. The soft coo of a happy baby." He looked disgusted. "Or the satisfied grunt of a man who has just had a beer and a babe brought to him at some local titty bar."

The door moved a little more. I was sure of it.

"Are you *list*-ening, *Ab*-bey?" Vincent jerked on my arm, and I nodded, trying not to cry out. "Good. Now, sounds. Did you know that the female body makes a certain sigh—a gasp, an intake of breath—when it is entered?"

I drew back from him, horrified.

He looked blissful and dreamy. "It is especially so the first time. An involuntary reversal of noise." His eyes turned cold. "Your friend, Kristen? She made the *best* noise." He leaned over to whisper in my ear. "De-licious."

Without even thinking about it, I hit him.

The slapping sound echoed off the tombstones, surrounding

us. We were both clearly shocked by my behavior, but I found my voice first. "How do you like *that* noise?"

An instant later the door behind us scraped full force and opened wide.

"Let her go," Caspian ordered in a deadly voice. I knew it wouldn't do any good—Vincent couldn't hear him—but I'd never been so happy to see someone in my whole life.

Then I saw the large chunk of marble in his hand.

"Did he hurt you?" Caspian asked me. I was too shocked by what he might do to answer. "Did. He. *Hurt. You.*" Caspian said again. I shook my head no, but he advanced anyway.

Vincent licked his lips and stared me down. "Like I said, I didn't think you had it in you."

"I have a lot more than that in me," I retorted.

"This is D., I presume?" Caspian asked, standing directly behind him now.

I nodded. "You were there that night, weren't you, Vincent?" I said. This might be the only chance I had to get answers, and I didn't want to waste it.

He looked angry, and then his face smoothed over. "I see now that Kristen was a mistake. The wrong one for me."

"So what, you led her on and then lured her to the bridge to finish her off? Did you push her in? Did you leave her there to die, all alone?" I had to know. The need to find out was ferocious.

He shook his head and put up his hands in a gesture of surrender. "I came back to see her. Things ended . . . badly. Is it *my* fault she slipped?"

"It *is* your fault if you broke her heart and left her there to cry. It *is* your fault if you saw her slip in after she reached for you and begged you to come back. It *is* your fault if you turned away and did nothing."

Murderous rage seeped through me, and I thought, just for the tiniest of moments, about letting Caspian hit him in the head with that stone. To let him bash Vincent's head against that rock so he could feel what Kristen felt. "If you did *any* of those things . . . then you're a murderer."

Vincent's eyes filled with an unholy fury, but his voice was calm. "Such accusations, Abbey. You have no idea if any of them are true."

I took a step toward him. "I *know* you did those things."

"Careful, Abbey," Caspian warned. "Don't get too close."

"He *killed* her, Caspian! He was the reason she was at the bridge that night."

"I know, but—"

Vincent suddenly turned to face Caspian. "Could you just

shut up? All this back and forth is really confusing. I'll get to you in a minute."

Caspian's jaw dropped open.

So did mine.

"You can *see* him?" I asked. "Who *are* you?"

"Not *who*," Vincent said, a tone of sheer entitlement in his voice. "*What*."

*Chapter Twenty-one*

# THE REVENANT

This is perhaps the reason why we so seldom hear of ghosts except in our long-established Dutch communities.

—"The Legend of Sleepy Hollow"

"I'm a Revenant," Vincent said.

"A what?"

"A *Rev-e-nant*," he repeated the word slowly, breaking up the three syllables. "What, you've never heard of me? I'm hurt."

Caspian came to stand beside me, and Vincent eyed him coldly. "I wouldn't get any ideas if I were you."

"I don't have *ideas*," Caspian replied. "I have plans."

Vincent's face changed, almost faster than I could tell what was happening, and it was like looking at a rapidly flickering movie screen. His features pulsed and faded, as if they were being broadcast across a blank canvas. He reached across me in the same instant, grabbing Caspian by the throat. "You may be dead, but that doesn't mean I can't hurt you."

Vincent lifted Caspian off his feet and tossed him against the mausoleum door like a rag doll. He hit with a sickening crack and slid to the ground. His eyes were closed.

I screamed, clenching my fists in panic.

"Interesting," Vincent said.

I tried to push past him, tried to rush over to Caspian, but he grabbed my shoulder and held on tight.

"Let me go you, bastard!" I yelled. "Oh God, if you hurt him . . ."

"What do you think I was *trying* to do?"

A sob escaped me, and Vincent looked around. "Unfortunately, now is not the time or place. But I will *take* what is *mine*."

I raised my hand to slap him again, and he thrust me aside. "I'll be seeing you, Abbey."

And with that, he turned his back and walked away.

My vision went blurry, and I realized I was crying. My legs gave out. I tried to stand, but they wouldn't work, so I had to crawl over to where Caspian was lying.

"Caspian," I whispered; my throat was raw and sore. "Casper . . . please. Open your eyes."

He didn't answer.

I touched his shoulder, but my hand went through to the ground. I tried again, and again, then pounded my fist against the grass in frustration. "Caspian!" I prayed to every god that was out there for him to please open his eyes.

Rocking back on my heels, I felt a keening moan erupt from inside of me. This wasn't supposed to happen. We were supposed to be together. It wasn't supposed to be like *this*.

"Abbey," I heard him say. "Abbey ..."

My eyes were blurry again with streaming tears.

"Caspian! Are you okay? Oh my God, I thought you were ... I didn't know what I thought. Just something bad." I couldn't help myself—I tried to touch his face and hit solid ground again.

He gazed up at me, looking like a fish out of water. "I'm okay ... just knocked the nonexistent breath out of me." He closed his eyes and murmured, "I think I slipped into the dark place."

"Don't go there again," I pleaded. "Okay?"

His eyes opened, and I could see their brilliant green reflecting back at me. "I won't," he promised. "Just let me close my eyes for a couple of minutes."

I nodded, and when I thought ten minutes had passed, I whispered, "Caspian."

I didn't think he'd heard me. But then his eyes opened and flickered to mine. "I'm here. I didn't go to the dark place."

"Good. I would have followed you there."

He looked startled by my statement, and after a moment of silence, cleared his throat. "Let's see if everything is in working order." He tried to stand and almost fell, but caught himself against the door. I clenched my fists. It was *so* hard not to be able to help him. But he managed on his own, and even cracked a grin at me. "I'm fine. Still dead."

"Don't say that."

"Why? It's the truth."

"I know, but . . . still." I scowled. "I don't need the reminder right now, okay?"

He fell silent and looked around us.

"He's gone," I said, answering his unasked question. "But I think we need to take a trip to go see Nikolas and Katy and tell them what just happened."

He nodded his agreement, and I stood too. Then we turned toward the path that led to their house.

It took us a while to get there, though, because the woods were dark, and it was tricky finding our way. When we finally made it, I led the way to their door and knocked loudly in case they were still asleep.

Nikolas answered right away, dressed in his usual overalls. "Abbey?" He cast a glance behind me at Caspian.

"I'm sorry it's so early, Nikolas. But we need to talk to you."

He waved a hand. "We are early risers. Is something the matter?"

"What's a Revenant?" I asked.

Nikolas paled and gestured for us to come in, scanning the woods behind us as he shut the door. Katy was sitting in the rocking chair by the fireplace, but rose when she saw us. I nodded my head at her, suddenly tired and overwhelmed and not in the mood for pleasantries.

After I introduced Caspian to her, we all sat down at the kitchen table, and I waited for Nikolas to explain. He stalled.

"How are you doing, Abbey? Would you like some tea? We could make some tea if you'd like."

I banged my fist on the table. "Answers, Nikolas! I need answers."

He looked shocked by my outburst, and I sighed loudly. "I'm sorry, but I've been up all night, my best friend's maybe-murderer followed me to the cemetery and almost attacked me, and then he threw Caspian into a mausoleum door. So, what's a Revenant, and how come you told me to pay attention because it might save my life, Nikolas?"

Nikolas and Katy exchanged a glance, and then suddenly Nikolas stood up, moving to the window. "This person who attacked you, he called himself a Revenant?" Nikolas addressed his question to the window and didn't look at me.

"Yes."

"What did he look like to you?" Nikolas asked.

"Black hair, blue eyes, expensive clothes, and a snotty attitude." A sour taste filled my mouth. "There was always something about him that got on my nerves. Even from the first time I met him, last year at my uncle's store."

"Did he have a particular scent? Or a beautiful voice?" Nikolas said, finally turning away from the window to face me.

"No, he . . ." My voice died, and Caspian gave me a questioning look. I was suddenly flooded with an overload of images. Melodic voices, and the taste of ash on my tongue. It was like I was remembering things I didn't even know I'd forgotten. "Wait. It's like . . ." I struggled for the words. "I'm remembering these strange people I've met. Twice, this guy and girl talked to me, and they had beautiful voices that sounded like music. And clear eyes. It was almost like looking into glass. I think the girl had blond hair. The guy had his dyed black. Before they left the first time, I smelled something burning. Like leaves. The second time, I tasted ash on my tongue."

I looked at Nikolas, confused as to why these memories were surfacing.

Nikolas returned to the table. "Is there anything else you can remember? This is very important, Abigail."

For some reason the slip of my proper name bothered me. It struck a serious chord, and I frowned. "There were these two people that came over for dinner the other night. They said they were real estate agents, new in town. The woman had red hair that I kept thinking was originally blond. And when she walked by me, she had on this strange perfume that smelled like ash. I thought dinner was burned or something, because I kept smelling it." I glanced at Caspian. "The man had a strange name."

"Kame?" Nikolas asked.

"Yes, how did you know that?"

Nikolas and Katy exchanged another worried glance, and I gripped the table edge as fear washed over me. "Guys, what's going on?"

"You are *very* certain that the first two strangers and the second two strangers you met were different people?" Katy asked.

I thought about it for a minute then said, "I'm sure. The first two, Cacey and Uri, were my age, and the other two, Kame and Sophie, were closer to my parents' age. And then there's Vincent Drake. He's the one who *told* me he was a Revenant." I looked back and forth between them. "Are they all . . . the same thing?"

Katy nodded, and Nikolas's eyes looked worried.

Leaning forward, I said to Nikolas, "Please tell me. What *is* a Revenant?"

He locked eyes with Katy. "A Revenant is sent to help the living half cross over to the Shade half. Caspian is dead, yet he's here, because he is a Shade. A shadow caught between two worlds. The black stripe is the brand that marks him as this. Did you have a near-death experience?" he asked Caspian. "Before your actual death."

Caspian nodded.

"That is when the mark came. You were destined to be one of us. I had a near-death experience of my own." He turned to look at me. "You are his other half, his living half. His partner and companion. Attuned to his frequency, in a sense, and destined to fill the missing piece of his soul." Nikolas rested his hand on top of Katy's, smiling lovingly at her. "A soul mate."

I gulped and peeked over at Caspian. He had his hands spread wide on the tabletop and was staring down at them.

Nikolas resumed talking. "Katy and I have been completed. We call it, in the Dutch language, *een koppeling*. A coupling. That is why we are here at this place. What happens when you and Caspian are completed . . . I cannot say."

Thoughts were slowing arranging themselves in my brain, and I started to put them together. "So all this living half and dead half, and crossing-over stuff . . . Are you saying . . . ?"

Katy looked at me and nodded. "You are going to die soon, Abbey."

The room grew very still, and everyone waited, all eyes on me. I let out a breath I didn't even know I'd been holding. "Oh."

"I am sorry we did not tell you before, when you came to see us," she said. "How does one bring up the nearness of death? But once the Revenants find you, a choice must be made. They found me a year after Nikolas and I had met. We both thought that perhaps it would be longer for you."

"That's why I urged you to reconsider," said Nikolas. "To stay away from Caspian. To pay attention to what I could not say, in a desperate hope that it would save your life."

"You *told* her to stay away from me?" Caspian asked.

Nikolas gave him a hard look. "Have you even seen two sides of a whole? There is usually a dark half and a light half. Now, between Katy and me, I know that I am the darker half. I have much blood upon these hands as a soldier for hire in my past life, and I'm betting that between you and Abbey, *she* is the light one. So what dark secrets do you hold, boy?"

Caspian looked angry. "Did you ever think that things might have changed? We don't live and die by the sword anymore. I may not *have* a lifetime of darkness to atone for. Maybe I just need her to be the star in my night sky. To hold back the darkness and to let me see the light." He looked at me then, and my throat went dry. "Or maybe it really is as simple as something in her fills the hollow in me. The black void disappears when we are together."

I linked my hands together and stared down at them, in awe of what he'd just said. His words filled my heart until all the cracks that had once been there were gone.

"If that is what she means to you, then you are the one," Nikolas said. "And I extend my hand."

I looked up in time to see them shaking solemnly, and I mouthed the words *I love you* to Caspian. He smiled his breathtaking smile at me, and my toes went numb.

Nikolas cleared his throat, and I blushed, realizing that my feelings were probably written all over my face.

"Okay," Caspian said, directing us back to the topic at hand. "So now we know why the Revenants are here."

"Actually, that is the problem," Nikolas replied. A fretful look was back on his face. "Revenants don't work alone. They are paired into teams of two, and only one team is needed."

"So when Katy . . . passed, and the Revenants were here, there were only two of them?" I asked.

"Yes."

"Why are there five of them now?" said Caspian.

"We don't know," Katy replied.

"Tell me more about this Vincent Drake," Nikolas asked me. "He was aggressive toward you?"

"Yeah, he was." I remembered that moment in the alley, and I shivered. "And he grabbed Caspian by the throat and threw him."

Nikolas shook his head. "That does not make any sense. Revenants help, not harm. This is a troublesome situation. I am fearful of what it means."

"It means that I'm going to die soon, *you* don't know what's going to happen to me and Caspian once I die and we're completed or whatever, and the Revenants may or may not be here to cause that death!" Everything suddenly felt like it was crashing down on me, and I buried my head in my arms.

"I think Abbey should go home and get some rest," Caspian said.

"I'm fine," I mumbled.

"No, you're not. You need to get some sleep and have some time to process this."

I lifted my head. "Hey, I know! We can go on the run. Leave town. If we stay away long enough, maybe Vincent and the Revenants will leave."

"They will find you, Abbey," Katy said. "It may take a month, it may take a year, but in the end it's only a matter of time."

"So is it like a bloodhound thing?" I asked. "They have my scent now?"

"Something like that," Nikolas said. "We are not certain of everything."

I laughed, and even I could hear the note of hysteria in my voice. "All I should have to do then is change my perfume. Ha! Great."

Caspian stood up abruptly. "Let's go."

He gave me a stern glare, and I reluctantly stood up too. "I could just stay here," I argued. "I'd be safe here."

"Home. Bed. *Now*," Caspian ordered.

"Okay, okay. It was just a suggestion. Geez."

He ushered me out of the house, and we found ourselves back on the path. I let him take the lead, and he did a good job of getting us back to the cemetery without any wrong turns into the forest.

It was almost dawn now, and we walked silently back

toward the main gate. Once we hit the path that would lead us there, Caspian stopped. "I want to show you something."

"Can it wait?" I was frazzled, full of raw edges and nervous energy. I really just wanted to get home and crash.

"It won't take long," he promised. "But you need to see this."

He turned to lead me to the side of the cemetery that I hardly ever went to. When we came to a stop, we were standing in front of two extremely old, faded red headstones. They were the type to have elaborate winged skulls and angels dressed as the Grim Reaper on them.

Or they would have, if they were still intact.

Now they were completely shattered. The fronts of them nothing more than cracked, bleeding stone. Carved names and dates were lost forever to time. I gasped as the sun rose, revealing the full extent of the damage. It was a horrible sight.

"I don't want there to be anything between us," Caspian said. "Do you remember when I told you about how I was angry and destructive?"

I nodded.

"I did this," he said quietly. "On my first day here, I was so frustrated, so mad that no one could hear me, I picked up a rock and threw it at them again and again. Smashing them to pieces so they'd be broken and unrecognizable . . . like me."

I gazed at him in disbelief. It didn't seem right. It didn't seem like him at all. "I heard about some tombstones being vandalized, but they said some kids did it."

Caspian shook his head sadly. "Not kids. *Me*. And I come here every once in a while to remind myself of it."

He held my gaze, and his eyes were highlighted by the sun. They were so vivid.

"This is what I always have to remember, Abbey." He flexed his hands and looked at them. "I might be invisible, but I can still touch things . . . *hurt* people." He looked away and mumbled, "Hurt *you*."

A sick feeling started roiling in my stomach, and I knew where he was going with this. Crossing my arms, I shook my head. "Oh, no. You are *not* doing this again, Caspian."

He looked at me with pained eyes, and I stalked closer, jabbing the air in front of him with one finger. "You broke my heart once before, during Christmas, with that I-just-want-to-be-friends note. You are *not* doing that again."

"It's better this way—"

"I'm not listening to you, and I'm going home now," I said.

He suddenly bent down to pick up a dead leaf from the

ground and held it out to me. Slowly closing his hand, he crushed the leaf. It crunched between his fingers, and when he opened his fist, only a pile of dust remained. "This is me. Dust. Ashes. I'm dead, and you have to face that."

Frustration and fury bubbled up in me, and I had to fight to keep a cool tone. "You know what? I *will* face that. Where are you buried?"

He blinked once. "What?"

"*Where* are you *buried*? I'm going to face it. I'm going to visit your grave."

"Why?" he whispered.

I leaned in, close enough for a kiss, and whispered back, "Because I love you, Caspian. I *love* you. I'll do whatever it takes to be with you." I held up my left hand. The red scratch that Vincent had given me was still clearly visible. I should have realized there was something more—*he* was something more— when he gave it to me. "And because I don't want any secrets between us either, I have to tell you something. I lied to you about this. About how I got it. Vincent scratched me when he stopped by my uncle's shop."

Caspian's face turned dark with fury, and for a second I thought he was mad at me for lying to him. "I am going to return the favor," he said, between gritted teeth. "Times ten."

He put out one finger and traced it down my palm, going right through it.

I felt the tingle all the way down to my toes.

"West Virginia," Caspian said softly. "Where we used to live. I'm buried in Martinsburg, West Virginia."

I crashed as soon as I got home, and when I woke up, thoughts of Revenants swirled through my head, darting like angry bees. But as I pushed my hair out of my face, I pushed the thoughts from my mind.

Right now there was only one important thing to take care of, and two potential roadblocks standing in the way.

I found Mom and Dad downstairs in the living room watching a movie. It was almost over, and I waited until the credits rolled before I sprung my big idea on them. "I want to go look at colleges in West Virginia," I blurted out.

Dad paused with the remote in his hand, mid-mute for the commercials, and Mom sighed happily. Her whole face lit up. "You do?"

They exchanged a *Can you believe this change of heart?* look, and I felt guilty for the lie. But not guilty enough.

"Yeah, there are some really great schools there, and with my senior year coming up, I'd like to rethink some of my options."

"We'll set everything up," Mom said excitedly. "Oh, honey, your first college tour! Such a big moment. We'll have to make sure to check out the campus and the dorms, of course, and—"

"*Mom.*"

"The town. You want to make sure the town is safe. A lot of people don't think about things like that."

"Mom!" I gave Dad a helpless look, and he grinned at me. "Mom, *stop.*"

She stopped. But the look of excitement was still there.

*Ah, damn it.* Now I felt bad. "The thing is . . . I want to go on my own." There was utter silence, and Mom's mouth gaped open.

"No."

"But Mom, I *really* want to do this, and I think it will be good for my independence. I'm growing here, and I feel like my feathers are getting all tangled."

"Feathers? What . . ."

"Baby bird," Dad said. "I get it."

I shot him a grateful look.

"How will you get there? Where will you stay? You'll be all alone." Mom's face crumpled.

"I can take a bus. And there are hotels there. I'll be fine. I'm seventeen. I can do this. In some countries girls my age are getting married, you know."

"M-married?" Her lower lip quivered.

*Uh-oh. Wrong thing to say.*

Dad came to the rescue. "Do you have any friends that could go with you, Abbey? I'm sure that would make your mother and me feel safer."

"Friends? Well, there's always Ben," I quipped. "He's dependable."

Dad nodded. "Yes, he is. You'll have to get separate rooms, though. And I'm going to call each night to do random bed checks. No bed hopping on this trip."

"*What?* Are you *serious*? He's a teenage boy, Dad. You actually *want* us spending unsupervised time alone together?"

"Well, considering the other options . . . He's been tutoring you, hasn't he? Has he made any inappropriate advances?"

"No, he's been the perfect gentleman."

"Then I think it's a good solution. He has a car, right?"

I nodded.

"See about making the arrangements, then." He patted Mom's hand. "Your mother and I will stay here."

Mom looked close to tears again.

"I'm serious about the bed checks though," Dad called,

when I got up to leave the room. "No funny business."

Shaking my head as I climbed the stairs, I wondered the whole way what planet I was living on and where my *real* parents were. Obviously, the ones in there had been replaced by pod people.

*Chapter Twenty-two*

# ROAD TRIP

Certain it is, his advances were signals for rival candidates to retire . . .

—"The Legend of Sleepy Hollow"

I talked to Ben about going to West Virginia with me, and he quickly agreed, saying that he was always up for a road trip. "Are you *sure* you don't mind driving?" I asked him again, cradling the phone to my ear.

"I don't mind, Abbey," he said.

"And I told you about the dad thing? He'll probably be obnoxious about calling to check up on me."

"You told me. Twice," Ben replied.

"Are you cool with dropping me off? I don't want you to be stuck hanging around."

"It's cool. My dad has a friend who owns a junkyard near there. I'll check him out."

"Thanks, Ben. I really appreciate this."

"What's the name of the college?" he asked.

Luckily, I was sitting in front of my computer, and I quickly turned to Google. "It's um . . ." I typed in *colleges in West Virginia*. A listing came up showing at least a dozen of them, and I scanned through. I couldn't believe my luck when Shepherd University popped up within ten miles of Martinsburg. "Shepherd," I said.

I clicked the link and arrived at the university's website. Pictures of tall buildings and smiling students littered the home page, and the "About Us" page said that it was a liberal-arts school. *Wow. Perfect.*

We decided to take the trip two days later, and I hung up the phone feeling a sense of accomplishment. This just might work. And the school looked pretty cool, too. Too bad I didn't have any plans to actually check it out. . . .

I wasn't sure how to tell Caspian about the trip, so I waited until the next day. I still hadn't figured out the best way to say, "Oh yeah, I'm going to be spending the entire weekend with Ben. *Alone.*"

We were in the mausoleum, sitting on the bench together, when he suddenly stood up. "I almost forgot. I have something I wanted to show you." He crossed over to his boxes, reached into one of them, and pulled out a tiny acid-washed blue-jean backpack.

"*Classy,*" I said, raising one eyebrow.

"I know, right? But I think you mean *classic*. This is vintage eighties style right here." Unzipping the backpack, he came over and sat back down. "What's even better, though, is what's inside." He pulled out a fistful of cassette tapes, and then produced a small, neon-pink tape player. "Portable."

"That *is* better." I grinned at him. The sight he made with the bright pink, girly tape player in his hand was comical. "It's your color, too. Pink."

"Matches my eyes." He held the player up and batted his eyelids.

"You made another trip to the thrift store, huh?" I said. "What did you leave this time?"

Caspian ducked his head and fiddled with the battery compartment. "I sort of, um, didn't?" He looked up at me. "I don't really have anything left, and there are only so many books a guy can read before he goes crazy. It's not an iPod, but at least it's something."

"I don't think they'll miss it. What songs did you get?"

He held out one of the tapes. "*Christmas Kids Sing the Blues,*" I read. "Wow, that's kind of an oxymoron."

He gave me a half smile and flipped through the remaining cassettes. "We also have . . . *Grover and Me Sing-a-long*, the Sheldon Brothers . . ."—he raised both eyebrows—"and . . . Debbie Gibson."

"Now *that's* what I call an eclectic music mix." I laughed.

Caspian put one of the tapes into the player, adjusted the volume to low, and pushed play. "I'm open-minded."

A mariachi band started up.

I wrinkled my nose at him. "Now we know what the Sheldon Brothers are."

He pushed stop and switched the tapes. An instant later soft piano and synthesizers came out of the tiny speakers. "Better than the mariachi band," I said. A female voice started singing.

Caspian tapped his foot along to the beat, and I gave him a skeptical look. "Really? You're enjoying this?" He cocked his head to one side but didn't say anything, while Debbie sang about silence speaking a thousand words. I raised an eyebrow at him.

"Don't you get it?" he said finally. "My silence is speaking a thousand words."

I rolled my eyes. "My silence is going to speak a thousand words too."

"Is your silence answering my silence?" he asked, a teasing

glint in his eyes. "Because my silence is getting very suggestive right now."

I blushed and looked down at my hands. *Will I ever get over this whole embarrassment thing around him?* I sure hoped so.

My phone beeped, and I took it out of my pocket, flipping it open in one fluid motion. Ben's number was there, and instantly, guilt flooded me. I still hadn't told Caspian about the trip.

I reached over to the cassette player and turned it off. The sudden silence between us was deafening. "Caspian . . . I need to tell you something."

His face changed. "Is it Vincent? Did he find you again?"

"No, no. It's not him. It's . . . I'm leaving tomorrow to go to West Virginia."

"To Martinsburg?" he asked quietly.

I nodded. "With Ben."

"Ben? Why?"

The words spilled out of me. "My parents wanted to go. Not to your grave, but to this college. Only, I'm not going to the college. I just told them that as a cover. So then *they* suggested that a friend go with me, and I joked about Ben, and . . . it just . . . worked out."

"Is he driving?"

"Yes."

"And you're staying there overnight? With him?"

"Yes."

"What time do we leave?"

"We're leaving at—wait, what? We, as in *we*? You and me?"

Caspian smiled an angelic smile. "Yes. You and me. I'm coming."

I opened my mouth to protest, but Caspian held up a hand and started ticking off each finger as he ran through a list. "I'm going because: One, Vincent Drake is out there, possibly after you. Two, the other Revenants are still out there, possibly after you. Three, *Ben* is going to be there with you. *Alone* ..." I snorted, and Caspian gave me a look. "I'm a guy. I know how his mind works."

"He has feelings for Kristen. Not me."

"Yeah, well, just wait and see what eight hours alone in a car can do."

"Six," I mumbled.

He held up a fourth finger. "Four, you're going to see *my* grave, and I don't want you to be alone. Five ..." He looked away, like he was trying to think of something else to add. "Five ... we'll get to spend quality time together. And I *love* the license-plate game."

One side of my mouth turned up in a smile I couldn't quite quell. "You're very persuasive, you know that?"

"I learned from the best, Arm-Twister Abbey."

Laughter burst out of me. Shaking my head, I said, "We're leaving at eight a.m. Don't be late."

"I won't." He grinned. "Pack extra snacks."

I tried to shove his arm and went right through him, laughing again as my hand bounced harmlessly off the bench. "Don't make me regret telling you about this. Or I'll let Ben talk about *Star Trek* the whole way down," I warned.

He groaned. "God help us all."

I shot him a teasing grin, but inside I was already worrying about the trip. One car. Two boys. Six hours. And I had to try to remember to only speak to one of them. *God help us all.*


The next morning Caspian knocked on my window at seven a.m., and I had to finish getting dressed knowing he was right outside the bathroom door.

Ben showed up at seven forty-five and gallantly hauled my suitcase out to the car, while Caspian stood around casting moody glares at him. I gave him a warning look, but he just ignored me, and I suddenly found myself wishing for some of Aubra's mom's Xanax. This trip was going to be *anything* but relaxing.

Before we left, Mom reminded me again to call her as soon as we reached the hotel, and Dad reminded me again that he'd made separate room reservations. On opposite sides of the hall.

I just nodded and tried to keep a cheerful look on my face, praying that I wouldn't break out into hives or anything. All I had to do was get in the car and leave the house. They'd never know.

Dad slipped me a fifty-dollar bill "for emergencies" after I hugged him, and then pulled out his wallet to give me two more twenties.

I looked down at the wad of bills in my hand.

"For fun," he said. I tried to say thanks, but Mom pulled me into an anaconda squeeze and wouldn't let go.

"Mom." She was cutting off my air. *"Mom."* My arms were going numb. "Okay, Mom! I need to breathe."

She squeezed me for a second longer and then reluctantly let go. Her eyes were wet, and there was a slightly panicked look in them as she pulled back. She tried to hug me again, but I stopped her.

"Mom, I have to go. We need to leave."

"I know, I know. Are you sure you have everything? And you promise you'll take pictures?"

I nodded. Of course, my camera had "accidentally" been left in my room, but she didn't need to know that.

She pitched her voice lower and cast a worried look over at Ben's Jeep. "Are you sure you'll be okay? With the . . . other thing? Do you have Dr. Pendleton's number, just in case?"

"I'll be fine," I said. "Bye, guys." I turned away from them before Mom could latch on again, and started walking to the car. Throwing my messenger bag into the backseat, I left the door open long enough for Caspian to climb in.

I had to cover my laugh with a fake cough when he whispered, "Anything but *Star Trek*. Please, dear *God*, anything but *Star Trek*."

Shooting him a quick *Behave* glare, I climbed into the front seat.

Ben started up the car, and we both waved as we pulled out of the driveway. Once we were completely clear of my parents, he turned and smiled at me. "Ready?"

"Ready."

"Ready," Caspian called from the back.

I pulled down the visor and flipped it open, using the pretense of fixing my hair in the mirror. Caspian met my eyes and winked. With an inward sigh, I shut the visor and steeled myself to play invisible referee.

Ben and I talked about the upcoming school year and what teachers we hoped we'd get, and the first two hours passed pretty quickly. Then the conversation moved on to our future plans and what we'd be doing *after* high school.

"I think it's really cool that you want to have your own store, Abbey," Ben said. "But why are you going to rent that dinky place downtown? You should open up a store in Manhattan."

I could practically feel Caspian's scowl from the back seat.

"Because she doesn't love *Manhattan,* you idiot," he growled. "She loves Sleepy Hollow."

Trying to pretend that I didn't hear him, I said, "I guess I'm just really attached to the town."

"Which you'd *know* if you spent five minutes actually paying attention to her," Caspian added.

"I don't know." Ben shook his head. "I just don't get it. The statistics are much better there. More volume, more customers, more profit."

"Higher overhead, higher taxes, less history," I rebutted. "I've given this a lot of thought, Ben. Trust me. Plus, it's something that Kristen was going to help me with."

Caspian leaned forward and whispered in my ear, "I think it's a great idea, Abbey. Don't listen to him. He's a schmuck. And by the way, have I told you how beautiful you look today?"

Ben was talking too, and I had to fight not to shiver at Caspian's words. I tucked a stray curl behind one ear, getting lost in the moment of having him so near.

"... did you ever find that out?" Ben asked. He looked at me expectantly.

"Sorry," I said. "Got distracted by a car. What was that?"

"I asked if you ever found out who that D. guy was, since you thought I was him."

Bad memories immediately clouded my mind, and I frowned. "Oh, yeah. I did. He was . . . a jerk."

"But Kristen was seeing him?" Ben said.

I looked out my window. Trees and houses rushed past in a never-ending blur. "She was seeing him, yeah. But I think she knew it was a mistake. When she wrote about him in her diaries . . . I think she realized that she was in over her head."

"Did these diaries mention anyone else?" He gave me a hopeful look, and I felt bad for him. I resisted the urge to reach out and put a hand on his arm.

"No, she didn't mention anyone else. Sorry, Ben."

"What about you and that guy you were dating?" Ben asked. "Are you still together? How come I never see him around?"

Fidgeting with my seat belt, I looked down. "It's . . . complicated."

"Complicated as in you guys broke up? Or complicated as in you're still together?"

"Um, I don't really know how to describe it."

Ben's face changed. "*Oh*. I get it. Friends with benefits."

"Good Lord, no," I blurted out. My face felt like it was on fire, so I opened the window to suck in a mouthful of fresh air. As soon as my face felt normal again, I turned back to Ben. "We're not, um, like that. It's just . . . complicated." *Drop it. Please drop it,* I mentally commanded him.

"I see," Ben said. Then, "Okay, no I don't. But I guess it's none of my business."

"Ding, ding, correct answer for ten bonus points," said Caspian.

I waved my hand in his direction to gesture for him to stop talking, and Ben glanced at me funny. "Bug . . . flying . . . gnat . . . thing." *Oh God, how much longer do we have until we get there? This car ride is going to be the death of me.*

"I thought he was an ass." Ben said. "You seemed really upset by him at school last year."

"It's cool now." I reached down to the radio, and held my finger over the power button. "Do you mind if I put on some music?"

He shrugged, and I scanned through the stations, trying to

find something good. I paused when I came to a familiar voice. Steven Tyler sang for a couple of seconds before Ben changed the station.

"Hey," I said.

"What? That song's almost over."

"Yeah, but I like it."

"Isn't it from an asteroid movie? *Doomsday* or something."

"*Armageddon*. The song is called 'I Don't Want to Miss a Thing.'" The memory of dancing with Caspian tugged at me, and I closed my eyes. A sudden lump rose in my throat.

"Going to sleep?" Ben asked.

I took the excuse. "Yeah, wake me up in an hour."

He changed the station again, and classical music filled the car. *Ugh*. I hated classical music. I wouldn't have a hard time falling asleep for real with *that* on the radio.

"Abbey. Hey, Abbey. Wake up, Sleeping Beauty." Caspian's voice was soft in my ear.

I picked my head up, neck muscles screaming in pain. I must have slumped over while I was sleeping. The driver's seat was empty. "Where's Ben?"

"He *left* you," Caspian said, sounding angry. "You were sleeping, and he didn't wake you up. And he thinks *I'm* the ass."

I looked around me. We were at a gas station, and I spotted Ben inside the store. "He just went in there."

"He should have woken you up," Caspian said. "Who just leaves someone alone like that?"

"But I'm not alone. I have you."

"*He* doesn't know that."

Caspian sat back and crossed his arms, glowering as Ben exited the store carrying a small paper bag.

"Be nice," I whispered.

"Tell that to *him*," he retorted.

Ben opened the door and sat the bag between us. "Oh, good. You're awake." He reached down and pulled out a bottle of Coke. "I wasn't sure what you'd want, so I got you this and diet. Oh, and a bottle of water."

I took the Coke from him. "Thanks, Ben. That was really *nice* of you," I said. Caspian made a rude noise from the back.

Then Ben pulled out a green and yellow bag and held it up, giving me a goofy smile. "Got some Funyuns."

I smiled back, and he started the car, heading onto the highway.

Popping the bag open, he held it out to me. "Want one? Come on, try 'em."

"Funyuns make you fart," Caspian said, and I exploded in laughter.

"What's so funny?" Ben asked.

I tried to stop laughing, but Caspian was leaning forward now, his face stuck right in between us. "Funyuns give you bad breath, too. Not very attractive to the ladies." He paused. "On second thought . . . enjoy your Funyuns, Ben!"

I had to bite the side of my cheek to keep from giggling. The fact that Ben had no clue what was going made it even harder to stop.

Caspian winked at me, and I took a sip of soda. Sternly telling myself to calm down, I tried to think up some excuse for why I was laughing. "I just thought that the name was funny," I said. "Funyuns. Are they fun onions or faux onions? It's funny . . ."

Ben shrugged. "Yeah, I guess the name is funny."

"So how much longer until we get there?" I needed a change of subject.

"About two and a half hours. Unless we get stuck in a wormhole."

I looked at him blankly. "A what?"

"Wormhole? You know, *Star Trek*? Because we watched the movie."

"Is that your favorite movie?" I asked. "*Star Trek*?" He nodded, but I cut him off before he could say anything further about it. "Okay, favorite *comedy* movie. That's not *Star Trek*."

He changed lanes on the highway, and we passed a truck carrying huge spools of wire. "*Zoolander*. What's yours?"

"*City Slickers*."

He gave me a surprised look. "Really? I wouldn't have picked that one for you."

"I know, right? It's such an old movie. But I love Billy Crystal. He's *sooo* funny. I like pretty much anything he's in."

He nodded.

"Do you know what Kristen's favorite movie was?" I said.

"No."

"*Back to the Future*. That's one of the things we had in common; we both loved old movies. But she loved Michael J. Fox, too. I mean, seriously, loved him. He came to New York City once for this promo project, some art show or something, and Kristen won tickets to go see him. She was *so* excited."

"Did you go with her?"

"No. I really wanted to, but she only won two tickets, and since she was under eighteen, a guardian had to go with her. You'll never guess what she tried to do, though."

Kristen's face swam in front of me, and my heart constricted painfully. Even the good things she'd done were still so hard to talk about.

"The night before they were supposed to leave, Kristen

called me and told me that she was sick so I'd have to take her place. I didn't believe her, so I went over to see. She had actually *painted red dots* on her face and told me it was the chicken pox."

Ben laughed.

"She felt so bad that I couldn't go, she was willing to sacrifice her ticket and give it to me."

"She really did that?" Ben said.

"Yup. Of course, I *made* her go, and she had a great time. Got to shake Michael's hand, and wouldn't wash it for a week. But I could never get over the fact that she was going to give up the *one* thing she wanted so badly, for me."

Ben and I fell silent, and stayed that way for another hour, until Ben saw a sign for a McDonald's. "Is this okay with you?" he asked, pulling into the parking lot. "I'm starving."

"Yeah. This is fine. I'm hungry too. But let's eat inside. I have to, um, use the restroom." Unbuckling my seat belt, I glanced into the rearview mirror.

"Take your time, Abbey," Caspian said. "I'll wait here."

I gave him a brief nod and then got out of the car, stretching my arms and legs as I walked into the McDonald's. Handing Ben some money, I told him what to order for me, then hurried to the bathroom. Soon we were back in the car and on the road again.

"The guy at the register said we only have about twenty minutes until we reach Shepherdstown," Ben said. "That's where your dad made the reservations, right?"

Reaching for my bag on the backseat, I carefully maneuvered around Caspian's leg and pulled out a piece of paper with the hotel address and confirmation number scribbled on it. "Yeah. We're staying at the Shepherd's Inn. I guess the town is too small for a Hilton."

"Sounds cozy," Ben replied. "Let's hope the sheets are clean."

"And the phones work," I deadpanned. "Otherwise, if my dad can't get through, we might have company tomorrow."

Ben followed the directions I'd printed out, and turned off onto a long gravel road. We bumped along, hitting potholes every couple of feet.

"Do you think they could have made this road any bumpier?" I asked, as I jolted out of my seat.

"Maybe they saved their money for the hotel. Jacuzzis, PS2s, plasmas, and a wet bar in every room."

"I'm *sure* that's what they did," I said. "Absolutely *positive*."

We bumped along a little farther until the road inexplicably smoothed out and turned into shiny blacktop. Combination movie rental–tanning stores started popping up, and it looked like we were heading back into civilization.

Ben eyed one of the combo stores as we passed. "Why would you want to go tan and then rent a movie right after? Or, alternately, rent a movie, then go tanning?"

A bait shop–Japanese restaurant popped up, and he looked at me with both eyebrows raised. "If I don't understand the tan-and-rent one, I *sure* as hell don't get *that* one."

"Haven't you ever felt like eating sushi after a long day spent in rubber boots and muddy water?" Caspian said.

I hid my smile as I looked out the window. "I don't know, Ben. Maybe the people here really like convenience?" He snorted but didn't say anything, and a large brick building with a striped awning came into view. A sign next to it proclaimed it the Shepherd's Inn.

"Guess we found it." Ben gunned the Jeep forward. "I hope it's not a hotel-slash-bowling-alley."

I snickered and then immediately felt bad for laughing at Caspian's home state, but he didn't seem to mind.

We parked and got out, each of us hauling our own bags, and Caspian followed behind me. The interior of the lobby was a *lot* more impressive than the exterior of the hotel, and I turned in several directions to take everything in.

Glass desks, vintage art, exposed modernized pipes, and brass light fixtures gave the place a modern twenties style with just a touch of steampunk. Even the clerk behind the desk was impeccably dressed in a stylish, old-fashioned business suit.

Ben checked us in, and I waited by his side as the clerk tapped away on her keyboard.

"Here we are," she said, then frowned. "I see a note on the reservation requesting rooms on opposite sides of the corridor, but the only rooms I have left that fulfill those requirements are the older rooms. Would you prefer two adjoining, updated rooms instead?" She looked at Ben, and then at me. Unsure of who to direct her question to.

"Updated rooms?" Ben brightened.

"We've just been bought out by Hilton, and our renovated rooms offer an in-room gaming system, complimentary snacks and beverages, free movies—"

"We'll take them," Ben said.

The clerk nodded and tapped another key. "And will this charge be staying on the credit card provided?" She looked down her nose at us, like neither of us could *possibly* have a credit card.

"Yes," I said firmly. "It's my dad's card."

There was more tapping, and then she produced two room keys. "Down the hall and to your left."

We followed her directions and came to rooms 304 and

306. Ben slid one of the cards into the reader, and a green light buzzed. The door to room 304 clicked open. "Guess this one's mine," he said, and walked in.

I slid my card into the reader for room 306. The door swung inward, revealing a room decorated in Parisian-style black and white stripes with small accents of red everywhere. Large pictures of metal gears and steam factories hung in glossy black frames on the walls.

Caspian followed behind me, and I dumped my luggage to the floor, then flopped down on the bed. He wandered around, checking the room out.

"Did you bring a bathing suit?" he asked suddenly.

I sat up. "No, I didn't think I'd need one. Why?"

He pointed over to the bathroom, which had a clear glass wall. The toilet seemed to be in a separate section, safely tucked away, but the shower was in full view.

"Because *that's* going to be fun."

*Chapter Twenty-three*

# A PERFECT MATCH

In this enterprise, however, he had more real difficulties than generally fell to the lot of a knight-errant of yore, who seldom had anything but giants, enchanters, fiery dragons, and such like easily conquered adversaries, to contend with . . .

—"The Legend of Sleepy Hollow"

I decided not to worry about the bathroom just yet—it wasn't like I could do anything about it anyway—and checked the room out for myself. I flipped through the TV channels, looked at the room-service menu, and tried out the gaming system, but I couldn't figure it out. It was some complicated thing, with twenty-nine buttons.

An hour later Caspian was sitting in the only chair in the room while I sat on the bed. "Have you ever stayed at one of those really ratty hotels?" I asked him. "With the seventies-style wallpaper and disco-ball ceilings?"

He nodded. "Once, when I was little, my dad had to go out of town for something, and I went with him. I don't remember where it was, but I remember the hotel. The room we stayed in had shag carpet and paneling on the walls."

"I know what you mean. Kristen's memorial service was held in this god-awful, tacky funeral home that had the same thing."

"I know," he said. "I was there."

"You *were*? I didn't see you."

"I didn't stay long. I didn't want to see you upset. I saw you at the cemetery earlier that day too. Sitting in a chair by a grave."

I remembered. I thought a shadow had been next to me. "I wish I would have known. I could have—" The room phone rang, cutting me off. I picked it up. "Hello?"

"Abbey, its Dad."

*Crap.* I was supposed to call them as soon as I got in. "Hey, Dad."

"How was the trip? Is the hotel okay? Are you alone in your room? The front desk clerk told me you're in adjoining rooms."

I closed my eyes briefly and massaged my temples. *Is he going to let me get a word in edgewise here?* "The trip was fine, Dad. We just got in, and I'm in an adjoining room because they're doing work on the other rooms. This is all they had available. And yes, Ben is in his *own* room." I avoided the are-you-alone question. That one was a lot harder to answer.

"Okay," he said gruffly. "Well, just remember, I'll be making random bed checks, so don't get any ideas."

I sighed. "I won't, Dad."

"Your mother says to have a good time and ask lots of questions."

"Will do. Bye, Dad." He said good-bye, and I hung up. Almost immediately, the phone rang again. I shot Caspian an aggravated look as I answered it. "Dad, this isn't—"

"Abbey, it's Ben. I just got a call from your dad too."

"Sorry, Ben. He's just being his normal, overbearing self."

"It's cool. You warned me about it. Hey, I'm gonna get a pizza delivered. You want some?"

"Sure. You know what I like." I cringed as I heard myself say those words. "On my pizza . . . I mean."

"Yeah, I get it. I'll call you when it gets here. Did you check out the movie channel yet? Some awesome stuff coming on at eight."

"I'll check it out." Hanging up the phone for the second time, I told Caspian, "Ben's ordering us a pizza."

"With a side of Funyuns?"

I stuck my tongue out at him. "*Nooo*, no Funyuns." I slipped off my shoes and crawled backward until I was propped against the headboard. The bed was *huge*, and the covers were made out of a fluffy white material that felt like I was being swallowed by them. As I stretched out, a pleasant drowsiness started seeping into my veins.

"Is it strange to be back here? So close to home?" I murmured to Caspian. My eyelids were heavy, and every time I blinked, they took just a little bit longer to open back up.

"Strange? Yes, but everything about this is strange. Are we here to actually look at my grave, or are we here to get away from Vincent Drake and the Revenants?"

"I don't know," I said drowsily, finally giving in to the long-reaching fingers of sleep that were pulling me down. "That's what I'm here to find out."

A loud rapping on the adjoining door had me sitting up straight, and I looked around wildly. I couldn't remember where I was. Then the luggage in the corner jarred me back into reality. The knocking continued.

"Caspian?" I croaked. My throat was dry, and I tried again. "Caspian?"

The red curtains stirred and parted. "I'm here." He was standing behind them, looking out the large window. "I'm right here, Abbey."

Relief washed over me, and I got off the bed, feeling my head clear with every step I took. My left foot was asleep, and I staggered slightly, but I made it to the adjoining door.

When I opened it, Ben was standing there with a pizza box in one hand. I wasn't very hungry, but I let him in anyway.

"You took forever to answer," he said, entering the room and putting the box down on a nearby table.

"I fell asleep."

He walked over to a low cabinet next to the TV and opened it. "I didn't order drinks, since we have the minibar. Can you believe this setup? What more could you want?"

I glanced at the incredibly well-stocked minibar. "Nice. Grab me a Sprite."

He grabbed the Sprite and a Coke, and picked up the TV remote. "Want to watch something while we eat?"

I helped myself to a slice of pizza and then sat on the edge of the bed. "Sure."

Ben carried the entire pizza box over to the chair and flipped through the channels while I picked at my piece. By the time he settled on *The Simpsons*, I was already done eating.

He stood up as soon as the show was over. "Mind if I take the rest of this?" He pointed to the pizza box. There were still three slices left, but I didn't want them.

"They're all yours. I guess I'll see you tomorrow, then?"

"Yeah. Oh, hey, what time do you want to leave? My dad's friend's junkyard doesn't open till ten."

"Ten is fine. Night, Ben. Sorry in advance if my dad calls again."

He walked to the door. "No problem. And if you need anything, you know where I'm at."

When he left the room, it felt like a sudden rush of energy went with him. The curtains moved, and Caspian came out. "Did you eat anything?" he asked.

"A couple of bites. I wasn't very hungry." The bed beckoned, and I lay down on my stomach with my head at the footboard. The TV flashed, and the words "Feature Presentation" came on; then intro music for a movie started to play.

Caspian sat down next to me, keeping a careful distance between us. "Closer," I whispered. "Come closer."

He moved closer.

I turned my head to stare at one jean-clad thigh. With one hand, I tried to trace the seams, but I slipped right through. My hand hit the bed, and I let it lie there, an inch away from him.

"Are you going to fall asleep again, Astrid?" he mused. "A guy could take offense at that. Are you trying to tell me I'm dull?"

I tried to shake my head, but only my cheek moved on the comforter, and I snuggled deeper into it. "You're not dull, Casper. You . . ." I searched my brain for the words he'd used before. "You exhilarate me."

His green eyes were the last thing I saw before I closed my eyes again, but I heard him lean down and whisper, "Thank you, Astrid. Sweet dreams."

The next time I woke up, I was really awake. No fuzzy-headedness and no disorientation. I blinked once or twice, wondering why it was still dark out, and rolled over to look at the clock. It was 3:12 a.m. Still nighttime.

My eyes quickly adjusted, and I could see Caspian sitting in the chair.

"Hi," he whispered.

"Hi," I whispered back. In the darkness the hotel room felt small and intimate.

"I moved over here because you were getting restless," he said.

"Okay." My stomach grumbled loudly and completely embarrassed me.

Caspian chuckled. "Hungry?"

"I guess. I didn't eat much pizza."

"I saw a vending machine at the end of the hall," he said. "I'll go get you some snacks."

"No, that's okay," I tried to protest.

"You need to eat something," he said as my stomach growled again. "Just let me go get something for you. Please?"

"But what if someone sees you? Well, not *you*, but you know. The snacks. Moving. On their own."

"It's three in the morning. No one's out there. I'll be quick." He stood up and turned on a small lamp by the TV. Then he turned to me. "Do you have any, uh, money? I'm all out."

I dug my wallet out of my pocket and handed him a couple of bucks. Then I remembered the minibar with all the snacks I could eat. I didn't bring it up, though. I had to pee, and if this was the only way to use the bathroom without him in the room, so be it. I'd just keep sending him out for random snacks.

And when it was time for a shower, I'd send him to the fourth-floor vending machine, with a very *long* list.

He grabbed the key. "I'll be back."

As soon as Caspian left, I hurried to use the bathroom. Then I washed my face and brushed my teeth. My hair was a *nightmare*, but it refused to be tamed, so I pulled it back into a ponytail. Next, I opened up my suitcase and rummaged through it.

Digging deep through the pile of clothes, I pulled out a set of white pajamas with red cherries printed all over them. They could hardly be called sexy, but they *were* cute. And the material was kind of clingy.

A soft knock sounded on the door, and I stripped out of my clothes and hurried into the pj's.

Caspian came in a second later, carrying a bag of pretzels, some chips, a breakfast burrito, and a candy bar. "A main course, two sides, and dessert." He dumped his haul on the end table, and then turned to me. "Cute. I like the mismatched buttons."

I glanced down. My buttons were all lined up wrong. "Oops." Turning my back to him, I called out, "Don't peek," and I straightened them. "Okay, all fixed."

Caspian's gaze seemed to linger on my top button as he said, "I liked it better the other way."

"Well, I can always undo it if you want." Hearing those words come out of my mouth, sounding *very* much *not* like I intended them to sound, I blushed and picked up the burrito. "I'm just going to heat this up in the microwave, and you can forget I said that, okay?"

His lips pulled up into a half smile, and he sat on the bed. I popped the burrito in and nuked it for twenty seconds before joining him. I ate in silence, and I got up to brush my teeth as soon as I was done. I did *not* want to have guacamole stuck in them.

When I exited the bathroom, he had one leg propped up on the comforter and was looking at a picture hanging on the far wall. I wondered how the rest of the night would go. Was he going to spend it in the chair, or on the floor? Or in the bed . . . with me?

"Tell me what you're thinking," he said suddenly, turning to face me.

"What I'm thinking? Why?"

"Because I can't *stop* thinking. And I want to know if you feel that way too." He looked frustrated. "Are you thinking about everything that happened? You should be. You should be thinking about why those Revenants are in Sleepy Hollow, and what that means. You should be thinking about Vincent Drake and how you can stay safe." He looked down at his leg and pulled at the fabric on his jeans. "You should be thinking about me, Astrid. And how all of this is happening because of *me*."

"I am thinking about everything," I said. "But just one thing at a time. There's so much to take in. I have to compartmentalize it all, or it'll take over." His eyes met mine. "I'm afraid, Caspian. Afraid of tomorrow—today, technically—and what it will bring.

I don't want seeing your grave to drive me back to Dr. Pendleton."

"Then go home," he urged. "Leave this place."

"Go back to Sleepy Hollow? Where there are Revenants who are waiting for me to die? Or where the crazy boy who might have killed my best friend waits?"

"When you put it that way, it sounds—"

"It sounds crazy. I know. I might be safer here. But the most important thing to face right now is *you*."

"What will it prove? You already know I'm dead."

"I don't know," I said truthfully. "I guess it's because sometimes I forget." I reached out a hand to put on his arm and felt the soft covers instead. "Because other than *that*, sometimes I forget you're not really here and normal." I looked away. "Trust me, I'd like to forget about this, but I think it's important. It *feels* crucial. Do you know what I mean?"

"I just don't want it to hurt, Astrid," he said.

His words made my heart ache, and I gave him a sad smile. "Hurt is a part of life." I gestured between us helplessly. "*This* hurts. It *kills* me that I can't touch you, Caspian. Can't kiss you. Can't listen to your heart beating." I closed my eyes, feeling the tears threatening. "Can you turn off the light?" I asked in a wobbly voice. "If I burst into tears here, I really don't want you to see it."

A second later the room turned dark with a soft *click*.

"Don't cry, Astrid," he whispered into my ear. "Please don't cry. Your big eyes and pouty lips . . . they undo me. I can't take it. I'll do anything to make it better."

I scrambled backward and found one edge of the covers. "Sleep with . . . me?" I said hesitantly. "Just . . . be near me."

Silence was his only answer, and I felt foolish. He didn't sleep. So why would he want to just lie there next to me?

"Climb under the covers," he said.

His voice sounded closer, like he'd followed me up the bed. A wicked heat spread through me and made my skin ache. I pulled back the covers and slid between the sheets. The legs of my pajama bottoms rode up my shins, and I wiggled around to straighten them out.

"Are you settled?" Caspian asked.

"Mmm-hmm." I counted to a hundred, then said, "Are you, um, settled?"

"I'm here." He sounded too far away.

"Come closer. I like it when you whisper in my ear."

"I aim to please."

The shiver came back. He was *much* closer now, and I gave a happy sigh.

"Put your hand on your chest, over your heart," Caspian

said. I almost turned to ask him why. "No questions," he said, anticipating my move. "Just do it."

"Over or under my top?"

"Under," he breathed. "Skin to skin."

My body heated up again. Placing one hand over my heart, I felt it beating hard. Like a trapped butterfly frantically fluttering its wings.

"Close your eyes," he whispered.

I followed his instructions. Then I felt it. Just the slightest dip in the bed. If I hadn't been concentrating, I might have missed it. My left arm and leg tingled for a second, and then my right arm and leg tingled at the same time.

"Do you feel your heartbeat?" His words fluttered down across my face, and I knew that if I opened my eyes, I'd see him on top of me.

It should have freaked me out. Lying in bed with a boy who was practically pinning me down. And yet . . . he wasn't. He *couldn't*. It felt right with him. *Safe*.

And dangerous. And thrilling. And exhilarating.

I had to moisten my lips before I could answer him. "I feel it."

"If I could touch anything in the world right now, it would be your heart. I want to take that piece of you and keep it with me when I'm alone in the dark."

His voice ached, and I ached right along with him.

"I want to feel your heartbeat too," I whispered.

"Pretend," he said. "Can you do that? Pretend I'm alive and there's nothing between us. Nothing at all. I'm real and warm and *alive*."

My eyes flew open, and I could just barely make out the contours of his face. Holding my hand steady over my heart, I wished I could see his eyes. "Nothing is between us, Caspian," I whispered. "I'm your other half. So half of this? Half of this erratic thumping? Is yours. I'll carry your heartbeat in mine."

The covers bunched around me. He was clenching his hands. "How can you do it, Abbey? How can you love me? I have nothing to offer. Nothing to give you. I don't even know how long I'll stay like this. You'd be better off—"

"Stop," I commanded him softly. "Stop this."

"But Ben—"

"Would be better for me? Has more to offer me?"

He stayed silent.

"Don't you think I *know* that, Caspian? Don't you think I've thought about that?"

His voice was quiet, but he said, "You have?"

"Yes. I have. On the night of my birthday party. When I first came back. All those times I was trying *so hard* to get you out of my head. I've thought about it a million times."

He pulled back, and the space between us widened. I sat up slightly, leveraging myself on my elbows to lessen the space. "I don't say this to hurt you, love." The endearment slipped out without me even thinking about it. "I'm telling you this so that you'll know I made a choice. I *chose* you. Before I knew you were dead . . . and after."

"Say it again," he said. "Call me your love."

I wanted to touch his face so much, to make him *see* how much he meant to me, that my fingers ached with the wanting. "Love, love, *love*. I chose you freely, love. Before I knew about the Revenants and being your destined other half. I thought about all the ways I could be with Ben—"

"Oh God, Abbey," he whispered. "You're breaking my heart here."

"No," I said. "Don't let it. I'm sorry—I'm messing this up." I rolled away from him, pulling my knees up to my chest. Hot tears threatened to spill, and I jammed my hands into my eyes to stop them.

"I'm so jealous of him," Caspian admitted. "Every smile he earns from you. Every laugh. I'm jealous of a geek who watches *Star Trek* and eats Funyuns, for God's sake." He laughed bitterly. "I see the look on his face, and I know . . . I *know* how he feels. Even if he doesn't. Because I feel it too."

I swiped my hand over my face and swallowed.

"I'm sorry, Astrid," he said. "I know what you were trying to say."

"Ben's a great guy, Caspian. He is. But he's not *you*. You're . . . chocolate to his vanilla. It works for some people, but not me."

"With sprinkles?" he asked. "Sprinkles are good."

"Maybe nuts instead of sprinkles." I smiled into the darkness. "Anyone who can hang out in a mausoleum all day *has* to be a little nutty."

"I guess I'm the perfect match, then, for a girl who likes to visit a cemetery." He drew out every syllable so that it sounded like a love song.

I closed my eyes, savoring those words. "A perfect match," I murmured. "My other half."

*Chapter Twenty-four*

# FACE TO FACE

She was withal a little of a coquette, as might be perceived even in her dress, which
was a mixture of ancient and modern fashions, as most suited to set off her charms.

—"The Legend of Sleepy Hollow"

A muffled thump and the call of "Housekeeping!" woke me
up later that morning, and I put the pillow over my head
to try and block out the sound. A short burst of knocks echoed
on the door, and I groaned out loud.

"No thank you," I called, raising my voice so it could be
heard through the door.

They knocked again.

"I don't need any room service! Go away!" It was rude, but
effective, and they moved on to the next room.

I felt the sheet slip as I rolled to my side, but I only made
a halfhearted attempt to grab at it. It pooled around me, and I

felt the cool air on my exposed midriff. I snuggled deeper into my pillow . . .

And then my eyes popped open.

Caspian was lying next to me.

I yanked my pajama top back down. *It's no worse than if you wore a bikini*, I tried to tell myself. *Your belly would show then, too.*

But I couldn't meet his eyes. I was *sure* my face was completely red.

"So," Caspian said. "How did you sleep?"

My brain was stuttering, but apparently my tongue had no such problems. "Fine. Good." He leaned closer. I inhaled sharply at his nearness.

"I want to wake up with you every morning," he said. "Just like this."

That familiar shivery feeling stole over me again and made my brain go all fuzzy.

"I *should* call you a pervert," I finally replied. "For ogling me while I sleep."

"It was torture. To look and not touch . . ."

"Hey! Just how much looking did you do?" I said indignantly.

"Not . . . much." He grinned at me, his hair falling into one eye. "I'm just sorry that I don't have my sketch pad. The real crime here was not capturing such beauty."

I shook my head at him. "That is *such* a come-on line. . . . But now I need a shower, and you're going to have to leave the room and return when I'm done, or keep your eyes closed the entire time. And I'll know if you're peeking."

"I'm staying in the room with you. And I won't peek."

"I'm trusting you."

"Of course you can."

His face was serious, and I could tell he meant what he was promising. Heading toward the bathroom, I called out, "Okay, close 'em." He did, but I still glanced out at him to see if he was keeping his word.

He was.

I turned the water on, adjusted the temperature, and momentarily forgot all about Caspian as soon as the hot water hit me. The shower was relaxing and just what I needed. I seriously regretted it the moment I turned it off.

I dried off with a towel down from the rack, then wrapped it around me. Another glance at Caspian told me that he was turned away, watching TV.

As I opened the bathroom door, a cloud of steam escaped with me. The carpet was soft on my bare feet, and I scrunched up my toes, enjoying the feeling. The towel I'd wrapped turban-style around my head started to come undone, so I reached up to secure it.

Behind me the TV switched off.

I froze, aware that I had to be careful how much I moved, or else the towel wrapped around my body could slip.

Turning slowly, I locked eyes with Caspian, and he crooked his finger. Beckoning me to come closer.

I couldn't resist.

He stood up from the edge of the bed and met me halfway. I couldn't tell what he was thinking. My heart felt like it was going to burst out of my chest.

"Your cheeks are rosy," he observed. "And you smell good." He let out a small groan, and I backed up a step, suddenly feeling out of my element. My suitcase was on the floor behind me, and I bumped into it.

"I'm at a disadvantage here." I tried to laugh. Tried to distract myself from this strange moment that I didn't know how to react to. "You're fully dressed, and I'm only wearing a towel."

In an instant he pulled off the dark gray T-shirt he wore. The black interlocking circles of the tattoo on his left arm flashed when he moved. "Now we're a little more even."

Desire hit me like a rock as I gazed at his bare chest, and I wondered what his skin tasted like there. He was so . . . *male*. So beautiful.

I bit my lip to keep from moaning, and Caspian let out a sigh. "You are so unbelievably sexy right now."

A wicked little devil prodded me to be bad, and I took off the towel wrapped around my head, flipping my hair to one side so it slithered over my shoulder. Biting down harder on my lip, I whispered, "Hold on," and disappeared into the bathroom again.

I grabbed my bottle of lotion from the counter, returned to Caspian, and sat down on top of my suitcase. This time, I was the one to beckon him.

I braced my feet on the carpet. One knee was exposed, and I hiked the towel up a little bit more until my whole thigh was showing. The thought that I was playing with fire crossed my mind, but I pushed it away. I was in the mood to get burned. Scorched, even.

The scent of vanilla wafted around us as I opened the lotion and squeezed some into my palm. Caspian watched my every move intently. I slid my hand up and down my leg, smoothing on the lotion. The sensation was heightened by the fact that he was there with me. Beads of sweat gathered on my forehead, and I quickly wiped them away. "It's hot in here," I whispered.

Caspian licked his lips, and a muscle in his jaw clenched. "You have another."

"Another?"

"Another leg," he said.

I smiled. "You're right." Squeezing out some more lotion, I massaged my other calf and worked my way up past my knee. I closed my eyes, picturing his hand there, on my leg . . . warm and firm . . . sliding up the towel . . . caressing my skin . . . The lotion bottle suddenly fell out of my hand and rolled away, banging against the end table with a thud.

An instant later the lamp crashed to the ground.

I jumped and met Caspian's eyes. He looked just as startled as I was.

There was a knock at the nearby door and then Ben said, "Abbey? Are you okay?"

I let out a frustrated sigh and tucked my hair behind one ear. The pounding continued, and I glanced at Caspian.

"We'll finish this later," he promised.

Standing up, I felt a little wobbly in the knees and went to open the adjoining door.

"Remember, you're in a towel," Caspian called out.

I looked down and pulled it around me tighter. Cracking

the door open a couple of inches, I stuck my face near it. "Ben, I'm fine."

"Are you sure? I heard a loud bang."

"Yeah, I just knocked over a lamp."

"Are you almost ready to go?" he said.

"I just got out of the shower. I'm not dressed yet. Give me ten minutes."

"Oh. Okay." He backed away, and I shut the door.

Returning to my suitcase to get some clothes, I told Caspian, "We're leaving in about ten minutes."

"I'm ready," he said, folding his arms over his chest.

"Aren't you forgetting something?" I looked down at his bare chest. "Your shirt?"

His muscles flexed. "You seemed to like it better off. I could just walk around like this. No one would see."

My mouth went dry. "I, um . . . yes." Then common sense kicked in. "But I don't want to be distracted all day." I ducked my head and rummaged through the suitcase, pulling out some jeans and a black baby-doll tee.

In the bathroom I dried my hair and got dressed next to the toilet, privacy firmly in place. All my earlier brashness had deserted me. When I walked out, Caspian was waiting by the door. And his shirt was back on.

"I liked your other outfit better," he said.

"I have no idea what you're talking about." But I gave him just the tiniest of smiles.

"Just you wait until you're asleep," he threatened. "I'm going to ogle you until my eyeballs fall out."

I grabbed my cell phone from next to the bed, and right before I opened the door, I winked at him. "Promises, promises."

He grinned, and we went out to meet Ben.

We found Shepherd University pretty easily, and Ben dropped me off at the main campus. "You'll be able to find someplace to eat here, right?" he said.

"I'll be fine, Ben. I'm a big girl."

"Okay. I'll be helping out at the junkyard all day, so I'll be back around six."

I waved him off and waited until he was out of sight. Then I opened my cell phone and dialed the cab company that I'd preprogrammed in. Ten minutes later the cab was picking us up.

"Martinsburg," I told the driver. Caspian stayed silent beside me. Once we reached the downtown area, the cabbie asked where I wanted to be let off. We were next to a florist shop, so I said, "Here's fine," and thrust some money at him.

Caspian got out first, and I followed quickly behind.

As the cab sped away, I turned to Caspian. "Does anything look familiar?" The streets were empty, so I didn't have to worry too much about anyone seeing me talk to myself.

"Yes. Of course. This was home."

"Where do you want to go?" I asked him.

"That's up to you," he said. "This is your visit."

I nodded. "Do you want to walk around here for a while? You can tell me about the town."

He jerked his head in some semblance of a yes, and started walking. I hurried to catch up, and waited for him to say something. He stayed quiet for a long time.

Finally, as we passed a balloon shop, he spoke. "See that door there?" I craned my neck and saw a glass door. "I cut my foot on it. Sliced the top right open. There's this wicked metal piece that acts as a door stopper. But I had sandals on, and it went right over the top of them. Took twelve stitches to close up."

I cringed. I didn't like thinking about him bleeding.

We turned the corner and left Main Street behind. It just fell away. There one block, gone by the next. The streets grew dirtier, and the houses shabbier, the farther we went. Rowhouses sat crammed next to each other, practically one on top of the other.

"That's strange," I said to Caspian. "No kids playing outside. Since they're out of school, I'd expect to see them in the yards, or on the street."

"There weren't very many kids around when I lived here," he replied. "It's mostly elderly people who can't afford retirement homes. They can't really afford their own homes, either."

"Oh." That was sad.

At the end of the block Caspian stopped in front of a small gray house that sat right next to some railroad tracks. The windows were tiny and dirty, and there weren't any shutters. "Home sweet home," he said.

"This is where you lived?" I tried to keep the surprise out of my voice, but it wasn't what I was expecting.

He kicked a loose stone. "Yup. This was my house." Moving closer, he stooped to peer into one of the front windows.

I came up next to him and looked in too. "Is anyone home?" I whispered.

"There probably isn't anyone living here." He tried the door, but it was locked.

Two or three paint cans, half a dozen brushes, and some empty beer bottles littered the floor of the small kitchen. "Somebody's redecorating," I said.

Caspian sat down on a concrete slab in front of the house

and put his head in his hands. "I hope they rip up that damn carpet in the kitchen."

"Carpet in the kitchen? That's weird."

"Tell me about it. The whole house was rigged with duct tape and chewing gum. Faucets only worked half the time, the shower didn't have hot water, and you couldn't use more than two outlets at a time or the whole fuse box would blow. The house was a death trap."

He looked embarrassed, and I thought about the house that I lived in. Sure, it creaked and settled every now and then, but it was big and spacious and remodeled. I never had to worry about what plug I used, or whether or not I had hot water.

"It was still *your* house, and I'm glad I got to see it," I told him. "It's a part of your childhood."

"A part I'd rather forget." Caspian looked away from me and kicked at a stone again. "The only good thing about this house was the railroad tracks." He stood up. "Follow me."

He led me across the train tracks, and we came to a steep embankment that held a drainage pipe at the bottom. After climbing down, he reached behind the pipe and appeared to be wiggling a section of it free. "It's loose," he called up to me.

I stood at the top of the embankment until he motioned for me to climb down. In his hand was a small cigar box. He looked at me with such pride on his face that a sweet joy flooded my heart. "It's still here. My box of treasures from when I was a kid."

There weren't very many items, but he pulled them out one by one, showing me all of them. "Here's a Mike Schmidt baseball card, my favorite kazoo, a lucky rabbit's foot . . ."

"It wasn't lucky for the rabbit."

Caspian smiled at me and kept talking. "A LEGO man, a lucky medallion, and here . . . the best for last." He tipped the box over, and flashes of silver and copper winked up in the sun. "Give me your palm."

I held my hand out flat, and he dropped a completely smooth, flattened piece of silver metal into it. I glanced down, recognizing the stretched markings. "It's a quarter!" I said. "What happened to it?"

"I put it on the tracks and a train flattened it. Used to do it all the time when I was a kid. Here's a dime, a penny, and a nickel that are all flattened too."

He dropped the rest of them into my hand, and they clanked together. I closed my fist, feeling the cool smoothness, and imagined Caspian as a little boy.

"I bet you were adorable," I said softly. "When you were little."

He shrugged and looked back in the direction of the house. "I was the weird, quiet kid who drew pictures all the time. I had a couple of friends, but no one special."

I looked up at him, wishing I could have seen the little boy that he once was. "I would have been your friend."

He smiled at me. "I know you would have, Abbey." He thrust the cigar box at me. "Here. Take it."

"But I can't. They're your treasures."

He held the box out even further. "I know. That's why I want you to have them. They're all I have left of my childhood, and it's a piece of me that I want to give you."

Fear of rejection was written all over his face, and my heart almost broke for him. Taking the box, I put the coins back inside and cradled it gently. "Thank you, Caspian. I'm honored."

My words seemed to make him happy, and he beamed at me. It was contagious, and I smiled back. The warm sun beat down on our backs, and in that moment I knew there was no greater feeling in the whole word.

"Do you want to see my elementary school?" he asked, almost shyly.

"Absolutely."

I tucked the box under my arm, and we climbed back up the embankment. He took me behind his old house and down several roads, until we came to a small red brick building. MARTINSBURG ELEMENTARY SCHOOL 1842 was carved above the front door.

*Go Bulldogs!* was painted in faded red and white letters along the side of the building.

"Home of the bulldogs, huh?" I asked, walking toward the school.

"Best basketball team since . . . okay, since never. The team here sucks."

I laughed and spotted a side door. "Should we try there? Do you think it's open? What are the odds?"

"Not very good," Caspian said, but he followed me to it.

I gave the silver metal push bar a slight tap, and the door swung right open.

We crossed the threshold and entered into the school. The hallways had that classic stale smell to them—papers, erasers, new sneakers, and old cafeteria food—and I wrinkled my nose. "I hope they air this place out before the new school year starts."

Caspian didn't answer. He was too busy looking at rows of black-and-white class pictures hanging up in the hallway. Most of them were hidden behind dusty glass and faded wooden frames.

I turned to the pictures. "Are you here?" I tried to find him, searching for his hair, but the photographs were yellowed and grainy.

He put one finger on a frame, and I leaned in to see where he was pointing. Even with the washed-out coloring, I recognized the hair and eyes. "There you are," I whispered. He had on a plaid shirt and brown pants, his eager smile showing a missing front tooth. "I was right. *Adorable.*"

He turned and gave me the same smile as in the picture, and I giggled. "I knew it. You're still nine."

Caspian nodded and ran his finger over the glass one more time. "Feels like a lifetime ago." His voice was wistful, and then abruptly changed. "I have one more thing to show you. Out back."

We left the school, and he took me to where a small fenced-in playground stood. It was shabby, and obviously not very well taken care of. The peeling paint on the red-and-yellow monkey bars barely clung on, and the swing set had only two swings, both with cracked wooden seats. A small row of plank-wood bleachers had been set up in the corner of the playground, looking out at what passed for a baseball diamond.

Caspian led me there.

He bent down and looked under the first seat. "Down here."

I bent down too, and saw a mishmash of carved initials, just barely making out a *CV*. "You were here," I said. "I see your initials."

"I carved them on my first day of school. I saw some older kids doing it, and they lent me their pocket knife."

"How old were you?" I asked.

"Six, I think. Old enough to want to make my mark on the world."

I ran my fingers over the *CV*, committing the feel of it to memory, and sat the cigar box down carefully. "It's too bad we don't have a knife now. I'd like to add my initials there too. Maybe next time."

"If there *is* a next time." Caspian gazed at me with a serious expression, and the mood turned somber. I didn't want things to stay that way, so I hollered, "Race you to the monkey bars!"

I got a head start and was already hanging upside down when he caught up. All the blood was rushing to my head, making me feel dizzy. "I can't stay like this much longer," I told him. "Head rush."

He leaned down and stuck his face next to mine, gifting me with a beautiful smile. "I know the feeling," he said. "You give me a head rush all the time."

We left the playground around two, and I was surprised by the fact that I wasn't hungry yet. We went back to Main Street, and Caspian pointed to a little gas station on the corner. "Go get something to eat."

"But I don't want to."

"All you've eaten since last night was a bite of pizza and a burrito. You need to eat more. Go fill your stomach with some food. I'll wait for you here."

I wanted to protest, but he had a point. And the smells of relish and hot dogs drifting out of the store were slowly starting to awaken my sleeping appetite. . . .

I went inside and grabbed a bag of chips, a hot dog, and a can of soda. I practically inhaled the food, proving that I was hungrier than I thought, and went back to the counter to buy a pack of gum.

I popped in a piece of minty freshness and chewed thoroughly, hoping to disguise any leftover hot dog on my breath. Caspian was waiting outside the store, the sun reflecting off his hair. The white-blond color practically glowed. "Ready to go?" I asked him.

"Where to next?"

"The cemetery."

He led the way, and I followed him silently. As we walked, a cloud passed over the sun, dimming the light around us, and his hair didn't glisten anymore.

I tried to pay attention to where he was leading me, but I got turned around and couldn't tell which way we were going. He moved quickly, and I found myself jogging to keep up with him as we started down a gravel road.

A white clapboard church appeared, with a small graveyard directly across from it. There was a dark metal fence surrounding the cemetery, and a faded sign arched between the two main fence posts.

"Welcome to Saint Joseph's Cemetery," Caspian said. "My final resting place."

I placed one hand reverently on the metal post and took a deep breath. *This is it. I'm here.*

The tiny graveyard was vastly different from the one in Sleepy Hollow. There were no mausoleums, no ornately carved headstones, no statues of angels . . . no statues at all. Just simple, square granite markers punctuated with carved names and dates.

I stepped up to the first stone. It read: WALTER ROSE, BORN JULY 7, 1923, DIED AUGUST 21, 1983. There was no "beloved husband" or "he will be missed." Just an empty name with an empty date.

"I'm over here," Caspian said, and I looked up. He was standing by a small gray stone, clearly set apart.

Forcing one foot in front of the other, I moved purposefully toward him. This was what I'd come all this way for. To see him. The *real* him. I steeled myself for the possible tears that might come and concentrated on walking.

Left foot.

Right foot.

Move one, then the other.

His head was bowed when I reached him, and I felt myself falling. Suddenly, the ground was underneath me. Rough stone caught my fingertips.

*C*, for Caspian. *V*, for Vander. He was here.

I spread my fingers and touched the rest of his name. Closing my eyes, I imagined ...

*Caspian in a black suit, eyes closed, head on a white satin pillow. Polished mahogany surrounding him, then slamming shut. Sealed forever.*

*Fresh dirt. Rich and dark, landing with a hollow thud against his closed coffin. New grass. Growing slowly. Tiny blades appearing from little seeds planted so many months ago.*

The pictures reversed, and new images began to play.

*Black suit, head bowed, rain streaming down, at Kristen's funeral.*

*Crying over her grave on prom night. Caspian finding me at the river . . . saving me.*

*Starry skies. The necklace he made me. All alone in his crypt, bent over a small candle and working with his hands to make something beautiful.*

*Lying on my bed. Green glowing over our heads. My own private constellations put there so I could have them anytime.*

*The library . . . smells of books and old papers. His hand grasping mine. That black stripe falling into one eye.*

*A kiss . . .*

My eyes flew open, and I gasped. Caspian was beside me in an instant, kneeling on the grass. "Are you okay? Talk to me, Abbey."

With one hand on his name carved in stone, I steadied myself and brought up the other to his face. The feeling was stronger here, and I held my trembling fingers in place.

"It doesn't hurt, Caspian. I thought it would. Thought it might be too much to bear. But it's not." A sense of awe came over me, and I looked at him in amazement. "If I'm strong enough to handle this, then I'm strong enough to handle whatever else comes my way."

Silent words that I did not say floated on the tip of my tongue. *Revenants . . . death . . .*

Caspian turned his head slightly to move closer to my hand, and a thousand tiny charges erupted under my skin. "Do you feel it?" I whispered.

He nodded. "It must be stronger because I'm here."

I shook my head. "It's stronger because you're *here*." I pulled my other hand away from the stone and placed it over my heart. Keeping my gaze steady, I smiled at him. "I finally feel it now. The missing piece."

He gave me a confused look, so I tried to explain. "When Kristen died, it felt like my heart shattered into a million pieces. And no matter what I did, or how I tried to make it better, I couldn't. Then I met you. And it started to heal. The cracks went away, bit by bit.

"I didn't realize that all the pieces were there except for one. But now, being here, with you, It finally *fits*. *We* fit, Caspian. I feel whole. Here, in this place. And I'll do whatever it takes to hold on to that."

I brought my hand down from his face and folded both hands together on top of the gravestone. Almost like I was praying.

"Even if that means I only get to touch you one day a year.

I'll take it." I turned my face up and felt the sun's warmth. "I want *you*, Caspian. I want your body, your heart, and your soul. And any part in between."

I took another deep breath. This was the scary part. "That only leaves one question to be answered." I wanted to look away. I wanted *so badly* not to see hesitation, or reluctance, cross his face. But I had to know. "Do you want me?"

"Forever," he said. And in the quiet stillness, the hushed authority of a solemn vow ran behind his words. "I want you forever."

*Chapter Twenty-five*

# UNFORTUNATE

What passed at this interview I will not pretend to say, for in fact I do not know.

—"The Legend of Sleepy Hollow"

We stayed in the cemetery for the rest of the afternoon. When it was time to go back to Shepherd University, I met Ben there on time and we drove to the hotel. Ben talked about the junkyard the entire time.

I nodded my head and listened with one ear, but I wasn't really paying attention. My thoughts were on Caspian. I didn't know what would happen when we got back to the hotel. What *could* happen.

Ben suggested that we get Chinese for dinner, and I caught enough of the conversation to agree. "Yeah, sounds good."

He pulled into the bait shop–Chinese restaurant, but we

were both too grossed out to eat there, so I suggested that we find another one.

The closest place ended up being almost an hour away, but it was worth it, and we returned to the hotel with several boxes of leftovers. Ben carried them in and walked me to my door. I just wanted him to say good night already so I could spend the rest of the evening alone with Caspian.

He started fidgeting with the boxes as soon as I pulled out my room key. "Are you sure you don't want to take any of these?" He held them out to me. "You might get the midnight munchies."

"They're all yours."

He looked down at the floor. "Do you want to come watch a movie or something in my room, then? I feel bad. I didn't get to ask you anything about the school."

I slid my key into the card reader and pushed open the door. "That's what we have a six-hour car ride home tomorrow for. We'll talk—" The phone in my room started ringing and I glanced over at it. "That's probably my dad. I should get it."

Ben nodded and opened his door too. "See you tomorrow. Night, Abbey."

He sounded kind of disappointed, but I told myself that

I'd let him talk my ear off the whole way home. I'd buy him a bag of Funyuns, too. That should make him happy.

I crossed the room and reached for the phone *just* as it stopped ringing. My foot kicked something, and I reached down to pick it up.

It was the bottle of lotion I'd had this morning.

Caspian stood by the door, and he slowly came toward me. I scooted backward, dropping the lotion, and felt the hard wood of the headboard at my back. "Lie down," he commanded, with a slight tremble in his voice.

My knees turned to jelly.

I inched my way down onto the bed, stopping when my back was flat. "This isn't, um, fair, you know."

"No?" He leaned over me, and I blinked several times, trying to keep my thoughts straight.

"No, it's not. You use that sexy voice and I go all melty."

"Mmmm, melty? Is that the technical term?"

I could barely breathe. He was wreaking havoc on all my senses.

"We can't . . . *do* anything," I finally said.

"We can't?" He whispered in my ear, "Let's find out what we *can* do. . . ."

I closed my eyes.

"Are you cold?" he said. "You have goose bumps on your arms." His gaze fell to my hair, and he lifted one hand, almost as if he was going to touch it. "I like seeing you like this. Your hair is all wild."

"And witchy?" I teased, remembering prom night. When I babbled about my wild and witchy hair.

He smiled. "I'm thinking, yes. You definitely cast a spell on me. It drives me crazy."

"There you go with those pickup lines again."

He shook his head and lowered his face. We were nose to nose. Lips to lips. "You have no idea how much I want to kiss you right now," he whispered.

"How much?" I taunted.

He licked his lips. "Very, *very* much."

"If you had to choose between kissing me once right now and then dying, or living forever without my touch, which would it be?"

He didn't even hesitate. "I'd die a happy man, with the taste of you on my lips."

I tried *very* hard not to blush. "I'd make the same choice too."

"You would?"

I nodded, then closed my eyes.

450

The hotel phone next to me rang loudly and completely broke the mood.

Caspian groaned. "Ignore it," he pleaded.

"It's my dad. I know it is."

"He'll call back."

"He already called once and I missed it," I argued. Truthfully, I was feeling a little bit of relief at the interruption. I was getting completely carried away.

Caspian sighed, and sat up, moving away from me. "You're right," he said. "You should probably answer it."

I reached for the phone, trying to compose myself before saying hello.

"Hi, Abbey, it's Dad."

*Yeah, like I couldn't tell.* "Hi, Dad."

"I called earlier, but you didn't answer. Were you in Ben's room?"

"No, Dad," I sighed. "I wasn't in Ben's room. We went to get Chinese food for dinner, so that's why I wasn't here to pick up."

"I'm trusting you, you know," he said. "Both your mother and I are. Speaking of, she wants to know what you thought of the college."

I *so* wasn't in the mood to talk about that right now. "It was okay." I tried to think up something to tell him. "I wasn't really all that impressed by it, honestly."

"Did you meet the dean? What did you think of the campus? What's the curriculum like?"

How could I answer *those* questions? "Like I said, Dad, I wasn't really happy with it. So it kind of all passed by in a blur."

"Oh."

Inspiration hit. "I think I'll tour some more colleges closer to home. Maybe I'll find one there that's more to my liking."

"Oh, yeah?" He sounded happier. "That's a good plan. I'm sure your mother can arrange something." He chattered on for another twenty minutes. Finally I told him I had to get to bed, and I'd see him soon. He agreed, and I hung up the phone with another warning to "be good" ringing in my ear.

I glanced over at Caspian. He seemed to be waiting for my reaction. "*That* was fun," I said.

"I could tell."

"Do you mind turning out the light?" I asked him. "I really need to get some sleep. Long drive home tomorrow." Sort of true. But mostly I wanted the light out because I felt awkward that our moment had been completely interrupted thanks to my father's call.

He nodded, and hit the switch. The room was plunged into darkness, and I slipped off my pants and into my pajamas.

Something crunched in my jeans pocket.

"What was that?" Caspian asked.

I pulled out a cellophane wrapper. "Fortune cookie." Padding over to the window, I parted the drapes slightly and cracked it open to read what was inside. *Every gift comes with a price. Choose wisely.* Clutching the fortune tightly in one hand, I climbed into the bed.

"Good fortune?" Caspian asked, settling down on the covers beside me.

I rolled onto my back and looked up at the dark ceiling, silently wishing for glowing plastic stars. "Yeah. It was. I think I'm going to hold on to it."

He was quiet, and I said, "I miss my stars."

"I have mine," came his reply. "Right here next to me."

I rolled to face him, but I couldn't make out anything in the darkness. It was like talking to a shadow. "Sweet dreams, Caspian," I said. "Even if you don't dream, think of me."

"Always," he replied.

I closed my eyes, with a smile on my face and the fortune in my hand.

~ ~ ~

I got dressed quickly the next morning and packed my stuff in a hurry. Then I went into the bathroom and made a call. Gesturing for Caspian to follow me, I left the room.

"Where are we going?" he asked, once we made it outside.

"I have something I need to do. It won't take long."

When the cab picked us up, I told the driver to take me to the florist shop on Main Street. I asked Caspian to wait for me outside. He agreed, and I went in, unsure yet of what I was even looking for.

The florist greeted me pleasantly and asked if he could help me with anything. I told him I was undecided, and went to go look in the giant glass display cases. Most of them held roses. Pink, yellow, red, white, peach, and striped varieties of all kinds. My head was spinning just trying to decide.

Finally, I checked back with the florist. "I'm looking for something . . . maybe a spray of flowers? But I don't want it to look like it's for a funeral."

He pointed to several small baskets, filled with white and yellow daisies, and then to a fern arrangement. But I shook my head. They didn't feel right.

"Of course there are always roses," he suggested. "I could put together a bouquet for you."

"No. I don't think I want that. I'm just not sure *what* I want."

I turned away and glanced at the display cases again. Nothing was standing out to me there.

Then I saw a smaller display case, tucked away in the corner. A wild purple plant was the only thing in it. "What's that?"

He came over and lifted it out to show me. The delicate brass pot it was in was gorgeous but looked like it could hardly contain the plant. Blooms tumbled everywhere.

"This is the heliotrope plant," he said. "I'll give you a good deal on it. They're not usually sold in florist shops. It's a very old plant. This one came mixed with a recent shipment."

The purple flowers seemed to be calling out to me, and I touched a clump of petals. "I'll take it. And a single red rose, too."

"You know, the heliotrope has a very distinct meaning," he said as I pushed open the door to leave.

"It does?" I said. "What is it?"

"It symbolizes eternal love and devotion."

I smiled at him. "Perfect. It was meant for me, then."

He smiled back and waved as I walked out. I switched the plant to my left hand and turned to Caspian. "Can you lead me back to the cemetery?" He nodded, and we made it there about ten minutes later.

I found his headstone and knelt down to carefully arrange

the plant beside it. The blooms arched around the stone, almost lovingly, looking like they'd always been there.

"Heliotrope for devotion," I told him. "And a red rose for love. Eternal love and devotion."

I placed the single rose on top of the headstone, then pulled away suddenly. A sharp thorn had sliced into my thumb. Caspian had his eyes closed and didn't see what happened next.

But I did.

A drop of blood fell from my finger and splashed onto the flower. The crimson bead rolled, then spread across one perfect red petal. It blossomed there, like an ink blot, and I couldn't pull my eyes away from it. It was obscene and beautiful. Death and life, all rolled into one.

Footsteps behind me made me turn around, and an old woman dressed in black came walking across the graveyard. She stopped at the row of tombstones before Caspian's, and nodded to me. I nodded back. And decided it was time to go.

Running my finger over that *C*, one last time, I whispered, "I love you," and prepared to leave. As I passed by the woman, she looked up at me.

"Remember, child," she said, "you're never alone."

"You're right," I replied, looking Caspian directly in the eye. "I'm not alone."

~ ~ ~

We left West Virginia to head for home, as Ben talked on and on about some new car project he had planned now that he'd visited the junkyard. I had no idea what the difference was between an alternator and a carburetor, and I didn't really care to find out. But Ben was happy to try to explain.

Caspian kept looking out the windows the whole way home, and I distracted myself by talking about Kristen. We were only ten minutes from the house when I pulled out my phone to call Mom and Dad. But they didn't pick up.

I was about to try Mom's cell when Ben pulled into our driveway.

"Thanks for going with me, Ben," I said, when he came to a stop. "Really. You have no idea how awesome that was." I wanted to hug him or something, but I didn't know how awkward that would be.

He cracked his neck and rolled his shoulders. "I'm glad you asked me to go, Abbey." His eyes flashed to the clock. "I better get going, though. I was starting to feel pretty tired back there. I'll catch ya later?"

"Yeah, sure." I hopped out and grabbed my suitcase, briefly holding the door open for Caspian. "Don't fall asleep on the way to your house."

Ben laughed. "I won't." And with a final honk he drove away.

I glanced over at Caspian, trying to keep it discreet, certain that Mom was going to come flying out the front door any minute. "I'm gonna go in and greet the parentals," I said quickly. "I'm sure they're just bursting with curiosity."

"I'll wait in the backyard," he replied. "When you have a moment, slip out for a walk."

I nodded, then wheeled my suitcase up the front walkway. The door was unlocked, and I pushed it open, leaving my luggage near the stairs. "Mom, Dad," I called. "I'm home!"

Silence greeted me.

I walked through the kitchen, peeking into the living room and dining room along the way. They weren't in either of those rooms.

"Mom? Dad? Are you guys upstairs?" I yelled. "There better not be some type of let's-get-freaky-now-that-our-kid-is-gone alone time going on here! If I find chocolate syrup *anywhere* other than the fridge, I swear, I'm moving out."

Taking the stairs two by two, I sprinted to the top. Mom and Dad's door was closed, which was *always* a good thing . . . but mine was open. *I know I shut that before I left. If Mom thinks she can go in there and mess with my stuff while I'm gone, she is* sadly *mistaken.*

I pushed my door open all the way, getting ready to assess the damage . . .

And stopped cold.

The overhead lights were off, but dozens of candles covered the desk, my nightstand, the fireplace mantel . . . Long shadows leapt and danced along the walls, their tiny flames flickering wildly as if a sudden gust of wind had blown through the room. *What the hell is going* on . . . ?

I took a step closer and felt my eyes widen. Too wide; it felt like they were bulging out of place and would pop out at any second.

My bed was littered with roses. Long-stemmed, heavy-blossomed, bloodred roses. They covered the entire surface in a massive heap, dozens upon dozens of them. There was something vaguely familiar about how they were arranged, almost like a bunch of . . . funeral sprays.

And stretched out among them, in the center of the bed, arms crossed in a classic funeral pose was . . . *Caspian*?

I screamed. My stomach twisted violently, and I knew I was going to throw up.

Then his eyes popped open. "This is how you like 'em, right?"

My heart stopped as I recognized that voice. *Vincent.*

He sat up slowly, uncrossing his arms, and the likeness to Caspian was uncanny. He'd dyed his hair the same white-blond shade and had even put in the black streak angling across his forehead. His hair looked longer—he must have flat-ironed it to get the same style—and he was dressed in a black suit. I watched in horror as he came toward me.

"What do you think?" He stopped for a moment to straighten the lapels of his jacket. "Do I make a good dead guy, or what?"

My stomach was still roiling, but I couldn't tell if it was from shock, or fear.

"Aren't you going to give me a big kiss?" he said, advancing again. My knees started shaking, and I ground my nails into my palm to try to focus on something else. "Come *on*, Abbey." His voice turned hard. "I set all this up for you. The least you can do is show your appreciation. Do you have *any* idea how much it costs to get this many roses delivered?"

I dug my nails in so hard that I felt my palm start to get sticky. And still my terror was mounting.

Vincent finally reached me and ran a cold palm down my face. "Feel that? Why would you want to be with *him*, anyway? Necrophilia, Abbey." He shook his head. "It's not a pretty thing."

I tried to hold still, to not let him see my fear, but I couldn't tell if I was succeeding. He watched me closely, then suddenly smiled.

"Now," he said, bending low into a grand bow. "Would you consider this our first date? Or our third? *Technically*, we had that little outing in the cemetery and our meeting in the alleyway behind your uncle's store, so I think . . . Yes, this is our third."

"We haven't been on any *dates*, asshole," I said quietly.

He looked affronted. "What do you call *this*?" And spread his arms wide. "I brought you flowers, we have mood lighting, I'm all dressed up, and we're quite alone. That, my dear, is a *date*."

I snorted.

Vincent's face turned hard, and he leaned down closer to me. "Am I not pale enough for you? Not cold enough?" He yanked my wrist and held it against his chest. "This is the problem, yes? My heartbeat? Sorry, darling. I'm not *dead* enough for you."

Something about the way he said "dead" struck a cold spot inside of me. I knew I wasn't going to last much longer. Vincent was going to kill me.

Then his gaze shifted. "What's this?"

He caught sight of my perfume cabinet, my lovely brand-new perfume cabinet that Mom and Dad had worked so hard on, and pulled my hand. Forcing me to follow him as he moved toward it.

I dug in my heels, but he was too strong. My arm felt like it was being pulled from its socket.

"Leave it . . . ," I managed, "alone."

He cocked his head at me. "What was that? You have to speak up."

The pain in my arm increased, and red-hot pokers shot under my skin. I whimpered, then clamped my mouth shut.

Vincent ran one hand over the outside of the cabinet, then opened one of the drawers and grabbed a handful of glass bottles. "Speak *up*," he said. Opening his fingers wide, he released the bottles, and they went crashing to the floor.

The smells, and glass, went everywhere. A cloud of scent enveloped me, and I coughed once, trying not to gag.

Vincent opened another drawer.

"Stop . . . it," I pleaded. "Just . . . stop it."

But he grabbed a second handful and this time threw them gleefully to the floor. Tiny splinters of glass bounced and shimmered. Puddles of liquid started seeping into the wood.

"That's a wonderful noise!" he said. "A symphony of sound!"

I had a split second of comprehension, a clear, perfect understanding of what he was going to do, but still I couldn't stop it.

Vincent gripped my curio cabinet with both hands, lifted it up, and threw it against the wall, an angelic smile on his face.

"Noooooooo!" I screamed.

Pieces of wood cracked and splintered. What was left of my perfume stock still inside the cabinet drawers exploded, and the sound . . . was heartbreaking.

I dropped to my knees, heedless of the glass that now covered the floor. My fingers clenched into fists, and the fury that filled me was pure, unadulterated rage. Then, suddenly, I heard another noise.

It was my name, coming from Caspian as he charged through the open door and threw himself at Vincent.

They both fell to the floor.

Vincent seemed shocked to see him, and in that brief moment Caspian reared back and slammed his fist into Vincent's eye. He managed to get in another blow, this one to his jaw, and I heard the snap as Vincent's head whipped back.

Then, just as suddenly, Caspian went flying.

Vincent's hands were outstretched, like all he'd done was simply extend them, and Caspian landed against the fireplace mantel. The force he hit with was so strong that immediately a crack ran up against the wall beside him.

"Caspian!" I yelled. He looked stunned for a second, and then his head slumped forward.

Vincent got to his feet and came to me, grabbing my arm again. He pulled roughly, trying to yank me over to the window, but I couldn't get my balance. My knees went sliding across the floor, and I screamed as glass shards ripped through my skin.

He stopped, looking down at the bloody trail I was leaving behind. "Messy. Messy. Messy. So damn messy." A brief look of distaste crossed his face, and then he scooped me up into his arms. "Try not to get any blood on the suit," he said.

I struggled. As much as I could struggle with knees and legs that were torn and bloody, and him squeezing me tighter. It felt like bands of steel were wrapping themselves around my lungs, and I took a gasping breath. "Can't . . . breathe . . ."

Instantly he loosened his grip. But didn't let me go.

My tears came then. I was so completely broken down and overwhelmed that I stopped struggling and just cried. My whole body shook, and Vincent held me out away from him.

"Just kill me," I hiccupped. "Just do it already."

I felt an awkward pat on my head. "Why would I want to kill you, Abbey?"

"Isn't that what you're here for? Didn't you . . . Didn't you kill Kristen?" I tried to slow my sobs. "You said you were there . . . the night she died, and now I know about it."

"Of course I was. And I guess you could say that since I let her fall in, I'm responsible." He shrugged elegantly. "But don't you see, Abbey? It was my bad. I had the wrong girl. I thought *she* was Caspian's other half. I've really wanted *you* all along."

"Me? You wanted *me*?" A pain so intense and so searing that it felt like my heart was physically being ripped in two filled me, and I would have doubled over if I could. "You mean," I choked, "that *I'm* the reason Kristen's dead?"

"Yes." Vincent smiled down at me. "Yes, that's right."

An anguished moan escaped me, more wild emotion than intelligible speech, and I grabbed at my head. The pain was there. *In there.* And it was killing me.

"Now that *he's* found you, I can't kill you," Vincent continued. "Or else you two will be completed, and that would just ruin everything. No, I've got to make sure you stay perfectly . . . *alive.*"

Suddenly feet came pounding up the stairs, and angry voices echoed in the hall.

"They're coming," Vincent said. "But they can't do anything

yet. I've made sure of that." Then he whispered in my ear, "Don't even *think* about doing anything stupid. Stay. Alive."

Uri, Cacey, Sophie, and Kame burst into the room, and Vincent dropped me without a second's hesitation.

Sophie shot me a worried glance. "Are you okay?" she asked.

"Three's a party, but seven is a crowd," I heard Vincent say. "That means it's time for me to leave."

There was the sound of someone rushing past me, and then Kame shouted, "Vincent, wait!"

I looked up just in time to see Vincent run to the window and leap out of it. Uri and Cacey followed, but they stopped short.

"He must be protected," Cacey said. "He disappeared."

Uri's face was furious—he looked like he wanted to leap right out the window and chase after Vincent—but Cacey put a hand on his arm. She shook her head once. "Wait," she said. "There is still time to find out what he's after."

In the blink of an eye, all four of them were standing over me and reaching down. I had an absurd urge to laugh at what they were wearing. They were coming to collect me in matching *khakis*.

"It's okay, Abbey," Kame said. "We're here for you. Just trust us."

His voice was soft and beautiful, and I glanced at him, feeling myself get pulled under the endless ocean that was in his eyes.

*But I'm not ready.* It was the first thought that came to mind, and I said it out loud. "I'm not ready."

# ACKNOWLEDGMENTS

Many thanks go to:

The inspirations: Washington Irving, Sleepy Hollow, L.J. Smith, Caroline B. Cooney (I'm still your number one Fangirl), Elizabeth Chandler, George A. Romero, and Johnny Cash.

The team players: Michael Bourret, Anica Rissi, the Simon Pulse team, and Lee Miller.

The support system: fans, friends, and family.

Thank you one and all.

# ACKNOWLEDGEMENTS

# ABOUT THE AUTHOR

Jessica Verday wrote the first draft of *The Hollow* by hand, using thirteen spiral-bound notebooks and fifteen black pens. The first draft of *The Haunted* took fifteen spiral-bound notebooks and twenty black pens. She spends her days and nights buying stock in pens and paper. She lives in Goodlettsville, Tennessee, with her husband. Find out more at jessicaverday.com.